CW00517806

A Premature Apocalypse

The Dry Bones Society

Book III

DAN SOFER

First edition: June 2018

This book is a work of fiction. Any resemblance to actual events or persons, living or dead, is entirely coincidental.

ISBN: 0-9863932-7-4
ISBN-13: 978-0-9863932-7-3

www.dansofer.com

Cover Design: Damonza Book Cover Design

CHAPTER 1

"What was that?" Fahid said. The sudden noise in the dark tunnel behind him made the hair on the back of his neck bristle. Was somebody else there—or some*thing*?

Hisham slowed to a stop. "What?"

Fahid put his finger to his lips and listened. He could have sworn he'd heard the shuffle of feet, but now his ears only detected the distant drip of water. Was his mind playing tricks on him?

Hisham aimed the beam of his flashlight, tracing the electric cables that ran down the cement ceiling and casting long, eerie shadows along the endless gray walls.

He bared his teeth. "Scared of ghosts?"

"I'm not scared," Fahid lied. He still slept with a nightlight in the room he shared with his two older brothers, but he would never admit that to his friend.

"We're under the Enemy's feet now," he added. "What if they've found the tunnel?"

For months the two boys had shoveled dirt, mixed cement, and plastered the tunnel walls. In return, they received a hamper of Hershey's chocolate bars every other week. The tunnel started in a storage room beneath the UNRWA Hospital in Gaza City and wormed its way beneath houses and apartment buildings, crossing the immense border wall, and ending in an empty field at the outskirts of two Israeli farming villages.

Their work was not without danger. Fahid had lost two school friends to collapsing ceilings. Another had drowned when the Egyptians pumped sea water into a tunnel near the Rafah Border Crossing. Their own tunnel had surfaced in enemy territory two days ago, and now the threat of detonation by the Israel Defense Forces haunted their every step. If enemy soldiers had slipped into the tunnel behind them, they would cut off the boys from escape.

"They haven't found it," Hisham said. "C'mon. Let's finish up and go home."

They had to complete their survey by dawn so that tonight, the Arab fighters with their heavy packs would not trip on loose stones or slip in puddles. Such mishaps might detonate their bombs or trigger machine gun fire, killing their comrades underground and alerting the Enemy.

Faster, the boys pressed onward.

Uuungggh…

A low moan issued from the darkness behind them, the sound of an injured animal. A wolf?

The boys halted, and Fahid gripped Hisham by the elbow. This time, Hisham didn't mock him for being scared. His eyes were large and white; he had heard it too.

Hisham grabbed him by the shirt. "Is this a trick? Are you messing with me?"

"No. I swear it! Turn on the lights."

"We're not allowed to, remember? The current makes the tunnel easier to find."

The groan rose behind them again. A second voice joined the first; then a third. Not a lone wolf but a pack of suffering creatures. The voices sounded almost human—humans unlike any Fahid had ever encountered.

"What if it's *them*?" Fahid hissed.

"Who?" Hisham knew exactly what Fahid meant. Everyone had heard the stories even if they refused to talk about them.

Fahid swallowed his pride. "The Dead Jews."

"Those are lies," his friend said. "Lies told by the Enemy to plant fear in our hearts. The dead do not rise, certainly not dead Jews."

"But they do. They sprout from the ground, and now they rule the Zionist Enemy!"

"Nonsense!" Hisham said, but his arm trembled.

Mnnnnngggrrrrhhhh....

Hisham clutched Fahid's arm too. The groaning came louder now, closer. There was a scraping sound as well, the shuffling of a hundred feet over the rough tunnel floor toward them.

Hisham swore and waved the beam of the flashlight behind them. Fifty meters back, the tunnel turned a corner and disappeared.

"Come on," he said, and he pushed forward.

Fahid kept up with him, glancing back every few steps at the darkness.

The moaning continued. The boys quickened their pace, then broke into a desperate sprint. They ran and ran until they met the solid stone wall at the end of the tunnel. They turned around and pressed their backs against the wall. The flashlight beam faded into the dark. The unseen creatures were worse than any night monster Fahid had ever imagined.

Unngggrrrhhh...

The voices grew louder, ghoulish voices from the murky realms beyond This World. Hisham aimed his beam, which cut the black void like a laser but didn't extend far enough. He swore again and hit the switch at the end of the electric cable. Their eyes shuttered as fluorescent strips sizzled to life and white light flooded the tunnel.

Silence. Empty, blessed silence. No groans. No footfalls. Hisham exhaled a deep breath. Fahid did the same. They chuckled. But not for long.

Unngggrrrhhh!

The shuffling started again, faster and more urgent. The bright light had not dispelled the terrors beneath the ground.

Fahid's hand found Hisham's, which was cold and wet. Hisham did not shake him off.

"The ladder," Fahid muttered. They had hammered steel rungs into the rock wall of the shaft above them. Breaching the surface would expose the tunnel to the Israeli enemy, but anything was better than facing the monsters at their heels.

Hisham stared ahead but said nothing. Moments later, Fahid saw why and he wished his friend had not turned on the lights.

The first figure to round the corner of the tunnel had long gray hair, matted with dirt. The dead man's head lolled from side to side, his eyeballs rolling in deep sockets. His naked body was wrinkled and grimy, and his arms swung as unnatural forces dragged his feet forward.

Hisham squeezed Fahid's hand so hard it hurt. A second ghoul trudged behind the first. Then a third followed, a woman. A dozen more marched behind them. The army of the dead grew so thick, Fahid could no longer tell them apart. Young and old. Men and women. The mass of lumbering limbs closed in on them, slow but determined and unstoppable. Their groans echoed off the plastered walls, becoming a deafening roar of otherworldly misery. Deep below the ground, the boys shuddered, trapped between a horde of Dead Jews and the Zionist Enemy.

When the monsters stepped within reach, Hisham snapped out of their petrifying spell.

"Up!" he cried. "Now!" He gripped the first of the steel rungs and scrambled upward into the tall shaft.

Fahid followed, his dusty sneakers slipping on the smooth rungs as he climbed upward away from the groping hands of the undead. Then he collided with Hisham's legs and his ascent halted.

"Keep going!"

"I can't. The hatch is locked!"

Below Fahid, the Gray Ghoul ogled the first rung with glazed eyes. They were unnatural, mindless monsters; they couldn't climb a ladder, could they? As if in answer to Fahid's unspoken question, the ghoul gripped the steel, gave the rung a tentative pull, and heaved his body upward. Behind him, more Dead Jews followed.

"They're climbing the ladder!"

"What am I supposed to do?"

"Break it open!"

Hisham banged the base of his flashlight against the handle of the hatch. Nothing happened. He banged again and again, and yet again, until finally there came a metallic *crack*. A draft of cool air ruffled Fahid's hair, and Hisham launched upward.

Fahid raced after, clambering into the night and rolling onto the dirt and patchy grass. The full moon bathed them in pale light.

Hisham slammed the hatch shut. "C'mon!" He pulled Fahid to his feet. "Over there." He pointed to a clump of yellow lights a few hundred meters away.

"That's the Enemy!" Fahid protested. Moments ago, the Israeli village, with its schools and kindergartens, greenhouses and factories, had been their target.

"Rather them than those things down there!" Hisham dragged him forward and Fahid relented.

They sprinted in the night, crossing half the distance to the village before slowing. Crickets chirped in the night as they panted. Fahid's legs burned, the chill air searing his throat and lungs. They paused to catch their breath and smiled at each other in the dull light. They had escaped the monsters.

Then the hatch swung open, and the boys spun around. The Gray Ghoul climbed out of the tunnel and lumbered after them.

Letting out a cry, the boys dashed toward the yellow lights of the nearest village. The groans rose behind them, piercing the night like icy daggers.

Fahid sprinted for all he was worth. Then he crashed into Hisham, and they tumbled to the ground. Fahid got to his elbows and saw why his friend had stopped. A half-dozen bushes formed a semicircle around them. Their camouflaged legs ended in heavy black boots. Beneath their leaves, the barrels of machine guns glinted in the moonlight.

"Stop or I'll shoot," said one bush, in Arabic.

They had run straight into a trap. The boys stared at the commandos, their muscles twitching, the groans behind them growing louder, as did the shuffling feet.

Fahid cringed and clamped his eyes shut. Any moment, the cold claws of the Dead would dig into his shoulders, their sharp teeth into his neck. Or bullets would rip through his body, shredding his flesh and shattering his bones.

But five terrifying seconds later, Fahid still lay there, alive and whole. The groaning had settled; the footfalls ceased. An early morning breeze blew on his damp, sweaty clothes, and an unearthly silence reigned. He opened one eye, then another. The gunmen were no longer looking at him and Hashim, but beyond, their mouths open.

He exchanged a fearful glance with Hisham, and, very slowly, they turned around.

Instead of otherworldly ghouls, men and women shivered in the breaking dawn, pressing their arms over their naked bodies. Their backs had straightened, and they looked about with surprise and confusion, as though they had woken up in an unfamiliar place.

The Gray Ghoul blinked at them and cleared his throat. "Excuse me," he said, in Hebrew. "Are we in Heaven?"

CHAPTER 2

Wednesday morning, Prime Minister Moshe Karlin prepared to do what no person in his position would ever do. Well, no *sane* person.

He strode down a hallway inside the Knesset building, the seat of the Israeli Parliament, his two trusted advisors in tow. When he reached the designated conference room his hand hesitated on the handle. The group of oily politicians behind the door hungered to see him fail, and his proposition would weaken his new government. Was he making a mistake?

"Are you sure about this?" said Shmuel. The balding former reporter and current Minister of Foreign Affairs had come to know him very well over the past months.

Was he sure? Moshe had not even wanted this job. And he'd made mistakes before.

He'd been a workaholic in his first life. In his drive to expand his family business, he had neglected his wife, Galit, and his daughter, Talya, and almost lost them both.

Since waking up in the Mount of Olives Cemetery five months ago, he had learned his lesson but then discovered a new obsession. With his newfound popular support, he'd fix society. Goodbye cronyism and corruption; hello justice and equality. Utopia was one election away. This time, his ambition had sent him into the clutches of organized crime and almost cost him his life.

But just when he'd foresworn political activism, another miracle occurred. Moshe found himself at the helm of the Jewish State and in an unprecedented position to make good on his campaign promises. But he knew he'd better tread carefully. The establishment played dirty and would not surrender power without a fight. If his plan worked, he wouldn't have to worry about that.

Moshe winked at Shmuel. "Keep your friends close," he said, "your enemies closer?"

Shmuel frowned. "Not close enough to stab you in the back."

"I warned him," said Sivan, the other advisor. "They're our enemies." Her good looks and Louis Vuitton suit hid the featherweight prizefighter who had managed their winning election campaign and now served as Director General of the Prime Minister's Office.

Moshe gave his friends a brave grin. "Isn't it time we turned them into allies?"

Shmuel gave a short, humorless laugh. "That's asking for another miracle."

"Not a miracle. An offer they can't refuse."

He opened the door and made for the head of the conference table.

"Well, well, well," Isaac Gurion said. "If it isn't God Almighty, descending from on high to mingle with the mortals."

Moshe ignored the gibe from his former patron. The portly seasoned politician had turned sour ever since the elections. With only twelve seats in Knesset, his newly minted Upward party had more bark than bite, but Moshe needed the Opposition Leader's cooperation for his plan to work.

On the chair beside Gurion sat Avi Segal, Moshe's ex–best friend and Gurion's current protégé. Avi stared at the polished wood of the conference table, a somber expression on the face beneath the greasy fringe. During their last encounter, with mafia guns pointed at their heads, Avi and Moshe had spared each other's lives. In an unexpected show of maturity, Avi had taken responsibility for tearing Galit and Moshe apart, and his confession had helped mend their marriage. Yet here he sat on the Opposition bench, and Moshe would place no bets on where his loyalties lay.

"Gentlemen," Moshe said. He nodded at Rabbi Yosef, the neighborhood rabbi who now served as Vice Prime Minister, Minister of Education, and Minister of Religious Affairs. "Ladies." He nodded at Savta Sarah. Galit's grandmother filled the roles of both Minister of Finance and Minister of Justice while knitting a scarf. With so few trusted friends on the Restart list, they had to wear many hats.

Only Rafi, the Yemenite taxi driver turned Minister of Transport and Minister of Defense, was absent. Something must have come up. *No matter.* Moshe had already run the proposal by his cabinet before arranging the meeting.

The remaining members of the Opposition snarled at him, but he turned to all present.

"The time has come," he said, "to beat our swords into plowshares and work together to make our nation great. Sivan?"

On cue, Sivan opened her briefcase and distributed copies of the proposal to the seated politicians.

Gurion scanned the document and licked his lips, then frowned and patted his comb-over. "So now you're dishing out ministries? Is this another little ploy?"

"Show some gratitude, son," Savta Sarah said. "Moshe doesn't owe you a thing. He's doing this from the kindness of his heart."

Gurion rolled his eyes. "Thanks for the lecture, granny."

"That's Minister of Finance to you," Moshe said. "And Minister of Justice. You'll note that Savta Sarah has agreed to offer both ministries to your party."

That shut Gurion up.

"And she's right," Moshe continued. "We're running the tightest government in our country's history—with few ministers and low expenses to the taxpayer. Adding ministers won't make us look better."

Truth be told, Moshe needed their help. The tiny cabinet could juggle only so many ministries.

And Gurion's political feelers had not failed him—Moshe had an ulterior motive. Only a strong, broad government could pass the reforms needed to fix the country's problems. In short, Moshe needed Gurion onboard.

Gurion consulted the document again and raised his eyebrows. "You want us to do the work and give you all the credit?"

"The credit will be yours. Far more than you'll get for twiddling your thumbs on the opposition bench."

Moshe eyed Rabbi Emden, in his silk black suit and tidy bowler hat, and said, "Torah True will get Religious Affairs *and* Education. Rabbi Yosef will forgo them both in the interest of a national unity government."

Rabbi Emden stared at the table and nodded. The rabbi had remained reticent throughout the meeting and did not even meet Rabbi Yosef's gaze across the table. Moshe filed that away for later. Right now, he had a coalition to cement.

Gurion dropped the document on the table. "This isn't enough. We should get the premiership."

Moshe had to laugh. The man had chutzpah. By "we" he meant "me."

"Restart has a majority in Knesset. The nation didn't choose you as their leader."

"Rotation, then. We'll take turns at playing Prime Minister, switching every year. We'll even let you go first."

Moshe shook his head.

Gurion folded his arms. "We won't settle for anything less than the vice premiership."

Moshe sighed. Placing Gurion a heartbeat away from the premiership would not bode well for Moshe's personal well-being, but he didn't say that.

Instead, he said, "Restart won the election by promising a clean sweep of the establishment. If we put you in a top spot, we'd lose credibility. This government will do great things; you can be a part of that. The country can use your experience and skills. We need more unity, not more division. Why rot on the sidelines when you can make an impact?"

He let the words linger in the air like fairy dust. The members of the Opposition eyed the documents on the table and tried not to drool.

"How long do we have to decide?"

Moshe stifled a grin. The negotiations had proceeded faster than expected. During his days at the helm of Karlin & Son, his father's taxi dispatch business, Moshe had used deadlines to great effect in clinching deals; now would be no different.

"The agreements are ready for signing," he said. Sivan withdrew a second wad of documents from her briefcase and slid them down the table. "I've arranged for a press conference ten minutes from now. They're setting up in the next room."

Cries of protest erupted around the table. "Ten minutes? That's preposterous! We need more time!"

"We've wasted enough time," Moshe said. "Let's work together."

The assembled politicians pored over the agreements, and Sivan handed out pens. They would sign, Moshe could feel it. He would have his unity government and push through the new legislation with far less friction.

Justice. Equality. Those elusive values would become an everyday reality. But the coalition was the first hurdle; more lay ahead. Good thing Dr. Klein, his cardiologist, had implanted those stents in Moshe's clogged arteries. He'd need a strong heart to survive the rest of the way.

The door opened, and Rafi poked his head inside. "Mr. Prime Minister, a word?"

There you are. From the balding Yemenite's pinched expression and his unexplained absence, Moshe knew the matter was urgent.

He joined Rafi in the corridor outside where a team of uniformed military personnel waited. "What's going on, Rafi?"

"You need to see something," Rafi said. He looked over his shoulder to make sure no one was eavesdropping. "Your helicopter is ready to leave."

Helicopter? Moshe sent a longing glance toward the conference room. "But they're about to sign. And there's the press conference in ten minutes. Can't this wait a few hours?"

"No," Rafi said. "It can't."

CHAPTER 3

The IDF chopper headed west toward the Mediterranean coastline, then banked south toward the Gaza Strip. Moshe peered out the back-seat window and swore under his breath.

Perfect. Just what he needed—a war during his first month in office. Instead of making meaningful political change, he'd have to mobilize reserve forces and manage a military crisis. But if the Gazan border had flared up again, surely Rafi wouldn't risk a helicopter ride so close to the Strip?

"Over there," Rafi said, his voice a crackle in the headset over the roar of the rotors. He pointed.

Far below, a dozen streams emerged from empty fields on the Israeli side of the border wall and flowed toward the villages. The tributaries converged and pooled beside a clump of large brown military tents.

The chopper dived toward the encampment, and Moshe's stomach churned.

He squinted at the streams, which before his eyes, became long columns of moving human beings. Hundreds of them—no thousands—and they were all naked.

Dear Lord!

For months, volunteers at the Dry Bones Society had collected the newly resurrected from cemeteries across the country. The new arrivals arrived each morning, naked and confused, in dribs and drabs. Moshe had never witnessed such a large influx of resurrected people and never in the middle of nowhere.

The chopper landed at a makeshift helipad at the edge of the campsite. Moshe, Rafi, and Sivan disembarked, keeping their heads low to avoid the whining rotors.

A soldier stood at attention. "Prime Minister Karlin," he said. A badge depicting a sword crossed with a leafy branch perched on his shoulder. "I'm Brigadier General Levi. The Chief is expecting you."

He escorted them along the edge of the enclosure formed by lengths of plastic tape between metal stakes. On the other side, men, women, and children with rough blankets draped over their shoulders gaped at the people who had just stepped out of the giant metal bird.

The First Responder Guidelines, which Moshe had written for the Dry Bones Society, advised volunteers not to disorient the new arrivals with displays of modern technology. But the guidelines did not prepare the volunteers for such a wave of new members.

The Prime Minister and his entourage climbed into the back seat of a waiting Humvee and sped off. The driver rounded the tents, hurried past a stream of returning humanity, and then stopped beside a second Humvee.

Chief of Staff Eitan stood in green military fatigues, arms akimbo, as he observed the steady march through dark sunglasses.

"Seen nothing like it," he said, after greeting the visitors. A team of soldiers handed out blankets and directed the pale-skinned arrivals to the enclosure.

Moshe had trouble believing his eyes too. What could account for this mass of resurrected people?

"Is there a cemetery nearby? Mass grave?"

"Beats me."

"An old burial site or battlefield?"

"Unlikely. Our officers interviewed a bunch of them. They're from all over history. But they're sure making our regular jobs easy—they're surfacing from terror tunnels based in Gaza."

"Gaza?" Rafi said. "They don't look like Arabs."

"No sir, they do not. They speak English, mostly, although we're getting a lot of French and Spanish too."

Moshe rubbed his forehead. Europeans in Gaza—that made no sense at all.

Sivan said, "What's that noise?"

Moshe heard it too—a low moaning from further down the line.

"Oh, that," Eitan said. "Follow me. And try not to freak out."

He marched a few feet toward the eerie sounds, then stopped.

"Notice anything… different?"

The men and women lumbered forward like sleepwalkers, their heads hanging loosely at the shoulders, their mouths open, and their unseeing eyes glazed over.

"Dear Lord!" Rafi said.

"Oh my God!" Sivan gripped Moshe's arm. "They're like… like…"

"Zombies," Eitan said, and he cleared his throat.

A shiver ran down Moshe's spine. During the elections, Avi Segal had branded the resurrected as the unnatural undead and stirred up fears about a zombie invasion.

"That's how they emerge from the tunnels. After a few steps, they come to. Good luck falling asleep tonight, folks."

A vague memory roused Moshe from shock. "Resurrection Tunnels," he said, and won blank stares from his companions. "Rabbi Yosef mentioned those once. It's an ancient tradition. During the Resurrection, righteous people buried abroad will roll through the tunnels to get back to the Holy Land."

"Strange as this sounds," Eitan said, "that might explain it. Some tunnels merge with natural subterranean caves. The network of caves could run beneath the sea floor."

Moshe shook his head in wonder. "Another ancient prediction checked off the list. Rabbi Yosef will be glad to hear that. We must call in the Dry Bones Society."

"No way," Sivan said.

"You're right—this job is too big for the DBS. We'll need to allocate funds in the new government budget."

"I mean," Sivan said, "we can't tell anyone. This has to stay here."

Her refusal to help caught Moshe off guard. "But they'll need food and clothing and accommodation."

"Nobody can know about this. Not until the coalition is signed and sealed. Do you know what a media circus this will become if anyone finds out? Imagine this"—she framed the scene of lurching naked people with her fingers—"on prime time TV. An army of zombies is all the Opposition needs to make our lives a misery. We'll need time to spin this in a positive light."

She had a point. "OK, let's keep this top secret for now. Rafi, what can we do in the short term without causing a fuss?"

"We have emergency stores in case of war and disaster."

"Excellent. Release those."

"And fast," Eitan said. "We're running out of blankets and food."

Moshe asked, "What about shelter?"

"We're setting up campsites. But we'll need a long-term solution soon, especially if this keeps up." He glanced at the zombies and swallowed hard. "Winter is coming."

CHAPTER 4

Wednesday morning, Yosef tried not to retch.

"Minister Lev!" gushed Rabbi Mendel of the Torah True party. He gripped Yosef's hand over the large oak desk of Yosef's chamber within the Prime Minister's Office building. "Pardon me. I meant to say, *Vice Prime Minister* Lev!" He plopped onto one of the leather visitor's seats and took in the room. "I *love* what you've done with the place."

Yosef glanced around his new spacious room. The only thing he had changed since taking office was the framed photo of the Prime Minister, which now displayed Moshe Karlin in a stately blue suit and tie. Yosef still didn't feel like he belonged behind the heavy desk. If he was a fraud, he was now in very good company.

A few weeks ago, Rabbi Mendel's puppeteers at the Great Council of Torah Sages had branded Yosef an agent of the *Sitrah Achrah*, the evil Other Side. They had fired him from his teaching job at Daas Torah Primary. During the election campaign, Mendel's political allies had libeled Yosef on national television as an alcoholic pedophile. But now that Yosef had attained a position of power, Rabbi Mendel pretended that none of that had happened.

Yosef suppressed his gag reflex and held his tongue for the same reason he had not redecorated his office. Soon he would vacate the room along with his ministerial positions as part of Moshe's coalition agreement.

Yosef didn't mind.

"You're a good man," his wife, Rocheleh, had said. She had meant "gullible." A little less gullible now, after all he had experienced, but still she was right: he did not belong in politics. As a regular Member of Knesset, he'd be able to help Moshe pass laws in Knesset and still have time to counsel new arrivals at the Dry Bones Society.

He drew a deep breath. "How can I help you, Member of Knesset Mendel?" The greedy politician did not deserve the title "Rabbi." True rabbis had a working moral compass.

"About the coalition agreement," Mendel said. "As you surely know, the gravity and demands of the Department of Religious Affairs require a number of deputy minister positions that appear to be missing from the list."

Yosef guessed where this was going. "And you were wondering whether I'd have a word with the Prime Minister about adding a few jobs?"

Mendel winced at the word "jobs" but didn't let the veiled condemnation derail his greed. "Five positions, to be specific."

"I see." Five extra ministerial positions with the associated salaries and benefits. Moshe wanted to reduce government expenses, but for the sake of the coalition, he would compromise.

Now that he had Mendel's attention, Yosef wanted to scratch an itch of his own. "I'm curious—why you? Member of Parliament Emden has known me for years. Surely he'd be the one to approach me?"

Spite boiled within him and Yosef flushed with shame. He knew perfectly well why Emden hadn't shown his face. His former mentor and confidant had turned their years of friendship into a political weapon when he had exposed Yosef's secrets in the smear campaign. The memory was a knife twisting in Yosef's back.

Mendel touched his nose. "Rabbi Emden went home early. He wasn't feeling well."

Yosef gave a short and mirthless laugh. Did Emden regret the betrayal, or did he fear that his presence would hamper Yosef's willingness to cooperate?

"A speedy recovery to him," Yosef said. "I'll speak with the Prime Minister and see what he can do."

He dismissed Mendel, along with the poison in his own heart. The Torah forbade bearing a grudge. Soon, he'd be able to wave it all goodbye and leave the politics to the politicians.

The phone buzzed on his desk. "Yes, Ram?"

Of the many ministerial perks, the personal assistant had taken the most getting used to. The Knesset bureaucrats had tried to pair him with a pretty young girl. Although Yosef had not doubted her secretarial credentials, he had requested a male replacement. One smear campaign was more than enough, and Yosef did not want to feed the rumormongers.

Ram had not disappointed him, although his effeminate lisp created the nagging suspicion that the bureaucrats had played their little joke on him all the same.

"Tom Levi is on the line for you."

"Tom Levi?" The name sounded familiar.

"He says he represents the Temple Faithful."

Yosef remembered.

"The Messiah is coming," Gavri the grocer had told him, and so, early on the morning of Election Day, Yosef had rushed to the Old City. Dressed in white shepherd's robes and a matching cotton beanie, the bearded and drunken messiah had stood atop the Western Wall and attempted to walk on air. Then reality hit in the form of the hard-stone floor of the plaza, and the paramedics rushed his broken body away on a stretcher.

While the stunning failure of the Messiah on the Wall had brought Yosef face-to-face with his own naivety, the catastrophe had not discouraged the messiah's followers in the slightest. Then and there, his red-bearded spokesman had tried to rope Yosef into a scheme to demolish the Islamic

Dome of the Rock on the Temple Mount and to rebuild the Jewish Temple in its place. "I'm Tom," the lunatic had said. "Tom Levi." Yosef, the lunatic magnet, had fled the scene.

"Shall I transfer the call?" Ram asked.

"No."

"Schedule an appointment?"

"No! Tell him I'm unavailable."

"Yes, sir."

"Thank you."

Yosef exhaled, long and slow. A secretary provided definite advantages. Tom Levi would no doubt try again, but by then Yosef would have relinquished his ministerial position, and the lunatic would be somebody else's problem. *Good luck with that, Mendel. Ha!*

The phone buzzed again.

"Yes, Ram?"

"Reverend Adams is here to see you."

Yosef's pulse quickened. "Please send him in."

He stood and wiped his palms on his trousers as the broad-chested American burst into the room like a force of nature in an expensive suit. The silver-haired Christian gave Yosef's hand a mighty double-handed squeeze that threatened to dislocate the rabbi's shoulder. "Vice President Lev, my congratulations," he said in his Texas drawl. "What an honor to meet with you again." His ivory teeth glinted as he smiled.

"Vice *Prime Minister*," Yosef corrected.

"Right, yes, of course!"

Adams was not a stickler for details. He took a seat, and his spindly, briefcase-toting assistant followed suit.

Yosef's heart palpitated faster, and not just because he had to deploy his minimal English skills. He knew which question his benefactor had dropped by to ask, and Yosef's answer would break his heart.

The New Evangelical Church of America had created a wholly owned subsidiary, The Flesh and Blood Fund, to bankroll the Dry Bones Society. He had also given the nascent Restart party the infusion of funds needed to jumpstart their winning election campaign. Would he turn off the tap when he realized that his church's key motivation for supporting those enterprises had not borne fruit?

Adams got straight to business. "You're a busy man, so I won't hog your time. Tell me, Rabbi," a smile sparkled in his eyes, "have we reached the Roman Period?" He sent a gleeful glance at his associate, who smiled and blinked at Yosef with expectation.

Each morning, the dead returned from further back in history. Casualties of the Israeli wars had preceded resistance fighters of the British Mandate period. The hapless dead of the Ottoman Empire, and Islamic and Crusader eras, had followed.

"Yes, we have," Yosef said. "The Roman Period and *earlier*. We find professors to speak with the new arrivals. Latin. Ancient Greek. Aramaic. And, how you say, Phoenician? Or Proto-Canaanite? I forget." Yosef chuckled, but his delay tactics failed.

Adams leaned forward. "Excellent. So, has *He* stopped by yet to visit his colleagues?"

"He?" Yosef clasped his trembling fingers on his lap.

"Yes. *He*. With a capital H. Our charismatic friend. The Aramaic speaker."

"M-many new arrivals speak A-Aramaic. And some are very… charismatic?"

Adams's smile froze. It thawed. Then it evaporated. He flopped against the backrest, and all that good cheer left him like air escaping a balloon. He glanced at his concerned assistant, then at the wall behind Yosef. "I… I don't understand. Surely by now…"

He shook his head, and his eyes glistened. The reverend had predicted that his Savior would descend from Heaven to rejoin the resurrected of His generation. Although this Second Coming would have created very awkward theological issues for the rabbi, Yosef felt a stab of empathy.

Yosef had tasted bitter disillusion too. The Resurrection

rewarded the world's victims with a second chance at life. But then Shmuel had unmasked a suicide bomber among the members of the Dry Bones Society, and that understanding had come crashing down. Did a cold-blooded mass murderer deserve a second chance?

And so, ironically, just as Yosef reached the pinnacle of success and power, he had lost his naïve faith both in the rabbinate and in cosmic justice.

Yosef searched for words to comfort both his fellow believer and himself. "Perhaps this resurrection is not what we thought."

CHAPTER 5

Eli Katz glanced at the whiteboard on the easel that Noga had set up in the living room of his penthouse on Jaffa Road. He had not felt this hopeful in, literally, a thousand years.

"I like it," he said. "It's a great plan."

"Honest?"

"Definitely."

Noga jumped on him and kissed him long and hard.

Eli came up for air. "And it's looking better by the minute."

"You're not just saying that because I kissed you, are you?"

"Nope, although that did help. Hey!" He evaded her jabbing fingers. "Here's why I like it," he added, to avoid death by tickling. He cleared his throat and read the three-step plan out loud. "'Publish paper. Contact media. Meet Prime Minister.' It's short, simple, and doable. Once *Nature Genetics* gives us our academic creds, the newspapers will carry the story. Once the story spreads, Moshe Karlin will come calling."

Moshe Karlin was their leading candidate for the role of Messiah in the cosmic drama. The resurrected man had stormed the political scene overnight, winning over the country with a clean campaign that promised to end corruption and cronyism. He was also the man that God had told Eli to anoint. At least, so Eli thought.

Five months ago, the Thin Voice had sent Eli, also known as Elijah the Prophet, to anoint the Messiah at the Mount of Olives Cemetery. Eli had spotted three people at the rendezvous point. Later, he would identify them as Moshe Karlin, Rabbi Yosef Lev, and a mysterious blond Russian woman who worked at the Dry Bones Society.

Unfortunately for humanity, before Eli could anoint the Messiah, he crashed his Harley into a truck and woke up in the Shaare Zedek Medical Center. The Thin Voice had fallen silent ever since. In the hospital, Eli met Noga. She stole his heart, rekindled his faith in humanity, and saved him from the head of neurology, Dr. Stern, who had developed an unhealthy interest in Eli's speedy recovery.

In hindsight, Eli's motorcycle accident was yet another step in the Divine Plan. God had led him to Noga, but not merely to jump-start an ancient prophet's rusty motivation. Noga's doctoral research project identified Palestinian Arabs as the Ten Lost Tribes of Israel, a demographic that Elijah the Prophet was to uncover during the Messianic Era. To reunite the Twelve Tribes of Israel in the Holy Land was high on the to-do list of the long-overdue Messiah. Without the Lost Tribes, the moment of Redemption might slip away yet again.

As for Moshe Karlin, a charismatic new leader of the Jewish State made sense as the Messiah. His layers of Secret Service security, however, made bumping into him on the street impossible. "Hey, Moshe. How you doing? And by the way, you're the Messiah. Good luck!"

But the publication of Noga's findings in one of the world's most esteemed peer-reviewed academic journals would open the path to Moshe Karlin. Noga had submitted her paper last week, and they used the wait to hone the rest of their plan.

Eli frowned. "We're forgetting one critical thing."

Noga's face became a battleground of fear and uncertainty. "What?"

"Breakfast."

Eli fixed shakshouka in a frying pan—heavy on the tomato, light on the chili—and popped a few slices of bread in the toaster. Sitting at the island of his designer kitchen, they munched away while the sun warmed the Jerusalem skyline through the French windows.

"Things were easier in the past," he said. "If I wanted to give King Ahab an earful, I'd just wait in the woods for his chariot to pass by."

"You should speak with archaeologists," Noga said. "They'd learn so much."

Memories from his earlier life used to freak Noga out. After she located the Ten Lost Tribes and discovered that dead people were rising from their graves throughout the country, her boyfriend's longevity no longer seemed so far-fetched.

"Nah," Eli said. "Even if they believed me, it's anecdotal evidence."

"Right." Her eyes narrowed as she thought. "How did you know where to wait?"

"For Ahab? The Thin Voice."

"Figures. Everything's easier with a direct line to God's Mind."

"Yeah." He sighed.

Without the Thin Voice, he'd never know for sure whether Moshe was the Lord's Anointed. He was flying blind. But maybe that was the point. After centuries of false messiahs, maybe this time really was different. Maybe this time the Final Redemption would arrive.

Noga's phone rang. She washed down a mouthful of shakshouka. "It's Hannah." She answered. "Hi, Hannah. How are you?"

Noga listened, her brow tense. They hadn't expected to hear from her doctoral supervisor for weeks. Academic journals took their time to analyze and reproduce results before including a paper in their next edition.

"Aha," Noga said. She stared into space, and her expression slackened. Something was wrong. "I see."

She put down the phone. "They're not going to publish the paper."

"Did we miss the deadline?" A delay would set back their plans by months.

"No," she said. "We submitted in time, but they still won't publish it. Not now. Not ever."

CHAPTER 6

"Are you sure it's safe?" Ahmed asked Dara. He did not ask, "Is it legal?"

They stood on the edge of a dirt road on the outskirts of Jerusalem, the surrounding hills strewn with stones and wild grass. His new friend handed him a large rock from a large mound. Ahmed hefted the stone in one hand, wondering how far he could throw it.

"Yeah, sure. I've done it many times. And if you get shot, they pay more."

Ahmed hesitated. As much as he hated eating from dumpsters, he did not like the idea of getting shot. But he needed money. A roof over his head would be nice too, instead of that old tomb at the edge of the Mount of Olives. His friend's promise of employment had sounded too good to be true. And when something sounds too good to be true, you run for your life. He had learned that the hard way.

Still, he had to start somewhere. And if he had a job, maybe Samira would want to see him again.

"Murderer!" the older Israeli man had roared. In the group session room at the Dry Bones Society, he had tried to throttle Ahmed. He had recognized Ahmed from the bus, the day Ahmed had pressed the detonator button threaded through his sleeve and thrown the commuters into a fiery hell.

Keep dreaming, you fool. Samira knew what he had done; she'd never want to look on him again.

"What if we get arrested?" Ahmed asked.

He feared capture more than injury. If the authorities found out who he was, they would imprison him for sure. And they weren't the only ones who wanted to put his head on a spike. In his nightmares, Boris the slave driver found him, and his henchmen dragged Ahmed back to the life of hard labor he had fled.

His cousin Hasan would be next in line. "A double martyr," he had told Ahmed. "You will be a hero. No, more than that—a legend." Ahmed had accepted the second explosive belt but then aborted his mission. How would the suicide bomber pimp receive him now? Probably not with hugs and kisses.

"You worry too much," Dara said. "Here." He pulled a white-and-black-checkered *kaffiyeh* from a plastic bin and handed it to Ahmed. "Put that over your face and you'll be invisible. OK?"

Ahmed glanced at the clump of young Arab men in rough clothes, loitering across the road. What other options did he have? "OK."

An unmarked bus barreled down the road, kicking up dust, and stopped beside the mound of stones. The two friends got on, along with the other desperate young men. Instead of buying a ticket, they scribbled their names on a lined sheet of paper using a pen attached by a string. *Walid*, Ahmed wrote. The word meant newborn. His new life was not progressing as he had hoped.

"Where does the money come from?" Ahmed asked when they had found a pair of seats at a dusty window.

"Europe," Dara said. "Germany, mostly."

"What do Germans want here?"

"To help the Palestinians."

Ahmed chuckled. "You're kidding, right?" He got that too-good-to-be-true sensation again.

"Their money is no joke. Their non-governmental organizations spend millions of dollars here."

"Wow." A million dollars was an unimaginable amount of money. Where did those millions go?

When they got off the bus, he found out. Ten other buses offloaded similarly wretched Arabs at the meeting point. A few dozen more arrived with the same cargo as they waited. Some were kids; the youngest looked seven years old.

An army of Europeans in flak jackets and sunglasses smoked cigarettes and joked around in foreign tongues. Most of them held microphones or shouldered television cameras.

"We're starting," cried an Arab man, who seemed to be in charge. "This way."

Two hundred Arabs pulled *kaffiyehs* over their faces and marched down the dirt road, the cameramen flanking them. The crowd stopped twenty meters from what looked like an oversized call box surrounded by cement blocks where two Israeli soldiers watched cars passing on a paved road. The soldiers wore helmets, bulky equipment jackets with high lapels, and machine guns across their chests.

"Wait for it!" the Arab leader yelled. The cameramen were still setting up their tripods.

One soldier talked to the other and pointed toward the waiting crowd. Inside the call box, another soldier spoke into a telephone handset.

"Now!" the leader cried.

"Let the show begin," Dara said.

The first rock hit a soldier on the head. The man collapsed behind the cement barrier, and two of his colleagues dragged him into the call box. To Ahmed's surprise, none of the soldiers returned fire.

Ahmed turned to see whether the reporters had caught that, but they had their cameras trained on the Arab rioters.

Rocks bounced off the cement barriers and cracked the windows of the call box.

"Why aren't they firing?" Ahmed asked.

Dara laughed. "They're too scared. If they kill any of us by mistake, they'll go to prison. C'mon, throw something."

Ahmed looked at the rock in his hand.

"C'mon, give it to those sons of pigs! Killers of prophets!"

In his first life, Ahmed had worked at the Rami Levi supermarket in Talpiot. His boss, Yigal, had joked around with him in Arabic, asked after his family, and let him take Fridays off. And when Ahmed's own mother had turned him out on the street, the Dry Bones Society had given him food and shelter. Moshe Karlin and Rabbi Yosef had saved Samira from Boris and his henchmen. What if these soldiers were their brothers and sisters?

Dara glared at him. "No stones, no money."

Ahmed lunged forward and threw the rock with all his might. It bounced into a clump of grass at the side of the road.

"Man!" Dara said. "You have the worst aim ever." He chuckled.

While Ahmed threw wide, the others had no inhibitions. Rocks rained on the call box, then targeted the passing cars. A windshield smashed, and the car veered off the road, almost colliding with oncoming traffic, then returned to its lane and sped off.

After that, the soldiers stepped out of their shelter and aimed their rifles in the air.

Some rioters fled to the back of the crowd.

"Go! Go!" the ringleader said, and a group of Arab kids advanced on the soldiers, hurling curses and stones.

Camera shutters clicked as they captured the scene: Israeli soldiers firing over the heads of seven-year-olds.

Ahmed swore. He had seen a lot of messed up things in his life, but the choreographed riot with its pint-sized human shields left him speechless. Where were their parents? And how much would they earn for an injured child?

He had been one of those boys once. And so, the wheel turned.

A military van pulled up outside the call box, and soldiers poured out the back. Weapons fired, and Ahmed ducked out of the way. A cloud of white smoke billowed nearby. The gas burned his eyes and seared his throat.

"Fall back," Dara shouted. They ran away from the tear gas and back to the meeting point where the buses idled.

The show was over.

CHAPTER 7

Beneath the tall dome of the empty hall in the Knesset building, Avi reread the coalition agreement for the tenth time. The document was the answer to his prayers.

The Plenum Hall of the Knesset stood three floors high, the rows of seats arranged before the Speaker's dais in the shape of a candelabrum. As a member of the Opposition, Avi sat at the back.

Within a month, he had gone from sleeping on benches in Sacher Park to dozing off on the comfy chairs in Knesset. Who would have believed it?

His new fortune in life had placed him in a bind. He had landed his spot on the Upward party list by stirring up popular discontent for the Dry Bones Society and their "undead zombies." Boris the gangster was his patron, Isaac Gurion his mentor, Moshe Karlin his sworn enemy, and Galit his rightful girl. But on Election Day, his worldview had flipped one hundred and eighty degrees. Nothing makes a man see the error of his ways like a gun pointed at his head.

Mandrake, Boris's sadistic and psycho boss, had tied up Avi and Moshe and urged them to blow each other's brains out—right in front of Galit. When it came to the crunch, Avi couldn't do it. He had never wanted to kill Moshe, he realized; he had wanted *to be* Moshe. His rash entry into politics had almost killed the two people he cared about most. No longer could he blame Moshe for his own failings.

The revelations had not faded after his narrow escape from death, not even after Moshe's resounding victory in the elections. And so Avi found himself in Knesset, on the Opposition bench, while secretly he was rooting for Moshe.

For two weeks, he had haunted the corridors of Knesset, trying to be invisible. He avoided his party leader, Isaac Gurion, who radiated pent-up rage and frustration and often vented both on his subordinates. Avi had skipped as many Knesset sessions as possible, preferring to creep into the Plenum Hall when vacant, like now.

But Moshe's generous coalition agreement would set the world aright. He and Moshe would be on the same team again. They'd be buddies like in the good old days at Karlin & Son before Avi's mad jealousy had led him to betray Moshe and ruin everything.

The memory of Karlin & Son gave Avi an idea. He rushed out of the empty hall and sped down a corridor.

He found Gurion lounging in a committee room in the Kedma wing and chuckling with Rabbi Mendel of Torah True.

Gurion looked up at his flushed minion. "Hello, Avi. Getting some exercise?"

He's in a good mood. Great. Avi gave a quick smile. "About the coalition—I was wondering: is the Deputy Minister of Transportation position available?"

"Why, are you interested in *going places*?"

Gurion and Rabbi Mendel chortled again. Why were they so happy?

"I think I can contribute there. Before I entered politics, I worked in the, ah, public transportation industry, and—"

"You mean at Karlin & Son?"

The mention of that detail unsettled Avi. Gurion had done his homework. But would he wonder where Avi's loyalties lay now? "Well, yes," he said, "but—"

Another chuckle cut him short. Again, Avi was out of the

loop and two steps behind; he hated that.

"What if you were to *head* that ministry—wouldn't you do even more good?"

Him—Minster of Transportation? "Yeah, sure. But I'm not high enough on our list, and with the amount of positions Karlin is offering…" More chuckles. They were driving him crazy. "What?"

Gurion motioned for Avi to sit next to him and placed an arm around his shoulders. "We're not going to join the coalition, Avi."

"We aren't? But then how will we get any ministries?"

"By taking them. We're going to bring down Karlin's government."

The floor of Avi's stomach fell away. "Bring down the government—but how?"

"That's easy," Gurion said. "Together."

CHAPTER 8

"Mr. Prime Minister!" said a voice in the corridor behind him. Moshe had hurried from the chopper pad into the Prime Minister's Office building, hoping to slip into his room unnoticed, when the man called his name. Of all people, he had hoped to avoid the Government Secretary.

Moshe turned as the eager little man ran over. "Yes, Rubi. How can I help you?"

"The question is 'How can *I* help *you*?'" He gave a nervous chuckle. With his square glasses and rounded features, Rubi reminded him of an owl. "I hear there was a meeting this morning with Opposition MPs. My department's job is to coordinate between you and Knesset. If I'd only known in advance—"

Moshe held up his hand, cutting him short. "I know, you would have taken care of everything."

Since Moshe's first day in office, Rubi had pressured him to avail himself of his teams of bureaucrats. Moshe had selected an employee from the pool of secretaries but drawn the line at more sensitive roles. Like the intelligence agencies, the Government Secretariat was part of the entrenched establishment. Over the years, they had nurtured relationships with career politicians such as Gurion, and they resented Moshe's new upstart party that had stormed the halls of power. They probably feared that he aimed to terminate their comfy tenured jobs; on that point, they happened to be right. Could he trust them not to leak top secret information to their old pals? Considering that morning's events on the Gazan border, Moshe's decision seemed wise.

"It's not just the logistics," Rubi continued. "We have speech writers and spokespeople. A prime minister who wants to get things done can't do everything on his own."

"I appreciate your concern," Moshe said. "But I prefer to write my own speeches, and Sivan is managing our press relations. I'll be sure to contact you when the need arises."

He continued down the corridor, but the bureaucrat wasn't giving up. "At least let us help next time, I'm sure you'll see our added value. Will you be making any announcements soon?"

Moshe halted outside his office and studied the eager owl's face. Was he interested in proving his worth, or was he fishing for information? He must have heard of Moshe's sudden helicopter excursion. What else did he know?

"Mr. Prime Minister," said Ettie. Moshe's elderly secretary peered at him over half-moon spectacles from her desk outside his office. "The American Ambassador is waiting for you inside."

Interesting. "Is this a scheduled appointment?" He didn't recall any diplomatic meetings on his calendar today.

"No, sir. But he says it's very urgent."

Were the Americans going to pressure him into yet another Peace Process already, or had some new crisis arisen? Either way, he'd found the perfect excuse to brush off the Government Secretary. "If you'll excuse me…"

"Of course," Rubi said, and trudged away.

"Ambassador Smith," Moshe said in English, closing the door of his office behind him. He shook the burly American's hand and took his seat behind the Prime Minister's desk. "To what do I owe this pleasant surprise?"

The ambassador had presented his credentials to the new prime minister during Moshe's first week in office. Smith had been cool and dismissive, but today the ambassador greeted him with a broad, eager smile, his cheeks flushed with ingratiation.

"I am happy to bring Your Excellency an urgent message from the President of the United States."

"Wonderful," Moshe said and swallowed hard. *Here it comes.*

Smith's smile threatened to split his face in two. "The President would like to remind you of the special bond between our great nations. As the only liberal democracy in the Middle East, Israel shares with the United States not only political interests but a cultural and moral heritage."

Moshe shifted on his padded seat. Such an introduction implied a very large ask. What could the President of the United States want from the Jewish State?

"The President would also like to remind Your Excellency of the United States' long history of friendship with and support for the State of Israel, both financial and political. From sharing intelligence and generous military funding to vetoing hostile resolutions at the United Nations."

Moshe fought the urge to interrupt. That "friendship and support" had often fluctuated with changing American administrations, and always came with a catch. Their demands for action—and inaction—often endangered Israeli lives.

"Above all," Smith continued, "the American People have always felt a deep connection with the Nation of Israel and concern for its fate."

Moshe was learning the complex dance of political statesmanship. The steps included demands cloaked in compliments and accusations dressed as gratitude. Translated into plain English, the president's message meant, "You owe us big time and it's time to pay up."

Fortunately, Moshe could dance too.

"On behalf of the State of Israel," he replied, "I thank the President for his kind reminder. Please let him know that we are very grateful and deeply appreciate his nation's friendship and *ongoing* support."

He emphasized the word "ongoing." Translation: what's in it for us?

Ambassador Smith drew a deep breath and gritted his teeth. Beneath the veneer of cordiality, the career diplomat resented having to dance with Moshe Karlin, the former unwashed civilian. But orders from the President were orders.

"The President would like to formalize our special relationship by offering the State of Israel full membership in the federal republic."

Moshe must have misunderstood. "The federal republic?"

Smith pursed his lips. "In short, he's inviting the State of Israel to become a part of the United States of America."

"The fifty-first state?"

"Exactly."

"Wow." That was an unstatesmanlike thing to say, but Moshe couldn't control himself. "But… we're in the Middle East."

Smith shrugged. "Hawaii is in the middle of the Pacific Ocean. Alaska is on the other side of Canada."

"Forgive me for asking, Mr. Ambassador, but why?"

"The benefits are many. Any attack on Israel would be a declaration of war against the United States. The full force of the United States Army would stand behind you. Israel would no longer have to impose high taxes to fund its defense needs. Uncle Sam would take care of you. Your country would benefit from our international ties and credit rating. Israeli citizens would no longer require visas to visit or work in the United States."

"I understand," Moshe said. "But what I meant was, what would the United States stand to gain?"

Smith cleared his throat. "Of course, Israel would have to adhere to federal law. Israel would have to adopt the US currency and controls. Your Excellency would become the Governor of the State of Israel, and your government would integrate with the Senate and House of Representatives. We will make provisions to retain the unique character of the Jewish State as the homeland of the Jewish People."

Smith's eyes darted to the table. The ambassador was dancing around the topic, and they both knew it.

"But surely the United States doesn't need another state? Israel has been targeted for extermination by Muslim countries. Wouldn't this invite conflict?"

Ambassador Smith pouted as he mulled his next words. "The President feels that this is the right thing to do. In addition, the United States would gain access to Israel's resources."

A short laugh escaped Moshe's lips. "We have no oil or precious minerals, and little natural gas. Our main assets are technology and human resources."

"Precisely," Smith said, his mouth twisting into a knowing sneer. "In the Information Age, it's those resources that count."

Moshe wasn't buying it. The US already had access to the technology of Israel's start-ups and military. This sudden desire to adopt the Jewish State must somehow be related to the Resurrection. Did the American government, like Reverend Adams and his Evangelical Christians, believe that the world was approaching the End of Days? Were they hedging their bets ahead of Armageddon?

Smith seemed to have read Moshe's thoughts. "The times are changing," he said. "We expect that the State of Israel will be at the epicenter of that change. And, Your Excellency, we intend to be right there at your side."

Moshe had seen the posters with his portrait on the streets of Israel. "Welcome, King Messiah!" they read. Moshe hadn't let that go to his head. He wasn't the messiah; surely he would know if he was? With his rise to prominence, news of the Resurrection had spread across the world. Had the Americans contracted the same messianic fever?

Moshe swallowed again. He would have to tread carefully.

"Please thank the President for his very generous offer. Obviously, I'll have to discuss this with my cabinet. The coalition agreement we hope to sign soon will make the President's proposal much easier to implement. Please thank the President for his patience."

"Very well," Ambassador Smith said. He rose to leave. "One more thing. The President would appreciate it if you'd keep this offer secret. We wouldn't want other interested parties to create any obstacles."

"Of course."

Moshe shook his hand, escorted him to the door, and paced his office.

The fifty-first state! The proposition would be a hard sell to the Israeli public. But was accession to the United States in Israel's long-term interests? Moshe had hung his personal hopes on powerful friends before and paid the price; he did not want to repeat that mistake on a national scale.

There was a knock on the door before it opened, and Sivan entered.

"I've rescheduled both the coalition signing and the press conference for tomorrow."

"Excellent."

"And I think I've found the right spin for the developments in the south."

"The miracles never cease. What's the angle?"

She sucked in a deep breath. "The Sixth Aliyah."

As usual, Sivan's marketing genius had nailed the solution. Since the late nineteenth century, Jews had arrived in the Holy Land in waves, each known as an *aliyah*—an ascension or immigration. Some immigrants came to lay the foundations for a future Jewish State, others to escape persecution in Europe, the Middle East, and Asia.

By naming the recent influx of resurrected as the Sixth Aliyah, Sivan framed the phenomenon as the natural continuation of the first five mass immigrations. And why not?

Besides, anything was better than Zombie Invasion, the phrase that Gurion's Opposition would use if they ever got wind of these new arrivals.

"I like it!"

"Thought you would. Great, that's settled then. Now we just need to keep a lid on things until the coalition agreement is signed."

The intercom buzzed, and Moshe thumbed the speaker-phone.

"Yes, Ettie?"

"The Russian Ambassador is here to see you, sir."

First the Americans; now the Russians? "I don't suppose he made an appointment either, did he?"

"No, sir. But he says it's very urgent."

CHAPTER 9

"You know what this place needs?" Irina said, over breakfast. She glanced at the peeling wallpaper of Alex's kitchen.

Alex looked up from his cornflakes, his ponytail switching behind him. "A bulldozer?"

She laughed. His second-floor apartment in downtown Jerusalem had seen better decades, that was clear, but wasn't ready for the wrecking ball yet. The three-room rental with the chunky plaster and noisy plumbing had an Old World charm. It was an apartment they would remember fondly after moving to the suburbs.

"Flowers," she said. "Some color."

Over the past weeks, Irina had spent more evenings at Alex's apartment than her Dry Bones Society dormitory room; she'd come to think of the bachelor pad as home.

"Good idea," he said. He seemed relieved. Had he thought she'd planned to go through his wardrobe and discard his old T-shirts? Irina made a mental note to do just that later.

She and Alex had grown close since their random meeting at the Dry Bones Society. Beneath the bulging muscles, she'd discovered a gentleman and a kind soul. There was still so much for her to learn about the new man in her life. The Russian tattoos hinted at a difficult past. She had yet to meet his friends and family. A thrilling thought struck her—had he met hers?

Moshe Karlin and Rabbi Yosef had discovered her among the tombstones of the Mount of Olives Cemetery. Five months later, she still recalled nothing of her former life, and not for want of trying.

Alex had enlisted his neurologist friend to crack the mystery of Irina's sealed past. Despite the doctor's unorthodox methods, which had involved a dentist's chair, electrodes, and hypnosis, her former life remained a locked vault. "A lack of blood flow to the right temporal lobe, the seat of long-term memory," Dr. V had explained. "Usually the result of head trauma."

Traffic accident, she assumed. She shivered at the idea of her violent first death and pushed thoughts of her demise from her mind. The possibilities in her new life were far more interesting.

Alex finished his bowl of cereal. "Want me to drop you at the office?"

He meant the Dry Bones Society. With Moshe's move to the Prime Minister's Office, Irina had inherited the reins of the charitable organization. She and Samira, the Arab girl she had met early in her new life, had taken over his corner office in the DBS call center. Moshe didn't mind; running the country kept him more than occupied.

"Not today," she said. "I'm going south."

Alex raised his eyebrows. "South?"

"Special mission. Hush-hush. I'm scouting out development cities with basic infrastructure."

"More new arrivals than usual?"

"That's the strange thing. The numbers have leveled out since we hit BCE. Something's going on, but the details are still under wraps."

Alex looked at his wristwatch and downed the rest of his coffee. He grabbed his keys, kissed her goodbye, and stepped out.

Irina put the milk back in the fifty-year-old fridge and washed the bowls in the ancient enamel sink. Out the window, buses hissed and growled along Shamai Street.

A development town! Where would the returnees come from?

Although she enjoyed her work at the Society, the outing would provide a welcome break in the routine of day-to-day logistics and troubleshooting. She missed teaching the training classes, a task she now delegated to other volunteers to clear her schedule for her new responsibilities. At their rate of growth, soon she'd need to delegate even more. She also missed having Moshe and Rabbi Yosef around the office. They still maintained a keen interest in the Society's functioning, and the expansion into development towns might give them an excuse to get together.

Irina changed into the fresh clothes from the shoulder bag she had brought along last night. She still had a half hour before she was to meet Samira at the Central Bus Station, so she turned her logistical talents to Alex's wardrobe.

Among the stacks of jeans and T-shirts, surprisingly few called for the trash bin. His winter shirts collected dust beside two sweaters on an upper shelf. Alex did not hoard clothing and he hardly used the hanging space. She pushed the jacket and pairs of corduroy trousers aside, clearing plenty of space for her own clothes. Moving in with him made sense, seeing how much time she spent at his place. She'd raise the topic tonight, make him think it was his idea.

The floor of the closet might pose a problem. His pairs of sneakers, beach sandals, and a scuffed pair of leather boots took up most of the floor space. She'd need a separate closet for her own footwear, which, like the Dry Bones Society, displayed exponential growth.

A crack between the boots drew her eye. Shoving the footwear aside, she touched the floorboard and a square panel shifted inward. *Hello.* A secret compartment? The panel lifted easily in her hands to reveal a white shoebox. Was this where he hid photos of his ex-girlfriends?

Exactly how many young women had his bad boy looks reeled in? Judging from the weight of the box, quite a few.

Fighting a pang of guilt for invading his privacy, she removed the lid, and the mischievous smile fled from her lips. Inside the box, a large black handgun glinted in the dull light.

CHAPTER 10

"Ambassador Gurevitch," Moshe said in English. He shook the hulking Russian's hand and took his seat behind the Prime Minister's desk. "To what do I owe this pleasant surprise?"

Sparks of déjà vu tingled down his spine. Back-to-back surprise meetings with the world's superpowers were not the work of pure coincidence.

Gurevitch removed his military visor hat and took his seat slowly as though performing a squat. A dozen medals covered his heart, pinned to his tight brown uniform blazer. He sized up Moshe without smiling, drops of sweat massing on his bulbous forehead.

"Your Excellency has an urgent message from the President of the Russian Federation." The ambassador dabbed at his brow with an embroidered handkerchief.

"Wonderful," Moshe said. The sparks of déjà vu exploded like fireworks.

"The President would like to strengthen the ties between our great nations and invite the State of Israel to join the Russian Federation."

"Wow," Moshe said, breaking protocol for the second time that day. What was going on here? "Forgive me for speaking frankly, Ambassador Gurevitch, but Russia has not exactly been a friend of the Jewish State. Russia has armed and funded our mortal enemies and stood against us in international forums."

The ambassador overcame his befuddlement. "Yes, but imagine how the map would look with us on your side!"

"You'd abandon the Arab states?"

"Absolutely!"

The truth was well known: if Israel were to lay down her weapons, there'd be no more Israel; if the Arabs were to do the same, there'd be no more war. Peace in the Middle East—wouldn't that be an achievement for Moshe's first month in office! Peace in the Land was also an objective that Rabbi Yosef had assigned to the Messiah of David. Moshe swept the thought from his mind.

But the ambassador's offer raised questions. Was Russia willing to erase decades of power politics to bring Israel under her wing? And why were the world superpowers suddenly so desperate to adopt the Jewish State? This time he was going to get some answers.

"Level with me," he said. "This is connected to the Resurrection, isn't it?"

Gurevitch ran a tongue over his teeth, seeming to sense that the talk was not going his way. "We have known of this Resurrection for some time, Your Excellency. And our recent analysis indicates that you are now weaponizing the undead."

Weaponizing the undead? Moshe didn't even know what that meant, and he said as much.

Gurevitch's face whitened. "Soldiers that cannot be killed."

What was he going on about? "That's ridiculous. We have no such weapons."

"Please, Your Excellency, do not insult our intelligence. Our satellites have spotted your recent military activities on the Gazan border."

"But the resurrected are not immortal." Moshe had discovered this firsthand. He had suffered a second heart attack while in Mandrake's custody, and the thugs had revived him with CPR. Moshe reminded himself to deal with the local Russian mafia while he could.

Gurevitch rolled his eyes. "We waste time with these denials, Your Excellency. If these weapons of mass destruction should fall into the wrong hands, the resulting catastrophe could destroy the planet."

By "wrong hands" he meant the Americans, and now Moshe gazed on the full picture in all its crazy glory. The United States had satellites too, and they were not above spying on their allies. Noticing the military camps surrounding the streams of naked dead, their analysts must have reached the same outlandish conclusions.

So much for "shared cultural and moral heritage." The Americans wanted to adopt the Jewish State to obtain the new shiny toy in the Weapons of Mass Destruction store. Did all espionage think tanks employ wacko conspiracy theorists?

Moshe bit his lip. How could he allay the ambassador's fears without leaking news of the Sixth Aliyah—and without endangering his coalition agreement? So far, the Russian had seemed impervious to Moshe's attempts at denying the claims.

Or could that work in his favor?

Moshe folded his arms on the desk. "I cannot comment on any of that." Gurevitch leaned back in his seat, a self-satisfied smile creeping over his mouth. "Please thank your President for his generous offer. I will have to discuss this with my cabinet once we've solidified the new coalition."

"Of course." The Russian got to his feet and strutted to the door. "And Your Excellency?"

"I know," Moshe said. "This will be our little secret."

With another self-satisfied smile, the ambassador closed the door behind him.

Weaponizing the undead. Moshe would never have thought of such an abomination. *They think we're monsters.* For centuries, haters had accused Jews of the worst crimes imaginable: poisoning wells, murdering Christian children to bake their blood into matzo bread. Never mind that the Jews drank from the same wells and that Jewish law forbade the eating of blood. Haters project onto their victims the evil in their own hearts.

A knot formed in Moshe's innards. He was a poodle caught between two snarling Rottweilers. How long could he hold them off?

CHAPTER 11

Avi followed Moshe Karlin into the men's washroom and prepared to burn his bridges. Again.

"Psst, Moshe!" he hissed.

Moshe spun around. In his eyes, surprise turned to suspicion. He leaned against the counter of wash basins.

"What can I do for you, Avi?"

Avi checked under the doors of the toilet stalls. They were alone. He had spent the entire morning walking past Moshe's office and avoiding eye contact with his secretary. He didn't want his meeting with Moshe to appear in the visitors' log. So, he had floated in the corridors, watching the bureaucrats of the Prime Minister's Office come and go, until finally, he managed to steal a moment alone with Moshe. Thankfully, the Secret Service didn't shadow Moshe in the men's room.

"I've come to warn you," he said, keeping his voice low. His eyes darted to the entrance door, which could open any moment and destroy the opportunity. "Gurion is going to double-cross you."

Moshe folded his arms. "How so?"

"I don't know the details, but he's going to make sure the coalition fails."

"Before or after he joins?"

"All I know is that he's setting a trap. He said he's going to bring down the government."

Moshe glanced at his shoes. "And in return you want…?"

Avi shrugged. "Nothing."

"A seat on the Restart list? My eternal gratitude?"

The thought of switching to Moshe's camp had crossed Avi's mind. But Moshe had a majority in Knesset. He had no use for a turncoat MP. No, Avi was more valuable to Moshe behind enemy lines. He said, "I just want to help."

Moshe laughed. "Forgive me if I find that hard to believe."

The implied accusation stung. "I don't blame you for thinking that." He didn't need to list his offenses: deception; turning Galit against him; dragging Moshe's name through the sewers. "But, honest to God, I've changed. I'm risking everything by speaking with you now."

"Unless Gurion sent you. If I withdraw the agreement, then I'm the bad guy, and the Opposition finally has a fact to use against me."

"Gurion doesn't know I'm here. He'd fire me if he did."

Moshe frowned and shook his head. He wasn't angry, just sad. "Thanks, Avi," he said. "But I'll take my chances."

CHAPTER 12

"Where to, sir?" said Baruch from the driver's seat.

"Home," Yosef said. He ran his fingers over the leather upholstery of the backseat for possibly the last time.

Of all the perks due to a minister, Yosef would miss his personal chauffeur the most. Baruch, with his flannel fedora and perfectly groomed pencil mustache, seemed to have stepped out of an era when shoe polishing was an art and trouser length an exact science. He kept the black Audi in pristine condition, the air within redolent of lavender.

"Very good, sir," Baruch said.

The car pulled off, leaving the government precinct in Givat Ram and gliding toward the German Colony. As the light faded over Jerusalem, the world beyond the spotless windows floated by, quiet and peaceful.

"Cyndi?" Baruch asked.

"As always."

The driver's eyes smiled in the rearview mirror, as he pressed a button to play Yosef's favorite CD, Cyndi Lauper's Greatest Hits.

Yosef would miss Baruch. With the signing of the coalition, his driver and car would fall to the new minister. Yosef would have to make do with the pool of ministerial cars and drivers, or simply drive himself to work. To think that only months ago he had been content with his old white Subaru, which had run on hopes and prayers in addition to gasoline. How quickly one adjusted to the comforts of life.

Shedding his governmental responsibilities would provide another major advantage—the peace of mind to focus on his own spiritual growth. The Jewish High Holidays approached: Rosh Hashanah, the awesome Day of Judgment; Yom Kippur, the hallowed Day of Atonement; and Sukkot, the joyous Festival of Booths, when the righteous celebrated their favorable Divine verdict. Between political campaigning and the interminable chores of government, Yosef had little attention left over for the things that really mattered.

After months of obsessing about messiahs, resurrections, and politics, he longed for the simplicity of his personal religious regimen. Say your prayers, keep the Sabbath, and watch what you eat; God will take care of the rest. The world had ticked along well enough before fate had thrust Yosef into Knesset; it would continue once again without him. "The righteous," the Sages said, "have their mundane affairs handled by others."

Safely ensconced in the four cubits of his religious inner world, he wouldn't have to face the cracks in the mirror of external reality. He wouldn't have to wrestle with Divine justice and the other ogres of incongruous theology. Once more, he'd walk the Earth wrapped in God's invisible armor.

"*Aba*! *Aba*!" Simcha and Ari cried, as Yosef walked through the door of his single-story home on Shimshon Street. They jumped up and down in the living room, their earlocks flying, and their skullcaps of black velvet slipping from their heads.

Yosef didn't merit that hearty welcome every day, but today was no ordinary day. He planted a kiss on each little forehead, opened his briefcase on the dinner table of scratched wood, and handed each boy a sealed pack of laminated trading cards. Instead of soccer heroes, each card displayed the portrait and name of a famous rabbi.

"Thanks, Aba!"

Thank Ram, Yosef thought. His new secretary had gotten hold of the new editions on behalf of the Vice Prime Minister.

The boys tore open the nylon packaging and riffled through the cards with glee.

"Aba," Ari said, pouting with disappointment. "Where's your card?"

"Apparently, I'm not that important." Yosef didn't know who printed the cards, but they fell under the umbrella of the Great Council's influence.

"But Aba, you're the boss of the whole country!"

Yosef chuckled. "Democracy doesn't work that way. You don't get to tell everyone what to do. Being in government just means that everybody hates you."

He made the rounds, distributing kisses. Uriel did his homework at the dinner table, and little Yehuda, in pajamas, tested the flight capabilities of his favorite toy car.

"Yossi," said Rocheleh. Her head wrapped in a new flower print head covering, she pored over a thick brochure from Semel Kitchens on the counter. "What looks better—granite or Corian?"

Upon receiving his first ministerial salary, Yosef had signed a hefty twenty-year mortgage and purchased a larger property down the road. For the first time in their lives, the boys would sleep in separate bedrooms. Rocheleh had selected the seven-room house and was designing her new kitchen, which, Yosef suspected, would require a second mortgage.

Yosef glanced at the brochure. The kitchen counters looked identical to him. "Whatever you prefer," he said.

Rocheleh groaned. "You're no help at all!" But she smiled and gave him a delicate hug.

Their marriage had changed beyond recognition. Gone were the dismissive comments and accusatory stares. What a difference a comfortable salary made to *shalom bayit*, household peace! And how good it felt to say yes not only to their material needs but quite a few of their wants.

Whatever coalition agreement Moshe struck, at least Yosef

would keep his ministerial income.

A knock at the door snapped him out of his pleasant reverie. He peered through the peephole, and a very different emotion bubbled in his gut. Yosef opened the door, a hot flash of anger surging through his body.

Emden stood on the dark threshold, his shoulders hunched and his trademark bowler hat missing from his head.

"Call my office if you want to speak," Yosef said, skipping the usual friendly formalities. After all he had done, how dare he bother Yosef at home?

Emden gave Yosef a quick, guilty look. His eyes were red and sunken as though he hadn't slept in days. There was something both pitiful and disturbing to see the once proud and regal rabbi in this disheveled state. He looked sad. No, not sad. Frightened.

"This is a personal call," he said, his voice shaky, defeated. "May I come in?"

Yosef seethed. Emden had threatened him before in the guise of friendship. "If this is about the coalition, it can wait until tomorrow."

Emden flinched at the implicit rebuke. "No, Yosef. It's not that. I've resigned from Knesset."

The news caught Yosef off guard. Emden had held his eminent position at Torah True for years. Why would he resign?

"I've come to warn you, my friend," he continued. "Your life is in danger."

CHAPTER 13

Moshe followed his security detail into the Talpiot Police Station. How the tables had turned! During his previous visit, he had languished for hours behind the bars of a holding cell. Today he would call the shots.

The two receptionists stood at attention. Perky and Bored, as he had labeled them, sported identical blue uniforms and dark ponytails. This time they displayed broad toothy grins as well.

"The Commissioner is waiting for you," said Perky—or was it Bored?—and pointed at a long corridor of office doors.

Moshe nodded and smiled. This time he did not have to present his identity card.

As he passed the doors of offices, his presence of mind faltered. Prime Minister or not, the tables could always turn again. He had learned that lesson well. While Moshe was tied up in a dark abandoned warehouse, Mandrake had put a gun to his head and threatened to turn him into either a murderer or a corpse. Moshe's next move would place him in direct opposition to the sadistic mafia boss.

He knocked on the door at the end of the corridor, stepped inside, glanced at the Commissioner, and did a double-take. The large policeman with olive skin and barrel chest got up from behind the desk to greet him. "Mr. Prime Minister."

"Commissioner Golan, congratulations on your promotion." The name *had* sounded familiar. Months ago, Golan, then a homicide detective, had assisted Irina and Moshe in their attempt to discover her identity. They had failed, but Officer Golan had offered his calling card and sympathy.

His grip was warm and firm. "Thank you, sir. Any luck with our mutual friend? Irina, wasn't it?"

"Irina, yes. Still no leads and no memories."

"That's a shame."

"Yes, it is. But she's doing good work at the Dry Bones Society."

After the exchange of pleasantries, Moshe asked his security guards to close the door of the office, and he took a seat.

Again, he weighed the wisdom of prodding the sleeping bear. Only this bear was no longer sleeping.

"What can you tell me about a man known as Mandrake?"

Golan's Adam's apple jumped. "Russian mafia. Moved in a few years ago. Displaced the local cartels in Jerusalem and the rest of the country. Real nutcase. We've been itching to lock him up, but so far, we have nothing solid on him. Why do you ask?"

"What would it take to reel him in and dismantle his network?"

A smile spread across his face. "Organized crime? We'd need a new undercover program and better equipment. A lot of our resources are deployed to prevent suicide bombs and knife attacks."

"That's what I thought," Moshe said. "So I made a special provision in the new budget earmarked for fighting organized crime. It's time we made that a priority."

"Thank you, Mr. Prime Minister. We'd like that very much." His eyes lingered on Moshe. "You've met this Mandrake, haven't you?"

Moshe's fingers trembled at the thought of the warehouse, and he wasn't sure how much information he should share.

"I've heard enough to know we can't ignore him."

Golan nodded. "I'll take care of it."

"Good. Let me know if you need anything."

Moshe had set the wheels of justice in motion; now he could only wait.

He turned to leave, then paused at the door. "One of his operations runs in a warehouse off Pierre Koenig Street. They rope illegals into forced labor. The manager's name is Boris. Start there."

CHAPTER 14

In a dark chamber deep within the Malcha Technology Park, a red notification light flared. Mandrake placed his deck of playing cards on the glass table and turned to face his laptop. The cards helped him think. He'd done that a lot these past few weeks. Thinking and waiting. Now, it seemed, the time for waiting had ended.

A large, red letter A filled the screen as an encrypted call connected.

"Mandrake," said an electronic voice, the human qualities of the speaker garbled beyond recognition by distortion software.

"Yes, my lord," he said. The voice commanded respect. The voice had given, and the voice could take away.

"We have encountered some unforeseen developments," said the voice. "Proceed with Plan B."

A thrill shot through Mandrake's body, and his shoulder twitched. Plan B. He had hoped for this result.

"I understand."

The electronic voice spoke again. "Name your target."

Mandrake said the name out loud.

The voice repeated the name, seeming to savor each syllable despite the electronic garbling. "How appropriate."

"Preparations are already underway," Mandrake said. His

foresight had paid off, and now was the time to ask for a favor. "One request, my lord, if you will?"

"He's yours," the voice said, reading his mind. "When the End Time arrives, he's all yours."

"Thank you."

The screen faded to black as the call disconnected, and the red notification light bled out.

Mandrake smiled with anticipation. He'd had the pleasure of the target's company once before, and he had enjoyed bending him out of shape. This time, he'd break him.

"You're mine," he said in the dark. "Moshe Karlin, you're all mine."

CHAPTER 15

Eli offered the older woman a box of Kleenex.

"Thank you," Hannah said, and she blew her nose.

Noga's doctoral advisor sat on Eli's living room couch, wearing sensible slacks and smelling of a gender-neutral perfume. She had dropped by the penthouse with the letter she had received from *Nature Genetics*. There was something heartrending about watching the professor cry.

Noga said, "Did they explain why?"

Self-doubt flickered in his girlfriend's eyes. Noga had triple-checked her data and searched her conclusions for weaknesses. "Extraordinary claims require extraordinary evidence," Noga had said, quoting Carl Sagan. Eli had doubted the theory too, at first. Are Palestinian Arabs the Ten Lost Tribes? The results of her genetic research strained the limits of credulity.

Hannah blinked her eyes clear. "They didn't bother. They just called the idea 'ludicrous, sensational, and unworthy of serious consideration.'"

"Didn't they review the data?"

Hannah's short laugh sounded like a cough. "They probably didn't even read the whole paper."

"So much for academic neutrality," Eli said, but his attempt at humor failed to lighten the mood. Eli knew how they were feeling. He had been on the other end of incredulity. *Crazy. Delusional.* The condemnations hit harder than sledgehammers. He had succumbed to those pressures too, giving up his identity to win Noga's love. Would Noga give up on her convictions too? Right now, she needed his support.

"We can submit to other journals, can't we?"

"Academia is a closed, tight group," Hannah said. "Word has spread by now. We're the talk of the town. No self-respecting journal will touch our paper after that resounding rejection. My name is a joke. Appealing their decision will only make matters worse. I could lose my post at Hebrew U."

Guilt stabbed Eli's conscience. He had warned Noga of the scorn and derision she could expect for sharing her theory with the academic world. Then Hannah had supported her analysis and even found corroboration in the oral traditions of Arab tribes in the West Bank. Eli had hoped that the growing mountain of evidence would force skeptics to take them seriously. He had been wrong.

"What do we do now?" he asked.

Hannah shook her head. "Nothing. The Israeli-Palestinian conflict is too charged a topic. The same goes for anything that might appear to support Biblical prophecies. You can't reason with emotion. We can only wait, let things quiet down, and hope that someone might reevaluate the paper without prejudice."

Noga sat beside him like a wilted flower. If the first step of their plan had failed, there was no way they were going to share their discovery with the Prime Minister. The Ten Tribes would remain secret, the Messianic potential unrealized, and the Final Redemption out of reach. How long would the cosmic window of opportunity stay open this time? Waiting was not an option.

Eli had not spent his years fostering contacts in politics or academia. He had spent the last decade developing skills that were much more mundane. Could that too be part of the Divine Plan?

"What if we tried a different approach?"

Noga perked up at his words, and Hannah glanced at him with interest for the first time. Did the boyfriend have something useful to contribute? Noga and Eli had decided not to tell her supervisor about his identity. They already had one extraordinary claim to prove; adding to the list might tempt the scientist to flee for the hills.

"We've been aiming for a top-down solution. Convince the academics in their ivory towers and the information will drip down to the masses. But what if we started at the bottom?"

Hannah laughed again, scornful. "Science by press release?"

"No, not the media. Not at first. That's just another set of gatekeepers we'd need to pass. No tabloids either. We don't want people to group us with alien abductions and conspiracy theories. We want credibility, but of a different kind."

"What is he going on about?" Hannah said to Noga. The prospect of losing her job had shortened her fuse. His idea would not help her with that either, but they were beyond worrying about academia. Their goals aimed far higher.

Understanding blossomed in Noga's eyes, and she smiled. "I think I know where you're going with this," she said. "It's worth a shot."

CHAPTER 16

Yosef faced his former mentor across the dinner table, his shoulders tensed. Rocheleh had cleared the living room and herded the boys off to bed.

Emden sat there, his eyes lowered to the table, his hair unkempt beneath the black skullcap. By all appearances, he was a broken man, and pity muddied the hurt in Yosef's heart. Pity and fear.

Your life is in danger. The warning had gotten Emden through the door, and it had better not be another cynical ploy.

"I owe you an apology," Emden said.

"You've apologized before." The olive branch Emden had extended during the elections had been a political stick disguised as a carrot.

"You're right. I've made many mistakes over the past months. First and foremost, I was wrong to betray you. That is my deep and everlasting shame." He let the words float in the air, disarming Yosef. "I don't expect you to forgive me, but I hope at least to make it up to you in some small way. You see, I made another mistake, and in this, I joined the entire rabbinical leadership. We did not believe that the Final Redemption was upon us. We explained away the resurrected, so comfortable we were and set in our ways."

Yosef shifted in his seat. The resurrection on the street did not meet all the expectations of Jewish tradition, he would admit that. The flaws bothered him too. But what was Emden driving at?

"But since yesterday," Emden continued, "there can be no doubt."

Now Emden had surprised him. "The coalition?" he said. Had Moshe's offer changed the religious establishment's worldview?

"No, not that." Emden raised his gaze for the first time and studied Yosef. "Moshe hasn't told you? He must have his reasons. You'll find out soon enough."

"Find out what?" Was Moshe keeping secrets from him? Or was this Torah True's way of pitting Yosef against his dear friend and partner to create a rift in the Restart party? *Divide and conquer.* Yosef's shoulders tensed again.

Emden explained. "The teachings of the Final Redemption fall into three categories, Yosef. Restorative traditions predict a return to times of yore: The scion of David will rule again, reinstate the Temple sacrifices in Jerusalem, and ingather the Lost Tribes.

"Utopian traditions take this a step further: The Messianic Era will raise society to unprecedented levels. Food will be aplenty. Precious stones will cover the streets of Jerusalem. The Third Temple of Fire will descend from the Heavens. The nations of the world will grasp the tassels of our clothes in their thirst to learn our Torah, and the righteous will feast. In the end, we shall defeat even Death."

Emden swallowed hard. "But there is a third set of traditions, Yosef—the Apocalyptic. These traditions are the reason that the sages, even though they yearned for the Redemption, prayed that the birth pangs of the Messiah would not appear in their lifetime. A terrible war will rage, and the mighty armies of Gog and Magog will amass in Jerusalem. Natural disasters will rend the Holy City asunder. The monstrous Leviathan will roam the ocean depths, and the evil Armilus will attack the Messiah. Many will die; many more will wish they were dead. And the Lord Almighty will judge them all."

Yosef shuddered. He had heard many of the claims about the Messianic Era, but they had sounded far away and exaggerated. Coming from the usually calm and collected Emden, the predictions sent shivers through his every bone.

"Two messiahs appear in our ancient writings. The Messiah of David, the rightful King of Israel. But a second messiah will stand at his right hand. His life will be difficult, his sufferings many. He will die in that perilous time, so that the Messiah of David may live. It is because of the Second Messiah I seek you out now, my friend."

Yosef had seen the posters on the streets. "Welcome, King Messiah!" The banners carried the portrait of Moshe Karlin, the Prime Minister of Israel. But, after his recent embarrassing experiences with popular belief, Yosef had not taken the posters seriously.

"Wait a minute. Are you telling me that Moshe Karlin is the Messiah of David?"

"Look around you, Yosef. The dead are rising. The Jews are returning. And, only months after his resurrection, a political unknown controls the government and promises social justice?"

Yosef had searched long and hard for the Messiah. He had hoped to find him among the sages of the Great Council. Once upon a time, he had even considered Emden as a candidate. Yosef had cold-called hundreds of potential messiahs in the Bezeq Online Directory. He had rushed to the Old City's Western Wall to greet a self-proclaimed Messiah only to watch him plummet to the ground and leave on a stretcher. Yosef had exhausted all possibilities until he had toyed with the inevitable heretical conclusion that the Messiah was a comforting fiction invented by generations of miserable Diaspora Jews.

Had the True Messiah stood right in front of him all along? But if Moshe was the Messiah of David, who stood at his right hand if not the Vice Prime Minister? Yosef felt sick to his stomach.

"Please, my friend, listen to me. You must flee!"

"Flee where?"

"As far away as possible. Here." Emden withdrew a stack of airplane tickets from his pocket. "I'm leaving tonight with my family. I urge you to do the same before it's too late!"

Yosef read the destination on the tickets. "Hawaii?" This was insane. Emden had lost his mind. "You can't be serious!"

Emden held his gaze. "I quit the government and left Torah True. I have never been more serious."

"But why me? Even if I'm the Vice Prime Minister, surely the Second Messiah could be anyone?"

"Because, my friend, the Second Messiah has a name. He is also known as the Messiah of Yosef!"

CHAPTER 17

"Is everything OK?" Alex asked over breakfast, Thursday morning.

Irina forced a smile. "Yes," she lied.

Early in her second life, she had gone undercover, sneaking into a Zumba class to meet Galit Karlin. Adopting another persona had come so easily to her that she'd wondered whether she'd been a spy in her forgotten first life. The idea of living a lie seemed less exhilarating now.

Last night, she had slipped into bed early and pretended to be asleep when Alex came home. She had not wanted him to touch her before she discovered the truth about him, and today she would do just that.

Alex chewed his cornflakes and considered her. He did not seem convinced by her answer, and for once she wished the tough guy exterior had not come with an extra dose of emotional intelligence. "How was your trip to the south—did you find what you were looking for?"

"Far more than I expected," she said. While she and Samira had traveled by bus to Ofakim and Mizpeh Ramon, dusty development towns on the edge of the Negev desert, the large black gun had filled her mind. Why did a car salesman hide a scary handgun in his closet? And boxes full of bullets? Many people carried guns in Israel but in the open and on their person, in case of terrorist attacks.

Who was Alex Altman? She hadn't met his friends or family. Suddenly, the ponytail, biceps, and tattoos seemed to be hiding more than a sensitive soul. Sometimes appearances did not deceive. In her desperation to find love and belonging, had she overlooked the obvious?

Alex took his bowl to the sink and found his car keys. "Can I give you a ride?"

"I'll go in later. I have to run an errand or two." That was true enough.

"OK." He kissed her on her forehead, seeming to sense that more than that would not be welcome. "Have a good day."

"You too."

The moment the door closed behind him, she shot to her feet, returned the milk carton to the fridge, and grabbed her handbag. She listened at the door, waiting for Alex's footfalls to fade in the stairwell before she eased the handle down and slipped outside.

The engine of his car turned as she left the apartment building. She walked away from the sound, turned a corner, flagged down a white taxi cab, and got in the back seat.

"Follow that car," she said.

"The black Hyundai?"

"Yes. But don't get too close." *Always stay two cars behind.* She had learned that from a movie.

The driver chuckled, and they pulled off down Shamai Street. The cabbie wore a black leather jacket, and his hair gel smelled of fish. His eyes crinkled in the rearview mirror. "Checking up on your husband?"

She groaned within. A chatty driver was the last thing she needed but shutting him up would not improve her chances of success. "He's not my husband."

"Boyfriend?"

"Yes."

"You should dump him."

"Yeah?"

"If he hasn't married you by now, then he's stupid. I'd marry you right away."

"Oh, really?"

Irina had to smile. The black car turned again, flowing through downtown Jerusalem. They climbed Agron, passing Independence Park, then crossed the busy intersection at King George, descending into the tree-lined streets of Rechavia.

Most car dealerships had shops in Talpiot to the south, but Alex was heading west. Where was he going?

"So, what's this about—another girl?"

"No. It's… complicated."

Irina felt a pinch of guilt for following Alex. She'd never suspected him of cheating on her. He truly cared for her. Then why was she tailing him in a taxi? *Silly girl.* His morning detour was nothing diabolical. Alex ran errands too. She'd probably catch him red-handed at Home Depot buying plastic flowers for their apartment, to please her. Shame on you for doubting him.

The black Hyundai barreled down Herzog Boulevard, then slowed as traffic thickened, waiting in line to turn left toward the Malcha Mall.

Malcha Mall had a Home Depot. Her cheeks warmed with shame. But the mall didn't open until ten o'clock. Was he moonlighting at a department store?

The Hyundai slipped across the intersection just as the light turned red, leaving the taxi stuck in the line of cars.

"Don't worry," the driver said. "We'll find him. I have a sixth sense for finding people."

Irina rolled her eyes. She considered calling off the search and heading for the DBS when the light changed, and they rolled over the intersection and into the Malcha valley.

The square mall loomed to their right, no black cars in sight. The parking section had multiple floors, and, although the bays were still mostly empty, they'd waste a lot of time searching them all.

"Never mind," she said. "I think we lost him."

"Just a minute." The cabbie overtook an Egged bus, passing the entrance to the parking bay, and rounded the traffic circle.

He made a left instead of a U-turn and said, "Voila!"

A black Hyundai had parked on the side of the road opposite the Technology Park.

"What did I tell you—I have a sixth sense. There's your man."

He pointed. Across the street, Alex walked through the gate toward the tall main tower of the office buildings.

Alex, at the Technology Park? The sight reignited her curiosity. "Can you wait a few minutes?"

"I'm right here." The cabbie turned off the meter. "This one's on me. Anything for a damsel in distress."

Irina didn't have time to argue. If the slick cabbie thought he would get her number in return for his efforts, he was dreaming.

She crossed the street and headed for the gates, keeping the glass building of the guard station between her and Alex, in case he glanced behind him. The security guards checked the trunks of cars but paid no attention to the lone woman with the handbag.

Slipping through the gates, she made for a tree and peeked around the trunk. Alex was following the path that cut through the well-trimmed lawns and manicured hedges.

What was he doing here? Did he pick up cars from customers at their workplace?

Man-sized sculptures of Hebrew letters in reflective metal dotted the lawns. Irina followed, darting from an oversized Dalet to an arch-shaped Chet. If the engineers in the buildings peered out the windows at the gardens they'd think a crazy woman had broken into their Technology Park.

Alex walked full steam ahead, his gait rigid, without turning around once. If he had spotted her behind him, he gave no sign of it. He walked through the glass doors at the base of the main tower. Signs in the windows read The Open University and the names of a dozen other technology companies.

She waited in the cover of a large Vav and was about to dash toward the entrance when the doors opened, and a man stepped out. Irina's breath caught in her throat. She knew him.

His tweed jacket looked out of place in the Technology Park, as did the gray hair and mustache. He belonged in an abandoned warehouse in seedy Talpiot where the hopeless traded their freedom for a roof and two meager meals.

Irina had found herself among those lost souls until Moshe had risked his life to set her free. The man who had ruled the slave labor camp now shuffled down the path of the Technology Park with a smug expression on his face. His name was Boris.

CHAPTER 18

Ahmed broke into a sweat when he saw the line of dusty men. The unpaved street in the heart of Silwan was the last place on earth he wanted to hang out. Here in his old hometown, people would recognize him. His mother, or worse yet, Hasan.

"C'mon," Dara said.

"Can't you go for me?"

"You have to collect in person. Those are the rules. C'mon, it won't take long."

Against his better judgment, Ahmed stepped forward. The line led into the doorway of a low building. The men exiting the next door smiled and patted their pockets.

A dozen other men stood in line behind Ahmed and Dara. They met his stare, then looked away. Just another rioter collecting his wages. They didn't recognize him.

His mother's house lay two roads down. Would she acknowledge him if she saw him on the street? She had refused to let him stay. "You have your palace and your wives," she had said, as she'd shoved him out the door. "Enjoy your eternal reward." His visit had upset her picture of the world and threatened her newfound prestige as an *Um-Shaheed.*

Hasan had parked his yellow Mercedes sports car by the prefab hangar at the top of Silwan. Any moment now he might pass by and identify his traitorous cousin.

The line inched forward. Inside, he saw no Germans. The gruff man behind the table had a thick mustache and barked questions—"Name? How many stones? Any injuries?"—and handed out crumpled fifty-shekel bills. The Arab's manner had something of Boris, the Russian slaver, despite the Arabic and the rough worker's hands. Both men lined their pockets with the lives of desperate men.

Behind the money man, a younger, muscular Arab stood and ogled the advancing line of men. A large gun stuck out of his belt.

Ahmed lowered his eyes. *This was a mistake.* He would not let Dara talk him into doing this again. But who would employ a former suicide bomber with no identity card? The doors of the Dry Bones Society had closed to him. Never again would he bask in Samira's warm smile. A new name wouldn't change that.

"Hey, kid," Gruff Mustache said. "I said, 'Name?'"

"Walid."

He checked the name off a list. "How many?"

"Um, five."

"May as well have been none," Dara said, laughing. "His aim is crap."

Ahmed gave him a "what the hell are you doing?" glare, and Dara covered his mouth with his hand.

Gruff Mustache didn't seem to care. "Injuries?"

"Only his pride." Ahmed would beat Dara well and good when this was over.

The Arab held out a fifty-shekel note, and Ahmed snatched the money.

"Next!"

"You," said the gunman at the back. One hand touched his ear, the other rested on the handle of his gun. "Come here."

Ahmed's heart skipped a beat. The gunman was staring right at him. "Me?"

"I was just kidding," Dara said, the smile an old memory.

"About the stones. He threw them, I saw it."

The gunman pointed at Dara. "You stay."

Ahmed stepped forward, his limbs stiff, as though walking in a dream. Did the man know him? *What does he want with me?*

"This way." The gunman walked up a set of stairs at the back.

Ahmed followed, his limbs trembling. He climbed the steps, sweat slipping from his brow and down his cheeks. His senses intensified. Each passing second seemed like an eternity. The spiral cord of an earpiece sprouted from Gunman's left ear. The gun shifted in his belt as he moved, the back of his shirt damp with perspiration.

Ahmed was back on bus number eighteen, his backpack heavy with rusty screws and ball bearings dipped in rat poison. Any moment, the explosives would roast his sinful flesh in a ball of fire. Only this time, the end would arrive in the form of a bullet to the head.

The steps ended in a cement shell of a room. The only furnishing was a wooden desk. A man lounged in a chair, his legs and boots crossed over the desk. His hands rested on his head of wavy dark hair spiked with gray, his elbows pointing to the sides.

"Hello, cousin," Hasan said. "What a lovely surprise."

CHAPTER 19

Thursday morning, Galit Karlin reached into a brown packing box and withdrew a pink stuffed animal. Moshe had bought the teddy bear for the newborn Talya. If only she could reach back in time to that day and make things the way they were.

In many ways their lives had improved beyond their wildest dreams; in others, they felt broken.

"We need to close that, yes?" the mover guy said, in shaky Hebrew.

"I'm sorry." She dropped the bear back into the box. The team of strong Russians in dungarees worked fast and in silence. When they spoke, their Hebrew was stilted and accented beyond recognition.

Galit stood in the center of the living room. Empty of furniture, their home on Shimshon Street felt like an empty shell. Like her life. And it was all her fault.

Galit had believed Avi's lies, believed that Moshe had cheated on her. Her stupidity had led directly to Moshe's death. When he returned from the grave, she had fallen for other lies: Moshe was a ghost. No, he had faked his death and spent two years living it up with other women.

Moshe had not given up on her. But after tearing down the web of deceptions, he had discovered her own shameful secret: her affair with Avi.

She could blame Avi all she liked—and he had confessed his role in the drama to Moshe—but the damage was done. And she felt the difference. Although they shared a home and a bed, Moshe didn't look at her the same way. Each day he buried his head deeper in his work. Did he still love her?

So, she did the same. The move to Beit Aghion, the Prime Minister's Residence on Smolenskin Street, had kept her occupied for a week. She called movers to pack up and store most of their old furniture. The renters were arriving next week, and they had been particular about finding the house "clean and empty." Which reminded her, she needed to call the cleaning service to confirm their appointment.

"Mrs. Karlin?" one of the Russians called to her from the kitchen. "The other dishes are where?"

He held up Exhibit A, one of the few remaining dinner dishes of the set they had received for their wedding. The missing dishes had exploded against the walls of the kitchen and living room. She had thrown them, first at Moshe, then at Avi. Her cheeks burned with shame.

"Those are all we have left," she said. "On second thought, put them in the trash." Their new home had its own set of crockery and her days of Frisbeeing dishes were over. For one thing, the security guards outside the fortified Prime Minister's Residence would come running with machine guns. And Henri, the in-house chef, would use one of his carving knives on her if she dared to harm his precious kitchen.

The thought made her laugh. She'd have to be on her best behavior from now on.

The sound of knocking on the front door made Galit jump. After her experience in Mandrake's torture warehouse, loud noises startled her. A Secret Service guy peeked in the front door, and she breathed a sigh of relief. So long as Moshe stayed in office, their security detail would keep them safe.

"Mrs. Karlin? Some people are here to see you."

Had the renters arrived early? She did not want them to

see the house in its current state of disarray.

She strode to the doorway, and her jaw dropped.

A smiling middle-aged couple stood on the steps, trailing four large suitcases. A bald patch glimmered on the top of the man's head and the woman clenched her mouth tight, her eyes ready to stream. Behind them waited another family with three teenage children.

"Mom, Dad," she said. "What a surprise!"

CHAPTER 20

Ahmed froze to the spot. Hasan stared at him from behind the desk, his eyes filled with anger or disgust, Ahmed couldn't tell which.

A window stood open behind Hasan. Ahmed could dash across the room, dive through the window, and hope to break his fall on the heads of the waiting rioters. Sprawled across the chair and desk, Hasan would not be able to react in time, but the gunman at Ahmed's back would.

"Walid, is it?" Hasan said, a smirk spreading across his lips. "I like it. A fresh start. What do you think of my new digs?"

Ahmed released the breath he had been holding. Hasan had not used his real name or outed him for his failed mission. Was he not the grudge-holding type, or was the small talk a distraction, a playful moment of torture before his execution, the way cats toyed with mice?

Having no choice but to play along, he glanced at the walls of rough cement. "Could use some paint."

Hasan laughed, swept his legs from the table, and sat up. "I agree. Doesn't look like much but looks can be deceiving. I've been expanding. Diversifying." He got to his feet, stepped around the desk, and leaned against it. With a nod of his head, he dismissed the gunman, and Ahmed felt the tension ease out of his body.

"You had me worried, little cousin."

"Worried that I wasn't dead?"

Hasan laughed. "There is that. I wondered what had happened to you, disappearing off the face of the planet."

"You're not upset with me?"

"It's for the best. As it so happens, I have another opportunity for you."

"Another chance to kill myself?" The fear dissipated, and his anger at his cousin returned. Hasan had goaded him into killing himself. He was responsible for the pain Ahmed had endured and the impossible situation in which he found himself, and now he wanted to use Ahmed all over again.

"No, Ahmed. I'm done with that."

"For the Germans?"

He seemed surprised at Ahmed's inside information. "For the Shepherds of our nation." He meant the Imams, the spiritual guides of their community. Was this Ahmed's ticket back into the fold?

"What's the catch?"

"There is no catch, Ahmed. This time you will not die." Hasan winked. "You'll get filthy rich."

CHAPTER 21

With his many flight hours at the podium, Moshe had thought he'd get over his public speaking jitters. As he entered the auditorium in the Knesset's Negba Wing, he realized that he'd been wrong.

Reporters and photographers packed the three hundred seats and every inch of standing room. In the front rows, Knesset members waited with folded arms and crossed legs. The event would not be easy for any of them. Restart ministers were surrendering their hard-won positions, and members of the Opposition would have to swallow their pride.

Moshe had been ambitious. Too ambitious, according to Shmuel. Today, as he applied the final touches to his tower of cards, he only hoped that the whole thing wouldn't come crashing down.

Sivan met him halfway to the podium.

"They signed?"

She nodded and glanced at the piles of folders on a low table beside the podium. "You've done it. I can't believe it."

"*We've* done it," he said. "And to be honest, I can't believe it either." The tension of the last few weeks eased like steam from a pressure cooker. *We've done it.*

He drew a deep breath and marched to the podium. Camera shutters clicked as he surveyed the assembled politicians and news people. In the front row, Isaac Gurion patted his oily comb-over and frowned. Moshe would have to get used to that frown at cabinet meetings. But at least he'd be on Moshe's side of the table when the government passed the new legislation that the state so desperately needed.

In the next seat, Avi Segal mimicked his boss's expression. His last-ditch attempt to torpedo the coalition had failed. After all they had gone through together, he'd thought Avi would have had the decency to keep quiet and stop his machinations. Some people never changed.

Rabbi Yosef, Shmuel, Savta Sarah—the rest of the cabinet and all one hundred and twenty members of Knesset waited with bated breath for his announcement.

Keep it short; keep it simple.

"My fellow Ministers," he said, "Members of Knesset and the press. Thank you for joining us on this historic occasion. Despite Restart's dominance in Knesset, we have worked hard to form a new unity government, a broad coalition that includes all major parties, new and old." He paused to let the gravitas of this moment sink in.

"This was no small accomplishment. We've all had to put aside our personal agendas and grievances to come together as one for the sake of our beloved country. I have full confidence that together we will work hard to make life better for all our citizens."

A frenzy of clicking cameras set in during his final dramatic pause. "I call upon Isaac Gurion, formerly Head of the Opposition, and now a minister in our new unity government, to say a few words."

Gurion got to his feet and shuffled to the podium. As he gave Moshe a meaty double-handed shake, they posed for the cameras, and Moshe stepped aside.

"I would like to thank Prime Minister Karlin for his generous offer," Gurion said, following the scripted speech they had agreed upon. Then he lifted a folder from the pile of signed coalition agreements and opened it on the podium.

Sivan sent Moshe a concerned look. This had not been in the script.

Moshe gave his head a slight shake. *Not to worry.* Gurion wouldn't do anything stupid; he had too much to gain.

"He offered us power and money," Gurion continued.

Nauseating vertigo gripped Moshe, the "oh crap" moment of the cartoon coyote who has just stepped off a cliff. Gurion had abandoned the script altogether. *Oh, no.*

Gurion extracted the stapled pages of the agreement and raised them in the air. *What is he doing?* But Moshe already knew, and he was powerless to stop him.

"However," Gurion continued, "our conscience won't allow us to be a fig leaf for his corrupt government!"

A hush swept over the auditorium as Gurion turned to glance at Moshe, and, with a smile like a snarl, he tore the agreement to shreds.

Gurion let the scraps float to the floor along with the metaphorical cards of Moshe's meticulously constructed tower.

"Karlin spoke of a better life for all citizens, but he lied." Gurion jabbed a finger at Moshe. "He lied to us all. This very moment he's assembling an army of undead in the heart of our land. He's preparing a zombie invasion that will take our jobs, our homes, and, if he has his way, our very way of life!"

No, no, no! Moshe's face moistened. Cameras clicked. Reporters grinned like sharks smelling blood in the water. What a scoop!

Oh God, make him stop!

But Gurion didn't. "We will continue to fight for the common people against this unnatural—"

Sivan came to her senses first. She dashed to the podium, shouldered Gurion out of the way, and grabbed the microphone. "That's all for today," she said. "We'll take questions at another time, and provide details for the Sixth Aliyah, the new wave of returning Jews who are bolstering our country."

She disconnected and pocketed the microphone, and gathered up the remaining agreements, whatever good that would do. The coalition was dead.

Sivan motioned for Moshe to follow her out of the room, but Gurion's sneer transfixed him.

"You just made a terrible mistake," Moshe said. "It doesn't have to end this way."

"Oh, this isn't the end," Gurion said, his face contorted with hate. "This is just the beginning."

CHAPTER 22

Alex drew a deep breath and pushed through the glass double doors of the Technology Park tower. A man didn't often enter a lion's den voluntarily, but Alex had made his decision. Would he walk away unscathed?

Down a short passageway, elevator doors opened, and Alex collided with a middle-aged man with a tweed coat and fluffy gray mustache. The man grunted an apology in Russian and made for the exit. He did not fit the hi-tech yuppie stereotype. Then again, neither did Alex. But despite his tattoos and ponytail, the techies wouldn't give him a second glance. They'd write him off as a delivery man, not a criminal. Since meeting Irina, he no longer felt like a criminal either.

The elevator doors opened again, and he followed the signs for Magitek.

Irina remembered nothing of their shared past. That trick of fate had granted him that rarest of gifts, a second chance. The Girl had died, but Irina lived, and with her, he could build a future. But for that future to survive, Alex needed a miracle.

He pressed the intercom button at a thin glass door.

A redhead sat at the front desk of enamel white and studied her nails. *Where's Anna?* The gum-chewing blonde had manned the gates of Mandrake's headquarters for years. Had the boss moved again? Unpredictability was the crime lord's signature. Alex should have called ahead and made an appointment.

The receptionist blew a bubble, glanced up, and Alex realized his mistake. The door clicked open.

"Love the new hair," Alex said, in Russian.

"Thank you," she said, as though each word pained her like a tooth extraction.

"Don't blondes have more fun?"

"What?"

"Never mind." He walked toward the room at the end of the corridor. If things went well, he'd never have to speak with her again. If things went badly, he'd never see her again either.

He walked through the hive of cubicles, where hundreds of young men jabbered into headsets, then he stared at the security camera above a white door.

When the door clicked open, Mandrake was waiting for him with a broad smile.

"Sasha, what a surprise." His boss wore black jeans and a turtleneck. He placed a strong hand on the small of Alex's back and guided him to the framed mirror on the opposite wall of the antechamber.

"Were you expecting me?"

"I'm always hopeful."

Closed-circuit television cameras. Of course.

This time, the whoosh of the hidden panel didn't startle him as the wall slid sideways, and they stepped through the black portal. Unlike last time, they were not alone in the darkened command room. Men in black uniforms manned the terminals, and the soft plastic patter of their keystrokes filled the air.

Mandrake strode through the control room and opened another door. Inside, dim purple ambient light filled the office. His boss flopped on a low backless couch in the center, beside a low table with a laptop and a deck of cards. Mandrake's office; the lion's den.

He patted the spot beside him on the couch. Alex preferred to stand, but he obeyed.

"A drink?"

"No, thank you."

"Smoke?"

Alex shook his head. *Where to begin*? How could he phrase his request so that his old comrade-in-arms would not take it the wrong way? Was there a right way?

Mandrake lit up a cigar and blew a smoke ring. "You want out?"

Alex blinked at him. *How does he know?*

"How long have we known each other, Sasha?"

"Since Korosten."

Mandrake's smile widened. "Ah, the People's Primary."

Alex choked up at the memory of the Soviet orphanage. "You saved my ass, that first night. Those stupid kids didn't know what hit them."

They chuckled, two orphan boys standing up to a cruel, cold world. The Jew and his sidekick.

"We've come a long way from Korosten, haven't we?"

For a moment, he wasn't Mandrake, but Gennady, the tough kid with the hooked nose and love for all things magical.

"We sure have." Alex no longer knew the full extent of his friend's dealings, nor did he want to. Since the Girl's death, something had snapped within, and the old friends had drifted apart like continental plates, slow but inexorable.

Mandrake frowned. "Your timing is terrible. New opportunities are sprouting up every day. You could run an entire division of the Organization."

Alex stared into the purple gloom and said nothing.

"It's the Girl, isn't it?"

The mention of her made Alex flinch. "No," he said. "Not only that. It's been a long time coming."

Mandrake took a long drag on the cigar and exhaled. Two perfect gray rings floated in the air, and the smaller sped through the larger. "I understand."

"You do?"

"We had a good run together. All things come to an end. No hard feelings."

Once again, his friend had shredded Alex's expectations. "Thank you."

"Cigar?"

"Sure." Alex had walked through the lion's den and emerged without a scratch.

Mandrake lit the cigar from the glowing embers of his own and handed it over.

"I just need one last favor."

Alex coughed, from both the cigar fumes and the condition. He had counted his blessings too soon.

"What kind of favor?"

"A simple one. And the perfect way to wrap up your career."

Alex had a bad feeling about this. "Who's the target?"

Mandrake blew another perfect ring. "Our good friend Moshe Karlin."

CHAPTER 23

Thursday afternoon, Yosef planted his elbows on his desk and held his head in his hands. *Calm down, Yosef!* He closed his eyes and sucked in deep, long breaths. If Rabbi Emden's visit last night had unsettled him, today's two newsflashes had slammed into him like speeding freight trains.

Lying in bed last night, Yosef had mulled over Emden's tidings. Two messiahs? Yosef could not see the need. And the title "Messiah of Yosef" probably meant "a descendant of Yosef," the Biblical Joseph, as with "Messiah of David."

This Armilus character sounded like the Devil, and Judaism had rejected such dualism. God reigned alone and supreme; no creation could oppose His Divine will. Add to that the world wars, the Leviathan—the legendary sea monster destined to be slain in the Messianic Era, its hide used to form a banquet tent for the righteous—and precious stones in the streets of Jerusalem, and the whole story moved beyond belief. The Messianic Era would not overturn the Laws of Nature, Maimonides had written, and Emden's predictions of preternatural mayhem stretched even Yosef's credulity.

Besides, this resurrection, suicide-bombers and all, was probably not *the* Resurrection, and the Final Redemption lay far ahead in the future.

Having poked holes in the prophecies of doom, Yosef had

drifted off to sleep.

Today, however, Yosef had learned of the so-called Sixth Aliyah. The floodgates had burst, and waves of newly resurrected foreigners washed over the country. Yosef had nothing against the second-timers—he had sheltered them in his own home—nor did he fear that the State of Israel could not absorb them. He wasn't even troubled by the zombie-like behavior of the new immigrants before they awoke in the Holy Land. It was the theological implications of the phenomenon that had triggered his panic attack.

Jewish traditions had whispered of Resurrection Tunnels. Righteous individuals who had not merited burial in the Holy Land would walk upright through these subterranean pathways to the Promised Land. The Sixth Aliyah meant that yet another ancient prediction had materialized. Perhaps this resurrection was indeed *the* Resurrection, and the Final Redemption was at hand. And if so, could Yosef indeed be the ill-fated Second Messiah, the right-hand man who must die so that the Messiah of David may live? Yosef had yearned for the Redemption, but was he willing to sacrifice his life—to widow his dear Rocheleh and orphan his precious sons?

No! That made no sense. Yosef was just a simple neighborhood rabbi. He didn't belong on the stage of history just as he didn't belong in the office of the Vice Prime Minister. *Never mind.* Soon Yosef would relinquish his ministerial posts, including the Vice Premiership. He would be safe.

Then Yosef had learned of the second news item. The spectacular implosion of Moshe's coalition agreement meant that Yosef would remain Vice Prime Minister for the foreseeable future. As Vice Prime Minister, Yosef remained Moshe's right-hand man and next in line. *The Second Messiah has a name*, Emden had said. *The Messiah of Yosef!*

Yosef shuddered again. Emden had urged him to flee like Biblical Jonah, but Yosef knew how that story had ended. He could resign from the government, but the timing could never be worse. "Vice PM Resigns Amid Claims of Prime Minister Corruption," the headlines would read. "Prime

Minister's Inner Circle Flees Zombie Invasion." How could he betray Moshe at this time?

No, there must be another way. Emden was wrong. Yosef grasped at the facts that disproved his theory. Moshe had not discovered the Ten Lost Tribes; neither had he rebuilt the Third Temple. And where were the other signs of the Messianic Era—the war of Gog and Magog, the evil Armilus, the natural disasters, the devastation?

Yosef nudged the laptop on his desk to life and searched the Internet. According to Wikipedia, the Jewish Second Messiah would lead the Ten Lost Tribes of Israel and reunite them with the tribe of Judah. This warrior Messiah would wage war against Armilus and die in the battle.

Hah! Yosef had not located the Ten Lost Tribes, and he was no warrior. He scanned the references at the bottom of the article. They included ancient Jewish writings that the Jewish Biblical canon had rejected. *Enough!*

The intercom buzzed.

"Yes, Ram?"

"Rabbi Levi of Torah True is here to see you."

Rabbi Levi? Yosef didn't recognize the name. Was Torah True keen to join the government even without Gurion? The visitor might provide the escape hatch from public office that Yosef craved.

"Show him in!"

Yosef patted his hair and straightened the lapels of his suit jacket. This time he would be more receptive to the rabbis' demands. Let them be the Messiah of Yosef.

He stood as the door opened, and Ram showed the young rabbi in.

Rabbi Levi shook Yosef's hand but kept his head down, only the ends of his red beard peeking beneath his black hat.

When the door closed behind him, the young rabbi raised his head and fixed Yosef with a pair of radiant blue eyes.

Yosef's shoulders sagged. "You're not here for Torah True, are you?"

Tom Levi, the messianic cult spokesman, grinned like a

naughty little boy caught with his hand in the cookie jar. He sat down. "I'm glad you found time to meet with me, Rabbi Lev."

Yosef ignored the veiled recrimination. He could call security, but that might push the lunatic to more desperate measures yet. Perhaps all the little boy needed was some fatherly attention. "How can I help you?"

"You should take your job more seriously."

"As Vice Prime Minister?"

"No, your *real* calling. Vice Messiah."

Yosef almost swallowed his tongue.

"We've got work to do," Tom continued. He leaned back in the seat as though he lived there and glared at Yosef.

"Like rebuilding the Temple?"

"Among other things. Such as reinstating the priestly sacrifices."

"And how do you propose we do that?" Yosef didn't even want to debate whether sacrifices in the twenty-first century were a good idea.

Tom leaned forward and smiled his blissful, crazy smile. "The Temple Institute has already prepared the sacred vessels, and they've figured out the incense recipe too."

"And the Temple Mount?" Yosef asked. "Do you expect the Waqf to just hand over the Dome of the Rock so you can rebuild the Jewish Temple? They don't even allow Jews to pray at the site."

"Screw the Waqf and his golden dome. We'll bulldoze that monstrosity whether he likes it or not."

"The last time an Israeli Prime Minister visited the Temple Mount, the Arabs rioted."

"That's why the Prime Minister must come out, and soon."

"Come out?"

Tom rolled his eyes as if the answer was obvious. "Announce that he's the Messiah. Then he can get on with business, and nobody will dare stand in his way."

Yosef bunched his eyebrows and tilted his head. "I don't

understand. Wasn't your friend supposed to be the Messiah?"

"Who?"

"The Messiah on the Wall. The man you introduced at the Kotel."

"Oh, him. He died."

His matter-of-fact delivery of the tragic news shocked Yosef, and he couldn't resist a jab.

"Isn't he going to 'rise from the ashes'?" He raised his hand in the air, palm up—repeating the words and gestures Tom had used moments after the paramedics had carried away his former leader on a stretcher.

Tom shrugged. Talk of his dead friend seemed to bore him. "Whatever. That didn't work out. But our Moshe Karlin, he's the man!"

Yosef thought of the mangled body on the stone tiles of the Western Wall Plaza, of the giddy hope and expectation he had nursed in his breast that morning. This messiah idea was a dangerous business. He needed to cool Tom off before he did more damage.

"We all want the Messiah," he said, keeping his tone calm and devoid of sarcasm. "But we have to be very careful. Nobody can force the Redemption. We need patience. It's too early to jump to conclusions. We need time to think this through."

Tom ground his molars, staring absently at the wall behind Yosef. He shrugged again and got to his feet. "You do your thinking, but don't take too long," he said. "We've waited two thousand years. That's long enough."

CHAPTER 24

Maimonides riffled through the glossy magazine he had found on the side table of the waiting room. The lifelike paintings on the pages displayed a wide variety of animals and breathtaking vistas that he'd never glimpsed before. There was so much to learn—so much to see! Today he was taking the first step in his own voyage.

He glanced up at the secretary behind the desk, a young woman of about fifty years of age, who peered at him over her glasses, then returned to her reading. She had not forgotten him.

With difficulty, he read the cover title of the magazine. *National Geographic.* He had no idea what the words meant. English was the key to knowledge in this World to Come. Although the Dry Bones Society had provided an introductory course, he would need to master the language if he was to advance his studies.

Telephones. Mechanical carriages. Flying metal ships! The wisdom that humanity had accumulated over the past thousand years boggled the mind and burst the limits of the imagination. After his initial shock and disorientation, the thirst for knowledge overpowered him. He must study with diligence and discard his prior assumptions. Mankind had uncovered the secrets of Creation, and come what may, he would learn them too!

He turned the page and yet another picture took his breath away. Planet Earth in all her glory, a blue dot in the black vastness of space. The image astounded him each time. The Earth revolved around the sun, of course, not vice versa. This was so embarrassingly obvious when you thought about it. Men had landed their flying ships on the surface of the moon and returned home to tell the tale!

Questions multiplied in his brain; his ignorance was unbearable.

"Rabbi Maimon," the secretary said. "The President will see you now."

"Oh, thank God!" Maimonides jumped to his feet with the energy of a much younger man and strode toward the white door.

The President's office was neither very large nor ornate. Framed certificates and photos with various dignitaries lined the walls. A thin clean-shaven man smiled at him from behind his desk and got up to greet his visitor.

"Good morning, Rabbi Maimon," he said, in Hebrew. "It is an honor to meet you."

"The honor is all mine."

Maimonides sat in the vacant chair. The President had white hair. Good. The task ahead required a man who had devoted his life to studying.

They smiled at each other.

"Would you like a tour of the campus?"

"Maybe later."

"OK." The man cleared his throat. "How can I help you, then?"

Where to begin?

"I want you to teach me."

The man gave a good-natured chuckle. *Good.* A sense of humor. He would need patience, too. Lots of it.

"What would you like to learn?"

"Everything!"

Another good-natured laugh. "Could you narrow that

down for me?"

"Sir, in my first life I began my studies at a very young age. I learned Aristotle by heart and became expert in all branches of knowledge: Mathematics, Astronomy, Philosophy, and Medicine. I served as physician to Sultan Saladin and his royal family. And, of course, I wrote extensively on Jewish law and philosophy. I expect that my religious treatises supplied the final word on those topics. The modern sciences, by contrast, have advanced greatly since then. In short, Mr. President, I want very much for you to be my mentor and master, to teach me the knowledge of the New World."

The President of the Hebrew University blinked. This time he did not chuckle. Had he gone too far? Did the list of his achievements sound like the boastings of a braggart, one unworthy of the master's time?

The kindly man cleared his throat. "Rabbi Maimon, I don't think that is possible."

The words stung like a slap in the face. "Pardon me for asking, sir, but why not?" His fingers dug into the padded armrests of the chair.

"You see, Rabbi, the amount of knowledge we teach at the university is immense. Take the Faculty of Science. One can devote an entire lifetime to the study of one sub-branch of one sub-specialty and still not know all there is in that field, never mind an entire branch. You could devote many lifetimes to study and still only scratch the surface. And by then what you learned would already be out of date. You see the problem?"

"But surely a few intellectual giants have mastered all fields?"

The man just shrugged. "Impossible. The best you can hope for is a shallow knowledge of a handful of subspecialties."

Many lifetimes. He had started a new life, but the Resurrection was a one-off event. He could bank on, at most, another seventy years.

"But if no one man can understand everything, how do

you make critical decisions?"

"We don't. We rely on experts. And they, in turn, rely on other experts. Together, we can get a fuzzy picture of what's going on. The human brain just can't process all that information."

Maimonides' hands trembled on the armrests. So much knowledge, and all beyond his reach!

The President leaned over the desk and touched him on the shoulder. "Don't worry about it." When he sat down again, his eyes brightened. "I have an idea." He turned the computer screen toward his guest and typed away at the keyboard. "Let me introduce you to someone. Your new best friend."

Ten minutes later, Maimonides strolled along the stony paths of the campus grounds and sighed. Knowledge used to be the great leveler. Not everyone was born a king or priest, but the Crown of Torah lay waiting to be claimed by all who made the effort. But the days of mastering all the world's knowledge were gone.

Still, there was hope. He stared at the name scribbled on the square of yellow paper the President had given him. Even if he couldn't know it all, he could at least learn something about everything, and all thanks to his new best friend. This friend was always available and would never get tired of answering questions. His name was Google.

"Your Excellency!"

He turned to the source of the greeting. A plump man in a suit waddled toward him, trailed by serious young fellows in black jackets.

"Your Excellency!" The man stopped to catch his breath, mopped his forehead with a square of cloth, and brushed long strands of oily hair over his bald spot. "I'm so glad I found you."

"You've been looking for me?"

"Yes, yes! Our great sage and teacher, Rabbi Moses son of Maimon."

Maimonides straightened and found his smile again. At

least his works of Jewish law remained timeless. They would not go "out of date" to make way for some new discovery.

He cleared his throat. "How may I help you, my son?"

The plump young man turned serious. "A great sage such as yourself—isn't it time you took up your true calling?"

"Well, I'd be honored to join an academy for Torah study."

"Torah study?" The man laughed. "A sage of your eminence deserves far more than a mere teaching job. Do you know what they say about you? 'From Moses to Moses, none compares with Moses.' In other words, since the time of the Moses in Egypt, none has arisen like Moses son of Maimon. That's right! And the first Moses wasn't just a teacher; he was a leader."

"Oh." *A leader.* "I suppose I did guide the Jewish community of Fustat in spiritual matters. And I answered questions on Jewish law and practice from the entire Jewish world."

"Don't think small," the man said. "Think big! Men like you belong at the very top—at the head of the Jewish State!"

The head of the Jewish State. That did sound appealing.

"And who are you?"

The man gripped his hand and gave him a feisty, double-handed shake. "Isaac Gurion, at your service."

CHAPTER 25

Thursday evening after dark, Moshe slunk home to the Prime Minister's Residence on Smolenskin Street. He needed a hot bath and an early night; he'd get neither.

Constructed in the 1930s by a wealthy Jewish merchant, the mansion known as Beit Aghion had at various times housed a Yugoslavian king and Jewish fighters wounded in the War of Independence. As Moshe trudged through the arched doorways, he felt like a battered soldier, not royalty.

Galit stood in the hallway, a forced smile on her lips and a group of visitors at her back. Moshe's hopes for that hot bath and early night died on the spot.

"Miki!" Moshe said, extending his hand to his father-in-law. He hugged his mother-in-law too. "Ita!" Behind them stood another couple with three bored teenagers. "Dudu and Orit!" More handshakes and hugs for the brother-in-law and family. "What a surprise!"

Moshe hoped he hadn't overdone his display of excitement.

"Yes, it is," Galit said with a plastic smile. She hadn't known about the visit either.

"Join us for dinner?"

Henri, in his chef's white formal jacket and hat, served up platters of roast meat at the dining room table of polished oak, usually reserved for entertaining foreign dignitaries. He'd done a phenomenal job on such short notice.

"Miki, how long is your stay?" Moshe said, and sipped his red wine.

With his balding head and roving eyes, Moshe's father-in-law resembled a large rodent.

"Now that you're Prime Minister," Miki said, a knowing sparkle in his eyes, "we're back for good."

Moshe almost sprayed red wine over the embroidered tablecloth. He didn't dislike his father-in-law. They got along very well at a healthy distance—in their case, a ten-hour intercontinental flight. Galit's parents had not wanted their daughter to remarry her dead husband, and their sudden invasion of Moshe's home raised red flags.

"So, Israel's not going to be wiped off the map anymore?"

From across the table, Galit fixed Moshe with a chiding glare. After the Six Day War, Miki's brother had moved to New Jersey, convinced that the Arabs would make good on their promise to "drive the Jews into the sea." Soon after Galit and Moshe got married, Miki had joined his brother.

Miki dismissed the comment with a chuckle. "Not with you in charge."

Was that a compliment? Moshe's suspicions multiplied. "Where are you staying?"

Galit answered for her father. "They were going to stay at our old house, but seeing that we've rented it out, I invited them to stay here with us."

Moshe almost choked on a chunk of roast meat.

"Just for now," Ita said. "Until we find something long term."

"Wonderful," Moshe said. Just what he needed; a battle on the home front too.

After dinner, the men retired to the library for a drink. Moshe poured Glenmorangie into three tumblers and collapsed into an armchair.

"Everyone in the US is talking about the Resurrection," Miki said. "You can't imagine the excitement."

"Yeah?"

"It's all over the news. And you—they just love you."

At least somebody does. Moshe decided not to burden his father-in-law with his recent governmental failings. Things always looked better from the outside.

Ice cubes floated in the honey-colored sea in the glass, like icebergs waiting for the Titanic. *This is only the beginning*, Gurion had said. The bulk of that iceberg lay beneath the surface. Moshe would have to steer clear and chart a course into calm blue oceans.

"You look tired," Miki said.

"Running the country is tiring work."

Miki opened a box of cigars on a side table and lit up. Moshe, the non-smoker, declined his offer to join him.

"Take it easy," Miki said. "You'll wear yourself out if you keep on like this."

"I suppose I could do with a vacation."

"Vacations don't last forever. All that weight on your shoulders. You need to delegate if you're going to last a full term."

Finally, Moshe understood where the conversation was going. "You mean, by hiring helpers."

"Exactly."

"Like you?"

His father-in-law smiled. "You can always trust family."

"It's not that simple, Miki. Restart promised to get rid of cronyism, and the Opposition is already crying corruption. I can't just hand out jobs to my in-laws."

"Sure you can. You're the Prime Minister—you can do what the hell you like."

Moshe chuckled but shook his head. If only that were so.

But as the heady vapors of single malt whisky numbed his mind, his father-in-law's advice sounded less crazy. *Do what the hell you like*. Maybe he was right.

CHAPTER 26

Conflicting emotions crashed inside Alex as he parked his car between the gloomy stilts of his apartment building Thursday evening. Soon, he would be free. Against all expectations, Mandrake was cutting him loose. Alex would start life anew.

The path would not be easy. He'd have to find a new career. A legitimate career. His days of swindling were over. Nothing in his life had prepared him for this.

In a way, he had become like Irina. The thought comforted him. They would reinvent themselves together. Despite the difficulties, the sight of freedom on the horizon calmed him. Any struggle was worth that second chance.

He turned off the ignition.

Only one hurdle lay between him and that new life, and that final magic trick put everything at risk.

He got out of the car, locked the doors with the remote, pushed through the door of the apartment building, and climbed the stairs.

He'd find work in sales or start his own company with the money he'd stashed away over the years. Irina deserved a better home than the dingy two-room apartment in downtown Jerusalem.

He knocked and turned the key in the door of his apartment.

Irina sat at the kitchen table, her shoulders tense and her face drawn. She looked up as he entered, her eyes damp and bloodshot. A bad day at the Dry Bones Society? She had seemed edgy that morning.

A sudden suspicion wrenched his guts. Had memories of her past returned? No, that was impossible. "Retrograde amnesia," Dr. V had said. "Caused by a lack of blood flow to the right temporal lobe, the seat of long-term memory." The horrors of that first life had been sealed away forever. Or had they? He searched her eyes for clues.

"Hey," he said and placed his shoulder bag on the shelf by the telephone. She didn't reply. "You OK?"

Her voice strained and accusatory, she said, "What's this?" She raised her hands from her lap. In them, the Glock looked large and menacing.

Alex exhaled his relief. She had found his spare gun, that's all. "That's for self-defense." That was no lie. In his line of work, that need arose very often.

"Hidden in your closet with boxes of bullets?"

Alex sat down opposite her and smiled. He could handle this. "Many people have guns," he said. "This is the Middle East."

His words were not having the desired effect. What was really on her mind?

"Shouldn't this be in a safe?"

Alex laughed. She was overreacting, that's all. "This is a rented apartment. I'm not going to invest thousands in a safe, and the landlord won't either, believe me."

His words had no effect.

"What do you do, Alex?"

The change of topic unsettled him. "I told you, I work with cars. Buying and selling."

She looked him in the eyes. "At the Malcha Technology Park?"

Oh, crap. The gun had stirred her suspicions, and she had followed him. "No," he said. "That's our head office. I meant to tell you about that. Today I quit my job."

Her eyes teared up, and she shook her head. "Stop lying to me!"

The hurt and fear in her voice startled him. He'd do anything to save her from pain. That's why he had risked everything this morning. "It's true, I spoke with my boss, and—"

"With Boris?"

"Who?"

"Boris."

"Who's Boris?"

Irina gave him a brief sarcastic smile. "Gray hair. Mustache. Tweed jacket."

Alex remembered. The Russian guy with the self-satisfied smile had jostled him on his way out of the elevator.

"He runs the slave labor camp in Talpiot," she continued. "Shmuel, Samira, and I would still be trapped there if Moshe hadn't saved us."

Double crap. The older Russian had seemed out of place in the hi-tech park. Alex had almost collided with another of Mandrake's foot soldiers, and the coincidence had made him guilty by association.

Lies lined up in Alex's mind. He didn't know what she was talking about, and he had nothing to do with this Boris. Feigning insult, he could turn the conversation against her. She was paranoid or taking out her work frustrations on him.

The tactic would work. She'd feel bad, and he'd get off scot-free. But he couldn't do it. He'd told her enough lies, and it had to stop. This morning, he'd taken the first and hardest step, and if they were ever going to live happily ever after, he'd have to come clean. Well, not completely clean. If she knew the whole truth, she'd never want to look at him again. It was a thin rope to walk, but he had to try.

"You're right," he said. She shifted back, away from him, so he added, "But not the way you think." His words seemed to have calmed her, or at least prevented her from fleeing out the door. She still believed in him; otherwise, she would have left before he came home and avoided the confrontation.

He took a long, slow breath. *Here goes.* "I do work with cars, or at least I did until this morning. The work wasn't completely honest. For years I've worked for a criminal organization. The boss is my oldest childhood friend. We met in an orphanage in the Ukraine. I don't know Boris, but I suspect he works for the same organization."

She frowned, and a tear slipped down her cheek.

"I haven't been fully honest with you, I know, but I'm changing that. That's why I quit today. I'm done with all that." He reached over and grasped her hands in his. "I want a new start, to build an honest, new life together, the two of us."

Irina stared into his eyes, still suspicious, but she did not withdraw her hands. "And your friend is just going to let you go, no hard feelings?"

A laugh escaped Alex's lips. *No hard feelings.* Mandrake had used the exact same words. "It wasn't easy," he said, "but he knows I've been uncomfortable for a long time. And there's a small catch."

"What catch?"

"He's given me one last job." Alex swallowed hard. "And to get it done, I need your help."

CHAPTER 27

Sunday morning, Avi's dress shoes squelched in a muddy patch of grass beside the Menachem Begin Expressway. "A treasure hunt," Gurion had said, before dispatching him to the highway that cut through Jerusalem from north to south. *More like a wild goose chase.*

Was this a joke—or payback? Gurion knew everything about everyone. Had the Opposition leader learned of Avi's attempt to warn Moshe Karlin of the planned betrayal?

A lot of good that had done. Moshe had not listened. Why should he have? He'd dismissed Avi's risky gesture as a clumsy ploy to bury the coalition before it was born. Despite Avi's best efforts, his dream of joining with Moshe had died with the coalition, and he was stuck doing Gurion's bidding.

Avi glanced behind a bush beside the fence of Gazelle Valley, the urban wildlife park. Nothing.

Beyond the fence, a baby gazelle eyed him and chewed grass.

"Yeah, I know," Avi said aloud. "This is stupid." He made for the next turnpike and groaned as mud seeped into his socks.

Maybe Moshe would listen to him next time. If there was a next time. Gurion kept his cards close to his chest, telling Avi only what he needed to know. This time he had only told him where to go and what to say. Even if he found his target, what did Gurion hope to gain? If anything, the move would push him further from the seat of power.

Moshe would know what Gurion was up to. But would he believe Avi if he told him what Gurion had instructed him to do?

Avi halted. In the shadow of the turnpike, a figure crouched.

Avi drew closer, picking his way through the twigs and autumn leaves. The man huddled over a small campfire. The letters DBS appeared on the back of the grimy bathrobe that had once been white. A thick mane of dark hair hung low over his back.

At the crackle of a leaf under Avi's shoe, the man turned. He had a long, thick beard and large, dark eyes. Smoke and the sweet scent of roasting meat wafted from the stick in his hand, which ended in a skinned rabbit.

Well, what do you know? Gurion had been right.

"Good morning, sir," Avi said. He was to be polite and persuasive. "Sorry to disturb you."

The man stared at the intruder. "Five years," he mumbled. "Five years!"

Whatever. The hobo met the description but appeared to be out of his mind.

Avi kept to the script. "A great statesman such as yourself should take up his true calling."

The man cocked his head to one side like a chicken. Had the words gotten through to him?

"Five years!" Theodore Herzl cried. "Five years too late!"

CHAPTER 28

"There's a leak," Sivan told the ministers at the round conference table. "I know it."

"Don't look at us," Shmuel said.

Moshe interceded. "Nobody's making accusations."

He had called the urgent cabinet meeting in the Government Room of the Knesset building Sunday morning to discuss their new plan when Sivan had aired her suspicions.

"Somebody talked," she said. "How else did Gurion find out about the tunnels?"

"Any of those soldiers could have told family and friends," Shmuel said.

"Unlikely. The IDF blocked cellular communications for the entire area and canceled all home visits. The Chief of Staff or the intelligence chiefs are to blame. They owe their positions to the previous administration. We should replace them all!"

Moshe sighed. "It might not be their fault. A rogue staff member could have leaked. We'll weed out the bad guys in time, but for now, we need damage control. Sivan?"

She said, "As you know, we're calling it the Sixth Aliyah."

"Nice!" Savta Sarah said. She turned to Moshe. "She's good!"

"Indeed. Sivan will present the details to the public this afternoon and try to calm things down. The Dry Bones Society has stepped in to help and located absorption towns for the new arrivals. But that's not why I called you together. I wanted to discuss our new way forward." He glanced around the table. "Where's the Minister of Defense?"

The assembled ministers shrugged. Rafi's unscheduled absence was never a good sign, but Moshe had to push on. He'd update him later.

"Our coalition efforts failed. Fine. We'll drag them into the future, kicking and screaming."

Calls of agreement rose around the table. *Do what the hell you like.*

"We don't need their votes. It's time we got down to business and drafted our new legislation. This is our chance to fix the State, and it might be our only chance, so let's make it count. Minister of Finance?"

Savta Sarah cleared her throat and shuffled a stack of papers. "Our team did the research you requested, Moshe. The situation is appalling. Our deficit is at an all-time high and growing. Half the country lives in overdraft, and ninety percent of the wealth belongs to ten tycoons. It's shameful!"

"As we suspected," Moshe said. "What can we do about it?"

"We can use common sense. Money doesn't grow on trees. Spend less than you earn and pay off your debts. We studied other economies, as you asked, and the data backs this up. In addition, we need to open the market, encourage competition, and incentivize small businesses."

"Excellent. Move on to a proposal. Talking of opening the market, Minister of Foreign Affairs?"

Shmuel said, "We need to strengthen our economic ties with other countries. Asia and Africa are hungry for our technology. Our back-channels indicate that Saudi Arabia, Qatar, and Yemen want to normalize diplomatic relations too."

"Wonderful!"

Sivan said, "It must be the Resurrection. There's nothing

like a monopoly on life after death to win new friends."

"But that goodwill won't last forever," Moshe countered. "Shmuel, move forward with those trade agreements. We'll need to schedule diplomatic visits to solidify our new friendships and—"

The door opened, and Rafi entered, breathless. "Sorry I'm late."

He stepped up to Moshe and whispered in his ear. *Oh, no.* Moshe had been expecting something like that, but not so soon.

"What's the matter?" Sivan asked.

Moshe let Rafi share the tidings.

"We've sighted an American aircraft carrier in the Mediterranean, ten miles off the Haifa coast."

"No harm in that," Shmuel said. "They're an ally."

"At the same time," Rafi continued, "a Russian aircraft carrier has moved into the Gulf of Aqaba and is heading for Eilat."

Moshe sighed. There was no way around it now.

"There's something you should know." He told them about his urgent meetings with the ambassadors, their offers and their unshakable belief that the Jewish State had turned the resurrected dead into weapons of mass destruction.

"But we've done no such thing, have we?" Sivan said.

"Of course not. But nothing will convince them otherwise. Each side wants to get their hands on our imaginary weapons before the other superpower does."

"Should we be worried?" Rabbi Yosef asked.

"Things don't turn out well when superpowers think you're hoarding weapons of mass destruction. Just ask Saddam Hussein." Around the table, the ministers shifted in their seats. "We'll keep stalling and hope they come to their senses. Meanwhile, we've got work to do. Where were we? Minister of Interior, what can we do to cut bureaucratic red tape?"

Rabbi Yosef opened his mouth to speak when knuckles rapped on the door and two uniformed police officers entered the room.

"Excuse me, Mr. Prime Minister," one officer, a young man, said, his cheeks red with obvious discomfort. He must have drawn the short straw.

"We're in the middle of a confidential meeting." Where were the Knesset security officers when you needed them?

"I understand that, sir. But I'm afraid you'll have to come with us."

"What?"

The officer handed Moshe a document printed on official stationery. "This warrant comes straight from the Attorney General. We need you to come with us for questioning."

"Right now? That's ridiculous!" Surely the Prime Minister had rights too. "On what charges?"

The officer's lips trembled. "There's a list."

CHAPTER 29

Ahmed watched in awed silence from his seat of honor at the main table on stage. Men gawked at him from the packed rows of the event hall in Bethlehem. He wore a new suit beneath a white robe and a *kaffiyeh* of distinction on his head. Beside him, Imam Basel sang his praises into a microphone. Had the martyr promises finally come true?

No! He had committed a vile and cowardly crime and cut short innocent lives. The hell he had crawled through in his second life wouldn't atone for a fraction of his guilt. This event was a show, a charade. Hasan had told him nothing of his new job, only freshened him up, changed his clothes, and deposited him at the hall. Once again, he was a tool in cruel hands. He was sure of it.

And yet… this felt so good.

"A hero," the Imam declared, "and a warrior. Our son returned to us at this critical time to fulfill his destiny. He is a sign from Above of comfort and consolation. Of redemption!"

In the crowd, men smiled, and their eyes sparkled with hope. Because of Ahmed. After months of suffering, the lost sheep had returned to the warm embrace of the fold.

The speech ended. Imam Basel hugged him. Well-wishers lined up to shake his hand, then drifted to the tables laden with food and drink. Ahmed's cheeks hurt from smiling, his elbow from countless handshakes.

When the line ended, a short, rotund woman in a black burka drew near, the corners of her eyes wrinkling through the slit. The only woman at the gathering, she had sat at the edge of the table of honor, and now she pounced on him and squeezed the breath from his lungs.

"My Ahmed!"

"Mother?" He choked on the knot of emotion in his throat. At the end of their last meeting, when he was friendless and alone, she had turned him out onto the street.

"I knew you would return, my boy," she said. "Forgive me for not letting you stay. How was I to know that you are the One?"

The knot of emotion dropped to the pit of his stomach. "The One? Mother, what do you mean?"

She gave his chest a playful tap. "Always so humble. I must hurry off. See you soon!"

"Mother!"

But Dara had taken her place. "Ahmed, is it?" he said. He was still wearing his filthy street clothes. "So, you hid your real name and the fact that you're a *Shaheed.* A resurrected *Shaheed*! Sorry, I didn't know. Otherwise, I would have bowed and kissed your hand."

"Knock it off." His mother's words had broken the spell. "This whole situation stinks." He glanced around for Hasan.

"What do you mean? You're a hero. You're the man!"

Ahmed spotted his cousin, who wore a fancy suit and handed one of the organizers an envelope.

Ahmed stormed over to him. "What's going on?"

Hasan smiled and clapped him on the shoulder. "Great job, cuz!"

"Cut the crap! I'm the One—what does that mean?"

Hasan herded Ahmed aside, the smile still painted on his face. "Calm down. This is a good thing for you, and it comes from the very top."

"Imam Basel?"

"Higher. From the Shepherd himself."

"The Great Imam?"

Hasan nodded. The spiritual leader of the Palestinians had gone into hiding years ago. The Great Imam had said that he, Ahmed, was the One!

"What does that mean?"

"You, my cousin, are the long-awaited Mahdi."

"Who?"

Hasan lowered his voice. "You know, the Guided One."

Ahmed still understood nothing.

"The Redeemer who appears at the Resurrection and destroys evil. Got it?"

What had Hasan been smoking? "You're crazy. I'm not a redeemer."

"Don't look at me. This comes from Above."

Ahmed wasn't buying it. He wasn't special, and Hasan had lied to him before. "Give me my money, and I'll be on my way."

Hasan gave him a charming smile. "You'll get your money. There'll be so much, you won't be able to carry it all. You'll wipe your ass with hundred-shekel notes. But what's your hurry?" He slung his arm around Ahmed's shoulder. "Stick around. Trust me, you do not want to miss the after-party."

CHAPTER 30

Late that afternoon, the tycoon exited her private gym on the twentieth floor. Radiating heat and soaked to the bone, she marched toward the elevator. She'd told Itai, her personal assistant, to have her helicopter ready in an hour, and so she did not have time for the balding man in the tacky suit who waddled toward her.

"Shirley, my darling!" Isaac Gurion crooned, his smile wide enough to swallow her whole.

She glared at Itai, who threw up his hands in a mime of defeat, and mouthed the words, "He wouldn't leave."

Gurion leaned in for a kiss.

"Don't touch me," she said, without breaking her stride, "I'm sweaty." Thank goodness for small mercies.

Gurion jogged beside her to keep up. "Now I know that you're very busy," he said, and he made her laugh. Busy, indeed; the slimy politician had no idea.

That morning she'd met with her lawyers to sign the contract for an apartment complex on prime Tel Aviv property. The luxury tower project—her third that year—had posed zoning challenges, and she'd deployed an extra set of incentives and kickbacks to get the mayor on board.

In the afternoon, a museum opening had moved her to tears, dedicated as it was to the memory of a dear friend. That left an hour for TRX with her personal trainer before the gala dinner that evening.

She wasn't sure why the Whatever Organization was honoring her with the Whatever Prize, but awards always meant that said organization required more donations.

"But," Gurion continued, "this matter is both urgent and of great interest to you."

"What do you want?"

"That's what I love about you," the politician gushed. "Always to the point."

"You were saying?" The elevator doors were only a few meters away. Gurion had her ear for ten seconds, tops.

"A new joint venture," he said.

The little man sure had a nerve! "As I recall, our last joint venture flushed a truckload of money down the toilet."

"Karlin stole that election!" he cried, red in the face.

She pressed the button for the elevator and chuckled. "Tut-tut, Isaac. It's not like you to lose your cool. He beat you fair and square."

A spiteful fire burned in the silly man's eyes. "And now he's set his sights on you!"

Her smile dropped. "What do you mean?"

"He wants to open the markets and increase competition. Level the playing field."

Level the playing field. Demagogues had been threatening to make life difficult for decades. Once in power, they always came around to her way of thinking. But Moshe Karlin was not your garden-variety politician, and he didn't come from money either. He'd be a problem.

"How can you be so sure?"

"I have eyes and ears everywhere."

She swore under her breath. Even fat little silly men had their purpose in the grand scheme of things. "How much do you need?"

Gurion smiled, and the image of a penguin in an oil slick rose in her mind. "I knew you'd understand."

CHAPTER 31

Ahmed could not believe his eyes. Platters of fish and meat covered the tables in the garden of the mansion, along with a dizzying variety of cold drinks, cakes, and fruit. Steam rose from the swimming pool and into the crisp night air. On the deck and lawns, young, beautiful people smiled and danced, their bodies swaying to the enchanting beat of the sensual music. Had he finally entered Paradise?

A luxury car had carried Ahmed to the mansion in Bethlehem, and for the first five seconds, he had stood at the edge of the garden and gaped. The revelers did not appear to be martyrs or saints. Especially not the girls. Clad in frilly underwear that barely contained their curves and high-heeled sandals that drew his eye to the shapely contours of their bare legs, they gyrated to the rhythm, raising their arms and kicking back their heads. There were so many of them!

A hand draped his shoulder and snapped him out of his trance. "Welcome to Paradise, cuz!" Hasan said. He had taken off his suit jacket and swirls of chest hair peeked through his unbuttoned shirt. "How do you like your new home?"

"I can stay here?"

"For as long as you want. Look at those girls." He leaned in to whisper in Ahmed's ear. "A little secret—they're not virgins." He laughed as Ahmed's cheeks burned. "Trust me, cuz, it's better that way. Here, have a few of these." He held out a bowl of yellow M&Ms, and Ahmed scooped a handful. "Easy! Just one or two. Knock 'em back."

"What are they?"

"They'll help you relax, enjoy yourself."

"Drugs?" Hot anger rose within him again. He knew this was too good to be true! This was a trap.

"Chill out, Ahmed." Then he raised his voice. "Hey, everyone! The Mahdi is in the house!"

The revelers turned to them and cheered. Some raised beer bottles and wine glasses in the air. "Drugs," Ahmed hissed, "*and* alcohol?!" Islam outlawed all intoxicants.

"You worry too much, cuz."

"Hey!" Dara came up behind them, smelling good and dressed well. Hasan had sent him upstairs for a shower and change of clothes. "What did I miss?"

Hasan ignored him and waved to a tall young woman, who smiled and sashayed over to them. "This is Fatima," he said to Ahmed. "She'll take care of you."

Fatima bowed her head. "It is an honor to meet you, Mahdi." Her voice was soft and sensual.

Ahmed was about to say that he was not the Mahdi, but she drank him in with those deep, dark eyes and his tongue forgot how to form words. Instead, he swallowed the pills in his hand.

"Be gentle," Hasan said, a smile in his voice. "It's his first time."

"Then we'll make it memorable."

We? Ahmed's legs turned to jelly. He used all his willpower to stop his eyes from stealing a glance at the rest of her.

"Go on," she whispered. "Don't be shy. Feast your eyes. But we won't stop there."

Ahmed obeyed and glanced down the length of her. The porous clothing left little to the imagination. His breath came fast and shallow. The small part of his brain that could still think made an observation. She had said it again, hadn't she? *We.*

Fatima glanced to the side with a smile, and two more divine beauties strode up beside her. Taking his hand in hers, she led him into the house.

"Hey, what about me?" Dara called, but nobody was listening.

Fatima led them up a set of stairs. The other two girls fell in beside him and rested their hands on his waist.

Ahmed's heart thumped in his ears. The music swirled around his head and grew softer as they reached the upper level. He floated on air.

Soft red light filled a bedroom. The girls pushed him back onto a bed of soft linen.

Fatima smiled down at him, while the two girls climbed onto the bed.

"I've never served a Mahdi before," said one. Her voice was flowing honey. Her fingers caressed his chest, sending goose bumps over his flesh.

"We're so lucky," said the other. Her hands loosened the buttons of his shirt.

Ahmed was the Mahdi. Everyone was saying it. And why not? He had died a Shaheed and awoken from death. *I am the Mahdi.*

Their fingers traced a path from his torso to his trousers.

He inhaled sharply and closed his eyes. In his mind's eye, a different girl stood over him. Her smile was warm and welcoming.

Samira.

The demure girl at the Dry Bones Society had snuck back into his thoughts, the way she had stolen into his heart. She must hate him now, knowing what he had done. The moment she had discovered his crime, heartbreak had glazed over her kind eyes, and Ahmed had fled from her sight.

But the girls on the bed didn't hate him. They adored him. In their eyes, he wasn't a murderer, but a redeemer.

I am the Mahdi. One day, Samira would see that too.

Ahmed's clothes melted away. The mattress shifted and

fabric ruffled as the girls undressed.

Their soft hands were on him again, exploring and soothing. He pretended they were Samira's hands.

Yes. Samira would understand now. She'd give him a second chance.

CHAPTER 32

"Is this a joke?"

The middle-aged woman pulled her shopping cart up Jaffa Road on Monday morning, no doubt on her way to the Machaneh Yehuda open-air market. She had paused when Eli had walked up to her, flashed his charming smile, and handed her a flyer.

How times had changed. Eli had spent centuries avoiding direct human contact, interacting only enough to keep his ear to the ground for changes in culture and language. Relationships would only blow his cover and compromise his Divine mission. Today, however, he mingled with the common people.

"Not at all," he said. "This is based on a scientific genetic study."

"Oh."

She glanced again at the flyer's title, "Have We Found the Ten Lost Tribes?" After hooking the reader's attention, the flyer pushed the reader down a slippery slide. "New scientific research has discovered the Ten Lost Tribes of Israel in the most unexpected of places."

Eli said, "Be sure to visit our website, and see for yourself." He pointed to the URL in large letters at the bottom of the flyer: TheTenLostTribes.org.

Her eyes brightened. "I'll ask my grandson to find that for me. He's a wizard on the computer. Thank you!"

"You're welcome."

He moved on to the next passerby.

Web design. Copywriting. Internet marketing. By creating the OpenGen website, Eli had inadvertently acquired the exact skillset he would need for his grassroots campaign to spread the word of the Ten Lost Tribes. Perhaps he had lost the Thin Voice because he no longer needed it? The Boss sure worked in mysterious ways.

Noga approached at a brisk walk.

"How's it going?" he asked.

"Great. I need more flyers."

Eli reached into his shoulder pack for a fresh pile of color leaflets.

"The website really adds a lot," she said.

"Authority building," he said. "Just like the photos." They had selected stock images of white-coated scientists and the familiar double-helix of DNA. The website created the impression that established research institutes backed the study.

"How are the ads doing?"

Eli consulted the Facebook Ads app on his iPhone. "Picking up. So far we're popular with millennial men and middle-aged women."

Noga laughed. "I can't believe this is actually working."

"Neither will Hannah," he said, and Noga laughed again. The idea of distributing leaflets to the masses had appalled her doctoral supervisor.

It was so good to see Noga happy again. He said, "The world has never been smaller. Soon everyone will know."

"And then the media will come calling?"

"If we can't go to the Prime Minister…" He trailed off.

"Then he'll have to come to us!"

She looked at the handful of flyers. "I'll need more of these. It's crazy down there." She pointed toward the side street that led to the pedestrian mall on Ben Yehuda Street.

"Have they come here to learn about the Ten Tribes?"

She laughed again. "I wish. There's an event."

His interest piqued, Eli escorted her back through the alley. She had not been kidding. A river of humanity, tourists and locals, pooled from the side street tributaries and flowed down Ben Yehuda toward Zion Square.

Above the heads of the crowd on the small square rose a platform. A podium with a microphone stood empty on one side of the dais, a dressed table on the other, beneath a banner that read, in large golden letters: "Welcome, Kings of Israel!"

Behind the table sat a royal panel of three men with serious beards and large golden crowns on their heads.

"What the hell?"

CHAPTER 33

Avi jogged down Ben Yehuda Street toward Zion Square. He was late and empty-handed. Gurion did not react well to the failures of his underlings, and if he suspected that Avi was collaborating with Moshe, this failure would only confirm his suspicions.

He waded through the thick audience toward the stage in the middle of the square. Spectators covered the sidewalks and overflowed into the streets, and police officers redirected traffic.

Gurion must have serious connections and money to pull off the event. For Avi's own anti-zombie demonstration a while back, he had leaned on Boris and his murky underworld ties and still received a smaller turnout.

He spotted the politician beside the dais and called to him from the barrier of yellow police tape. Gurion waved to an officer to let him through.

Gurion smiled as he considered the crowd, in a good mood. "Where's Theodore?"

"He wouldn't come."

"My instructions were clear—"

"He's cracked. Barely understood what I was saying. Kept going on about 'five years' or something. Trust me, you wouldn't want him here, anyway."

"Doesn't matter," Gurion said. "I found something better."

He nodded toward the stage where three bearded guys sat at a dressed table. They wore flowing purple robes and golden crowns. The name tags on the table read "King David," "King Saul," and "King Solomon." "You found them—the actual kings of Israel?"

Avi had heard of historical personages returning among the resurrected—Herzl had been one of them—but he was sure major biblical characters would have made the evening news.

Gurion sneered through his teeth. "No, you idiot. I wouldn't bring actual kings here. We need famous names that will win popular support but won't turn around and elbow us out of the way later. Maimonides didn't take the bait—he prefers his books—so I had to improvise. I took three drunks off the street, cleaned and dressed them up, and promised them a crate of wine for their trouble. They look pretty convincing if I do say so myself."

Avi swallowed. Gurion's mad plan was starting to make sense. He'd use the kings of yore to breed discontent with the current government, then step into the vacuum when Moshe stepped down.

Avi had to warn Moshe. Had he heard of the gathering already? A Channel Two news van straddled the curb on Jaffa Road. Moshe would know how to counter Gurion's deception. He glanced around but saw no sign of the Prime Minister or his cabinet members. Avi had to stall the event, to buy Moshe some time.

"What about Karlin?" Gurion gave Avi a quick, searching glance, so he added, "What if he shows up and interferes?"

"I wouldn't worry about your old friend." Gurion grinned with renewed enthusiasm. "Right now, his hands are very, very full."

CHAPTER 34

Monday morning, Galit rolled over in bed to find Moshe's side empty and cold. He had left early and without saying goodbye. Last night, he had come home late and hardly said a word to her.

Her stomach cramped. Her worst fears were materializing. *He hates me.*

She lay in bed for a while. Being First Lady had its advantages and sleeping in was her favorite. The housekeeper made sure Talya was awake and fed before the Secret Service dropped her off at kindergarten. Now that she had cleared out and cleaned up their home on Shimshon Street, she had to deal with her visiting family.

Galit climbed out of bed and freshened up in the adjoining bathroom. She had eaten breakfast in her pajamas in her old home—her own home. In the Prime Minister's Residence, she had to dress up.

In the kitchen, the chef whipped batter in a baking tub.

"Morning, Henri," she said.

"Good-a-morning, Mrs. First Lady. Pancakes?"

"What's the occasion?"

"Our *new* guests, of course," he said. From the subtle sneer with which he said the word "new," he made known his disapproval of the interlopers. "They have quite an appetite.

This is their third batch."

A lump of embarrassment formed in her throat, and she gave the chef an apologetic smile.

Her nephews were in the games room, judging from the sound of ping-pong balls. Her father lay across the living room couch, his stomach rising and falling through his wife beater undershirt while he stared at infomercials on the big screen.

"Morning, Dad."

"Morning." He didn't look up.

She picked up the dirty plate he had left on the polished side table.

Greta, the housekeeper who reminded her of a German governess from old movies, had asked her to be extra careful not to scratch the antique furniture, and Galit lived in continual fear of her stern looks.

"Dad, what did we say about cleaning up?"

"Thanks, dear." He popped a cigar in his mouth and reached for a lighter.

Something snapped inside her. Galit snatched the cigar from his mouth.

"Hey, what was that about?"

"It's time you got dressed, don't you think?"

"What?" He stared at her as though she had spoken Chinese.

"You know—get a job, find a place to stay. You're eating us out of house and home!"

"I think the State of Israel can afford it."

"No, we can't!" she said, louder than she had intended.

Fear and frustration surged through her, as she sobbed. Her father stared at her, his eyes wide and confused.

"What's going on?" Galit's mother had arrived in a bathrobe, curlers in her hair. She threw an accusatory glance at her husband. "What did you say?"

"Nothing!"

She hugged Galit and walked her to the bathroom.

"He hates me!"

"Your father?"

"No. Moshe. We never talk."

"Well, dear, he's been pretty busy. He is the Prime Minister, after all."

"It's not just that." Galit weighed telling her mother the truth of her complex history with Moshe and Avi, then thought better of it. "It's complicated," she said.

"Hush now. Every relationship has its ups and downs. How often do you think I've wanted to throw your father out onto the street, hey? Sometimes, I wish I had." She searched Galit's eyes for a sign of comfort.

How could Galit make her understand? She alone was to blame. Moshe had done nothing wrong.

She said, "It's like there's a wall between us, and I'll never break through."

Her mother thought awhile. "Be patient, dear. In time, all walls crumble, and he'll bounce back when he's ready. Just make sure you're there for him when he does."

CHAPTER 35

"I demand to see the Commissioner!" Moshe said. He was losing his patience and fast.

Yesterday evening, the police officers had dragged him to the Talpiot Police Station for questioning regarding undisclosed charges. He'd been very polite and cooperative. This was all a big misunderstanding. They'd sort it out. The new Police Commissioner was his partner in fighting organized crime. And his efforts seemed to be working—they had released him on condition that he return to the station first thing in the morning.

This morning, however, they had kept him waiting a full hour, along with his lawyer and security detail, in a small interview room. Now he wanted answers too.

The young officer at the interrogation table shook in his boots. "The Commissioner is unavailable at present."

The kid was just doing his job, but enough was enough. "Then he'd better become available. I have a country to run. I can't wait here all morning."

"I'm sorry for the delay, Mr. Prime Minister. I'm sure—" But he didn't finish. A door clicked open behind Moshe, and the officer sighed with relief. "Oh, thank God."

Commissioner Golan swaggered into the room. "Mr. Prime Minister. Apologies for the delay." He dismissed the officer, sat down, and dropped a thick manila folder onto the interview table.

He leaned back, stretched his shoulders, clicked his neck, and opened the folder. Gone was the eager and easy manner of their first meeting, and no flicker of recognition registered in his dark eyes. "We want to question you about some criminal charges that have come to the attention of the Attorney General."

Criminal charges! Moshe had hardly had enough time in office to do anything illegal.

"What are the charges?"

"We'll get to those shortly." He glanced down at a list on the top page. "Do you have your attorney present?"

"Yes."

"Do you realize that anything you say can and will be used against you in court?"

"Yes. Mr. Commissioner, let's skip the formalities and cut to the chase. We've both got a lot to do." He did not say "like fighting organized crime," but he hoped his eyes conveyed the message. "What are the charges?"

"Corruption."

Moshe wanted to roll his eyes. Like his foot soldiers, the Commissioner was stretching out the interview far longer than necessary. "Can you be more specific?"

Commissioner Golan inhaled and glanced at the second sheet. "Child labor."

"What?!" That was preposterous.

"Says here that, for the past two years, you have employed a minor to do menial labor in your home on Shimshon Street."

"That's news to me. Who was the alleged worker?"

"A Miss Carmel Schneider."

It took a few seconds for Moshe to make the connection. "The babysitter? Since when is hiring a babysitter considered corruption?"

"The babysitter," he repeated. "Are you sure?"

"Yes."

"And that was all she did?"

"Yes."

"And Mrs. Karlin will corroborate that version of the story?"

"Yes. There is no story here, so there's not much to corroborate."

"Good."

"Can I go now?"

"There's more." He leafed through the pages of the file. "Is it true that your in-laws have moved into the Prime Minister's Residence?"

Moshe shifted on the hard seat. How on earth did he know that already?

"They're visiting; they haven't *moved in.*"

"So, they're paying the government for their food and lodging?"

"Do you have in-laws, Commissioner?"

"Please answer the question."

"No, of course not. They're our guests."

"I see. It seems that the residence received a delivery of cigars. Very expensive cigars. Were these for diplomatic consumption or for your guests?"

Oh, crap. Moshe pictured Miki lighting up in the library. He had assumed that his father-in-law had owned the cigars, but now it seemed that Miki had turned his stay into an all-inclusive vacation. "I'll have to look into that," he said. "I don't keep track of every item ordered at the residence."

Commissioner Golan grunted, stared at the papers, but said nothing.

"C'mon, Commissioner. What's going on here? We're both just trying to do our jobs. Last week I increased your budget for organized crime—"

Golan looked up, and Moshe regretted his words instantly. "Are you trying to bribe me?"

"No. Of course, not. I'm just reminding you that we're on the same side. Now, are we done?"

Golan glanced at his wristwatch. "We'll be done in five

minutes."

Five minutes? Then it hit him. Isaac Gurion was behind the charges, and the Opposition Leader knew Moshe's every move. Sivan had suspected a leak; Moshe had discovered an open fire hose.

Moshe would deal with Gurion later. First, he had to end this interrogation—this diversion—and get back to governing. Golan was in Gurion's pocket. Corruption existed, all right, and its roots ran deeper than Moshe had thought. If Gurion could buy the Commissioner, others could too. And Moshe had entrusted him with the war on organized crime!

"That's enough." Moshe straightened his suit jacket and got to his feet. "This meeting is over. Tell your men to open the door and let us go."

Golan held his gaze. The command had wounded his pride. "Or else what?"

Indignation boiled within Moshe. A dozen juicy threats came to mind, but Golan would turn them all against Moshe as an attempt to obstruct justice.

But Moshe didn't need to make threats. The door shuddered in its frame. The table shifted on its legs, inching toward the wide-eyed Commissioner as though it had come alive. And then the ground shook beneath their feet.

CHAPTER 36

"Are you sure this is the right place?" his friend asked.

Ahmed nodded and pressed onward, entering Clal Center on Jaffa Street. Dara peered at the tired floor tiles and blackened windows of the decaying shopping mall with doubt. Ahmed hid his own hesitation.

An arrow pointed the way to the Dry Bones Society. The last time he had set foot in the Society, he had come under attack. The balding man had recognized him from bus number eighteen and pounced on him with the fury of a much younger man. *Murderer!* Samira had looked on, her eyes clouding over with disbelief, then disappointment, and Ahmed, unable to lie to her, had fled.

"I hope this girl is worth it," Dara said.

"She is."

Hasan had warned them not to leave the mansion in Bethlehem, their new home. For his own protection. As word spread, many would seek out the Redeemer, and Satan's followers might wish him harm.

"Better than the girls last night?" Dara chuckled. "That's hard to imagine."

Ahmed's shaved cheeks warmed again at the memory. He had brought his new friend along to increase his status in her eyes—a witness to support his claims—but perhaps that had been a mistake.

"She's different," was all he said.

Would she recognize him today? Hasan had filled his closet with white satin robes and shiny suits. New clothes for a new man. No longer did they call him Ahmed, or even Walid, only Mahdi. Believers bowed their heads at the sight of him; they muttered praise and whispered prayers. Samira should be proud. She should welcome him with joy. Once again, he would bask in the warmth of her smile.

The quiet unnerved him. The bustle from the Absorption Center on the fourth floor had always echoed down the central pier of the Center. Had the Dry Bones Society moved? The offices of the Call Center would hold the answer. Wherever she was, he would find her.

Avoiding the rickety elevator, he led Dara to the stairs. The third-floor corridor brought a fresh wave of memories: Savta Sarah calling to him, leading him to his first warm meal in his second life; Samira stepping up to their table, that demure smile on her lips. "She'll take care of you," the old lady had said. Longing surged in his chest, an intense, painful yearning for that lost moment. The time had come to reclaim what was his.

He marched down the corridor, passing the Absorption Center, to the main offices and the doors with the words "The Dry Bones Society" emblazoned on the frosted window. Ahmed inhaled, puffed out his chest, and knocked twice.

At that moment, his courage fled. What if the old man answered? Surely others would recognize him. Would they cry murder and pounce on him again to finish what the old man had started? Dara's presence would make them think twice. He had been wise to bring his friend, but was the entire visit a mistake?

As he made to retrace his steps, the handle turned, and a young woman with olive skin and a green hijab stood in the doorway. The sight of her sent a bolt of lightning through his heart. Samira radiated calm and welcome, and his concerns evaporated. He had come home.

"Ahmed?" The welcoming smile faded. She looked over her shoulder, then down the corridor. "What are you doing here?"

She did not curse him or chase him away, although concern wrinkled her beautiful features.

"Can we talk?"

She glanced at the watch on her wrist. "I have to go in five minutes."

"Five minutes is fine!" His soul soared. He'd trade a year in Boris's purgatory for five minutes in her presence!

She relented. Inside, she led them past the cubicles and buzz of the Call Center to the manager's corner office with the large windows. At the door, Ahmed turned to Dara. "Give us a moment?"

"Sure."

He closed the door behind him. Samira leaned against the desk. Something had changed in her. She stood taller and held his gaze longer.

"Is this your office now?" The office had belonged to the founder, Moshe Karlin.

Samira smiled. "In part. Irina and I run the Society, now that Moshe and Rabbi Yosef are in government."

Government. There had been an election the day Ahmed had failed to blow up. The day Ahmed had become Walid. Restart had launched Moshe and the Rabbi into Knesset.

"We've been so busy," Samira continued. "You cannot imagine. Waves of new arrivals. New Absorption Centers in other cities, mostly in the south. I was about to head over there when you arrived."

Her excitement infected him. "Do you still lead the welcoming sessions?"

She laughed. "There's no time for that anymore, and too many sessions. Teams of volunteers and society members handle that."

"I pity the new arrivals," he said. "You were so good at that."

Her cheeks flushed, and she glanced at her feet, her mouth forming the demure smile he had missed so much. "I still keep an eye on their training," she said, "to make sure they're doing a good job."

They smiled at each other, the recent past a long-forgotten nightmare. Five minutes was not enough.

Her eyes took in his clothes, and she got serious again. "Why are you here, Ahmed?"

The question made his eyes moisten. He didn't belong here with her. "To see you," he said. "I too have changed. You'll hear about me soon. They call me Mahdi. The Guided One," he added when she shook her head. "The Redeemer. I'll be addressing a gathering at Al-Quds University tomorrow. The word is spreading. Samira, this is my true destiny!"

Samira didn't lower her head. She did not mutter praise or whisper a prayer. "You're a Redeemer?"

The skeptical note in her voice spiked resentment in his chest and tried his patience. Other girls, far more desirable in their makeup and high heels, had felt honored to keep him company, to satisfy his every desire, but this outcast girl doubted him?

"*The* Redeemer," he said, keeping his temper in check. "This is the reason I returned. The Shepherd has decreed that I am the One."

"The Shepherd?"

"The Great Imam."

"You met him?"

"No, but he has spoken."

She lowered her eyes again. Had she finally understood?

"Ahmed," she said, her voice soft and calm, pleading. "Do not make the same mistake twice."

The same mistake? "There is no mistake—"

"Please, Ahmed. Listen to me. The shepherd tends the flock, and the sheep believe he is their friend. But the shepherd is not truly their friend. They realize this when they enter the slaughterhouse, but by then, it is too late."

Ahmed's anger flared again. Why couldn't she be happy

for him? Why did she have to invent flaws in his newfound fame and fortune?

He opened his mouth to chide her, to refute her words, and humble her, but he didn't get the chance, for at that moment the windows shuddered in their frames and the building shook.

CHAPTER 37

Clutching a small handbag, Irina stepped into the airy antechamber of the Prime Minister's Office on Kaplan Street in Jerusalem's Givat Ram neighborhood. She stepped up to the guard desk and flashed her visitor's pass. Although Moshe had granted her free access to the buildings of the government precinct, today she felt like an infiltrator and a traitor.

You're not doing anything wrong.

Alex had come clean. He had confessed his criminal past, the past he was leaving behind to start a new life with her. And she believed him. One last task stood between them and that new life, a job as simple as it was seemingly harmless. If all went according to plan, she'd settle the matter today.

The heels of her pumps clacked over the stone tiles as she made for a corridor. Moshe had given Irina and other members of the Dry Bones Society management a tour of the Knesset and Prime Minister's buildings during his first week in office. Although she often thought of Moshe and they discussed Society matters on the phone, she hadn't seen him in over two weeks.

Moshe's secretary munched a sandwich at her desk outside the Prime Minister's office.

"Morning, Ettie."

Ettie looked up from her newspaper and swallowed her

mouthful.

"Irina, welcome back."

With graying hair and half-moon spectacles on the edge of her nose, Ettie would not give Moshe's wife any cause for jealousy, no doubt one of the reasons that Moshe had selected her from the list of State secretaries.

"Is the Prime Minister in?"

Confusion passed over the secretary's face for a moment—or was that concern? "Not yet."

"Oh." Moshe's absence would compromise her plan. She should have made an appointment, but she didn't want to leave a trail.

Knock it off, Irina. You're not doing anything wrong. No matter how often she repeated her mantra, the very fact that she was acting on the orders of the criminal underworld made her feel dirty.

"When will he get back?"

That concerned look again. "I can't say. Soon, I hope."

"I see." Was something the matter? Prime ministers were busy people. He was probably stuck in meetings or attending to any number of crises in the Jewish State. All in a day's work.

She settled on the waiting bench and straightened her skirt.

Alex had worked for the underworld. The thought still made her shudder. The same organization as Boris, although Alex hadn't had any direct dealings with the slave driver. Thank goodness for that.

Moshe had sacrificed all he had to extract her from Boris's slave trade. By comparison, Alex's path to freedom sounded too easy. Was there a catch hidden somewhere, a consequence that she hadn't anticipated?

She cared for Moshe. At one point, she had loved him. She'd never knowingly hurt his career, never mind put him in danger. Would she regret this? Criminal elements had tried to harm Moshe before. They had abducted him and his wife on Election Day, and, although Moshe had not gone into the details, their battered and bruised state indicated that the experience had not involved polite talk and cups of tea.

Irina crossed her legs on the bench.

No, there was no harm in this. She wouldn't be proposing anything new. People already shouted it from the street corners. The move would boost his popularity and strengthen his standing. She'd just be giving Moshe a little nudge in the right direction.

She glanced at her wristwatch. Fifteen minutes had passed. Today wasn't the best day for this. She positioned her legs to stand when a familiar bearded man walked up to the secretary's desk.

After a short, hushed exchange, the secretary turned toward Irina, and the rabbi followed her glance.

"Irina, good to see you." Rabbi Yosef smiled and made for her.

She stood. "Good to see you too." The rabbi had gained a few more worry lines on his face and strands of gray in his beard. Government work had taken its toll.

The worry lines deepened. "Is everything all right at the DBS?"

"Busier than ever, but good. Is Moshe around?"

"I hope so." There it was again. The people in government were doing a lot of hoping. The premonition returned. "Let's talk in my office."

He closed the door of his room when they were inside, and Irina settled in the visitor's chair before the desk. Moshe smiled at them from the framed photo on the wall, an Israeli flag behind him.

Rabbi Yosef took his seat. "Moshe's still with the police."

"The police? Is he OK?" Had Moshe been in an accident?

"They took him in for questioning yesterday. Some sort of corruption probe."

"But he's only just taken office. He hadn't held a public position before."

"Exactly. It's probably nothing, trumped-up charges from the Opposition."

Irina sagged in the chair. Isaac Gurion and Avi Segal had bombarded Moshe and Rabbi Yosef with smear campaigns during the election. She'd have thought they'd stop dragging his name through the mud once he ruled the country. Apparently, she had been wrong.

"Poor Moshe," she said. "After all he's been through."

The rabbi raised his eyebrows, a gesture both of empathy for Moshe and pessimism for any cessation of hostilities. "This all has to stay between us."

"Of course."

"Maybe I can help you—while Moshe is out?"

The rabbi was right. He could help her. In fact, he'd make the job much easier for her. "Rabbi Yosef, I have a question about the Messianic Era."

"Sure, go ahead." At the mention of religious doctrine, the rabbi seemed to relax. This was his area of expertise. Moshe had questioned him about the Messianic Era before proposing that they run as an independent party in the elections.

"The Messiah is supposed to rule the Holy Land and bring justice to the Land?"

"Among other things," he said, and his eyes narrowed. "Why do you ask?"

"I was just thinking. You've seen the posters around the city. People have been talking. Could Moshe be the Messiah?"

There—she had said it. She had done her part, and now the rabbi would do the rest.

Rabbi Yosef laughed, not in surprise or delight, but irony. His eyes hardened.

"What?" she asked, and her brow moistened. Did he suspect she was acting on behalf of others? Would he ask who had sent her?

"Nothing. Just… you're not the first person to ask me that."

Irina breathed again. She was not the first. Others had made the same suggestion. The mission had a greater chance of success, and she shared the burden of guilt with others. *What burden of guilt? Knock it off!*

"I understand," the rabbi continued, "why people would think that. Moshe came out of nowhere and shot to the top. He's trying to fix the system. But the Messiah is supposed to do many other things as well: rebuild the Temple in Jerusalem; bring back the dispersed tribes of Israel. It's hard to see those things happening soon."

Irina couldn't believe her ears. A month in Knesset had worn down the rabbi's indomitable optimism. "What about the Resurrection—isn't that one of the signs?"

He shrugged. "A great miracle, nobody can deny that. And another sign of the End Days. But is it *the* Resurrection? Many of the details do not match traditional expectations. And there are so many other signs that have not come to pass."

Irina stared at the man behind the desk. Was this the Rabbi Yosef who had physically bounced with excitement at her return, who had gushed about the approaching Redemption with unshakeable confidence? The man before her doubted the miracles that surrounded him. He would not aid her mission; he'd stand in her way.

"Signs?" she asked. "What other signs could we need?"

He stared at the desk, and his lips trembled. "Wars," he muttered. "Disasters. For example—" But he didn't complete the sentence.

A teaspoon tinkled. They stared at the coffee mug on his desk, which shifted over the polished wood. And then the walls shuddered.

CHAPTER 38

"Are they for real?" Noga said.

Among the masses around Zion Square, Eli gaped at the kings on the dais. The scene was wrong. Very wrong.

How could this be? Had the Boss raised the former kings from their tombs and crowned them anew without him? A deep pit opened in the floor of his stomach. Had the Thin Voice abandoned him, not because his mission no longer required Divine intervention, but because the Boss had replaced him with another prophet?

A rotund man in a suit bounded onto the platform and took the podium. He gave the crowd a sincere stare and patted his sweaty comb-over.

"My fellow citizens," he intoned, and his voice reverberated between the buildings and stores of downtown Jerusalem. "This is a historic day. Behold the return of your kings of old, the mighty kings of Israel!"

Whispers circled among the crowd, fermented excited chatter, and erupted in cheers.

The man pointed with his arm. "I give you King Saul, the first King of Israel; King David, the Sweet Singer of Israel; and the mighty King Solomon, the Wisest Man on Earth."

At the mention of their names, the kings rose from their seats and bowed for the crowd. A chant rose among the masses. *David, King of Israel. Alive, alive and well!* Men in white knitted skullcaps danced and waved their arms. An old lady broke into sobs. Little boys climbed onto their fathers' shoulders to get a better view of their royalty.

Then the realization hit.

"That's not them," Eli said.

"Who?"

"The kings. They're imposters."

"Are you sure? It's been a long time."

"Three thousand years," he said. "I kept to the north mostly. I only saw David a few times and at a distance. But he wasn't a redhead, and he had a much smaller nose. The real Saul would rather fall on his sword than sit next to him, End of the World or not. As for Solomon, he wasn't *that* fat."

The sweaty man on the dais raised his hands for silence. "Alas, my friends. Our rightful kings will not rule again."

A stunned silence descended on his audience.

"'Why?' you ask. Because one brazen man has usurped their God-given rights and stolen the crown for himself and himself alone!"

Boos resounded from every direction, then the crowd fell quiet to hear more about Public Enemy Number One.

"You know who I'm talking about—the wicked villain, Moshe Karlin!"

Eli and Noga exchanged a look of shock. Was he really accusing the current Prime Minister of being the anti-Messiah?

"That's right!" the man roared into the microphone. "King Karlin sits on their throne and lords over us. But he hasn't stopped there. His hunger for power knows no bounds. Thirsting for your blood, he has opened the gates wide for a zombie invasion. And while you struggle to keep your homes and your very lives, he feasts on the fat of the land, filling his pockets with our beloved country's wealth."

"This is crazy," Noga said.

"Not crazy," Eli said. "Evil. Who's the prophet?"

"Not a prophet," she said. "A politician. Isaac Gurion, head of the Opposition."

"That explains it." Eli glanced around. The mob was growing angrier by the minute. In a different generation, Eli would have marched over to the raised platform. He would have challenged the imposters and rained fire from Heaven. But the Magic had fled, along with the Thin Voice.

He grabbed her hand. "Let's get out of here."

"Why?" Her eyes widened.

He nodded toward Gurion on the stage. "I have experience with false prophets. They never end well."

They pushed through the crowd, cutting a path back toward the pedestrian mall on Ben Yehuda.

Gurion's voice boomed behind them. "At this very moment, the police are questioning *King* Karlin regarding multiple counts of the darkest corruption. We, your faithful servants, will not rest until we have removed the usurper from our midst. Down with King Karlin!"

"Down with the king!" the people chanted, their faces twisted with rage. "Down with the king!"

Noga squeezed his hand. "Wait—did you feel that?"

He had—a tremor along the cobblestones. The mob stamped their feet in time to their chant. Could a thousand feet cause the ground to shudder?

The earth shook again. Voices cried out around them, this time not in anger but surprise. A bulky man in a checkered shirt bumped into Eli. "Sorry!"

Eli turned around. People held onto each other to keep their balance, bracing for another jolt. Fear filled their eyes. On the dais, the kings gripped the table, like a raft in a raging sea, while the false prophet jumped down the stairs and disappeared into the crowd, a rat abandoning ship. But was that ship sinking or merely buffeted by a large swell?

The answer came in the form of an eardrum-tearing *crack*. Before their eyes, the dais shifted to the side, then plummeted like a rollercoaster car, and the entire platform, along with the podium, the table, and the "kings," dropped out of sight.

Women shrieked. People pushed and shoved each other, as the ground split and shattered beneath their feet. The earth parted, the buildings falling away on either side, as jagged fissures raced from Zion Square and snaked up the cobbled streets.

"Get back!"

Eli pulled Noga away from the widening crevasse, pressing into the packed walls of humanity as, around them, people slipped and fell, screaming and flailing, into the chasm. Great chunks of the torn road rose into the air as though God Himself had taken a chainsaw to the planet's crust.

Patches of cobblestone crumbled into the void. Eli cried out as he forced his way forward, away from the fissure, pulling Noga after him. Another crack sounded and Noga cried out. Her hand slipped from his.

He turned, dropped to his knees, and peered over the edge. She hung by her fingertips from a rock ledge a few feet below the surface. "Eli!" The dark chasm yawned beneath her.

"Hold on! I'm here." He pulled at a chunk of sidewalk, testing that it held, then reached down with his other hand. "Take my hand!"

His fingers brushed hers, half an inch from the rock ledge. No, not a rock; rather, a large translucent stone that refracted daylight into his eyes. *What is that?*

"I can't let go," Noga said. "I'll fall!"

"No, you won't. Just reach out with one hand."

Another shudder knocked the fleeing masses to the ground, and Noga shrieked.

Eli reached further, willing his body to stretch, to grab her wrist and pull her to safety. Noga's eyes projected terror and disbelief.

"You can do it."

She reached for him, and he gripped her fingers for all he was worth. He couldn't hold her much longer. "Good. Now grab the next ledge." He eyed another handhold, another shiny outcrop further up. She did it. He heaved upward. Her boot found traction on the wall of the fissure, and she inched toward the surface.

A smile flashed across her face for the first time since the ground had opened. She was going to make it. Soon, they'd roll back onto solid earth.

Then, with another loud *crack*, the ground gave way beneath him, and they fell.

CHAPTER 39

"What's the damage?" Moshe asked the ministers around the conference table. He had called an emergency cabinet meeting in the Government Room as soon as he got back to Knesset.

Sivan glanced at the data sheet she had compiled. "The earthquake hit a magnitude of seven point two on the Richter scale and tore downtown Jerusalem to shreds. Buildings within a ten-kilometer radius show damage. There's concern about aftershocks."

"Casualties?"

"Dozens dead, a hundred missing. But the main danger is the aftermath. Electricity and water services are down across the city. Three gas installations exploded. A dozen roads are unusable. In short, the capital's a mess. And the cellular networks are down—overloaded by people trying to contact their loved ones."

Moshe sank into his chair. With zombies on the march and his coalition in ruins, he faced trumped-up corruption charges, while superpowers flexed their muscles at the borders. As if that wasn't enough, now he had to deal with a major natural disaster—and all in his first month!

"Gurion's going to go to town with this."

Sivan shook her head. "Unlikely. He led an antigovernment protest this morning at Zion Square. Something about replacing you with the Kings of Old. The earthquake hit during the middle of his speech. Eyewitnesses say the ground opened, swallowing the stage and everyone on it. Gurion hasn't been seen since."

Silence reigned in the Government Room.

"Dear Lord." Moshe had aimed to outmaneuver Gurion, his virulent critic and rival, but he'd never intended him any physical harm. The timing of the earthquake was uncanny. To the casual observer, God had taken Moshe's side. Moshe glanced at Rabbi Yosef, who seemed to sink deeper into his chair.

"I wouldn't get complacent," Sivan said. "The Opposition is already spinning this against you."

She pulled out her phone and played a video clip. Rabbi Mendel of Torah True spoke into a Channel Two microphone, the sirens and strobe lights of emergency vehicles in the background. "This is the work of Moshe Karlin," he said, "He's plunged the nation into turmoil to distract our attention from his corruption charges."

"He has got to be kidding!"

Shmuel said, "So much for 'acts of God.'"

"There's been looting too," Sivan continued.

Moshe never understood how people could take advantage of a national tragedy to steal. "The police won't be enough. We'll need to call in the army to protect businesses until we can get a handle on the situation."

"It's not just the businesses that need protection. The rift exposed diamond deposits in the ground."

Had he heard her right? "Diamonds?"

"And other precious stones. People have been hacking away at the disaster site with hammers and picks, and many have fallen into the fissures."

Moshe didn't know what to say. He'd run out of exclamations. The situation became more bizarre and surreal each passing moment. He turned again to Rabbi Yosef—was this another sign of the Messianic Era?—but the rabbi kept his eyes on the table.

"Moshe," Rafi said, snapping him back to practical concerns. "The army is already stretched thin with the Sixth Aliyah. We don't have the manpower for this."

Moshe considered all the pieces on the board. *Why the heck not?* "We don't, but others might. Shmuel, let's meet right after and put things in motion."

Sivan glanced from Moshe to Shmuel, and back. "What's the plan?"

Moshe glanced at the walls. Gurion had learned about the Sixth Aliyah, and the Police Commissioner knew the goings-on at the Prime Minister's Residence. The Knesset Government Room might be no different.

"I'll tell you all soon. Sivan, we need to address the public and calm everyone down. Meanwhile, those not involved with disaster management, push ahead with the new legislation."

He adjourned the meeting, and the ministers rushed to their tasks.

Sivan caught him at the door. "What's with the secrecy?"

He threw another glance at the walls. "You were right about the leak," he whispered. "It's worse than we thought. Gurion's people know everything we say and do. At Knesset and at home."

Sivan's lips parted as the realization hit. "They've bugged us?"

Moshe nodded.

"I'll have the Secret Service do a sweep."

"Our offices too."

"I'm on it."

Moshe met Shmuel in the hallway. "Let's walk and talk. It's time to call in favors."

CHAPTER 40

Monday afternoon, Yosef wandered through Ground Zero in a daze. Large stretches of street and sidewalk had broken away and pointed heavenward. Jets of steam spouted from the immense dark chasm. The air smelled of burnt wood, gas, and rotten eggs. He hazarded a glance over the edge. Precious stones glittered along the walls of the rift. *This can't be.*

As both Vice Prime Minister and Minister of the Interior, he needed to see the situation on the ground in person. Leaving his security detail at the military cordon, he strolled down what remained of the Ben Yehuda pedestrian mall. Buildings on either side leaned away from the fissure like so many towers of Pisa. A steaming hole was all that remained of Zion Square. It was as though he had stepped onto the Hollywood set of a disaster movie.

A man crouched at the precarious edge of the crater. Soldiers walked over and grabbed him by the shoulders. Diamonds, large and encrusted in dirt, trickled from his pockets as they dragged him to safety.

Natural disasters will rend the Holy City asunder, Rabbi Emden had said. *Precious stones will fill the streets.*

Had the Messianic Era truly arrived? Was his life in danger?

But the list was not complete. Elijah had not returned, nor

had the Third Temple of Fire descended from the Heavens. Leviathans did not swarm the oceans. And, as far as he was aware, human life still ended in death.

Did this disaster even qualify? Earthquakes were a natural phenomenon. The timing was remarkable, but Israel did lie along the Dead Sea Transform, a well-known fault system. Tremors shook the Holy Land every couple of decades. The Galilee earthquake of 1837 had almost leveled the cities of Safed and Tiberius. This was just the worst tectonic event in recent history.

A golden crown lay amid the rubble. Yosef picked it up, the thin plastic crown of a child's Purim costume. *The Kings of Old*, Sivan had said.

"Mr. Vice Prime Minister!" said a voice in English. The soldier who approached him had the same southern drawl as Reverend Adams, his uniform the patchy earth colors of digital camouflage. "We've secured the site."

"Excuse me!" said a soldier with a thick Russian accent. He wore a different patchwork uniform and a green beret. "He means that *we* secured the site!"

Moshe had called in both the Americans and the Russians. Both armies had aircraft carriers stationed off Israeli waters and had airlifted the commandos to Jerusalem within an hour.

Now Yosef stood between the fighters of rival superpowers in the heart of a torn and bleeding Jerusalem. Rabbi Emden's voice whispered in his ears again. *The mighty armies of Gog and Magog will amass in Jerusalem.*

"Both of you," Yosef said. "Together!"

The soldiers scowled at each other, then backed down. For the moment, Yosef had averted World War Three. His small country had enough troubles.

Yosef continued his survey. A fleet of ambulances with the Red Star of David insignia carried off the remaining injured, and extraction teams rappelled into the crevasse to search for the missing.

"Rabbi!" A soldier ran over to him. An American. What new disaster had the day brought?

The soldier dropped to his knees at his feet. "This is the End, isn't it?" The soldier grabbed the string tassels that stuck out from Yosef's belt. "Teach me, Rabbi!" Tears flooded his eyes. "Teach us your Torah. Save us!"

Yosef moved his mouth but failed to find the right words in English or any other language. *The nations of the world will grasp the tassels of our clothes in their thirst to learn our Torah.*

While Yosef blinked in amazement, two of the soldier's compatriots walked over, patted the teary soldier on the back, and hauled him away.

Another sign. Another portent. Yosef's fateful death drew one step nearer.

The ground shook again. Yosef crouched down, steadying himself with his hands on the broken cobblestones. Metal groaned as a street lamp collapsed and shattered.

When the tremor subsided Yosef got to his feet. An eerie sound made him turn around. A throaty groan, not quite human. The jungle nightmare whimper of suffering. The noise had emanated from the steaming chasm.

Yosef inched closer to the broken edge. Then a large, grimy hand clamped onto the lip of the crevasse, and Yosef jumped. A second hand joined the first.

A survivor! A survivor with thick, rough fingers. Yosef took another step forward when a large shaggy head poked above the surface. Large unseeing eyes stared right through him and curdled his blood.

Yosef stumbled backward. He had seen no one like him. The survivor's brow ridge protruded over his eyes. He had a broad, projecting nose and a small chin. Was this an earthquake survivor, or something very different?

With a grunt of effort, the man leaped over the edge and stood erect on solid ground. Well, almost erect. Thick swirls of hair coated his body, but not one scrap of clothing.

A second manlike creature climbed out behind him. And a third. Within seconds, two dozen hairy hominids—the females only slightly less hairy—stooped over the trembling rabbi, who had just noticed another key detail. Hairy or not, none of them had navels!

The creatures shook their heads like wet dogs, blinked their eyes, and took in the street scene with visible curiosity.

The leader of the pack considered Yosef, cocked his head to one side, and said, "Ook?"

CHAPTER 41

Isaac Gurion staggered down Shamai Street, his suit trousers torn and flapping at his shins. His ribs hurt, the side of his head was damp and sticky, his ears rang, and dust coated his entire body. He didn't care about any of that, only the anger that raged within. *He tried to kill me. The bastard tried to kill me!*

He pulled his iPhone from his breast pocket of his jacket. The screen was a web of shattered glass. He tossed the lifeless device into the gutter, pushed through the doors of the Dublin Irish Pub, and climbed onto a stool at the bar.

He tossed a crumpled fifty onto the grimy wood.

"Whisky," he said, his voice like a croak.

The bartender delivered a glass tumbler with two fingers of golden liquid. Gurion knocked it back, and the alcohol stung the bite marks on his tongue. The ground still shook beneath his feet, but the liquids in the bottles behind the bar didn't.

"More!"

The bartender complied.

The ringing in his ears subsided to a low hum, and the chatter of a television screen made him turn. A newscaster babbled away, and a photo of Moshe Karlin appeared on the screen.

"In the wake of today's catastrophe and despite recent

corruption charges, Prime Minister Karlin's approval ratings are higher than ever."

"You'll pay for this!" Isaac growled at the screen. The couple at the corner table eyed him. "What are you looking at?" he yelled. They turned away. Bloody cowards.

He dropped another crumpled note on the counter. "Turn that crap off."

Again, the bartender complied.

Gurion sipped his drink and closed his eyes. In his mind's eye, the dais lurched sideways. He dived off the platform, and seconds later, the ground swallowed it up.

Demons, Avi Segal had called them. Unnatural and undead. Hyperbole, Gurion had thought. Election propaganda. Now he understood. Karlin wielded supernatural forces. He raised the dead and conjured earthquakes to smite his rivals. He had no limits and zero inhibitions. How could a mortal man, as powerful or rich as he may be, contend with an enemy like that?

He slurped his drink and savored the pain of his open wounds. He'd find a way. If he had to sell his soul to the Devil, he'd take Karlin down.

"Unfair, isn't it," said a sonorous voice beside him.

On the next stool sat a black trench coat. A bald head rose above the lapels.

"Who the hell are you?"

"Your protest was going so well. Even I wanted to believe in the Kings of Old. You could almost smell the desire and the fear."

Irritation smoldered inside. The stranger knew more than he should, and Gurion did not enjoy being on the uninformed side of a conversation.

"What do you want?"

"To help a friend in need."

The trench coat turned, and Gurion came face-to-face with an immense beak nose and large, sensitive eyes. The man smiled. His poise and measured speech spoke of patient plans and an iron will. A man with no limits and zero inhibitions.

Gurion patted his comb-over, located the greasy strings of hair at his ear, and pasted them into position.

"What do you have in mind?"

"You deserve better, Mr. Gurion. Much better. Pick a card."

A deck of cards fanned out in the man's hands, face down. Gurion had no patience for parlor tricks, but he humored him and selected a card.

"Hello, King of Diamonds," the man said.

Gurion turned the card over. He was right.

His new friend gave him a toothy smile. "One king alone may sit the throne. Don't you agree?"

CHAPTER 42

Eli woke up with a start. Bright light shuttered his eyes. He made to cover his face with his hands, but his arms wouldn't budge. Thick straps held them at the wrists. His ankles too. He tried to sit up, and another hard restraint pressed into his neck. He writhed on the hard, flat surface at his back to the hum of fluorescent lights. The place smelled of formaldehyde. *Where am I?*

He craned his neck to turn his face away from the harsh light. The ceiling sagged and curved inward, the inside of a tent. A metal trolley stood beside the hard metal bed and contained medical implements: scalpels, hypodermic syringes, and sterile cotton swabs.

Then it came to him—the earthquake at Zion Square. Noga reaching for his hand. Him clutching her fingers, heaving upward. They were safe, on solid ground. Then they fell.

A hospital. Of course. A field hospital! That would explain the tent, if not the silence. But what kind of hospital kept patients strapped to metal tables?

The light swung away and a man in a blue surgical mask and cap stood over him. Blue penetrating eyes evaluated him through rimless spectacles.

"Welcome, Mr. Eli Katz." The mask muffled the voice, but Eli still made the connection.

"Dr. Stern?" Eli's muscles relaxed, and he fell limp against the cold metal slab. He was back at the neurology ward of the Shaare Zedek Medical Center. But the hospital had looked very different. "Thank God it's you. Can you help me with the straps? Where are we?"

"Somewhere safe. You were lucky I found you. The hospitals are very crowded."

Eli's muscles tensed again. They were not at the hospital.

"Where's Noga?"

"Don't worry about her. For now, you just need to relax. You'll need your strength."

"Have you seen her? We were together when… when…"

"Hush now." The doctor made no move to undo the straps. Instead, he stabbed a large syringe through the lid of a sealed vial and pulled back on the plunger.

"What is that?"

"This will help you relax."

"I don't want to relax. I have to find Noga." Dr. Stern extracted the syringe, pushed the plunger, and a jet of liquid sprayed into the air. "No, Doctor, please." This wasn't real, this was a nightmare. "Help!" he shouted. "Somebody, help me! Help!"

The doctor maintained an eerie calm. "Save your strength. Nobody can hear you here. And besides, the city is in chaos. You're just one more missing person." He swabbed Eli's shoulder with an alcohol pad.

"You can't do this. Let me go!"

The doctor's cold blue eyes locked on his. "You were right, you know."

The needle pricked Eli's skin. "Ouch! Right about what?"

"When you emerged from your coma at Shaare Zedek, you claimed to be Elijah the Prophet and over three thousand years old. You said you had to fulfill your destiny and anoint the Messiah. I didn't believe you then, but I do now." The doctor lowered the surgical mask and smiled. "But you got one thing wrong."

The doctor's face swam in circles. "Oh, yeah? And what

was that?"

"Your destiny wasn't to anoint the Messiah." His words echoed as the room spun and faded. "Oh no. Your destiny was to meet me."

CHAPTER 43

Ahmed stepped up to the podium, his fingers trembling on his cue cards. Below the stage, three hundred faces stared at him in silence. Cold sweat trickled down his temple. His lips quivered. The audience this morning was much larger than that of the event hall in Bethlehem—and an impressive display of popular support for the Mahdi, considering the havoc of yesterday's earthquake. But the size of the turnout had not caused his nerves.

Black flags lined the expansive courtyard between the faculty buildings of Al-Quds University in East Jerusalem. The flags honored Hamas and Islamic Jihad, and although the terrorist organizations would have applauded Ahmed the suicide bomber, they would not like the words he had decided to say today.

A man cleared his throat. And another. *Why was the Mahdi silent?* From the front row, Hasan gave him a plastic smile, his eyes widening with a silent demand: *Get on with it!* Sitting there among the dignitaries in his fancy clothes, his cousin had forgotten their argument earlier that morning. The sight of him hardened Ahmed's resolve.

He leaned into the microphone. "Yesterday's earthquake was a sign," he said, his voice loud, echoing off the facades of white Jerusalem stone. Not *his* voice; the Mahdi's.

"A sign of a new era ahead," he continued. "A time when we will stop talking about struggle, because victory will already be ours. The End Times."

Heads nodded in the crowd, like so many sheep. They bleated their agreement.

The shepherd is not their friend, Samira had said.

Ahmed turned to the next cue card. The words spoke of God smiting the Jews in downtown Jerusalem. They called for a Final Intifada, in which the entire Arab world would unite to wipe the Jewish Stain from the Middle East.

He looked up, away from the cards, at the blue heavens.

"A time," he continued, in his own words, "of forgiveness and reconciliation. An end to the hatred in our hearts and the lies in our ears."

Murmurs of confusion circulated among the herd, unaccustomed to a message of peace from their leaders.

He skipped to the final card. "Tomorrow," he said, raising his voice to counter the rising hubbub, "meet me at Al Aqsa. Bring your sons and fathers, daughters and mothers. Each has a part to play in the final chapter of our story. Only together, as one, our hearts filled with unwavering belief, will we succeed where others have failed."

He turned from the podium and hurried to the stairs, ready to flee. A tight throng of men blocked his path to the base of the platform. Not masked men in black with knives and Kalashnikovs, but elders with kaffiyehs and ingratiating smiles, each eager to shake hands with the promised Mahdi. He shook their hands. In their eyes, he found not anger but gratitude.

"*Shukran!*" Hassan shouted. Thank you! He pushed between the well-wishers and their Mahdi. "So much to plan! So much to do!" He grabbed Ahmed by the arm and marched him away.

"What the hell do you think you were doing there?" he hissed when they reached the cover of an arched passageway. "Your instructions were very specific. Are you trying to get us both killed?"

Ahmed clenched his jaw. His gamble had worked, and he would not throw away his winnings. "I want to see the Shepherd."

Samira's words had loomed in his mind ever since their short reunion. She was right—he had no idea who was behind Hasan's actions. If Ahmed was being led to another slaughterhouse, he had better find out soon, and the only way to know for sure was to hear it from the Shepherd himself.

Hasan ran his hands through his hair. "I told you, that's impossible."

"Then get ready for more surprises. Next time, at Al Aqsa." Hasan had paraded Ahmed before the world as the Mahdi; he couldn't touch him. And he knew it.

Hasan punched the air and cried out, "Fine! I'll take you to the Shepherd. But from now on you do exactly as I say."

Ahmed tried not to smile like an idiot. For once, he had outsmarted his cousin; he would meet the Great Imam himself.

"Promise me!"

"OK, I promise. I'll do exactly what you say." Once he had met the Shepherd, why shouldn't he?

"Good. You'll see your precious Shepherd. But trust me, you'll regret it."

CHAPTER 44

Irina burst out of her corner office at the Dry Bones Society. With their recent activity in the south, thanks to the Sixth Aliyah, the Jerusalem office had grown quiet. Deceptively quiet. Then, yesterday, all hell had broken loose. She was going out of her mind.

Manic hominids ran around the Call Center, grunting and whooping, while frantic society members tried to catch up.

"Get down from there!" she cried.

One of the new arrivals had climbed out of the third-floor window of the Call Center and strolled along the outer ledge above Jaffa Street.

"Get back in here, right now!"

Like most of the new arrivals, the hairy imbecile could not wrap his head around the idea of clothing, and now he pressed against the window, giving her an uncomfortable close-up of his nether regions. She groaned.

"Do something!" she yelled, her gaze falling on the nearest bystander, Ben, a lean twenty-something and one of the non-resurrected volunteers.

"They don't listen," he said, throwing his hands in the air. "They don't even understand what we're saying."

He was right, of course. The cave dwellers also had no clue about private property or personal hygiene, and the dormitory upstairs smelled like a zoo.

"Where's the professor?" Irina said over the ruckus. "Professor!"

Professor Grommet shuddered at the sound of his name, as he nursed a paper cup of coffee to calm his nerves. The academic had doctorates in linguistics and anthropology and had helped them communicate with resurrected men and women in Assyrian, Babylonian, and even Sumerian.

Irina raced in his direction, dodging a pair of thick-browed children as they played catch with the swivel chairs.

"Help us!"

"It's no use," the professor said. "Their language is too primitive—mere grunts and gestures. We could try sign language."

"Sign language—are you kidding me?"

"Chimps can learn sign language, and these, ah, *members*, are far more advanced. Neanderthals, I assume, or Homo erectus."

Irina didn't know what he was talking about, and she didn't care. She had hundreds of semi-humans in her care, and the kitchen had run out of bananas. And today she'd seen more of their "members" than she could stomach.

She made for the front door. Samira needed backup in the Absorption Center. She had worked overnight to get the generator running, and the water had returned that morning, but the new residents were not making life easy. If she didn't make progress soon, she had half a mind to call pest control.

At the door, she collided with Alex. His eyes wandered to the charging hominids. "Not a good time?"

"Nothing gets past you."

"We need to talk. It can't wait."

In the mad panic at the Society, Irina had forgotten her own personal troubles.

They stepped into the corridor, and she closed the door.

"Will he do it?"

Irina looked over her shoulder by reflex. Her mission to the Prime Minister's Office on behalf of Alex's criminal handlers still made her feel like a traitor. "No. I didn't get to speak with him, and Rabbi Yosef didn't like the idea. I don't think Moshe will either. With all that's going on, he doesn't have time to think about it."

Alex gripped her shoulders. "Then we have to leave. Now!"

"But we're in the middle of a crisis, Alex. When things settle, I'll try him again."

"It doesn't work that way. The people I work for, they don't accept excuses. We must disappear now while the whole country is in chaos. This might be our only chance."

Irina glanced down the corridor. The muffled noise of pandemonium continued unabated behind closed doors.

How could she abandon Samira at a time like this? The Society needed her.

"I saved some money," Alex continued. "We can get new identities. New lives."

A new life. Since Moshe and Rabbi Yosef had discovered her among the gravestones on the Mount of Olives, that was all Irina had ever wanted—a new life with a man she loved.

"Tomorrow?" she said. The word was a plea.

Alex scrunched his lips, and his chest heaved. After a moment that seemed to last an eternity, he nodded. "Tomorrow."

CHAPTER 45

"Horrendous!" the Texan said. "Preposterous!"

Reverend Henry Adams gripped the armrests of the seat before Yosef's desk with large, manicured hands, his face red.

"Yes, yes," Yosef said, in English. What had so upset his benefactor? "You mean the earthquake?"

"No, no. That was a sign from the Lord Above and a blow to Moshe's detractors."

Yosef swallowed hard. "You mean the… monkey-men?"

The early hominids had amazed Yosef too but not shaken his worldview. *How* God had created humanity didn't really bother the rabbi. But representatives of the earlier stages in human evolution might disturb those who clung to a more literal reading of Genesis.

The reverend's brow wrinkled. "Monkey-men?"

"Never mind. Ah! You mean the accusations against Moshe. Of, eh, corruption?"

"No, of course not! I won't dignify those with any attention."

Yosef scratched his beard. Which of the many recent troubling events had infuriated the reverend so?

"Did you receive our email, Rabbi?"

Yosef nudged his laptop to life. Coordinating emergency activities throughout the country had left him no time to check his Inbox. He turned the screen to allow the reverend a better view. The message from that morning contained a single link, and Yosef clicked it.

YouTube played a news broadcast from Al Jazeera. "High hopes are spreading across the Arab world that the End Time has arrived," said the clean-shaven Arab presenter. "In the wake of a major earthquake that wreaked havoc and destruction on Jerusalem, a Mahdi-claimant has arisen in the Holy City and won hearts and minds across the Muslim world."

The clip cut to a grainy handheld video of a young Arab in a smart suit, white cloak, and headdress, who spoke into a microphone at a podium. He looked vaguely familiar.

"Known only as Ahmed, the former suicide bomber rose from the ashes to lead the faithful to a new era of victory."

The Arab kid from the DBS! *The suicide bomber!* Yosef said nothing. If the boy had aroused Adams's ire, Yosef had better not tell him that the Dry Bones Society had fed and housed the boy on his dollar.

The camera cut to the tree-lined grounds of the Temple Mount. Opposite the towering golden Dome of the Rock, a group of workers in blue overalls shouldered building materials and constructed a raised platform.

The narrator continued. "Preparations are underway for the largest ever gathering at Al Aqsa tomorrow when the Mahdi will deliver his message."

Something in the images caught Yosef's eye, but then the clip ended, and Reverend Adams gave Yosef a stern, expectant look.

"What is this Mahdi?" Yosef asked.

"The Messiah."

"Ha!" So the Muslims believed in a Messiah too. "And this is a problem?"

"Rabbi Yosef." The reverend sounded disappointed. "Our Daddy running late is one thing, but an *Islamic messiah*—unacceptable!"

"I don't understand."

"Nature detests a vacuum; left alone, the empty space fills

with evil." He made a sucking noise to illustrate his point.

"And this messiah has filled the vacuum?"

"Exactly. He will lead people astray in the hope that he's the real messiah. If he's the only contender, that is."

Adams straightened on the chair and cleared his throat. "Now I know what I'm about to say is unexpected. Believe you me, we don't take this lightly. But after long and careful discussion, our board feels that there is no alternative."

Yosef got lost in the long words, and the reverend seemed to notice. "In short," he concluded, "we want Moshe to know that the New Evangelical Church of America stands behind him."

Adams seemed to be waiting for a response.

"And?" Yosef said.

"And we will back Moshe when he claims his rightful title."

The meaning hit Yosef like a raging buffalo. "You want Moshe to say he's the Messiah?"

Dear God, what was wrong with everyone? First Emden, then Irina, and now—of all people—Reverend Adams himself. Did they all want Yosef dead too?

"But he's Jewish!"

Adams winked. "So was Jesus." He became serious again. "I know this may seem surprising and counterintuitive. Believe me, this Resurrection of yours has created enough theological issues for us."

"It has?"

"Of course. If this is the afterlife, this reunion of sinful body and pure soul, then—excuse me for saying so—what a letdown! People have endured all kinds of suffering in the hope of entering the pearly gates of Heaven, only to get thrown back right where they started—in this cesspool of sin and folly! Is this the eternal bliss we yearned for?"

Yosef didn't understand the reverend's poetic language, but he got the gist. Was this the World to Come—Heaven on Earth?

"Never mind the theology," Adams continued. "We'll

work that out later—Moshe will be a son of Jesus, or an incarnation, or what have you. To be clear, he'll have to step down when Christ does appear. But, for now, a Moshe is far preferable than an *Ahmed*!"

"But Moshe never claimed that he's the Messiah."

"What's stopping him? The move is bound to win popular support. The people are already screaming it from the rooftops. In his time, we've seen miracles and wonders, and first and foremost is the way he won that election!"

Yosef stared his imminent death in the eyes. If Moshe Karlin was the First Messiah, did that make Yosef the Second?

"Moshe Karlin is the Messiah," Adams said, and he gave the desk an authoritative thump. "Get the word out now, before it's too late. C'mon, Rabbi. What have you got to lose?"

CHAPTER 46

In downtown Jerusalem, Moshe smiled for the cameras, his arms on the shoulders of the Israeli relief workers at his side. He took care not to accept photo ops with the American or Russian soldiers. There was no need to inflame superpower rivalries.

The camera operators gave the thumbs-up and Moshe headed for his cavalcade, flanked by his security detail. The torn streets and lurching apartment buildings smelled of dust and disaster, but, all things considered, the catastrophe could have turned out far worse.

In the back seat of the ministerial SUV, he hit a speed dial button on the phone, and Sivan's face appeared on the display. "What's our status?"

"Power and water are back up, and so are key access roads. The light rail will take longer. Only a handful of citizens are still missing, and we've relocated residents in unsafe buildings to temporary housing."

"How temporary?"

"We'll have to bulldoze much of the city center to rebuild it. The Ministry of Tourism is talking of designating ground zero as a national monument and museum. The projected tourism revenues will more than cover new housing projects. And then there are the diamond and mineral reserves the earthquake uncovered. We've listed a public tender for the mining rights. Those will add tremendous revenues to State coffers."

"Great job."

"And you were right about the bugs. The sweep found monitoring devices in almost every office. The committee rooms too."

Moshe's hunch had paid off. "Gurion's work?"

"Probably, but we don't have a direct link to him yet."

"Pity he's gone. We'd press charges of our own."

A message flashed on the screen.

"About that," Sivan said, but Moshe cut her off.

"The American Ambassador is on the line. Let's catch up in my office." He touched the display, and Ambassador Smith's face filled the screen. His eyes were red and puffy.

"Mr. Ambassador," Moshe said, ready to apply a thick layer of heartfelt appreciation.

"How dare you!" The ambassador's mouth twisted with rage. "After all we've done for you." So much for "Your Excellency."

Moshe threw up his hands. "Hold on a minute. What are you talking about?"

The ambassador didn't seem to hear him. "The Russians—you picked the Russians? You're messing with the wrong administration. We'll bomb you into the stone age before we let the Ruskies get their paws on your undead army!"

"We've done no such thing, Mr. Ambassador! Believe me, you're our closest ally. Always have been."

"Oh, yeah? Then you better clear that up real soon, Mr. Prime Minister. Or else!"

Another message flashed on the screen. The Russian ambassador. *Crap!* He'd done nothing to indicate he'd sided with the Russians, and he'd only told his cabinet of the offers in broad terms. Who in Moshe's camp would have done something so stupid?

"I will," he said, "right away." His stomach juices swirled

as the vehicle took a corner. Another touch of the display and the Russian Ambassador's face filled the screen.

"You little worm!" Gurevitch snarled as he spoke and emitted drops of spittle. "We will squish you underfoot!"

"What? Why?"

"Don't play stupid with me, Mr. Prime Minister. The whole world knows you've handed your technology to the Americans. You take our kindness but spit in our face. You will pay the price."

"Mr. Ambassador, there's been a mistake!"

"You can say that again. See you in hell!"

"But we haven't—!" The call cut out.

What in God's name was going on? How could they both think he'd betrayed them and partnered with the other superpower? A third message flashed on the screen. Sivan was already calling him back.

"Put on Channel Two," she said. "They've been playing it in a loop."

"Get the cabinet together. I'm on my way."

Moshe fumbled with the controls, found Channel Two on the television feed.

Well, what do you know? Isaac Gurion stood at a podium, back from the dead. The slimy politician raged into a microphone. "He tried to kill me in broad daylight. In the process, he destroyed our capital and murdered innocents."

Moshe shivered. Did people believe that?

Gurion spoke with visible glee, a crazed smile on his face.

"But mass murder isn't enough for our dear Prime Minister, oh no," Gurion continued. "Yes, blood couldn't satisfy his lust for power and personal gain. Foreign soldiers fill our streets. He's sold our nation to a superpower. A mass murderer and a traitor! And now his undead soldiers are on the march and will not stop until they have conquered the entire world!"

"Dear Lord." Moshe had preferred Gurion when he was dead. His claims were contradictory and absurd. If Moshe craved power and had a personal zombie army, why would he bow to a superpower? But devastation and loss had racked the nation, and fear and suspicion didn't always respond to reason.

Besides, Gurion's target audience was not the average Joe but the superpowers. Gurion had confirmed their worst suspicions: the undead army was real and Karlin had partnered with their archenemy.

In his bid for power, Gurion had jeopardized the existence of the Jewish State. This wasn't another diplomatic crisis; this was Armageddon.

As they neared the Knesset compound, the cavalcade slowed. Protestors massed in the streets. Not long ago, Moshe had stood outside, chanting slogans at ministerial vehicles. The crowds appeared more menacing from behind the tinted windows.

The placards called to "End the Occupation" and to send the "Traitors to Jail." They were talking about him! A man with wild hair pressed his pudgy face to the glass. "You killed our friends and family!" he said, the window muffling his angry cry. "You'll hang for this!"

Moshe doubted that. Israeli law didn't hold with capital punishment. Besides, he had murdered no one. Gurion and his cronies had chosen the wrong time and place for their libelous campaign. An act of God had struck them down, literally, and the people still blamed Moshe!

The car lurched forward, and the protestor stumbled away. Soon the security gates closed behind them.

Moshe opened the door before the vehicle came to a complete stop, and he ran for the entrance. In a corridor, halfway to the Government Room, Shmuel called to him.

"Moshe, a package arrived for you."

"It'll have to wait. I've called an urgent cabinet meeting."

Shmuel shook his head. "Moshe, you need to see this."

CHAPTER 47

Eli came to, confused and groggy. His tongue lolled in his mouth like a slug and tasted of burned rubber. The tent flaps floated above him. He lay on the same metal table, his limbs restrained by thick straps. How long had he been out cold? He had to get out of there pronto, and not only to find Noga.

Dr. Stern had gone insane. He had kidnapped Eli from Shaare Zedek and tied him to a dissection table. The doctor had rambled on about immortality and destiny. Eli had preferred the skeptical Dr. Stern who had threatened to send him to the Kfar Shaul Mental Health Center. Now the tables had turned. What experiments did the mad neurologist want to run on him? He had better not stick around to find out.

He listened for movement but heard only the beep of a heart monitor. No sign of Dr. Stern or anyone else. He pulled at the restraints. The effort drained his strength, and he stifled his groans.

The Magic. Elijah the Prophet had rained fire from heaven. He had caused drought, created bottomless pitchers of oil and flour, and he had revived the dead. Dealing with a few leather straps should be child's play.

He willed his breathing to calm, his heart rate to slow. Closing his eyes, he found that invisible muscle at the center of his brain.

Flex. Turn the straps to dust. *Flex.* Make them disappear! *Flex!*

He moved his arm, but the bonds held fast. Eli swore under his breath. He wanted to cry out. *There's no magic*, Noga had told him months ago. *No miracles.* She had doubted his claims then. Now she believed him, but it made no difference. He was useless. During the earthquake, he had failed to protect her. She might be dead, and he wouldn't know.

Tears burned his eyes.

No! She had to be OK. There was a chance she had survived, and she might need his help. He wasn't going to give up on her.

He turned his head to the side, blinking back the tears. The metal trolley still stood inches away from the table. If the bed had wheels, he might just be able to reach it.

With every ounce of strength, he rolled to his right, until the leather straps cut into his skin. The table shifted. *Yes!* He relaxed, drew a deep breath, and repeated the action.

The table clicked against the trolley. He stretched his hand through the restraint as far as possible, gripping the edge of the trolley and pulling it flush with the bed. He dug his nails into the gauze sheet beneath the medical instruments, dragging them closer, and his quivering fingers touched the thin, rounded handle of a scalpel.

Shoes clicked on the floor behind him, and he retracted his hand.

He closed his eyes and feigned sleep, but the accelerated beep of the heart monitor betrayed his anxiety.

"Good morning, Mr. Katz."

There was no point in pretending. Eli opened his eyes. "How long have I been under?"

"A day. You should be proud of yourself. We've been very successful."

A horrifying thought made Eli break out in a cold sweat. Had Dr. Stern operated on him while he was unconscious? He didn't feel the pain of stitches or the pull of bandages on his skin. "What did you do to me?"

The doctor walked around the bed and into view. "Don't worry, Mr. Katz. I drew blood, that's all. I'm not a monster."

Right, Eli thought. You just keep your patients tied up against their will in your private laboratory. *Keep him talking. Distract him from the trolley parked alongside the bed.*

"What progress have we made?"

The doctor grinned. "Do you know how long turtles live, Eli?"

The turn of conversation did nothing to calm his concerns, but the doctor had called him by his first name.

"I don't know. Twenty years."

Another parental grin. "Try again."

"Fifty?"

Dr. Stern moved closer and shifted the trolley away to sit on the edge of the bed. The scalpels rolled out of reach.

"The correct answer," Dr. Stern said, "is forever. They never die."

"What do you mean?" Eli would have heard of a thousand-year-old turtle if one had existed.

"They age. But at a certain point that stops. Their metabolism levels off, their cellular activity stabilizes. The phenomenon is called negligible senescence. Most people think that aging is just a fact of life, and the body must inevitably wear down, but turtles prove otherwise. If it wasn't for predators, disease, and road accidents, turtles would truly live forever."

"Oh." Now that sounded familiar.

"Unfortunately, studies of turtles have done nothing for mankind. Their biochemistry is too different. Believe me, I know."

"You have a thing for turtles?"

Dr. Stern didn't rise to the challenge of a witty response. Instead, he sat on the edge of the bed and stared at his hands.

"Five years ago, my granddaughter was born with Hutchinson–Gilford syndrome, a form of progeria. People with the syndrome age at ten times the usual rate. They don't live past their thirteenth birthday. That's how my interest in turtles began."

The doctor seemed to age right before Eli's eyes, and he felt a pinch of empathy for the man, despite his own current predicament.

Dr. Stern removed his glasses and wiped them with a lint cloth. "Genetics wasn't my specialty. I had much to learn, and I spent a lot of money to set up this lab. But I was getting nowhere. The gap between turtles and humans was unbridgeable. And then you came along."

"Me?"

"Scientific research tends to focus on the norm and to ignore outliers. But the outliers teach us the most. Your recovery from that accident—I'd seen nothing like it. Your cells regenerated beyond the ability of normal human cells, and they did not appear to age. You were an outlier. At last, I'd found my human turtle. The applications were endless: healing progeria; treating cancer; regenerating severed limbs; and the holy grail of human ambition, immortality."

Dr. Stern replaced his glasses. "And that's why you should feel proud. Yesterday, I hit a brick wall. No matter how I analyzed your DNA, the algorithms found nothing unusual. Just another male human genome. But then I turned my investigation to epigenetics and the non-coding RNA sequences that determine which genes to activate and which to suppress. Now there was something very interesting! The secret to immortality had been sitting there for millennia, locked away in our dormant DNA; and now we have found the key to open it."

"Then let me go," Eli said. "You've got my blood, my DNA, and RNA. You don't need me anymore."

"It's not that simple. The theory needs testing, and I might need you on hand for some time. You slipped away before; I won't make that mistake again."

Eli wanted to shout and hurl threats, but he kept his mouth shut. The doctor would only sedate him again.

Dr. Stern stood. "I'm sorry," he said. "But it's for the greater good." He patted Eli on the shoulder and left the tent.

Eli lay there in silence and focused on his breathing. When he had counted to fifty, he lifted his right hand from over the scalpel he had snatched from the trolley. *Sorry, Dr. Stern, but Noga needs me. The greater good will have to wait.*

CHAPTER 48

"Sir, we're being followed."

The captain of the USS Ohio swiveled on his bucket seat in the dim red light of the control room. When you were a nuclear-powered submarine on a stealth mission in foreign waters, a tail was not good news. They sped through the Mediterranean toward the coast of Tel Aviv, all fourteen thermonuclear warheads ready for launch. He could slice the tension in the air with a Ka-Bar knife.

"Followed by what?"

The junior officer at the sonar station squinted at the display. Johnson was a NUB, or newbie, with a shaved head and an eager expression, but he'd performed well so far.

"I don't know, sir," he said. "The sound signature is not in the system. Whatever it is, it's big."

"A boomer?"

The nuclear subs of other nations snooped around the oceans too. Friendlies operated at pre-allocated depths to avoid collisions. Non-friendlies were the problem. Something was cooking in the hallways of power, but Command had sent no warnings of potential underwater confrontations.

"Too big, sir."

"Whales?" They'd sighted a sperm whale off Malta last week.

"Negative. The target is way bigger than us."

The captain swore and ran a hand through his hair. A foreign sub would have lurked in the baffles, the sonar blind spot directly behind them. Unless they hadn't noticed the USS Ohio yet. That would explain why they were making enough noise to register on the passive sonar.

"Drop another hundred feet," he told the navigation officer. Then he grabbed the 1MC handset and pressed the broadcast button. The crew fell silent for the duration of the message. "Rig for ultra-quiet," he said, his voice echoing among the chambers of the pressurized tube. "All non-essential personnel, move to your racks at once."

He lurched forward as the accelerator disengaged and the sub lost speed.

"Toby," he said to his executive officer and second in command. "Make sure they shut off the water heater and reactor cooling pumps."

Toby nodded and hurried off, his boots clanking on the steel floor.

The captain held his breath while they floated one thousand feet below the surface. Over his ten years in the Silent Service, he'd seen a lot of crazy stuff, but a vessel that large appearing out of nowhere was a first. If they lay still, the threat might pass them by unnoticed.

"Still there?"

"Yes, sir," Johnson said.

The unidentified submergible had not spotted them. Otherwise, it would have slipped behind them and disappeared, or clamped down in full stealth mode, as they had. Unless… unless the craft didn't consider them to be a threat.

Terror gripped his heart as he remembered a science fiction film he had seen as a teenager. An alien spacecraft parked at the bottom of an oceanic abyss had gobbled human subs and drilling platforms. Was an extraterrestrial vessel, with technology and firepower far superior to their own, hunting them?

"Sir, they're closing in on us. Fast."

Crap!

"Battle Stations Torpedo!" the captain cried. "Ahead Flank Cavitate!"

The order meant "get the hell out of here and make a splash if you have to!"

The crew sprang into action, pushing buttons and pulling levers. Their sub's forward acceleration pressed the captain against the hard back of the seat. The XO returned to the control room, holding onto shelves and piping to keep his balance.

The sub could reach twenty knots, twenty-five at full throttle and in perfect conditions. That might be enough to outrun the foreign craft, but not its torpedoes.

"Any fish in the water?" Torpedoes, he meant.

"Negative, but they've picked up speed. They're gaining on us!"

If the foreign craft's goal was to freak them out, it had succeeded.

"Join the Navy," they had said. "Subs haven't seen combat since the Second World War, and nuclear warfare isn't a real threat." He should have gone for a desk job on solid ground.

"Any change?"

"They're almost on us, sir. No sign of slowing."

"Dear God!" They would ram them—a suicide mission one thousand feet beneath the deep. But no government had such a large submergible, never mind terrorist organizations.

The captain squeezed the 1MC handset. "Inbound! Brace for impact!" He had drilled the emergency procedures for many unlikely scenarios but never a high-speed intentional collision. He dropped to the floor and wrapped his arms around his seat.

Three tense seconds passed.

"Johnson?"

Johnson shook his head, failing to believe his eyes. "She's on top of us, sir. Now to starboard. Wait, no. Port. It's as if she's… swallowed us."

The captain shuddered. Heads turned to him, eyes wide.

"Outside pressure?"

Another engineer said, "Unchanged sir. We're still one thousand feet."

"She hasn't swallowed us," the captain said. "She's swimming circles around us." Time to test his theory. "Slow us down, nice and easy."

The hum of the engines fell.

"Johnson?"

"No change, sir."

Whatever was toying with them had perfect maneuverability in the ocean.

"Turn on the sonar speaker."

Johnson flipped a switch.

Two seconds passed in silence. Then a loud baritone gurgle made him jump. Biologics, for sure, but this wasn't the chatter of dolphins or the drone of whale-song. The sound was unlike anything he had heard before.

"Let's breach, nice and slow."

Metal groaned from the ballast tanks as air rushed in and expelled seawater.

The ascent took three long minutes.

"We've breached, sir."

The captain could tell. The vessel's rounded hull, optimized for underwater performance, pitched from side to side, the sickening rolls they experienced during surface transits.

"XO," he said. "You have the Deck and Conn."

"Sir!"

"Open the hatch."

Without explaining, he made for the stairwell. He had to see this with his own two eyes.

The wheel turned and the hatch lifted outward on its hinges. A few rungs further and he stepped into the blue sky. A crisp sea breeze ruffled his hair. The deep blue of the Mediterranean lapped at the immense, sleek bulk of the sub, and stretched to every horizon.

He twisted around at the waist. Behind him, the black sail of the sub towered above, a crown of sensory masts jutting into the sky.

They were alone. No sign of their mysterious escort. Had she shied away from the surface, preferring the cool, dark depths?

The captain was about to return to Command and Control when the waterfall sound of crashing water sounded behind him—the unmistakable roar of a breaching sub.

He turned slowly. A large black mass rose above the waves. The smooth slippery mountain rose and rose, its shadow eclipsing the sub.

That was no sub.

Barnacles speckled the slick blubbery hide. But this was no whale either. A flipper breached the water, like the wing of a Boeing 747. He followed the line of the elongated neck, which stretched on and on, passing over the tall sail of the sub and falling toward him.

The captain twisted around and came face-to-face with the creature. The head, tiny in proportion to its body, was taller than the captain. A wet warmth spread through his trunks and trickled down his leg. His muscles turned to stone.

Large reptilian eyes considered him with interest and blinked. Then the scaly lips parted, revealing rows of long, sharp teeth, and the sea monster smiled.

CHAPTER 49

"Don't go!" Galit ran after her father as he dragged his suitcase out the door of the Prime Minister's Residence. "Please, *Aba*."

Her family's arrival had overwhelmed her and heightened the tensions between her and Moshe, but the sight of her father storming out of her home clawed at her conscience.

"No jobs," he said. "No cigars. Searching through our stuff like we're common thieves!"

"But Aba, I told you. They were searching for bugs."

"Bugs, shmugs! We can tell when we're not wanted."

Galit's mother rolled her eyes at his histrionics but followed him.

"Mom, do something!"

"It's no use, dear. I'll call you when we land. Good thing we didn't sell the house."

Outside, her father handed the suitcase to a Secret Service agent, who hefted it into the trunk of a ministerial SUV. Her brother, sister-in-law, and their kids waited in the ample back seat of another SUV.

"Bye-bye, Granny and Grandpa!" Talya said.

Galit's mom leaned down to kiss her granddaughter. Her dad mussed Talya's head of dark curls.

Then he cursed. "Look at that crowd."

Galit did. Outside the gates, a throng of protesters blocked the street. When they caught sight of her, they hurled abuse.

"Murderers!" said one, an old lady in a green shawl.

"Traitors!" cried another.

"Run along inside," Galit told Talya.

The country had gone crazy. On Channel Two, citizens fought in the streets and peaceful rallies turned bloody as the cameras rolled. Now the barbarians were at the gates.

Galit stepped up to the open window of the SUV. "Are you sure it's safe to leave?" Did the storm clouds of anarchy have a silver lining?

"We'll sure as hell drive out of here!"

The car doors slammed, windows closed, and the SUVs advanced toward the gate. Galit didn't watch them go; her presence would only agitate the angry mob.

Back indoors, she threw herself onto the living room couch and burst into tears. A month after becoming the First Lady, her life had fallen apart. The entire country had followed suit. Earthquakes. Riots. Police interrogations.

A lifetime ago, when Moshe had told her about Gurion's proposal, she had known that politics would shove them into the public spotlight, but she hadn't expected the attention to be so cruel or unbearable. She missed the old days. Moshe and her against the world. Now they seemed separated by a chasm wider than that caused by the earthquake.

There came a loud knocking on the door. Galit wiped her tears and rose to answer.

Her father marched inside when she opened the door, his head cowed, but still seething.

"We're back!" her mother said, singing the words. Her brother and his family followed her in.

"Couldn't get out?"

"Your security people know how to handle them. But our flight was canceled."

"When's the next one?" Flights to the US left Israel many times a day.

"All flights to the United States have been canceled until

further notice. An executive order from the President himself."

"Your husband," her father growled, pacing the entrance hall, his hands balled in his pockets, "has wrecked our relations with our main ally. If only he'd listened to my advice. To any advice!"

Her mother shook her head and walked off to the guest rooms. "Time to unpack," she said. "Again. Have those lovely Secret Service men bring the bags up."

Galit blinked. Her conscience quieted. Beware what you wish for. Now she had to put up with her family—indefinitely!

More knocking at the door. This time, two uniformed police officers stood in the doorway, a string bean and a sweet potato, both with serious looks.

"Let me guess. More questioning?"

"Yes, ma'am," said String Bean.

"Moshe's still at the office. The Prime Minister has things to do besides talking with you."

The officers exchanged a look. "We're not here for the Prime Minister," String Bean said. "We've come for you."

CHAPTER 50

Tuesday afternoon, the cabinet members stared at the object on the conference room table—a large golden envelope with Moshe Karlin's name embossed in the center.

"When did it arrive?" Moshe asked.

"This morning," Ettie said. She had transported the letter to Knesset from the Prime Minister's Office building. Her manner had soured since the earthquake. Did his secretary believe the corruption charges or did she also hold him responsible for the earthquake?

"Security checked it?"

She gave him a look of reproach over her half-moon spectacles. "Of course. They said it's clean. No traces of anthrax. Or fingerprints. What's surprising is how it got here with no one noticing. Besides for the contents, of course."

Moshe picked up the envelope. Everybody else seemed to know what lay within and it was time he caught up.

"Thank you, Ettie."

Taking the hint, she left the room and closed the door behind her.

The card within, like the envelope, was gold. The thick paper had a satin sheen. He read the message aloud: "The Messiah Coronation. Wednesday, 12 PM. The Sultan's Pool, Jerusalem. Dress: Formal."

Moshe glanced about for the hidden camera. "Is this a prank?"

Shmuel said, "Someone went to a lot of trouble to pull it off."

Sivan said, "And somebody seems to think you're the Messiah."

"The mob outside would disagree. According to them, I'm a murderer and a traitor. Besides, the invitation doesn't say *I'm* the Messiah of this coronation."

"It could be a good PR move," she said.

"What could?"

"Crowning you as the Messiah. Things have gotten pretty weird lately: the Sixth Aliyah; earthquakes. People could use the crutch."

"Yeah, but what happens when they find out I'm not the Messiah?" The room fell silent. "Come on, you don't really think…?" He turned to Rabbi Yosef—he'd set them straight—but the rabbi wasn't there. "Where's Rabbi Yosef?"

"With Reverend Adams," Sivan said. "Last I heard."

"Ah." He'd have to argue this one alone. "I think I'd know if I was the Messiah. And I hope he'd do a better job. Who's behind this 'Messiah Coronation' anyway?"

"Nobody seems to know," Shmuel said. "A stage is under construction at the Sultan's Pool. The sign outside mentions the Jerusalem Cinematheque, but their office knew nothing about it."

Moshe pushed the letter aside.

"This is another of Gurion's diversions. We have bigger problems to deal with." He waved at the seats, collapsed onto a chair, and surveyed the ministers who had made it to the meeting. Once again, Rafi was missing. He sincerely hoped that this time he'd return bearing good tidings. "Sivan, can we speak freely?"

She nodded. "This room is clean of bugs."

"Bugs?" Shmuel said.

Moshe spelled it out. "Gurion's been eavesdropping on our every word since day one, and he's used that information well. On my way here, the ambassadors of both the US and Russia called. Each is convinced that we've made a secret pact with the other and that we're going to use our new weapon of mass destruction, the Zombie Army."

Savta Sarah said, "What Zombie Army? Those new arrivals can barely tie their own shoelaces."

"You're right, but the ambassadors won't listen. Gurion's got them both threatening war. We need to calm things down before matters really get out of hand. Sivan, we need to make another announcement. Shmuel, get both Presidents on the line. Not at the same time," he added.

On cue, the door opened and Rafi entered, breathless. "We have an emergency," he said.

"Take a number and get in line."

"This can't wait. We've sighted nuclear submarines off the Tel Aviv coast."

"US or Russian?"

"US. The Russian subs have entered the Gulf of Aqaba, on course for Eilat. They're all carrying multiple thermonuclear warheads. The aircraft carriers have ordered their troops to return."

Sivan said, "If they've made them visible, it's a warning."

"More than a warning," Rafi said. "Both sides are using their influence to isolate us. Foreign airlines have withdrawn from Israeli airspace. Other countries have canceled incoming El Al flights and grounded Israeli planes in their territory. They're preparing for war."

"Shmuel," Moshe said.

"I'm right on it." Shmuel left the room at a trot.

"OK, what's next? Rafi, when can we replace the foreign troops with our soldiers?"

"Right away. The Sixth Aliyah is slowing. If the Dry Bones Society and social services take over the relief efforts, we can redeploy the reserve units to the city."

"Excellent." The situation had seemed so fragile, but one by one, their problems had solutions. Divide and conquer.

Glass shattered behind him and he cringed. Alon, the ever-present head of Moshe's security detail, drew his handgun and moved to the edge of the window. Then he spoke into his sleeve. "Four agents to the gardens."

A rock wobbled onto the carpet at Moshe's feet on a bed of glass shards.

On the other side of the smashed window, two men hiked across the lawns, pickets waving in their hands. At the perimeter fence of the Knesset compound, demonstrators gripped the steel posts and pulled their bodies upward. Like their stone-throwing comrades, they were not content to exercise their freedom of speech.

Within seconds, four agents in black suits waded through the flower beds toward the intruders. When their quarry turned to flee they fired shots in the air. Ten seconds later, two ruffians lay face-down in the manure, hands cuffed, as they awaited justice.

"That's not a demonstration," Sivan said. "That's a lynch mob."

Her phone rang, and she answered. "What?" she said, clearly surprised at the news. She ended the call. "It's Galit," she said.

Moshe envisioned a similar mob outside the Prime Minister's Residence, and his pulse quickened. "Is she OK?" He should have returned her missed calls.

"The police have taken her in for questioning."

"On what charges?"

"They haven't said yet."

"Gurion, that bastard. Now he's coming after my family too?"

"And pushing the entire country toward nuclear war," Sivan reminded him.

Earthquakes. Civil unrest. Nuclear war. And now Galit in police custody. Not since his abduction by Mandrake's goons had Moshe felt so vulnerable. If only he *could* conjure natural disasters and take out his enemies. Gurion more than deserved it.

"He's gone too far," Moshe said. "This has to stop."

"He's hitting us from every side," Sivan said. "But we're stronger. We'll get through it."

"I hope so."

The door opened, and Shmuel rushed back in. *That was quick*. The Foreign Minister did not look happy. "We have a problem," he said.

"We know. Many."

"No. A new problem."

Moshe threw up his hands. "Bring it on. Things can't get any worse."

Shmuel's jaw wobbled. "Actually, they can. Much worse."

CHAPTER 51

Eli sawed at the strap on his right arm, trying to make as little noise as possible. If Dr. Stern walked in now, his escape gambit would fail.

His wrist ached from the awkward movement, and his neck hurt from lifting his head from the metal cot and straining to see what he was doing. Gripping the scalpel backward between his fingers, he jerked his hand inward, slicing the hardened leather strap with the surgical blade.

As the knife ate away at his restraints, he slowed his pace. The scalpel blade hovered an inch above the tender skin of his inner forearm. If he wasn't careful, he'd cut right through the strap and slit his wrist.

As he worked, the doctor's words bounced around his brain. Over three millennia, Eli had survived numerous life-threatening injuries. His longevity had been a miracle, the hallmark of his special Divine Intervention, and a necessary tool for his eschatological mission. But if Dr. Stern was right, God had not guided Eli's every step; he had merely tinkered with his DNA.

No longer was the Almighty a fairy godmother who popped out from behind the curtain of existence to save the day. He was a grandmaster who set plans in motion billions of years before the game began and watched from afar as the moves played out. Having discovered the natural mechanism behind his longevity, Eli felt less indestructible.

The scalpel blade lurched toward his wrist as the strap gave way, missing his skin by millimeters. *Phew!* He stretched his free arm, and then ran his fingers over the strap at his neck, searching for the buckle.

"The holy grail of human ambition," Dr. Stern had said. "Immortality." The words recalled other, much older declarations. "He will swallow Death forever," Isaiah had prophesied of the End Times. "The Lord will wipe the tears from every face."

Was the doctor right—was this his true calling, to safeguard the genetic key to immortality until the Messianic Era?

And what of the Thin Voice—did those Divine Whisperings have a mundane explanation as well? Was he both remarkable and delusional? The Thin Voice had led him to the Mount of Olives and to Moshe Karlin. Was Moshe truly the Messiah or was their abortive meeting the random side effect of a runaway imagination?

He unbuckled the second strap. Eli sat up, reached over, and made short work of the remaining restraints.

Right now, he had only one mission—to find Noga. She needed his help. And if anything had happened to her… *No! Don't even think it.*

He turned off the ECG and ripped the electrode stickers from his chest. Shifting his legs over the edge of the bed, he eased his bare feet onto the cold cement floor. His legs supported his weight. This time he had broken no bones. The thin hospital gown flapped at his thighs. He needed clothes. The tent had no storage cabinets. Where had Dr. Stern stashed his things?

After taking a step forward, something pulled at his groin, holding him back. A catheter tube. *Oh, gross.* He detached the drainage pouch, and the loose tube dangled to his feet. *Freedom first; catheter later.*

He limped to the doorway of the tent, a set of overlapping flaps, parted them slowly, and stepped through. He found himself in another tent, another makeshift hospital room. A heart monitor beeped on a stand, and a respirator wheezed.

A sudden premonition tied his insides in a knot. He tiptoed toward the cot and the still form of the woman beneath the sheets. An oxygen mask covered her mouth and nose. As he drew closer, the knot in his gut tightened. *Oh, no!*

He touched her arm. "Noga, wake up!"

She didn't open her eyes; didn't move at all.

"Noga, we have to get out of here."

"I would advise against that," said a voice behind him.

Dr. Stern stood at the tent flap, his hands in the pockets of his lab coat.

"What have you done to her?"

"Saved her life. For now." His words were not a threat, only a sad diagnosis.

"What's wrong with her?"

The doctor stepped up to the gurney and gazed at Noga. "She was comatose when she arrived at Shaare Zedek. That level of brain trauma is irreparable."

Brain trauma. Irreparable. No! It couldn't be.

"Usually," Dr. Stern continued, "I'd advise the next of kin to pull the plug." He looked Eli squarely in the eyes. "You're her only hope."

CHAPTER 52

In the passenger seat of Hasan's yellow Mercedes, Ahmed's heart bounded like a terrified rabbit. The sports car zoomed along the dirt roads of Samaria north of Jerusalem, kicking up dust and cutting corners, as Hasan blared the horn at donkeys and their drivers. Hasan's reckless driving was not the only cause for Ahmed's adrenaline rush.

Little old Ahmed was going to meet the Shepherd—the Great Imam himself! No, not Ahmed; the Mahdi. Only a select few in a generation merited this honor. Ahmed had chosen the finest suit from the closet in his room and now racked his brain for clever questions. The Mahdi should prove himself worthy.

Hasan leaned his arm on the door and said nothing, a scowl on his face. The meeting must have cost him a lot of favors. At first, Ahmed had doubted whether his cousin had access to the Leader of the Generation, or whether the Shepherd even existed. The Great Imam had avoided the public eye for years and lived in great secrecy and austerity.

His money was real enough. Ahmed had grown used to his new life: the hot showers and clean clothes; the soft bed and fresh linen; the fridge and cupboards full of every imaginable delight.

But those material benefits had not impressed Samira. She

would not approve of the harem of beautiful young women that had served him so eagerly that first night either. Ahmed blushed at the memory. He'd better keep those details to himself.

Hasan turned right at a signpost pointing to Ramallah, his hometown.

Ahmed returned to the question of what to say. He'd start off with lavish thanks. Ahmed was not worthy of the title and mission that the Great Imam had bestowed upon him. He'd beg forgiveness for his ignorance, but inquire about the end goal of his mission, and ask the Shepherd's advice on how best to fulfill that destiny.

Ramallah panned by in the passenger window. Ahmed had never ventured into the city, notorious for its seething refugee camps and terrorist training grounds. The houses and apartment buildings on the outskirts had resembled the dilapidated housing of Silwan.

The inner belly, however, painted a different picture of life in the West Bank. Luxury hotels and technology centers stood tall with fresh marble and rounded edges that gleamed with tinted windows. Modern mansions stood in spotless Jerusalem stone, with paved driveways, manicured gardens, and fountains—the opulence reserved for the well-connected.

Some of the flock had grown filthy rich while others blew themselves up. *Why do we raise our little boys and girls to love death?* He didn't have the guts to ask the Great Imam that. Maybe one day he'd find the answer, after Al Aqsa, when his fame had spread throughout the land—throughout the world! Then, even Samira would kiss his feet.

The car pulled up beside a vacant lot beyond the luxury suburbs.

Hasan got out, leaned against the car, and lit a cigarette. Ahmed climbed out of the passenger seat and brushed off his suit.

"Is this the meeting point?"

Had the Imam's security guards selected a random spot for their face-to-face, to avoid capture?

"Go on, say hello." Hasan waved his hand at the empty lot. "Greet your Shepherd."

Ahmed scanned the vacant lot but found no Imams or security personnel, only a dented, burned out metal barrel. "I don't understand."

Hasan swaggered over to him and pointed at the battered bin. "There he is. Speak your mind. Talk all you like."

Was his cousin making fun of him? "The Shepherd is an old barrel?"

"You wanted the truth. Here's the truth—nobody's seen the Shepherd in years."

That made no sense. "The money," Ahmed said. "The speech. How do you know what he wants?"

"He drops off his instructions in that bin. Every week, every month. Whenever the Shepherd feels like it. The money too." Hasan dropped the cigarette in the dirt and ground the stub under his shoe. "This stays between me and you, OK? You can't tell anyone about this place. Understand?"

"No!" Hot anger boiled in his chest. Hasan was lying to him. Again. "You said I'd meet the Shepherd and ask all my questions."

"Go ahead. He's listening. Just don't expect any answers." He chuckled.

"This isn't funny, Hasan. You're calling meetings, telling people I'm the Mahdi when you've never even seen the Shepherd, never heard his voice."

"Keep your voice down, cousin. That's the way things are here. The leaders keep their heads down or they lose them. They still call the shots and pay the bills."

"Oh, yeah? And what does he say right now?"

Hasan rolled his shoulders. "Why don't we find out?"

He strutted to the bin, lifted the jagged metal lid, and reached his arm inside. When he withdrew his arm, he held a dusty burlap sack. He opened the mouth and peered inside.

Ahmed walked over. This was another trick. Hasan would whip out a dead rat and laugh when Ahmed jumped. But there was no rat, no trick.

"Here," Hasan said, his face blank and glistening with sweat. From the sack, he extracted a large golden envelope. "It's addressed to you."

CHAPTER 53

Boris strutted into the Magitek offices Tuesday afternoon, feeling on top of the world. The secretary at the white front desk looked up and popped her bubble of gum.

"Afternoon, Anna."

He had always sensed that the buxom Russian gave him *that* look. Others might have interpreted her deadpan as boredom, but Boris knew better. She was warming to him, and as he climbed the rungs of the Organization, she was turning red hot.

"He's waiting for you."

Boris nodded and continued his swagger down the corridor, through the busy cubicles of the Call Center. Not long ago, the thought of a face-to-face with the Boss had made him tremble. The revenues of his branch of the Organization had dipped, thanks to the nosy intervention of Moshe Karlin, his former slave, and Mandrake had called in a third party to get close to Karlin. Boris had feared that the Boss would terminate him.

Since then, Boris's luck had improved. He had redeemed his career—and extended his life expectancy—by running a special operation to infiltrate Israeli politics. The mission had culminated with the capture and subjugation of Moshe Karlin himself, bringing their interactions full circle and with a sweet dose of poetic justice.

Now Mandrake had entrusted him with a new task, one that would drive the final nail into Karlin's coffin. The preparations were right on schedule. Unlike that earlier meeting with the Boss, this time Boris did not fear losing his head.

He looked up at the camera at the end of the corridor, and the white door clicked open. Once inside the antechamber, he walked up to the mirror at the far wall, and a panel shifted sideways. Boris walked through the dimly lit control room, ignoring the technicians at their data terminals, and knocked on the door of Mandrake's office.

The door clicked open.

Mandrake waited for him on the low backless couch in the center of the chamber, draped in purple ambient light. He looked up from the laptop on the coffee table.

"Enter, my friend. Have a seat."

Boris obeyed. He settled on the couch beside his boss, close but not too close. He glimpsed a large letter A on the screen before Mandrake shut the laptop.

The gesture upset Boris's confidence. Mandrake didn't trust him. Had Boris misunderstood the purpose of the meeting? Instead of a pat on the back, had his boss summoned him to deliver something far less pleasant? With Mandrake, he never knew what to expect.

"Are we ready for tomorrow?"

"Yes, sir. We're all set."

"I'm pulling you off the project."

Boris's heart dropped into his trousers. He had been looking forward to watching Karlin meet his end. Had Boris messed up? Had someone libeled him to his boss behind his back? Or perhaps he'd done nothing wrong, but Mandrake would kill him to keep the secret safe. These might be his final moments; he'd better use them well.

"The stage is set," he said, in his defense. "All the pieces are in place. As you instructed."

"I know, my friend. But I have another task for you." He considered Boris, his large intelligent eyes bridged by a beak nose, like a raptor considering its next meal. "Do you believe in the Devil?"

Boris swallowed. These questions were better left unanswered. His boss had a thing for stage magic and the theatrical, but the sudden turn to the supernatural worried him? Had Mandrake lost his mind?

"Should I?"

"Of course not. But it is a useful idea. As the story goes, the Devil was once God's favorite angel. Until he rebelled. But even then, I suppose, God couldn't bear to destroy him." Mandrake fixed him with those large, intelligent eyes. "There's a devil in our midst, Boris, a traitor who requires elimination. It's very sad, really. A dear, old friend. I don't have the heart to do it myself."

Boris highly doubted that. Beneath the amicable facade, cold blood ran through veins of steel. Had Mandrake just compared himself to God? *Whatever.* Boris knew what was expected of him.

"Let me do it for you."

Mandrake gave him a warm, appreciative smile. "I'll tell you the story in full, my friend. I think you'll enjoy this task. It involves an old friend of yours too."

Mandrake slid two photographs on the table toward Boris. He didn't recognize the first photo. The devil, he assumed. The second, he recognized only too well.

Well, well, well. Full circle, indeed.

CHAPTER 54

Yosef pored over the holy books on his desk in the Vice Prime Minister's Office, Reverend Adams's words ringing in his ears. *Moshe Karlin is the Messiah.*

But how could Yosef know for sure? He needed more information. In the past, he had turned to Rabbi Emden and the Great Council. Who was left to guide him now?

The task was impossible. There were too many variables, too many contradictory traditions. This wasn't even his job. Elijah the Prophet should make these decisions. But where was he?

He must not get this wrong. The stakes were too high: the world's Redemption; and Yosef's life.

If he was going to make any progress, he had to reexamine his assumptions, and not just about the Messiah.

"Is this the eternal bliss we've been hoping for?" Adams had said. Yosef felt the stab of disappointment too.

For centuries, the dispute had raged among the sages. Did the Future Reward require the reunion of body and soul in This World, or did that eternal bliss belong to the World of Souls alone?

When Moshe had awoken in his second life, he had remembered nothing of the World of Souls. What was the soul, anyway? Did the soul even exist? If the body was all we had—all we were—then what of eternal reward? The axioms of life, the very ground beneath his feet, wavered over a dark abyss.

He closed the heavy tomes of Talmud.

Body and soul. God and Satan. Dualism appeared in many guises. But there was only one God. No devil encroached on His dominion. Was the body-soul divide an illusion? The six hundred thirteen commandments sanctified life in this world. But if we have no incorporeal existence, then the Resurrection made sense. Without the Resurrection, there could be no afterlife. The World to Come was the here and now, just later.

Yosef's phone vibrated. The text message from an unknown number contained a single word: BOOM.

Yosef's guts clenched. He made an educated guess as to the identity of the sender. How had he obtained Yosef's personal mobile number? The same way he had sneaked into his office under false pretenses. Had the sender graduated from persuasion to bomb threats?

A sudden apprehension made Yosef nudge his laptop from slumber.

The YouTube clip from the reverend's email still displayed on the screen. Yosef clicked play and skipped to the end. A jarring detail in the video had gnawed on the edges of his consciousness, but he couldn't put a finger on it. On the Temple Mount, men in blue overalls constructed a dais opposite the golden Dome of the Rock ahead of tomorrow's mass gathering.

Yosef played the section again. One worker had caught his eye. The man kept his head low as he carried a package on his shoulder. The shot was distant and pixelated, but Yosef knew the red beard and sparkling eyes beneath the flat cap.

Oh, no. Yosef guessed what he was up to and had to stop him.

Yosef grabbed his desk phone.

"Ram, get the Police Commissioner on the line. It's urgent!"

CHAPTER 55

Avi heard the voice of a ghost when he stumbled into the offices of Upward on Keren Hayesod Street. The ghost was cackling.

Avi halted, then winced as his arm in the plaster cast swung forward. The last time he had met a ghost, Moshe Karlin had returned from the dead and wrecked his life. Was this happening all over again?

He peered around the corner and blinked his eyes. *This cannot be!* He had seen Gurion on the platform, giving forth at the microphone, when the ground had collapsed.

Avi had danced sideways, as cracks tore through Zion Square, and he fled for his life. Looking over his shoulder, he saw the entire platform disappear into a gaping hole as if swallowed by Godzilla.

Then the earth flipped Avi like a burger, his arm slamming into an iron street pole. He had known pain before, but never like this. Bright lights sparked before his eyes as the mob surged ahead, tripping over his legs and trampling his injured arm until the world faded to white.

He awoke in Shaare Zedek hospital, a fresh cast on his arm. After an overnight stay for observation, the nurses released him. Only when he'd left did he realize his luck. The hospital had generators and water reserves. Outside, the situation was bleak.

He called his parents—the screen protector of his phone had shattered in his back pocket—and walked to their apartment in Wolfson Center. They'd never been so happy to see him. Gurion's stage had descended into the belly of the earth, and they had assumed that Avi had followed close behind.

He lay on the couch, munched his mother's honey cakes, and sipped sweet tea boiled over a gas burner. With Gurion gone, Upward would disintegrate, and when his term in Knesset ended Avi would need a new job. That gave him time. Few administrations lasted a full four years, but something told him that Moshe might break that rule.

Moshe. Avi had tried to warn him. He'd even tried to spy for him behind enemy lines. Now the Opposition was in disarray. With Gurion as his champion, Avi hadn't bothered to invest in warm relations with the other party members. If he was to be of use to Moshe, he'd need to butter up the next in line, or his days in politics were numbered.

The emergency services had done a great job. Within a day, they had reinstated critical services, and life had gone back to near normal. Soldiers filled the streets and kept downtown under wraps. They had to—according to the rumors, the fault line was encrusted with diamonds!

And so, Tuesday afternoon, Avi made his way to Keren Hayesod Street to figure out which way the political winds were blowing.

At the door, he heard Gurion's voice, and he was laughing. Was that a recording? Gurion was gone. Had he survived, he would have nothing to laugh about either. But when Avi stepped inside, sure enough, there he was—Isaac Gurion in the flesh, alive and well—if a bit scratched up—and chuckling.

"Isaac—you're alive!"

Gurion glanced at him but continued cutting a newspaper with a pair of scissors.

"Were you resurrected?"

Gurion glared at him. "Don't be ridiculous. I'm not one of

them. Oh, no." He hummed to himself as he cut along the edges.

Avi looked to the others in the room. A group of aides and Upward members of Knesset stood to the side and watched their leader from a safe distance, fear in their eyes. Avi wasn't the only one to have noticed the change.

He drew near. Gurion cut around the frame of a photo in the newspaper, a photo of Moshe Karlin. The headline read, "PM Karlin: Israeli Sovereignty Unshakable."

"Are you OK?"

"Never been better." Gurion cackled. Discarding the newspaper, he kissed the photo of Moshe and pinned the cutting to the corkboard on the wall. He stepped back to consider his handiwork.

"Long live the king," he muttered, and he giggled again.

That's it. Gurion had escaped the earthquake with his life but lost his mind. But his sudden adulation for Moshe Karlin gave Avi hope.

"Is this the new plan?"

"What?"

"Is there a new plan to defeat Karlin?"

Or, Avi thought, *will we join him at last?* He must have said something hilarious because Gurion crumpled into a fit of teary laughter. Avi looked at the bystanders, who were not laughing, but cringing.

Gurion recovered and stared at Avi as though seeing something beautiful for the first time. "We're not going to defeat Karlin," he said, his old venom returning.

Then his arm was a blur and with a loud snap, the scissors lodged into the corkboard, the blades planted smack in the middle of Moshe's face. "Oh, no. We're going to kill him."

CHAPTER 56

"You should have told me," Eli said. He sat beside the hospital gurney. Noga lay beneath the sheets, unmoving, her breathing shallow.

Dr. Stern stood beside him. "You were in a bad state and needed rest. Besides, we could have lost her any moment. I feared that you'd despair and slip away. I couldn't risk losing you again."

Eli stroked Noga's hair. For the hundredth time, he called her name.

Irreparable. This couldn't be the end. They had set her plan in motion. Soon the entire country would know the truth about the Lost Tribes. They were so close to their goal. Noga had to be there to see it.

"I'll do it," he said. "Whatever you need to heal her."

"We must move quickly; her vitals are falling. The good news is that we don't have to manipulate her DNA. That would require equipment far more advanced than I've cobbled together here. But this treatment is obviously very experimental. Normally we would perform lengthy testing and clinical trials."

"But that could take months," Eli said.

The doctor nodded. "More like years. I think I've identified the epigenetic activators associated with your healing abilities, as well as the aging inhibitors. But to generate those in the lab will take more time and equipment. Our only option is to harvest the activators from you directly."

Harvest. That sounded painful. "Whatever you need. And you can skip the theory. Just tell me what to do."

"We need your blood."

"My blood?" At the mention of the b-word, Eli felt lightheaded.

"We're in luck. You're Type O Negative, the universal donor."

Eli swallowed hard and held out his arm. "How much do we need?"

Dr. Stern gave him an apologetic frown. "A lot. A transfusion is the only option. Bring in the gurney."

Eli nodded. He rushed through the tent flaps, wheeled in the metal bed, and positioned it alongside Noga, while the doctor arranged the blood equipment. At the sight of the needles, Eli's head spun so he climbed onto the gurney and lay down. He turned his head away and stared at Noga.

Once upon a time, people had thought that bloodletting was healthy. Eli had never bought into that. "Ouch," he said, as the needle punctured his skin.

"Sorry about that," the doctor said. "The nurses do the blood work at the hospital."

"Yeah, I can tell."

The tube warmed against his skin as his lifeblood flowed. A metallic taste filled his mouth, and a white frost accumulated at the edges of his vision.

Think of something else, something good.

When this was over, he'd take Noga out for a juicy steak dinner. They'd clink their wine glasses together and watch their website traffic climb.

An electronic alarm sounded from the ECG. The beep of Noga's heart had slowed and the numbers on the display shifted.

Dr. Stern walked over and disabled the alarm.

"What's happening?"

"She's losing blood pressure. Her systems are failing."

"Then do something!"

"I am!"

Eli's chest shook as fear ripped through him. Noga lay right beside him, her life seeping away, and he was powerless to save her. He reached out and held her hand in his. *This can't be happening. You can't let this happen, God!* Noga had reignited his will to live; she had renewed his faith in humanity. Without her, he might as well give up.

"There," the doctor said, his voice soft and far away. "She's connected. Now we wait."

Tears dripped from Eli's eyes onto the metal gurney, and the world frosted over.

CHAPTER 57

Numbness spread over Moshe's body as the stranger delivered the news. The scientist's lips moved but Moshe no longer understood the jargon. The tidings had frozen his brain. This was the end of the road. And not just for Moshe. For everyone. Humanity's plans and schemes, hopes and dreams—everything anyone had ever done—all amounted to nothing. This was, literally, the end of the world.

Moshe held up his hand to interrupt. "Let's start over," he said. "Where did you get that?"

He pointed to the image on Professor Stein's tablet computer: a blurry white speck on a backdrop of inky black.

"The Hubble Space Telescope," he said. "NASA forwarded us the images an hour ago." The professor, a slight man with tidy gray hair and lined cheeks, headed the Israeli Space Agency, a division of the Ministry of Science and Technology.

"And we're looking at an asteroid?"

"Correct. That's a large body of rock. This asteroid, PK-7, originated in the Asteroid Belt between Mars and Jupiter." He talked slower than before and used simpler words.

"And this asteroid is heading for earth?"

"Yes."

"Are you sure of that?"

"PK-7 will hit Jerusalem tomorrow at twelve oh-three

PM."

Moshe couldn't argue with that level of specificity. During a nighttime hike in the desert hills outside Eilat, he had admired the shooting stars. Meteor—and asteroid—showers happened all the time, didn't they?

"Has this sort of thing happened before?"

"An asteroid of this magnitude? A bunch of times."

Moshe relaxed his death grip on the armrest of his chair. This had happened before. How bad could it be?

Professor Stein continued. "The last one hit sixty-five million years ago and wiped out the dinosaurs."

"Oh." That sounded less positive. "And what can we expect from this PK-7?"

"The main impact will obliterate everything within a twenty-mile radius and leave a deep crater."

"I see." Israel would lose her capital along with her important religious and archaeological sites. The loss would injure tourism revenues, but the country would survive. Jerusalemites could evacuate the city within a day. But the professor wasn't done.

"Of course, the region lies near a major fault line, so the impact event will trigger severe earthquakes across Israel."

"Worse than Sunday's earthquake?"

"Far worse."

Moshe felt the blood drain from his face. He'd have to beg the foreign troops to return. Major population centers would need to evacuate, perhaps across the border.

"Shmuel, get the ambassadors of the USA and Russia on the phones. We need to resolve that diplomatic crisis and beg them to allow flights to leave the country and save as many people as possible!"

"Sorry, sir," Professor Stein said. "But I wouldn't bother." The professor was a real downer. Moshe would not be inviting him to official cocktail parties. "The aftermath of the asteroid strike will be much worse than the initial damage. The impact will eject large amounts of dust and ash into the atmosphere. This dust cloud will spread over the planet, blotting out the sun. Photosynthesis will cease. Within weeks ninety-nine percent of life on Earth will perish."

A short, incredulous laugh escaped Moshe's lips. "But humanity will survive, right? We have technology and science..."

Professor Stein shook his head. "Even the deepest nuclear-powered bunkers will eventually run out of supplies. We're talking total annihilation. They call it Planet Killer Seven for a reason."

Moshe stared at the faces of the cabinet members around the conference table, the last cabinet of the State of Israel.

"How did we not know about this earlier?"

The professor cleared his throat. "The asteroid was in a secure orbit and not on any astronomical watch lists. It appears that the unusual solar flare a few months ago tugged the asteroid just enough to send it our way. Until today, Mars had blocked the asteroid's trajectory from Earth's line of sight."

Silence reigned in the room. Scientists had attributed the Resurrection to the effects of an unusual solar flare. The solar flare had given, now it was taking away.

"On the bright side," Professor Stein said, and all eyes clung to him for a shred of optimism, "CO2 levels will decrease markedly after a few hundred years, and the planet will cool. Climate change will no longer be an issue."

The assembled ministers gaped at him. If humanity was extinct, nobody would be left to worry about climate change.

Moshe's father's voice whispered in his ears. *A Karlin never quits.* A final spark of resistance flared within.

Moshe slammed his fist on the desk. "Then we have to prevent it. At all costs. We'll shoot it down or land astronauts on the surface and nuke it to pieces."

Professor Stein coughed. "Hollywood physics do not apply. All the nukes in the world would be unlikely to change the outcome."

"There's no hope of escape?"

The professor frowned. "Bomb shelters will crumble. Tidal waves and fires will follow. The few to survive the impact will die of hunger and disease."

"So, this is the end—there's nothing we can do about it?"

"That sums it up pretty well."

"Thank you, Professor."

"You're welcome." He reached out and shook Moshe's hand. "It's been a pleasure to meet you, Mr. Prime Minister. Our team at the Space Agency wanted you to know that we're very proud and think you could have really fixed the country. Best of luck to you all."

The professor left the conference room.

The cabinet members pondered the situation in stunned silence. Failed coalitions and corruption charges—even earthquakes and imminent world wars—no longer seemed important. Nothing mattered. Tomorrow, they were all going to die.

"Has the news hit the press yet?" Moshe said.

"That's the strange thing," Sivan said. "Nobody's mentioned it. Not in Israel, not the international media either."

"Then I suppose we'll need to tell the nation ourselves."

"Bad idea," Shmuel said. "People will panic. Our last minutes will be pandemonium."

"He's right," Sivan said and wiped a tear from her face. She had agreed with Shmuel; the world really was ending. "It's too late to do anything, and nothing we do will make a difference."

Moshe got to his feet, and the world shifted and swirled around him. He was a rudderless ship on a choppy ocean in the dead of night. He'd faced the fearsome waves before, but this time no safe shore beckoned on the horizon.

"We owe our citizens the truth," he said. "The news will leak soon enough; at least they'll hear it from the government first. I'll prepare a final statement."

He took one last look at his cabinet, his loyal supporters through the highs and lows of the last stormy months of human history. They looked to him for guidance and inspiration, but what hope could he offer? This time they would all go down with the ship.

"Thank you," he said. "For your service and your friendship."

CHAPTER 58

Late that afternoon, Yosef paced the foyer of the Talpiot Police Station and glanced at his wristwatch. He'd been waiting an hour—an hour too long. If his suspicions were right, something terrible was about to happen.

He approached the front desk. "Officers," he said. The two young women at the desk might have been identical twins. Both sported dark ponytails, and both had told him to wait. "This is a matter of life and death—when will the Commissioner see me?"

"Sorry, Mr. Vice Prime Minister," said the one. "But the Commissioner is very busy. You'd best try him again tomorrow."

She got up and swung a handbag strap over her shoulder. "Can you give me a ride?" she asked the other. Their resemblance was uncanny, and Yosef wondered how their coworkers told them apart.

"Sure," the other replied. She stood and swung an identical bag over her shoulder.

"You're leaving?" Night had fallen an hour ago, but Yosef had assumed that law enforcement didn't keep strict business hours.

"You're welcome to call the Police Hotline. They're open twenty-four/seven."

And with that, they were off.

In what twisted world did the Vice Prime Minister have to wait hours for the Police Commissioner to discuss a matter of *piku'ach nefesh*, life and death?

Yosef's business couldn't wait any longer. He looked over his shoulder. A telephone rang down a corridor, but no officers were in sight. For the first time, Yosef regretted forgoing the security detail usually assigned to the Vice Prime Minister. He could do with some backup now.

He walked around the reception desk and down a long corridor, scanning the signs on the doors of the offices. The Commissioner's room was at the far end.

Yosef knocked once then turned the handle.

Commissioner Golan looked up at his unannounced visitor, annoyance passing over his face for a moment.

"Mr. Vice Prime Minister," he said, without rising from his seat. "What an unexpected honor." He sounded anything but honored.

"Pardon me for intruding, but this is a matter of life and death."

Golan leaned back in his chair and indicated for Yosef to sit in the visitor's chair. He did.

"I have reason to believe there will be a terrorist attack on the Temple Mount tomorrow."

Golan said nothing, so Yosef plowed on. "During the speech of the, ah, Mahdi."

"The Arab Messiah?"

Yosef swallowed. "Yes."

Golan smiled. "Afraid he'll beat the Prime Minister to the punch?"

"The Prime Minister has never professed to be the Messiah."

Golan snorted. "Not yet. But that would be convenient, wouldn't it?"

Yosef had expected the Commissioner to send Special Forces to sweep the Temple Mount for explosives. Instead, he had accused Yosef of political schemes.

Focus on the facts. "A news clip from yesterday shows workers preparing the Temple Mount for the Mahdi's speech. One of the workers is Tom Levi. His cult aims to destroy the Dome of the Rock and rebuild the Jewish Temple. He told me that himself. I think this Mahdi has pushed him to act now. Today, he sent me this."

Yosef displayed the text message on his phone.

Golan said, "You think he'll blow up the Temple Mount along with the Mahdi's followers?"

"Yes!" Finally, Yosef had gotten through to him. "An attack on the Temple Mount would cause interfaith tensions to explode."

Golan nodded. Surely, he would do everything possible to prevent that.

"Mr. Vice Prime Minister," he said. "Let's be frank. This is about the corruption charges, isn't it?"

"What? No!"

"Another cynical attempt to direct our attention away from the Prime Minister's crimes. His wife's crimes too."

"No! Please listen to what I'm saying. People will die if we don't act."

Golan just smiled. "Let me guess, you want the police to cancel the Mahdi's speech, for their own safety, creating a media storm and removing the other messiah from the scene all in one stroke. Brilliant, I must admit. But I'm not falling for it."

Yosef couldn't believe his ears. Had the Commissioner heard a word he'd said? "The earthquake was not a cynical trick and neither is this."

"I wasn't talking about the earthquake." Golan glared at him. "Haven't you heard the news? According to your boss, terrorist plots are the least of our worries tomorrow. You people really should get your stories straight."

"What news?" What was he going on about?

Golan turned his laptop to face Yosef. "See for yourself. Straight from the Prime Minister's Office."

The front-page article on Ynet displayed a grainy photo of

a bright object in a black sky. A star? "Breaking news," read the headline.

Yosef read the first paragraph and fell off the chair.

CHAPTER 59

Dani Tavor wheeled his Samsonite carry-on bag into the international departures terminal at Ben Gurion airport and almost had a heart attack. As a celebrity, he was not used to waiting in line, but now he stood at the end of the mother of all lines.

Every Israeli and his sister had shown up at the airport with bulging suitcases and sharpened elbows. The few travelers not arguing at the top of their voices with the airport staff looked about with glum, doomsday faces. A few of the glazed glances stirred with momentary recognition at the sight of him.

Dani was having nothing of it. He whipped out his iPhone and dialed his daughter Liat's number, but got that annoying "out of service, try again later" message. He swore under his breath. Liat, her husband, and the grandkids had set out a half hour before him, but he couldn't spot them in the crowds. He hoped they had boarded a plane and would leave this Godforsaken country in time. Had they reserved him a seat?

With a final huff, he gripped the handle of his carry-on bag and marched on, flanking the unruly line, and made for the El Al Business Class reception desk. Into the bag he'd stuffed a change of clothes, a wad of hundred-dollar notes from his safe, and his Lifetime Achievement Award from the

Tel Aviv House of Journalists.

He rounded the corner and halted. The Business Class counters stood empty. He swore again.

In recent years, he'd arranged charters for his travels but as of today, all planes had fled the Middle East. Not for the first time, he wished he could afford a private plane. Fame in Israel came with all the annoyances but few of the perks. Today, however, his talk show career might just save his life.

He returned to the long line of Economy Class check-in desks. Flashing his fetching smile at the woman at the front, he cut in.

"Excuse me," he said. "Just a question."

The woman turned on him, ready to offload her frustrations and fears on the cheeky older man when that flash of recognition sparkled in her eyes. "Oh. Hi!" She ran her hand through her hair and smiled. "Honey, it's Dani Tavor!" She nudged her geeky husband in the ribs, who looked up from his phone. Their three kids gawked at him from behind the suitcase trolley.

"Thank you!" Dani gave them a free sample of his trademark penetrating stare, then turned to the clerk behind the desk. "My daughter reserved a seat for me earlier. I've no luggage to check in."

The clerk had exhausted her quota of smiles for the day. "Dani Tavor," she said, as she typed at her keyboard. "Nope, sorry. Nothing here. Where are you flying?"

"Anywhere."

"I'm sorry, you'll have to buy a ticket like everyone else."

Like everyone else—the nerve!

A finger tapped him on the back. "Hey," the husband said. "We were here first. Get in line."

Dani ignored him. "I'll take whatever you have," he told the clerk. "The further away, the better."

She glanced at the screen. "The only seats left are to Timbuktu."

"I'll take it!"

"Do you have a visa for Mali?"

"I'll use my foreign passport."

The clerk reached out, so he handed over his mint condition German passport. His mother had barely escaped the Holocaust, and her former nationality had allowed Dani to apply for German citizenship. As with many Israelis, he had procured the second passport "just in case." His forward thinking had paid off!

"That'll be fifty thousand."

He almost choked. "Fifty thousand shekels—for Timbuktu?"

The clerk wasn't joking. "No," she said. "Fifty thousand *US dollars*. When the exchanges open tomorrow, the shekel will be worthless."

The airlines had no shame—to take advantage of refugees, fleeing for their lives! He'd do a special exposé on airline extortion when he got back. But he wouldn't be back. Tomorrow an asteroid would obliterate the country. But still, fifty thousand US dollars!

"Move along," the clerk said.

"I'll take it." He held out his Visa Platinum Card. "Here, take my fifty thousand dollars."

She did. Good thing he'd removed the limit on his card. He glanced over his shoulder at the lines of desperate fellow travelers. How many of them could swipe fifty grand on their cards? There weren't enough seats for them all anyway, poor things.

In his lengthy career, he'd covered tragedy and sorrow, but he'd never looked the victims in the eyes hours before disaster struck. Oh, well.

The clerk printed the ticket and wished him a pleasant flight.

On the way to passport control, newsrooms displayed on muted television screens. "Breaking news," flashed the ticker in red. But for a change, the talking heads were smiling. Why were they still in the studio?

A familiar self-satisfied face filled the screen. Dani drew near. Isaac Gurion, that old devil, had survived the earthquake. What mischief could he possibly be stirring up during the final hours of the Jewish State?

"Asteroid Hoax," read the ticker.

What? He moved close enough to hear Gurion speak.

"Do not be fooled," Gurion said, looking calm, a beatific smile on his lips. "And do not be frightened. The apocalypse Moshe Karlin has promised is yet another lie. Fear not. Tomorrow, your true Redeemer will arrive."

Dani stared at the fifty-thousand-dollar airline ticket in his hand and he swore again.

CHAPTER 60

Galit stared at her husband's face on the television screen. This couldn't be real. She'd had Henri whip up a dinner of Moshe's favorite foods to comfort him and make up for the trouble she'd caused.

She'd spent the morning at the Talpiot Police Department, answering questions about the new First Lady's spending habits and use of state funds. The investigation was another travesty, she knew, but she still felt responsible. She had become another front in the political war against Moshe.

That, and the return of her family to the Prime Minister's Residence. They would be staying much longer than anticipated. A fancy dinner would not solve that problem either but would give comfort in these trying times.

"He'll bounce back when he's ready," her mom had said. "Just make sure you're there for him when he does."

She watched her husband deliver his recorded statement from the Prime Minister's Office, the Israeli flag behind him, and her petty concerns faded to nothing. In a matter of hours, a speeding chunk of cosmic rock would succeed where armies and haters had failed for decades—to annihilate the Jewish State. The screen switched from Moshe's serious face to an image of the asteroid.

The diplomatic dinner table, set to perfection by the kitchen staff, would go to waste. Who could eat at a time like this?

The door opened, and she ran to the entrance hall. Galit overheard Moshe speaking with his security detail. He used the words with which he had concluded his televised address. "Head home and spend time with your loved ones." Alon nodded and left.

Moshe turned around and met her eyes. Giving her a brave grin, he walked up to her and held her face in his hands. "I guess we won't be conquering the world after all."

"I never wanted the world," she said. "Just you."

He gave her that sad grin again and kissed her on the forehead. He wasn't angry with her. Moshe had always weathered her moods and outbursts with patience. Another trumped-up charge from the Opposition wouldn't make him turn on her. She should have known that.

"Dinner's ready," she said, a tear in her voice, hoping to find something positive in their last hours. "We'll have one hell of a final meal."

Moshe forced another smile, then trudged down the corridor to their bedroom.

Her father had sidled up beside her. "What's for dinner?"

Some people always had an appetite, end of the world or not. "Didn't you see his address?"

"Oh, yeah. Sneaky move."

"Sneaky?"

"That'll keep everyone busy for a while and deflect attention from the scandals. It's better than faking a war and easier to clear up after. Phew! The astronomers got it wrong. Sorry for the scare. Maybe I underestimated him. It's brilliant."

"You think Moshe made that up?"

"Don't look at me. That's the analysis on Channel Two. The timing is too convenient." Her father cleared his throat. "Shall we serve ourselves?"

"Go ahead." Galit made for their bedroom. She knew Moshe. He wouldn't make up something like that.

She knocked on their door. Hearing no response, she turned the handle. The room was dark, the lights off, and curtains drawn against the street lights. "Moshe?"

A soft grunt came from their bed. She walked in and sat on the edge of the bed. His head poked out from the bedspread.

"You coming to eat?"

"I failed you," he said. "We're all going to die, and I can do nothing about it."

"It's not your fault. You don't have to carry the world on your shoulders."

"We had the superpowers on their knees yesterday. Now they all want to see us die. If I'd just chosen one…"

Galit didn't know what he was talking about. He didn't share details of the government's inner workings with her, and she accepted that. But she didn't need to know the details. She knew her husband, and he always did the right thing.

"It'll be OK."

"No, Galit. This time it won't." He gave an ironic laugh. "They all think I'm a messiah, but they're wrong. I'm done."

She shushed him and stroked his hair. He was always the one calming her down over some silly, inconsequential nothing that had set her off; she'd never seen him so devastated and drained of life. Moshe had returned from the dead. He had faced off criminals, shaken up an unfeeling bureaucracy, and beaten the political establishment at its own game. He'd beat this too. She knew it. But not like this. "C'mon Moshe. You're not done yet."

"I am," he said, his voice louder, harder.

He pulled the covers over his head, knocking her hand away. Hurt flashed in her mind. *We've only got a few hours left on this Earth and he wants to be alone?*

She left the room, slamming the door behind her, and leaned against the wall. The hurt boiled away, leaving a silt of gloom. *We're all going to die.* She'd never taken that possibility seriously. Moshe always swept in to save the day. He was her personal Superman. But with Moshe in this state, she ran out of hope.

Hearing a knock at the front door, she ran to answer. She opened without thinking, forgetting the mass of demonstrators outside the gates. But no angry protesters waited on the threshold as the door swung open, only one man.

A series of emotions swept over her: revulsion and rage, and then pity. He hung his head, the face beneath the oily fringe for once devoid of guile and cocky self-assurance. The plaster cast on his left arm hung in a sling. When he looked up, fear flashed in his eyes.

On the welcome mat stood Avi Segal.

CHAPTER 61

"What are you doing here?" she demanded.

On the threshold of the Prime Minister's Residence, Avi avoided Galit's glare. After his deceptions and betrayals, he had no right to be there, but now he forced himself to look her in the eye. "Is Moshe home?"

Home. Moshe belonged here, not him, but Avi had to get inside at all costs. Moshe's life depended on it.

"Shouldn't you be with your pal, Isaac Gurion?"

"I left Upward. I quit politics."

Her short, dismissive laugh told him that she didn't believe a word. He didn't blame her, although, after their experiences in Mandrake's warehouse a month ago, he had hoped that she would have softened.

They had sat side by side, bound to their chairs and gagged. Avi had refused to let their mad tormentor kill Moshe. Later, when memories of Moshe's first death came flooding back, Avi had risen to her defense, and shouldered the blame for their unfaithfulness. He had deceived and betrayed them both.

The traitor in Avi had died, but earning back their trust would take time. Now time was running out. For what it was worth, he had to try.

"I need to speak to Moshe."

"About what?"

"His life is in danger."

She shook her head. Not the response Avi had hoped for, but the words seemed to have worked. She stepped aside and let him enter.

The hall of the Prime Minister's Residence had the high ceilings and fancy paintings of a museum. A glimmer of pride for his friend warmed his heart. *Look how far you've come, my bro.*

Galit closed the door behind them. "I guess you didn't get the memo. We're all going to die."

"I mean immediate danger. Gurion's gone crazy. He's not interested in defeating Moshe; he wants him dead. I tried to warn Moshe before, but he wouldn't listen to me. You must tell him. What?"

She shook her head again and considered him with a sadness that bordered on pity. "When I said 'we're all going to die' I wasn't being philosophical. 'All men must die.' I mean, we're all going to die tomorrow—every person in the State of Israel. The rest of the planet too, probably. We're expecting an asteroid strike at noon."

"What?"

She shrugged. "Check the news if you don't believe me."

We're all going to die. Did Gurion know? Would that make any difference?

"Then why are you still here? You should get as far away as possible."

"There's an international embargo. Most countries have pulled their planes and taken our aircraft hostage. Our neighbors have closed their borders, and tsunamis are expected in our waters."

"Dear Lord. What's Moshe going to do?"

Galit glanced down a corridor. "He's… not in a good state. I couldn't get through to him. I've never seen him so depressed."

"But he always has a plan. He always knows what to do."

"Not this time."

"Mommy," said a youthful voice. Talya padded toward them in her pajamas, rubbing her eyes with the back of her hands. She saw him, and her eyes widened. "Uncle Avi!"

She ran to him, and he lifted her into his arms. He gave her a great big hug and breathed in her little girl scent. She had called him *Aba* in the past when Avi had tried to erase every trace of Moshe and take his place. How he had missed her.

"Can't sleep, sweetie?"

"I had a nightmare," she said. She opened her eyes wide. "There was a witch."

"There are no witches," he told her. "Everything will be OK."

Her eyes brightened. "Will you put me to bed?"

Avi looked at Galit, and she nodded.

"Yay!"

Avi lowered her to the floor. "Lead the way."

He tucked her in and waited outside the door until her breathing came slow and regular.

He found Galit at the table of a large kitchen in cream paneling, a glass of red wine before her.

"Want a drink?"

"Yes, ma'am."

She poured a second glass and placed it before him. The dry red had a bitter aftertaste. The second sip was easier on the palate.

"I'm sorry," Avi said, apropos nothing. "I really screwed everything up."

"Not everything," she said. "Despite your best efforts."

Avi didn't mind the humor at his expense.

"For what it's worth," she said. "I forgive you." She took another swig of wine.

"You do?"

"Sure. We wouldn't want to die angry at each other, would we?"

"Do you think Moshe will forgive me too?"

"I think he has it in his heart, but I can't speak for him.

You'll have to ask him yourself, and good luck with that."

Avi gulped his wine. Moshe, depressed and stuck in bed—he never thought he'd live to see that. "I think I'll pass. If you couldn't get through to him, then I have no chance."

He topped up his glass from the bottle. They'd need more of those. At least he hadn't caused *this* catastrophe. Hanging out with the Karlins in the Prime Minister's Residence—he couldn't think of a better way to spend his last hours.

He put down the bottle and opened his mouth to share that thought with Galit, but he didn't. Instead, he stared at Galit. She held the glass to her lips, frozen, staring into space.

"You OK?"

"We can't get through to him," she said.

"OK."

"But someone else might."

Avi smiled. He knew who she had in mind. It was worth a shot.

CHAPTER 62

Moshe Karlin emerged from a deep sleep with a premonition of impending doom. The dawn chorus of birds reached his ears, distant and muffled through the window pane. He lingered in the warm embrace of the soft mattress and silky sheets.

In his dream, he had risen from the dead to become prime minister. He'd create justice and equality—alone if he had to and without the treacherous bureaucracy. Despite his meticulous plans, he suffered defeat and betrayal. None of it mattered. A rogue asteroid sped through outer space to pulverize the State of Israel and snuff out life on Earth.

That was just a dream. What a relief!

Unlike his other nightmares—the rickety bridge over the dark chasm, his father and grandfather on the grassy bank moving further away with his every step forward—this dream had seemed so realistic!

Soon, he'd roll out of bed, have breakfast with Galit, and drop Talya at kindergarten on his way to work. He had big plans. Karlin & Son would expand to Tel Aviv, then north and south, completing the vision of his late father, David Karlin, of blessed memory.

But as the features of the room emerged from the dark, the gloomy premonition returned. This wasn't his house on

Shimshon Street, but the Prime Minister's Residence on Smolenskin.

His nightmare was a reality, his struggles for naught. He could have spent his time better lazing at home with Galit and Talya. They were the reason he had wanted to make the world a better place.

He should reach out to them now, to hug and console them, but his body had turned to lead. What consolation could he offer? Everything would *not* be OK. Everything would cease to be. He had failed them. He had failed his father, his grandfather's legacy, and his nation.

The mound of impossible obstacles cast a dark shadow over him. Had he really thought he could play prime minister? He was completely out of his league.

A Karlin never quits. Moshe hadn't quit; the cosmos had quit on him. Time had run out; history was ending.

He released a long, defeated breath and discovered that he wasn't alone in the early morning gloom. On a chair beside the bed sat an old lady.

"Good morning, Moshe," she said, her eyes large and sad through the thick lenses.

"Savta. Where's Galit?"

"Outside. She's worried about you."

His conscience twinged. While he wallowed in self-pity, Savta Sarah was holding things together, and she had suffered far worse ordeals than him.

"She wants to talk to you but has forgotten how. So she brought me here to speak for her."

Another sting of guilt. Lately, he'd returned home from work sapped of strength and with little energy for family life. Since their trauma in Mandrake's warehouse, Galit had lurked in the shadows, and he had not pulled her near. Was he still angry at her? Would they die without working through their complicated history?

"Nobody thought they'd live," Savta Sarah said, slipping, as she did, into the past. "At first we did. But after a few weeks, we learned the truth—the only way out of the camp was through the chimneys." She stared at the ghosts in the dim light of the bedroom.

Moshe knew Savta's stories by heart. The SS men who took her father. The cattle train to Auschwitz. Her ballsy survival antics in the nascent Jewish State. But she had never spoken of life inside the death camp. Until now.

"Some lost their will to live. Others became animals, stealing crusts of bread and snitching to the guards—anything to survive another day. But some people chose the third option. They helped others, if only with a kind word. They held prayer groups in secret even though discovery would mean certain death."

She shook her head. "They didn't do those things so that God would save them. We heard no news of the war. Nobody left that place alive, and as far as we knew, no one ever would. They did those things because, in their final moments, they wanted to live well."

The twinge of guilt became a stab of shame, and he turned away.

"We all die," she continued. "We can't control that. The only thing we can control is how we live."

CHAPTER 63

The click of a closing door woke Avi. Early morning sunlight seeped through blinds on the kitchen windows. He leaned over the kitchen table, three empty wine bottles at his head. His chin ached from the pressure of the tabletop, his forehead from leaning on his plaster cast.

He had fallen into a drunken slumber. Heels clicked over the corridor tiles as Savta Sarah approached the kitchen. She'd entered Moshe's room hours ago, and Avi tried to divine the success of her visit from her expression.

Galit stirred on the living room couch. "What did he say?"

"Nothing."

"That took a long time," Avi said.

Last night, Galit had tried to call Savta, but the cellular networks were still down. Despite Gurion's misinformation, millions of Israelis were trying to finagle a way off the sinking ship. Moshe had dispersed the staff of the Prime Minister's Residence, each returning home, so Galit had found a bunch of car keys and placed them in Avi's hand.

After failing to locate Savta Sarah at the Knesset, the Prime Minister's Office, and the Dry Bones Society, he visited her small apartment in Katamon. Savta had answered the door wearing an apron. The world might be ending, but Savta was cooking.

Galit and Avi had waited outside the bedroom door. After fifteen minutes, they had retired to the kitchen. Another fifteen minutes later, they'd opened the second bottle of wine.

Savta shrugged. "I let him sleep. He needed his rest, and he'll need all his strength today."

"Does he have a plan?" Avi asked.

"Time will tell."

Avi jumped as a door burst open, and Moshe strode down the corridor, wearing a suit and knotting his tie. "Morning," he said.

Galit launched from the couch and converged with Moshe at the kitchen. He pecked her on the cheek. "Coffee?"

"Sure. I'm making." She put on the kettle.

Moshe whipped his phone from a pocket and dialed.

"Sivan," he said. "Yes, I'm at the Residence."

The networks were up again. Either the panic had subsided or most people had already left.

"Yes," Moshe continued. "Get the ambassadors on the phone. Both of them. No, not the ambassadors—get the presidents! And bring in Professor Stein. Whatever it takes. I'm on my way." He ended the call.

Galit handed him a coffee mug, and he took a sip. "Excellent." He drew her near, and she gasped as he gave her a long, hard kiss. "Thank you," he said. "You're a lifesaver. I'm nothing without you." She blushed, and tears streaked down her smiling cheeks.

He turned to her grandmother. "Savta, what do you say we pass some legislation?"

"Great idea."

Avi wanted to ask what was going on. An asteroid was about to blast them to smithereens and Moshe wanted to sign new laws?

Moshe's eyes turned to Avi. "What's he doing here?"

"He found Savta," Galit said. "And helped put Talya to bed."

The Prime Minister looked Avi over as if for the first time

and nodded. "Thanks, buddy."

"Moshe," Avi blurted. "Gurion's gone mad. He wants to kill you."

"Then tell him to get in line. We've got a planet to save."

Yes! Avi was back at Karlin & Son, at Moshe's side. They were a team again, working together to meet a common goal.

"How can I help? I can drive you."

"No."

The word nipped Avi's enthusiasm in the bud. *He doesn't trust you.* Why should he?

Moshe stepped forward and tapped him on the shoulder. "I need you to hold the fort." He leaned in to whisper. "Take care of Galit and Talya, in case anything should happen to me. Can you do that?"

"Yes, sir."

"Great." He took another gulp of coffee, put down the mug, and pulled Galit in for another kiss.

She teared up in his arms again. "Ready to conquer the world?"

"Ready or not, here we come."

She straightened his tie, stepped back, glanced at the floor, and didn't seem to know where to put her hands. "Be careful," she said. "Come back to me."

"I'll do my best."

With a final wave goodbye, he and Savta Sarah walked out the front door.

"He'll come back," Avi said. The words were designed to comfort Galit, but he clung to them too. "He always does."

CHAPTER 64

Moshe sat upright in the command chair of the Knesset's War Room and prepared for the negotiation of his life. The results would determine the length of that life, the lives of his citizens, and all life on the planet. *No pressure.*

"OK," he said. "Put them on."

The world came into sharp focus. The scent of destiny wafted in the air, and Moshe's body tingled. Every experience since the day of his birth had been preparing him for this moment. Every deal he had sealed, every challenge he had overcome, even his failures. Everything rode on these next few minutes.

In the gloomy depression of his bed that morning, he had gained an insight. He'd been doing things wrong. Alone, he'd never achieve justice and equality, never mind save the world. He needed help. Lots of it.

He glanced around the polished table, looking each friend and cabinet member in the eye, sending silent messages of faith and gratitude. Only Rabbi Yosef was missing. Efforts at contacting him had failed and they could delay the call no longer.

Many great men and women had sat around this table and other tables throughout history. Many had given their lives for this two-thousand-year-old hope. Moshe had reached this day thanks to them, and he would honor their memory. He would not let them down. And if he failed, he'd go fighting.

"Here we go," Sivan said, as the conference call connected.

Two rectangles displayed on the large mounted television screen. A grandfatherly statesman in a blue suit and red power tie grinned at them on the left. A bald eagle spread its wings over the circular seal of the President of the United States of America on the wall behind him. On the right, a stony face frowned at the camera. A double-headed eagle struck a symmetrical pose on the Russian Federation coat of arms. The Russian wore a similar suit of blue and red. The leaders of the world's two superpowers seemed to employ the same fashion stylist.

"Mr. President," Moshe said. "Finally, we speak face-to-face."

"Mr. Prime Minister." The American's head wobbled in a gesture of mocking self-satisfaction. "Or should I say, the last Prime Minister of Israel. You should have accepted our offer while you could."

The Russian's visage reddened with rage. "How dare you! A joint conference call—and without warning!"

"My apologies to you both, but I could see no better way to prove my point."

"This had better be good!"

Moshe turned to the Russian. "As you must have noticed, Mr. President, we have no agreement with the United States. And," he turned to the American, "from your counterpart's reaction, as well as the lack of Russian assistance in this time of desperate need, you can see that we've made no pact with them either."

The Russian leaned in and growled. "Do you think I'm an idiot? The two of you could have staged this."

"And why would we do that?"

"Because you are liars! The Americans are embarrassed by their inability to save you, their new fifty-first state, and now you need our help."

Reading between the lines, Moshe glimpsed confirmation of what Professor Stein had explained only minutes ago—that, in an ideal world, there *was* something they could do to avert the demise of the Jewish State.

He'd have to appeal to the best within the heart of each leader.

"You're right," he said. "I need your help. Seven million Jews, Muslims, Christians, and others need your help. With prompt action, you can save us. History will remember you as heroes. Do nothing, however, and our blood will be on your hands."

The American wobbled his head again. "I'd say your blood is on God's hands. We didn't send that asteroid your way. Who are we to second-guess the Almighty or sabotage His plans?"

Both presidents chuckled. *And they think we're the monsters.*

"As you know," Moshe said, "the asteroid will not destroy Israel alone. The dust cloud will suffocate all life on Earth. By helping us, you're helping yourselves and saving millions of your own people."

The Russian shrugged. "We'll take our chances. Your tiny country will absorb the main thrust of the impact, but our mighty nations will survive."

"I'm inclined to agree with my Russian counterpart," the American said. "Besides, thanks to all those zombie apocalypse movies, half our citizens already have bunkers and stockpiles—you name it! Many will perish, but the American people will endure. Considering the threat of your new weapons of mass destruction, we call that an acceptable loss. Oh, and don't bother appealing to the sympathy of our citizens. We've blocked news of the asteroid from the media. Consider NASA's notification of your space agency a personal courtesy."

In Moshe's periphery vision, the cabinet members shifted in their seats. The superpowers had partnered up against the Jewish State. Moshe's appeals to virtue and self-interest had fallen flat, and it was time for Plan C. When desire fails, use fear.

"You're right," he said. The change in tone subdued the laughter. "I lied to you." Now he had their attention. Suspicion flashed in their eyes, the concern that they had miscalculated and fallen into a trap.

"I told you that we had not weaponized the undead. The truth is, we have. Zombie super-soldiers. Unkillable. Unstoppable."

The Russian slammed his hand onto his desk. "I knew it!"

Moshe continued, "We've been amassing our zombie armies for months. I expected you to reject our plea for help, so I've already unleashed the undead on the world."

"You're bluffing," the American president said. "Our satellite footage shows that the troop buildup on the Gazan border has dissipated, not increased."

"That's because we've deployed them in subterranean tunnels. Until now we used the tunnels to hide the buildup of undead warriors, but this morning I gave them their marching orders. Tens of thousands of zombie soldiers are on their way to you as we speak. They only respond to my command, and unless I call them back, they'll be arriving at your capitals two days from now."

"Dear Mother of God," the American President said. He slapped his palm to his forehead. "What have we done?"

The Russian's skin turned paper white. "Turn them back at once!"

Moshe plowed on. "Dust clouds won't interfere with these weapons. They don't need food or sleep. By our projections, within a month, only one superpower will remain." Moshe paused for dramatic effect. "The Dead."

The presidents of the world powers shouted together, their pleas and promises forming an unintelligible ruckus.

Moshe raised his hands for silence, and the leaders obeyed. "Here's what we're going to do."

CHAPTER 65

That morning, Yosef opened and closed his mouth like a stunned fish. His wife had asked a simple question, but he had no idea how to respond. It was all so confusing.

Last night, Moshe had addressed the nation on TV. An asteroid would hit Jerusalem at noon. Then the news channel had switched to Isaac Gurion, who explained with an angelic calm that there was no need to worry, the world was not ending, and the Prime Minister's fear tactics would not distract anyone from his corruption charges.

Having no television, Yosef's children knew nothing of this, and their blissful ignorance made his decision only harder.

"Yosef," Rocheleh repeated, "is there school today or not?"

He had shared the news with his wife. "I don't know."

She placed her hands on her hips. "Well, if the Minister of Education doesn't know, who does?"

Yesterday evening, Yosef had tried to reach Moshe on the phone, or Sivan or anyone on the cabinet. Every time, he received a "network unavailable" message. This morning, the networks had resumed service, but his calls went straight to voicemail. On Emek Refaim Street, stores opened, buses zoomed, and commuters rushed to work as usual. What was going on?

"I don't know," he repeated. He had not issued an order to close the schools today.

"Well, if they're not going to school, *you* keep them occupied."

That settled it. "OK," he said. "Take them. Just check that the teachers are there too."

Rocheleh shook her head at his dillydallying and made for the front door. "Come on, boys. Let's go."

Yosef kissed them goodbye and wished them a fun day. He hoped he'd see them again.

He tried Moshe's number for the twentieth time. Voicemail.

Where was everyone, and why was Yosef out of the loop? Moshe wouldn't have invented an asteroid threat. But if it was real, how could the country carry on, business as usual?

He dialed another number. "When choosing between an uncertain outcome and a certain one," the Sages of the Talmud instructed, "prefer the certain one." Following their advice, Yosef focused his energy on another imminent catastrophe.

"Thank you for calling the Israel Police Service," the now familiar recorded female voice said. "Our operators are busy with other calls. Please wait or dial nine to leave a message."

Yosef exhaled a puff of frustration. Did the operators expect citizens caught in the middle of a terror attack to hold the line as well?

As usual, Yosef waited. He needed answers. Certainty. Elijah the Prophet. But Elijah was last seen disappearing into the heavens in a fiery chariot. The prophet dropped by Passover meals and circumcision ceremonies around the globe yet remained invisible. He was not the sort of person Yosef could call on the phone. At the right time, Elijah would appear out of nowhere in a cloud of smoke.

But now time was running out.

Elijah, where are you?

CHAPTER 66

Eli blinked his eyes open. He lay on a metal gurney in a tent. His bones were sore, and a tube yanked at the crook of his arm. Last he remembered before passing out, Noga's blood pressure had dropped as her body's systems collapsed. Had she survived?

He turned his head away from her, afraid of what he might see. A long plastic line ran from a suspended pouch to Eli's other arm. An infusion. He had lost a lot of liquid.

Beyond the transparent pouch, the doctor hunched over a desk. Eli tried to divine Noga's fate from the doctor's posture.

Then the chair swiveled, and the doctor hurried over to him, a steaming paper cup in hand.

"Have some tea," he said. "And there's a six-pack of mineral water in the corner."

"Is she…?" Eli began.

Dr. Stern smiled. "Her vitals are back to normal. I disconnected the transfusion a half hour ago."

Oh, thank God!

Eli rolled over, and there she was. Her chest rose as she breathed, but the eyes above the oxygen mask remained closed. "Did she wake up?"

"Not yet. We need to be patient."

Eli followed the doctor's orders. He drank his sugared tea and guzzled water. Noga's improving health gave him strength. Her body was recovering. But what of her mind? *We need to be patient.*

Eli flopped on the chair beside the gurney.

"Is there another laptop? Internet?"

Dr. Stern glanced at the jumble of medical apparatus on the desk. "Here, use this." He handed Eli an iPad.

Eli logged into the analytics portal for TheTenLostTribes.org. Visitor statistics had climbed yesterday morning, a sign that the Facebook campaign was working, but then, in the afternoon, the hits dropped off.

The earthquake. A natural disaster of that size must have caused havoc. Researching the Ten Lost Tribes would no longer appear on the average citizen's list of priorities.

He searched for news of the earthquake in Jerusalem and clicked through to an article on the Ynet news site. The front page covered the aftermath of the earthquake: electricity and water outages, gas explosions. Downtown Jerusalem looked like a war zone, with soldiers on every street corner holding up their hands to turn away reporters. Were those Russian uniforms?

A more recent editorial called for the Prime Minister's immediate resignation and ranted against his cynical use of natural disasters for political ends, such as the earthquake and the… the *asteroid scare*?

The earthquake had been real enough—Eli could vouch for that—but was Karlin stupid enough to invent an asteroid strike out of whole cloth?

He tapped back to the front page and the breaking news ticker. The headline sent cold shivers down his spine.

"What the hell?"

A man in a suit spoke into a bouquet of press microphones. Eli recognized him. He had first sighted the oily politician at Zion Square on a stage beside three imposter kings. The Earth had devoured the stage, but the ringleader had survived to make another speech.

Eli read the quotation and shook with righteous indignation. The lying creep was trying to usurp Eli's destiny.

"Oh, no you don't," he said, his voice a growl.

"What's that?" Dr. Stern asked, without looking up from his laptop.

"The news. This Isaac Gurion thinks he's Elijah the Prophet."

Dr. Stern smirked. "I thought that job was taken. He must be delusional."

Eli's fingers tightened over the iPad. "I know his kind. I've hunted them all my life. He's not delusional; he's a false prophet."

CHAPTER 67

Yosef dashed into the Talpiot Police Station to find the reception desk empty. He had arrived before the secretaries. After a few seconds of frustration, he realized this might work to his advantage.

He charged down the corridor to the sounds of ringing phones and muffled conversations, expecting at any moment to hear authoritative voices challenge his right to wander around the station.

Yosef would demand immediate action from the Commissioner. He was an elected minister of the State of Israel. That counted for something, didn't it? Yosef had never made a threat in his life, but if it came to that, he would. A governmental committee appointed police commissioners. Yosef could use his sway to put the fear of the Lord into the civil servant and galvanize him to avert the imminent tragedy. And if Yosef's intuition proved wrong, he'd live with it.

The corridor ended, and he reached his destination without objection. Yosef knocked twice on the Commissioner's door, then tried the handle. The door was locked. The Commissioner was getting a late start as well.

Yosef returned to the reception area. He perched on the edge of the hard, plastic seat, then got up and paced the room. Last night he had become familiar with every floor tile, every crack.

He halted. Had the police changed their minds about Moshe's announcement? Had they gone home to spend their last hours with their families? The murmurs of telephone chatter disproved that theory. He followed the sounds, determined to ask the first officer he encountered when the doors opened, when the twin receptionists strolled into the station.

Yawning and bleary-eyed, they dropped their handbags behind the desk. Yosef approached the counter. "I need to see the Commissioner. When will he be in?"

The women glanced at him, and without a word, they turned their backs on him and disappeared around a corner. Yosef drummed his fingers on the counter. He heard their idle chatter and the whistle of an electric kettle. Another long minute passed before the women returned, each nursing a mug of coffee. They took their time sitting down and arranging their desk equipment before one of them registered his presence.

"How may I help you?"

"Same as yesterday. I need to speak with the Commissioner."

"Do you have an appointment?"

"No, but we spoke last night. He knows what this is about."

That seemed to satisfy her. She put a phone receiver to her ear and sipped her coffee.

She put down the phone. "He's not in yet. Please wait."

Yosef wanted to pull out his hair. "When will he be in?"

The secretary shrugged.

He forced a smile and returned to his seat.

Over the next fifteen minutes, another four officers arrived, greeted the twins, and moseyed along the corridor to their offices. So far, no commissioner.

The relaxed atmosphere at the police station indicated that Moshe was losing the PR battle. Was the asteroid a hoax? Sivan had used many creative ploys to herd public opinion in the desired direction, but the end-of-world scenario sounded extreme even for her.

After millennia of human suffering and struggle, of hopeful waiting, would God destroy his Chosen People in one fell swoop? What of the Messianic Era? Even the prophecies of doom ended with the eternal rule of Heaven. The story of humanity had to have a happy ending.

Yosef approached the reception desk again and received the same answer, topped up with a "Please be patient." Yosef returned to his seat, and the receptionists returned to their nail polish.

Be patient.

Yosef *had* been patient. The Jewish People had been extremely patient. While they waited for their Messiah and the shofar blast of Elijah the Prophet, they had endured persecution and genocide. When would the waiting end?

Yosef wrung his hands. Right now, hundreds of men and women gathered on the Temple Mount, unaware of the danger.

This was Yosef's fault, in part. He had brushed Tom Levi off. But Tom Levi was no idiot and he had stopped waiting.

Yosef blinked. When madmen acted, how can the rest of humanity sit and wait?

A sudden gust of determination lifted him to his feet, and he charged at the reception desk.

"This can wait no longer," he said. "Where is the Commissioner? You must have a way of reaching him." Both twins opened their mouths to object, but Yosef cut them off. "Try his home number and his mobile. This is a matter of life and death!"

The raised eyebrows told him that the women seriously doubted his claims, but the one on the left raised the phone again. This time, she spoke to someone.

After a short conversation of monosyllables, she put the phone back down. "The Commissioner has taken the day off. Please come back tomorrow."

Yosef snapped. "You have got to be kidding me! Then get

me somebody else. There will be an attack on the Temple Mount today! A bomb!" The women stared at him as though he was insane. "I'm the freaking Vice Prime Minister! Do something!"

More plastic smiles.

"I'm sorry," Lefty said. "You'll have to speak with the Commissioner. Tomorrow."

He huffed and puffed and stormed off. What a colossal waste of time!

Baruch, with his flannel fedora and perfect pencil mustache, leaned against the black Audi on the curb. He swung the back door open for Yosef, then hurried around to the driver's seat.

"Where to, sir?"

"The Old City," Yosef said. He had stopped waiting.

CHAPTER 68

Moshe rounded up his broadcast and glanced at the camera in the Prime Minister's press office for the last time.

"And so," he said, "my fellow citizens, our plan is in motion—our only hope to save our nation from destruction. I urge you all to gather your loved ones, go home, and wait in your reinforced rooms. Those without such rooms must move to the nearest public bomb shelter. Within the next hour, we'll learn our fate. May God be with us. *Um Israel chai!*" Long live the People of Israel!

The red dot above the camera blinked out, and the operator gave the thumbs-up. An assistant removed the microphone from Moshe's lapel and shook his hand. "It's been an honor," she said.

"Here too. I hope we meet again. Now go home."

He drew a deep breath and exhaled. Things were out of his hands now.

Sivan met him at the door. They speed-walked down the corridor toward their waiting cars. "The broadcast went out?"

Sivan tapped at the screen of her phone. "Yes, and posted on all government sites and social media accounts. There's a breaking news bulletin starting soon on Channel Ten. Radio too."

"Great. Join us at the Prime Minister's Residence. We've

got a bunker and the best popcorn in town." He had invited his cabinet to join him too.

"I'll take you up on that," she said. "But first I have to pick up Cleopatra."

Moshe gave her a quizzical glance. He hadn't heard of any ancient Egyptian queens turning up at the Dry Bones Society.

"From the cat parlor."

"Oh, right. She's welcome too."

"Thanks!" At the ping of a notification, she looked at her phone. "Oh, crap!"

She stopped in her tracks, and Moshe glanced at her phone too. The Channel Two news displayed the face of Isaac Gurion. This would not be good.

Sivan turned up the volume. Gurion smiled at the camera, his face radiating calm. "Do not let the asteroid scare deceive you. Join us now one and all at the Sultan's Pool and behold your Redeemer! Prime Minister Karlin himself will be in attendance."

"What?" Moshe said. "Avi was right. He's gone insane."

The newsreader said, "Thousands have gathered around the Messiah Coronation Center at the Sultan's Pool outside Jerusalem's Old City." On the screen, a bird's-eye view of the narrow valley was displayed. Thick crowds of people flowed toward an immense black rectangular structure in a grassy knoll below a short bridge. "Unnamed sources claim that the Messiah may already be inside the building."

Sivan said, "The bastard is going to crown himself the Messiah."

Moshe looked at the thousands of innocent bystanders. Even Professor Stein's most favorable projections predicted widespread damage and destruction in Jerusalem.

He said, "And all those people are going to die."

CHAPTER 69

"More tape!" Irina yelled.

She had spent all night putting a lid on the pandemonium of their simian ancestors, when this morning, a video clip had appeared on the official Facebook page of the Prime Minister's Office, and the Dry Bones Society once again exploded with activity.

Volunteers stuck cardboard and plastic bags over the windows to prevent shattering. They toppled desks to create reinforced crawl spaces. Not designed as a residential complex, the meager bomb shelter beneath Clal Center could not house the entire dormitory of the Dry Bones Society. They had to improvise.

"Here!" Samira called from across the Call Center, and she tossed Irina another roll of duct tape. They had an hour to secure the site, and Irina had to fit in secret plans of her own. The asteroid was real. Moshe had dispelled the confusion and given them the instructions they needed to survive. All the cardboard and overturned desks in the world would not protect them from a direct hit, but Moshe's ballsy plan gave them hope for survival.

A handful of volunteers ran for the front door, little backpacks on their shoulders. "Hey, where are you going?"

Ben gave her a guilty look, then continued out the door.

"Where are they going?"

"The Sultan's Pool," Samira said. "The Messiah Coronation."

"The what?" Moshe had not mentioned that in his address and he had warned against staying outdoors.

"It's Gurion's work," Samira said. "Let them go."

How people could believe a word that slimy politician excreted, Irina could not understand.

She completed blocking her current window, then paused. Alex stood at the front door.

"We're out of time," he whispered when she came near. "We have to go now."

"But the whole country is in chaos. The asteroid—"

"We can worry about that later. If we don't disappear now, we're dead anyway."

Irina cast one last glance at the Call Center. Samira kneeled on the floor and sliced cardboard sheets into window-sized squares with a box cutter. Others shifted desks and boarded windows. There was no way to explain her sudden need to leave without exposing her friends to the criminal world.

"OK," she said.

Alex took her hand in his and led her outside and down the corridor. They passed the Absorption Center, her job. The Dry Bones Society had been a temporary home. Now she must build her own home, with her man.

Alex had parked his car on the pavement behind Clal Center.

"Did you bring my bag?" Irina said.

"Which bag?"

"The things I left at your place." Irina's bag contained clothes and toiletries to get her through their first week on the run.

"I haven't been back since yesterday. It's too risky. They might be watching."

"Where did you sleep?"

"In the car." He grinned.

That seemed a bit paranoid to Irina, but Alex knew what

they were up against. "Then I'll go." His lips tightened, so she added, "I'll be quick—I promise. In and out."

"OK," he said. "But I'll wait a few blocks away."

"No problem."

Shamai Street was only a few turns away through downtown Jerusalem. The car crossed over King George, and Alex stopped at a back street on the edge of Independence Park.

"Be back quick?" he said.

"In and out," she promised, and, leaving him with a hurried kiss, she jumped out.

The streets of downtown Jerusalem seemed empty for a Wednesday morning. The few people she encountered rushed off and didn't seem to notice her. A hurtling asteroid and messianic frenzy had created the ideal conditions for two lovers to escape into thin air. The thought thrilled her. They were embarking on an adventure into the unknown, just the two of them.

She paused at the corner to scan Shamai Street from a safe distance. Finding no unfamiliar cars in the parking bay and no suspicious men hiding behind newspapers, she walked beneath the stilts of Alex's building and punched the code for the front door. She skipped up the two flights of stairs, glancing up in case a thug had arrived ahead of her. Then, her heart pounding in her chest, from both the climb and the tension, she slid her key into the hole and walked inside.

Her bag lay on the kitchen table. Closing the distance in two strides, she grabbed the bag, slipped the strap over her shoulder, and turned to leave. She gasped. A man stood between her and the door. He wore a tweed coat and pointed a large black gun in her direction.

His gray mustache shifted as he smiled. "Nice to see you again, Irina," Boris said. "It's been too long."

CHAPTER 70

Ahmed stood in the wings behind the stage. This was his first visit to Al Aqsa and his last.

The murmur of the waiting crowds beyond the partition buzzed like the hum of twenty thousand bees. He checked the order of his cue cards with shaky fingers. The golden envelope could mean only one thing—he was nearing the slaughterhouse.

Hasan stepped in front of him, straightened the turban on Ahmed's head, and adjusted the collar of the white robe. Ahmed's cousin looked pale and his forehead glistened, but not because of the late morning sun. The drop-off bin in Ramallah meant that Hasan was also in the dark. For years he had danced for unseen puppeteers, blindly accepting their money without ever understanding their true intentions. Did he also sense that the end was drawing near—for them both?

"You look perfect, Mahdi," Hasan said. "Remember our agreement and keep to the script this time."

Ahmed nodded. Although Hasan had not fulfilled his promise to introduce him to the Shepherd, he had done his best. Was he not a victim too?

"Because if you don't, this time I'll blow your brains out myself."

His empathy for Hasan evaporated.

Hasan gave him a final clap on the shoulder. "Good luck." Then he rushed away to his seat of honor among the other dignitaries in the front row.

Alone at last, Ahmed turned to his last urgent task before stepping before the crowds to meet his fate. This task he could not fulfill in person.

"Dara!" he hissed. "Dara!"

With a whish of fabric, his friend appeared, all smiles and pride. "Here I am, O Mahdi. Your faithful servant is ready for your commands."

"Enough of that, you idiot. I have an important mission for you."

"Anything for my Mahdi."

"This is serious." He withdrew the sealed white envelope from the folds of his robe. "I need you to take this to Clal Center. Give it to the girl, Samira."

Dara accepted the letter and sniffed it. "A love letter—can I have a peek?"

"This is serious, Dara. And urgent. Take it to her right away, and only to her."

"What, now? And miss your historic speech? First, you disappear on me this morning, and now you chase me away?"

"Yes, now. Please, my friend. This means more to me than any speech."

Dara's shoulders sagged. "OK, my friend. But try to drag out your words, I don't want to miss the after-party." He winked and hurried off.

Good. The favor would also keep his friend far from the slaughterhouse that awaited.

Ahmed sucked in air, filling his lungs. He had been preparing for this day a long time. Everything he had experienced in his second life had led here. Today, he would meet the Shepherd, and he would prove that he had learned his lesson. This time, he would face his fate with honor.

He forced his legs to carry him around the partition and onto the stage. The excited murmurs rose as his sandaled feet trod over the white carpet that led to the white podium.

Placing his cue cards on the podium, he glanced beyond the microphones.

Beneath the clear blue canopy of heaven and crowned by the towering golden Dome of the Rock, Arab men of faith covered every inch of the Temple Mount plaza. Dignitaries in kaffiyehs and turbans filled the first five rows. Guards of the Islamic Waqf in dark trousers and white collared shirts lined the aisles. Beyond them stood the endless mass of pilgrims. The common folk wore their finest clothing and waited for their Redeemer.

This time nobody spoke ahead of Ahmed. The good tidings had spread, and the Mahdi needed no introduction. Besides, Hasan had said, rival imams and political figures had lobbied so fiercely to stand at his side that choosing any of them might spark a conflict that would engulf them in flames for decades.

From the front row, Hasan nodded at Ahmed to begin.

"My friends," Ahmed began, reading from the cards, his voice bursting from immense speakers around the expansive plaza like the voice of God. "You have seen the signs. Today we begin a new era. A time when we no longer talk of struggle, because victory is already ours. The End Times."

Cheers erupted throughout the crowd. The ecstatic hope of the crowd surged through him like a drug, and a smile spread across his face without bidding. *Yes! An end to their struggles.*

From his vantage point, the pilgrims at the back were dots of color, shapeless sheep in the herd, their murmurs of relief, contented bleating, secure in their trust of the Shepherd.

If only he could channel that power for good. The struggle should end, not because one side has defeated the other, but because the struggle was an illusion, a deception created by cruel shepherds to satisfy their own base desires.

But by telling them, he would break his promise to Hasan and risk the wrath of the Shepherd.

Would the people listen? In Bethlehem, the audience had not stoned him for heresy; they had warmed to him and gripped his hand. No doubt his words had surprised them, but they had longed to hear that message of peace.

He glanced at the next card. It spoke of the sons of pigs and killers of prophets, of yet another *intifada* and days of rage, of martyrs and streets flowing with infidel blood. And of his coronation later that day when he would strike the first blow that would start the Mother of All Wars.

The excited murmurs settled, and an expectant hush washed over the sea of eager faces. In the pregnant silence, fifty thousand men held their breath. How would the Mahdi bring The End? How would he snatch that final victory from the jaws of struggle and stagnation?

The courage Ahmed had nurtured behind the partition fled. How could he take on the Shepherd? How could he overturn centuries of hatred? He should turn and run. Run and hide. Hasan's assassins would catch him one day, but at least Ahmed would not stain his soul again with innocent blood.

His sweaty palms slid over the sides of the podium. His lips trembled, and his tongue dried up in his mouth.

A ripple in the sea of spectators drew his eye. An inlet had formed at the side of the crowd. The inlet widened as people pressed against each other and struggled to move away from the disturbance. In the center of the clearing stood a man.

Then the man shouted at the top of his voice. Another murmur spread over the waters, as the lone madman parted the sea, crying out and waving his arms.

Fingers of cold terror closed over Ahmed's heart as the man ranted and raved. Ahmed knew the madman, who now directed his words at him!

CHAPTER 71

Moshe dialed a number on a landline in his office, ready to concede defeat. He'd plead and beg—whatever necessary to save lives.

"You don't have to do this," Shmuel said, sitting beside him. "Chances are, we're goners anyway."

Most other cabinet members had left for the Prime Minister's Residence, where they'd follow the operation from the relative safety of the bunker.

Moshe gave him a brave smile. "I'm an optimist." Then he covered the mouthpiece with his hand. "It's ringing."

Shmuel lifted the other receiver to his ear and covered the mouthpiece.

Moshe's pulse thumped in his ears. Although they had traded threats and blows via press releases, he hadn't spoken with his adversary directly since the coalition had imploded. Now Moshe came crawling on his knees. *Pick up, Gurion. I know you're waiting for my call.*

Why else had the politician done this? His so-called Messiah Coronation was an exercise in brinkmanship. For Moshe, it was a catch-22. If he accepted the invitation, his presence would be proof of his haughty, overbearing rule. King Karlin, Gurion had labeled him, a corrupt dictator who holds himself above the law. If he didn't show, Gurion might claim that golden crown for himself, riding the wave of messianic fever to the crest of public opinion. And while Moshe deliberated, thousands of citizens waited in the open, putting their lives in graver danger with every passing minute.

It was a game he couldn't win and so he wouldn't play.

The line continued to ring.

Had Moshe misunderstood—was Gurion intentionally trying to increase the death toll so that, even if Moshe averted total annihilation, he'd still shoulder the blame for thousands of casualties? Or had Gurion's hatred blinded him to the dangers of the asteroid?

The call connected.

"Well, well, well," said the familiar, greasy voice. "If it isn't King Karlin himself."

"Hello, Isaac."

"We're waiting for you. The table is set. All that's missing is our Savior."

Moshe scanned his options one last time, but no way out presented itself. All good things came to an end.

"You win," he said. "Call off this coronation of yours and send those people home. I'll stand down. I'll resign as Prime Minister, dissolve the government, and appoint you as my interim replacement. I'll dismantle Restart too and leave politics forever."

"Moshe, Moshe," Gurion said, sounding injured. "What do you take me for?"

"Don't take my word for it. I'll sign a declaration or whatever you want. Just send those people to their bomb shelters." Moshe eyed Shmuel, who nodded. He had to reveal their plan; at this point, there was no harm in doing so. "We've set a process in motion. There's a chance we'll beat the asteroid, but even in the best-case scenario, there will still be widespread destruction. The crowds outside the Messiah Coronation Center will die if they stay out in the open…"

He trailed off. Gurion was laughing.

"Sorry," Gurion said, recovering. "I couldn't hold back."

"It's real, Isaac. Check with NASA. Check with any astronomical organization—they'll all say the same thing. The asteroid is—."

"I know, I know." Gurion's voice quavered with residual humor. "I never doubted you, King Karlin."

Avi was right—Gurion had lost his mind, and in his insanity, he would slaughter innocents. "Think of the people you've gathered outside, Isaac. Their families, their children."

"I don't want you to resign, Moshe. Oh, no. I want much more than that. You tried to kill me. Now come here and face me like a man." His voice became gruff with pent-up fury. "This isn't politics, Moshe; this is personal."

The call cut out.

"He's gone mad," Shmuel said. "He wants to get at you, even if it means killing thousands."

Moshe got to his feet. "You should head for the Residence now."

Shmuel gaped at him. "You can't be serious."

Gurion had cornered him. "I need you to oversee the operation while I'm gone."

"Don't go there. That's exactly what he wants."

"I need to warn those people. They're there because of me. I should have denied the rumors that I was the Messiah while I could. Now they'll only listen to me."

"But he'll murder you. He practically said so himself."

Moshe gave him another brave smile. "I hope it won't come to that."

CHAPTER 72

Yosef had never entered the Muslim Quarter of the Old City alone and for good reason. Most attacks against Jews occurred there. But today Yosef walked past the knot of Border Guard soldiers at Jaffa Gate, and into the unfamiliar labyrinth.

Every second counted. He hurried along narrow alleys that squeezed between high walls of white stone. Decades of sun and rain had worn the cobblestones smooth. As he delved deeper, the metal street names on the walls no longer bothered with Hebrew or English, only Arabic.

An Arab man, rough and unshaven, glared at Yosef. A woman, covered from head to toe in a flowing burka, averted her eyes. With his velvet skullcap and fringes flying from his belt, Yosef dared not ask for directions. A lone Jew in the Muslim Quarter was vulnerable; a lost Jew was asking for trouble. For the second time that day, he regretted forgoing his security detail.

The trickle of pedestrians became a steady flow, and Yosef knew he was moving in the right direction. As he bustled along, he searched for a solution to an imminent problem. Of the eleven gates to the Temple Mount, non-Muslims could only enter through one, Mughrabi Gate, via a ramp next to the Western Wall Plaza. Tourists had to schedule their excursions in small groups and during limited visiting hours. Yosef had not scheduled a tour for today, and he approached from the north. How on earth would he get past the Temple Mount guards?

As the foot traffic thickened, the number of robes and kaffiyehs increased. Yosef flowed with them, until, turning a corner, he glimpsed the tall arch of the Gate of the Tribes.

An immense leafy tree cast a shadow over the arched gateway. The crowd meandered between metal dividers, bolted to the ground. A battery of men in dark uniforms eyed the worshipers, assault rifles slung over their shoulders, as the visitors passed beyond black crowd-control barriers emblazoned with the word Police.

Once through the gate, Arab men massed on the green expanse, exchanging smiles and pointing to something to the south and out of sight.

A month ago, Yosef had waited in line outside of the Western Wall Plaza to greet a different messiah. He had tasted the ecstatic rush that now reflected in the eyes of the Arabs. This time, he hoped the gathering would not end in mass tragedy.

The line advanced. A young bearded officer with olive skin and mirror glasses raised his hand at the sight of Yosef. "You can't go in there." His voice had the harsh guttural inflection of an Arabic speaker.

"I need your help," Yosef said. "There will be an attack on the Temple Mount by Jewish extremists."

"Whoa, slow down, Rabbi." The officer motioned for his colleague to stand in for him as he led Yosef to the side.

He raised his sunglasses onto his forehead. "What attack?" he said, his voice hushed.

"Have you seen a man with a beard—a redhead?"

The officer shrugged. "Buddy, most people here have beards."

"This one is Jewish. I saw him on the Temple Mount. It was on the news. He must have planted explosives."

The officer did not look impressed. "What makes you

think that?"

"His cult wants to destroy the Dome of the Rock to build the Jewish Temple in its place. By any means. He told me so. We need to evacuate the area."

The officer looked over his shoulder at the thousands of worshippers on the Temple Mount. "That won't be possible. And you are?"

The officer clearly didn't recognize him. Yosef had hidden from the cameras ever since the election campaign. "I'm the Vice Prime Minister of the State of Israel."

The officer didn't stifle his laugh. "And I'm the Genie of the Lamp."

"This isn't funny. I'll hold you personally responsible for whatever happens."

"Run along, Rabbi. Don't make me arrest you."

Yosef had feared this scenario. *Don't panic. Be firm.* "I've spoken with Commissioner Golan!"

At the mention of the Commissioner, the officer's smile disappeared. The Commissioner hadn't heeded Yosef's warning either, but saving lives justified the half-truth.

"Last I heard, it's business as usual."

"Then you're not up to date."

"One moment." The officer pulled out a walkie-talkie and spoke in Arabic.

Oh, great. Had Yosef expected the guard to take his word? The Commissioner's office would expose Yosef's deception. If he wound up in a holding cell, he'd have no chance of averting the tragedy.

On loudspeakers beyond the wall, a voice boomed in Arabic, and a cheer rose from the audience like the crashing of waves on the seashore. The gathering had begun, the Mahdi addressed his unsuspecting crowd, and Yosef stood on the wrong side of the wall.

Starry-eyed worshippers poured through the gates and into harm's way. How could he stand idly by as they rushed to their death? The ruins of the Jerusalem Temple, the most sacred spot on earth, chosen by God to bring peace unto the world, would soon become the scene of a terrible crime that would sow suffering and conflict for generations.

Stop waiting, Yosef. Do something!

With a sudden jolt of wild desperation, Yosef stepped up to the nearest worshipper.

"Don't go in there," he said. "Something terrible is about to happen!"

The elderly Arab sneered at him from beneath his kaffiyeh and hurried along.

Yosef accosted the next in line, grabbing him by the arm. "Go home—you are in danger!"

"Hey!" the officer called behind him. "Stop that!"

Heavy boots clapped on the stone courtyard behind him.

"All of you—leave this place! Run for your lives!"

A hand gripped his shoulder, but Yosef ducked and dived sideways, evading the officer's grasp. He cut back and sprinted for the open gate.

As the gate grew larger, Halachic qualms flashed in his mind. Jewish law prohibited Jews from treading on the holy ground of the former Temple but permitted almost anything to save even a single human life. How many men, women, and children would perish if Tom Levi executed his cruel plan?

His legs carried him forward. Crossing the threshold, he almost slammed into the burgeoning crowd of Arab worshippers. The Temple complex was much larger than he had imagined. And so green! People flowed over the lawns and around the towering golden dome, its octagonal base tiled in blue, yellow, and green. The white stage stood before the Al Aqsa Mosque to the south.

Yosef had expected the guards to apprehend him by now. Glancing over his shoulder, he discovered why they had not. The black-clad police officers glared at him from the threshold. The officer with the sunglasses spoke into his walkie-talkie, his forehead glistening with sweat.

Ha! The Israel Police entered the Temple Mount only to escort tourists and catch terrorists, delegating the management of the holy site to the Jerusalem Islamic Waqf. Mass gatherings such as today were especially sensitive, and a charging group of armed Israeli officers in the middle of the speech would create a diplomatic incident of international proportions. Yosef had a few seconds before the officers got permission to grab him.

He scanned the worshippers for a red beard. None paid him any attention, their eyes fixed on the white-robed figure on the stage. The Mahdi's voice roared from the many loud-speakers.

Tom Levi would stay far away for the detonation. Yosef had better search for the explosives. Where had he placed them? What did explosives look like? And if he found them, what could he do to prevent them from detonating?

Nothing. Time was running out. He had to clear the place, and if the police would not help, he'd do it alone.

"Hey!" he cried at the top of his voice.

Two men at the edge of the crowd scowled at him, then returned to the spectacle on the stage.

Yosef ran south along the flank of the standing audience.

"Hey! All of you! Shoo! Get out of here. You are in danger. The Temple Mount is about to explode. Leave now!"

The speech continued unabated. Yosef's ranting had won only short-lived glares of irritation and shushing. What was this Jew doing here, interrupting their Messiah's speech?

He glanced back. The officers were running toward him now. His time was up. If only they had believed him.

He charged at the crowd, waving his arms and roaring like a raging bull.

That did it. The worshipers in his path lurched away from the raging Jew, clearing an opening in the mass of bodies.

"Your lives are in danger!" he declared. "Leave this place! Leave now!" He walked on, the horrified robed men edging away from the ranting madman, their eyes bulging.

Yosef pressed on, walking deeper into the crowd, repeating his mantra at the top of his voice and waving his hands. On and on he charged as the mass parted like the Red Sea.

The Arabs stared at him from an arm's length away. Did they understand a word he was saying?

He spun around, pleading with them, imploring them to flee, and discovered that the opening had closed behind him. The path had become a small air pocket within an ocean of Muslims. The police officers peered at him from the sidelines, their rage replaced with fear and concern for the trapped Israeli civilian.

Then the Messiah on the stage fell silent. The susurrus of a thousand whispers circled the crowd like a host of murmuring spirits. The worshippers blinked at Yosef, their surprise turning to annoyance and edging toward outrage. In their eyes, he read their thoughts. *An infidel in our midst! An intruder at our holy site!*

When the Messiah spoke again, his tone had changed. Yosef didn't understand a word, but he guessed the meaning as the clearing shrank and the crowd closed in on him. Not all the worshipers were old and frail. A dozen rough hands clamped onto his arms and prodded him forward. He fell over but didn't hit the ground. More hands gripped his legs, lifting him overhead, stretching his limbs in every direction.

He glimpsed blue skies above, and pain shot through his joints. Closing his eyes, he braced for the worst. His life was at the mercy of the mob now. He muttered a final prayer—*Shema Yisrael!* Hear O Israel!—when another voice echoed in his mind.

Your life is in danger!

CHAPTER 73

Eli sat at Noga's bedside, stroking her hair and willing her to wake up. Her vital signs had returned to normal hours ago, but she remained unconscious. Misinformation was tearing the world apart at the seams—on the one hand, fear of extinction by rogue asteroid; on the other, hope in a false messiah. Eli needed to go out there and fulfill his destiny before time ran out, but how could he leave her in this state?

"How much longer will it take?" he asked.

Dr. Stern looked up from his desk in the private field hospital. "I don't know. Judging by the speed with which her body recovered, I thought her mind would follow soon, but—"

"How long?" Eli had not meant to shout.

Dr. Stern lowered his eyes, looking old and haggard. "A few minutes. A few years. Never. Nobody's tried this treatment before, and she was out for so long. Maybe too long."

An anguished gasp escaped Eli's mouth. This was why he had avoided entanglements with mortals. Love might last forever, but humans didn't. Only Eli. Dr. Stern had located the Fountain of Youth in Eli's epigenetic makeup, but the discovery had come too late for the only girl who mattered.

Dr. Stern returned to the comfort of his computer screen.

"Don't do this to me," Eli whispered, addressing Noga or

God—he couldn't tell.

Had Noga served her purpose in the cosmic drama and become expendable? Did the same apply to Eli as well?

Months ago, lying in his hospital bed and mourning the loss of his powers, Eli had suspected that God had abandoned him. Perhaps he had lost the Magic because there would be no Redemption. Had God finally given up on humankind? That same depressing scenario rose in his mind now. In the time of Noah, God had promised never to send another flood. But there were other ways to wipe out humanity.

According to Moshe Karlin, at noon today, an asteroid would slam into the country, pulverizing the Jewish State. The impact would inject the atmosphere with enough dust and ash to create a year-long winter that would extinguish ninety percent of the planet's living creatures. Had humanity become expendable too?

He grasped Noga's hand. Was she better off asleep? That way, she wouldn't see her dream die and her world blasted into oblivion.

Her fingers twitched in his hand, and Eli bolted upright. "Noga?"

The eyelids fluttered.

He stroked her hair. "Noga, can you hear me?"

She opened her eyes and stared into his. "Eli?"

Her voice was soft and weak, but she was looking at him and she knew who he was. Eli couldn't hold back. A tense halting laughter jerked his body, and he bawled into her hand.

A chair shifted as Dr. Stern rushed to her bedside.

"Why are you crying?" she said. "Aren't you happy to see me?"

Eli wiped the tears from his cheeks, while Dr. Stern stood over them, his eyes glistening.

"Never been happier," Eli said.

Her eyes shifted back to him. "How long have I been gone? Does Karlin know about the Ten Tribes?"

Eli shushed her. He wanted to tell her that everything

would be fine, that she should rest and take it easy. There would be time to talk about everything. But that wasn't true. "It doesn't matter," he said. "You're OK. That's enough."

"No," she said. "We have a job to do." She struggled to sit up.

He placed a hand on her shoulder, holding her back. "Don't worry about it. You need to rest."

"Then you must do it," she said. "Go on without me. Promise me."

He looked at Dr. Stern, whose brow furrowed with unspoken questions. *Karlin? The Ten Tribes?*

"The thing is," Eli said, "it's too late."

"It can't be!"

There was no way around it now. "I'm so sorry," he said, "but it is. An asteroid is heading for Jerusalem. Karlin said so on the news. We have an hour left. I'd rather spend that hour with you."

"No," she said, shaking her head.

"I didn't want to have to tell you, but it's the truth. It's over, Noga. I'm sorry."

"No," she said. "It's only over when we stop trying."

Dr. Stern cleared his throat. "The asteroid scare might be a hoax."

"Then we have to try!"

"It doesn't matter. Isaac Gurion, that false prophet, has set up his own Messiah Coronation. It's underway right now."

"Who's he going to crown?"

"That's unclear. He claims that Karlin will attend the ceremony, but he hasn't said who his messiah will be."

"Then this is our chance. Maybe our final chance to get through to Karlin."

She might be right. "But… I don't want to leave you."

"Do it for me, Eli. We've come so far, you've waited so long."

He had waited long, but now that the moment had arrived, he faltered. Was this really about Noga, or, without the Magic and the Thin Voice, had he lost his nerve?

Dr. Stern jerked his head to the side, and Eli joined him a few steps away for a hushed consultation.

"Humor her," he said. "It might raise her spirits and aid her recovery."

Eli grasped around for more excuses. "What if you need me for another transfusion? Or your granddaughter? She needs treatment too."

As unpleasant as the transfusion had been, Eli would go through it a hundred times to spend his last hour with Noga.

The doctor's face slackened at the mention of his granddaughter. "That won't be necessary. She died two months ago." Dr. Stern seemed to crumble as he spoke the words.

Two months ago. During his stay at Shaare Zedek, Eli had evaded Dr. Stern's probing about his speedy recovery, desperate to conceal his identity. If he hadn't, the doctor's granddaughter might have lived.

"But," the doctor added, "it's not too late for Noga, or for this other little project of yours."

Another memory from Shaare Zedek rose in Eli's mind. *Never delay*, Oren, his roommate had said, shortly before his untimely death. *Or you will lose her.*

Eli stepped back to the bed. "OK," he said. "I'll do it." The smile on her face made his decision worthwhile. "But I want you feeling much better when I return."

"Deal!"

He kissed her, long and hard, then turned to Dr. Stern. "I need clothes."

CHAPTER 74

"If you don't mind me saying," Moshe's security chief said from the driver's seat later that morning, "this is a bad idea."

Alon might be right. Outside the windows of the SUV, people poured into the road beside the Mount Zion Hotel and the Jerusalem Cinematheque, thick as bees in a hive. In sweaters and ski caps, the common folk had hit the streets to greet their Messiah.

Moshe had set out for the Sultan's Pool with a single guard and without his usual cavalcade. The rest of his security detail he had sent home to their families. Yesterday, protestors had jumped the Knesset perimeter fence and hurled rocks at his window; would this gathering turn violent too?

The citizens didn't seem angry. Sighting the SUV, pedestrians jumped out of the way and let them pass. Many waved at the tinted windows or gave the thumbs-up.

As they rolled onto the bridge over the Hinnom Valley, Moshe learned why. A sequence of large images was displayed on a two-story billboard: a golden crown, Moshe's own likeness, and a turbaned young Arab.

What was Gurion up to? Spinning lies like webs, he had lured Moshe to the Messiah Coronation. Once caught in his sticky trap, would Moshe be able to wriggle free?

Let Gurion spin his webs. Moshe had his own mission to

complete, and then he'd hightail it to the Prime Minister's Residence.

"Stop here," he said.

"Sir, I recommend that you stay inside the vehicle."

"I'll stay close."

The SUV idling on the curb of the bridge, Moshe swung the door outward.

"There he is!" a man said.

More excited voices spoke. "That's him. That's Moshe Karlin!"

Moshe cringed, expecting a rotten tomato or a hook to the jaw. Instead, he found hopeful smiles.

He smiled back, crossed the road, and stepped up to the railing.

The Hinnom Valley squeezed between Mount Zion and the rise of modern West Jerusalem. The corner where the mountains converged had served the Ottomans as a reservoir. Today, the so-called the Sultan's Pool functioned as a stadium for open-air concerts.

Moshe leaned over the low stone wall of the bridge and peered through a gap in the Plexiglas barrier. This concert had sold out.

People blanketed the tidy rows of seats on the valley floor. Vendors moved between the rows, selling drinks and snacks. A red carpet ran along the main aisle and ended in a huge, black, boxlike structure, at least several stories tall, that dominated the stage. This Messiah Coronation had involved some serious preparations.

Alon joined him at the wall. He faced the street and unbuttoned his jacket, allowing free access to the holster at his side.

Moshe lifted the bullhorn he had packed for the ride and placed it between the Plexiglas dividers. Then he climbed onto the low wall and held down the press-to-talk button of the handset.

"Friends," he said, broadcasting his voice into the valley. Heads turned heavenward at the sound of the voice from above. "Fellow citizens. I know why you're here."

Voices cheered below; hands clapped. Bystanders filmed him on their mobile phones.

"You've heard unbelievable things in the media and from the Prime Minister's Office. Some are easier to swallow than others. We don't want to believe that our lives are in danger, or that the world we know is ending. It's much easier to hope that things will be OK."

The morning breeze played with his hair and caused feedback on the megaphone. He released the button. Every head turned to him. In the tense silence below, a man coughed. He had their undivided attention now.

He pressed the button again. "People exploit our desires and fears to get what they want and with little consideration for others. So, I've come here to tell you the ugly truth. The asteroid is real. We are all in great danger. The government is working to minimize the damage, but you must go home now, collect your loved ones, and take cover in the nearest bomb shelter."

Somebody cried out below. "You'll save us!"

Cheers erupted, then the voices chanted. *Kar-lin! Kar-lin! Kar-lin!*

Moshe enjoyed hearing his name as much as the next guy, but his supporters would remember Moshe Karlin in a very different light after their country got pulverized and they lost their loved ones.

"I should have said this a long time ago," he said into the handset, and the chant died down. "There are no magic wands. I cannot perform miracles or conjure natural disasters. I'm just a human being like you. And I am not the Messiah."

There, he had said it. Had they finally gotten the message? Voices echoed below. They were laughing. What was so funny?

The loudmouth cried out again, "That's what they said you'd say!"

The chant rose again. *Kar-lin! Kar-lin! Kar-lin!*

Moshe glanced at Alon, who shrugged. Once Gurion had

planted the seed of hope, how could he prove that he wasn't the Messiah? He glanced at his golden wristwatch, the piece Gurion had given him a lifetime ago for running with Upward in the elections. Under thirty minutes to impact. He needed a new tactic and fast.

"OK," he said. "If I say I'm the Messiah, will you go home?"

Cheers and applause.

What did it matter? He squeezed the talk button again. "Fine. Your Messiah commands you to go home and take cover. You have less than thirty minutes to reach safety. Go!"

More cheers below. His audience stood, but the crowds didn't run for the exits. Instead, they clapped. Another chant emerged. "Show us! Show us! Show us!"

Moshe released the button and swore under his breath. There was no winning with these people.

They wanted a show. Fine, he'd oblige. If he couldn't get through to them, he'd find someone who could.

"Isaac Gurion," he said into the loudspeaker. "Show yourself. You wanted to meet face-to-face. Time to show yours."

All eyes turned to the black box on the stage. The dark, foreboding structure recalled the warehouse where Mandrake had held Moshe captive. Whatever he did, Moshe should not go down there.

"Come on out, Isaac. Stop hiding."

As if in answer to the taunt, a loud *clank* issued from the box. A door-shaped rectangle fell away from the front of the box and crashed to the ground. All present waited with bated breath, but not a soul emerged from the box.

A new chant rose from the crowd. "Mo-she! Mo-she! Mo-she!"

The dark opening beckoned.

Gurion was running this show. Moshe wasn't the Messiah, and the people needed to hear it from Gurion.

"Mo-she! Mo-she! Mo-she!"

Fine!

Moshe climbed off the stone wall and returned to the

sidewalk. Abandoning the megaphone, he descended the ramp into the Hinnom Valley and the Sultan's Pool. The chant grew louder with his every step.

Let Gurion have his way. Let him hurl insults and accusations. If that was the fastest way to send his believers home, Moshe could handle it.

Moshe stepped into the arena. People rose from their seats and clapped their hands as he passed. He waved and pressed on, Alon at his heels.

The box rose five stories above him. Would the walls fall away as the door had, to reveal a dazzling stage to the delight of the audience?

He stood opposite the open doorway and peered inside, but the dark passageway faded into shadow.

C'mon, Isaac. Where are you?

The gaping hole called to him.

Moshe glanced at his wristwatch. Time was running out for the citizens in the arena. He'd have to end this charade quickly. He turned to Alon. "Wait here."

"But sir—!"

"It's OK. Gurion won't harm me in public, and I can't exactly walk onto the stage with an armed escort."

He stepped forward, and the crowd cheered. Another few steps and he was inside the box. The inner walls were of painted wood. Three meters in, the passage turned left.

Hinges creaked behind him, and he turned back. The door rose from the floor with a whoosh, snuffing out daylight, clicking shut, and entombing Moshe in darkness.

Oh, crap!

What a colossal mistake. Avi had warned him that Gurion wanted to kill him. But Moshe had not listened and now he had walked right into a trap.

Calm down. He won't kill you. Gurion wanted a public confrontation. He wanted to flaunt his power and hand Moshe a resounding defeat. He wouldn't resort to murder, would he?

Moshe had to get out of the box right away. He felt his way forward, retracing his steps to the door. His hands searched for a handle. He pushed outward, but the door wouldn't budge. He threw his weight at the wall, ramming with his shoulder and all his strength.

Then something hard slammed into the back of his skull, and he slumped to the floor.

CHAPTER 75

Ahmed watched as the rabbi's body floated over the crowd toward him.

"That's it," he said into the microphone. "Gently now."

The sight of the rabbi in the clearing, one bearded Jew in a sea of Muslims, had slapped Ahmed back to his senses and decided his internal conflict. He could not let this dear man die before his eyes. The rabbi had lost his mind, or he had a very urgent and important reason for risking his life. Either way, Ahmed would shelter him as the rabbi had done for him.

The body reached the end of the standing masses. "Now, place him on his feet." The befuddled men obeyed their Mahdi.

The rabbi stood, his shoulders hunched, every muscle in his body tensed for sudden flight. He looked up at him.

Ahmed beckoned with his hand. "Come here," he said in Hebrew. "Don't be afraid."

Many heads turned in the crowd and mouths tutted. Most of the crowd had not known the identity of the strange man they had supported over their heads, and the Mahdi's use of Hebrew now confirmed their suspicions.

The rabbi, clad in a black suit and skullcap, a brown beard streaked with white, and the white tassels of religious garb pouring from his belt, climbed the steps of the stage and inched toward the podium, his eyes filled with apprehension and focused on Ahmed.

Questions floated in the whispers of the multitude. What was a Jew doing here—and onstage with the Holy Mahdi?

In the corner of Ahmed's eye, Hasan writhed on his seat, his fists balled. This was not in the script. The Shepherd would exact a price for the failure. His cousin was probably weighing the benefits of rushing onto the stage to execute him on the spot, against the alternative of fleeing for his life. For now, he remained seated.

Ahmed had made his decision. The rabbi had forced his hand, and he was glad of it.

He laid a hand on Yosef's shoulder, and the rabbi flinched. "Welcome, Rabbi Yosef," he whispered. "Be not afraid."

The rabbi swallowed, not entirely at ease yet. He said, "We're in danger..."

Ahmed cut him short. "Nobody will harm you while you're with me."

The agitated murmuring of the masses below grew with each passing second. He had to calm them while he could.

"This man," Ahmed continued, speaking into the microphone in Arabic, "saved my life, and the lives of other Arabs. He took them into his home when they had nowhere else to go. Fed them. Clothed them. In return, he asked for nothing."

The whispers had settled, and in the many eyes, he saw anger turn to surprise and curiosity. As in Bethlehem, he sensed the thirst for a new message and a budding joy akin to relief.

"This man is not your enemy. Our enemies are lies and fear." At the edge of his vision, in the front row, Hasan twitched and buried his face in his hands.

Ahmed would pay for this later, and pay dearly, but for now, he rejoiced. This would not undo his terrible crimes, but for once he would spread light instead of darkness. He thought of Savta Sarah and Moshe Karlin. Most of all, he thought of Samira. By the time she heard of his speech today, it would be too late for Ahmed, but she would remember him with pride.

"We will only triumph," he continued, the words pouring from his soul, "when we realize that the true foe is not this nation or that, this belief or that, but the hatred we sow in our hearts."

He felt a tug on his arm. "Ahmed," Rabbi Yosef said. "There are explosives on the Temple Mount. We must ask everyone to leave at once."

The warm euphoric feeling fizzled in an instant.

"What explosives?"

"There are terrorists who want to destroy the Temple Mount, along with everyone here. A man with a red beard. He must have planted explosives all over."

Ahmed felt the blood drain from his cheeks. It was one thing to deliver a new message of hope, but to follow it with the threat of violent death?

The rabbi was not lying. At once, Ahmed understood why he had burst onto the mount and endangered his life.

While the two men on the stage conferred, the whispers resumed.

Ahmed cleared his throat. "This man saved my life. Today, he has saved us all. Now, listen carefully," he added, "and please, do not panic."

CHAPTER 76

Savta Sarah glanced at the next paper on the Speaker's podium.

"Item twenty-four," she read into the microphone. "The Tax Reform Law. I trust you all are familiar with it."

By "you all" she referred to the three Restart members of Knesset who had joined her in the Plenum Hall. They nodded their heads.

"All in favor, raise your hands."

Three hands rose in the air.

"Very well. Mrs. Secretary, please note that the law has passed."

The previous twenty-three laws had passed without incident and in record time. Today would go down in history as the most productive day the legislature had ever known.

"Mrs. Speaker," a man in a black suit called from the back row. "I must object again!"

Well, almost without incident.

Rabbi Mendel of Torah True had turned up and objected to every word that came out of her mouth. The nerve!

"Yes, Member of Knesset Mendel?"

"You cannot pass laws with such a low level of attendance!"

"We've been through this before, Mr. Mendel. This legislation requires no minimal quorum, and—"

In true Knesset tradition, Mendel didn't let her finish the sentence. "And," he spluttered, "you cannot pass laws with a single reading."

She rolled her eyes. "Again, Mr. Mendel, the first law we passed lifted those requirements for the legislation proposed today."

"But... but..."

She ignored the thorn in her side, turned the page, and ran out of pages. "Mrs. Secretary, have we reviewed all the items on our schedule?"

The Secretary, Mrs. Weinreb, a delightful young woman in her sixties, had tended to the red tape with a rush of taps on her keyboard. Working with professionals was such a pleasure.

Mrs. Weinreb read from her screen. "Let's see. We passed the Tycoon Law, the Law of Limited Government, the Tenure Abolition Law, the Anti-Cronyism Law, Land Registration Law, the six Transparency Laws, and the Law of Free Negotiation...."

That had been Savta's own modest contribution. Store owners could no longer complain when she asked for a discount. By law, she had the right to ask.

Mrs. Weinreb finished going through the list. "I think that covers everything."

"Excellent. Then it's time to go home."

Savta Sarah left the papers on the podium and made for the exit where Rafi waited. She put her arm in his, and they made for the car park. The Minister of Defense had stayed behind to make sure she left the building and got to safety in time. Moshe had seen to that, lovely boy.

"How did it go?" he asked as they strolled through the Knesset corridors.

"Very well. It's about time the country ran freely and fairly."

"Yes, indeed. I hope we get to see that in practice."

"Me too."

Outside, he held the door of the car open for her. "To the Prime Minister's Residence?"

Moshe had invited her to watch the operation from the safety of the Prime Minister's bunker. "Not today," she said. "Take me home. I defrosted all that meat; it'll go bad if I don't get to work soon."

"You're cooking—today of all days?"

"Rafi, dear, if we survive this, there will be celebrations. And celebrations need food."

CHAPTER 77

From the driver's seat, Alex reached over and opened the glove compartment. He grabbed his Glock and checked the cartridge before lodging the gun between his legs. Something wasn't right.

His black Hyundai idled a short walk from Shamai Street. Irina had left to collect her things fifteen minutes ago. She should have been back by now.

He had spent so long under Mandrake's wing that he'd never imagined how it felt to be on the wrong side of him. By now the crime lord had realized that Alex would not deliver on his final mission.

Nobody left the Organization. After all he and Mandrake had been through together, Alex had believed that he'd be different. He'd been kidding himself. In hindsight, he should have disappeared without a word. Instead, Alex had opened his big mouth and triggered the fulfillment of his worst fears.

Had Mandrake even expected him to follow through or had he assigned him an impossible mission, one he would surely fail? His twisted mind enjoyed creating that semblance of justification. Mandrake didn't crave the moral high ground; he had strangled whatever conscience nature had endowed him long ago. But the moralizing seemed to give him a sadistic pleasure, to torture a man with the idea that he had brought Mandrake's cruelty down on his own head.

A hundred terrifying scenarios flashed through his mind: Irina slumped over, a tidy round hole in her forehead; Irina strapped to Mandrake's man-sized red dartboard, pleading for her life.

He should never have allowed her to return to his apartment. Now she had fallen into Mandrake's hands, and only one more decision remained: was Alex going to follow her?

He swore and thumped the steering wheel with his fists. Why had she popped back into his life and turned everything upside down? Not that he'd been happy before; her death had torn him apart. But at least he had been alive. Now, Mandrake saw him as a traitor, and in this line of work, traitors didn't live long.

You idiot! Alex had deluded himself that he could redeem his past, that he and Irina could live happily ever after and leave the terrors of the past behind. Now he had lost everything: his love, his oldest friend, and the only career he'd ever known.

Only his life remained. For how long, he didn't know. If he wanted to keep breathing, he'd better shift the stick into Drive and never look back.

A blond woman appeared around the corner of the building and his heart jumped in his chest. The woman spoke into her phone, a handbag tucked under her arm, and marched on. She wasn't Irina.

Alex punched the wheel again. Then, leaving the motor running, he opened the door and got out. He shoved the handgun into the back of his jeans and beneath his jacket.

He couldn't do it. Not again. Alex had given her up once before, and the trauma had ripped his soul.

He walked around the back of his apartment building, scanned the street for Mandrake's thugs, and continued to the entrance. This second chance wouldn't come again. He'd already decided. A dozen times, he could have walked away, out of her life. Each time, he had returned. If he abandoned her again, his soul wouldn't tear; it would shrivel and die.

What point would there be in breathing?

Shoving fear and indecision out of his mind, he focused on the task at hand. This was a job, like any other, but this time, he was working for himself. For Irina.

He punched the code into the keypad and pushed through the door. Taking the steps two at a time, he landed on the balls of his feet and glanced up the pier, gun in hand, searching for killers lying in ambush.

He reached the door of his apartment without incident and touched the handle. Had the fear all been in his head? Had she taken a bathroom break?

Unlocked, the door swiveled inward. He checked the corridor, then stepped into the kitchen.

Irina stood by the counter, facing him, her arms hugging her chest. He exhaled a pent breath. She was alive! But her fearful eyes flitted to the side where a man slouched in a kitchen chair—the gray-haired man in the tweed coat from the elevator. The man stared at Alex, the revolver in his hand trained on Irina, while a smile spread beneath his bushy mustache.

Alex could slug him, but not before the man fired his gun at Irina, and, at this range, he wouldn't miss.

Before Alex could decide what to do, the question became moot. Thick arms slipped under his armpits, lifting him off the floor and spreading his arms wide like useless wings, while tough hands shoved his head downward. His gun clattered to the square tiles of the old kitchen.

"Finally," Boris said. "The man of the moment has arrived."

CHAPTER 78

Yosef stared at the crowd of Arabs below the stage. Moments ago, they had seemed ready to rip him limb from limb; now, they were helping him catch a terrorist.

"A redhead," he whispered to Ahmed, "with a beard. Not an Arab." The former suicide bomber translated his words into Arabic and spoke them into the microphone.

Headdresses shifted from side to side as worshipers conferred with each other and glanced around the Temple Mount.

"They should spread out and leave the Temple Mount in an orderly fashion using the nearest exits." Ahmed nodded and translated. The masses dispersed, exposing the neat lawns and cobbled pathways of the wide enclosure, and clustered at the exits.

Yosef's heart thumped in his ears. Any moment, the stones and trees could burst into flame as the charges detonated around them.

A clean-shaven Arab from the front row approached the stage and yelled at them. Yosef didn't understand the angry words, and he was glad for it. Ahmed stared the man down but said nothing. Then the Arab stalked off.

The lines at the gates shrank as the Temple Mount emptied. Had Yosef sounded a false alarm? Had Tom planned merely to disrupt the gathering? Yosef could live with that.

A commotion broke out, and voices shouted. A half-dozen white-robed Arabs burst back into the Temple Mount, pushing and shoving another man. Their quarry stumbled forward and fell to the ground. The *kaffiyeh* fell from his head, revealing a head of red hair.

"Get away from me!" he cried in Hebrew, and even at the distance, Yosef recognized Tom Levi's voice.

"What do we do with him?" Ahmed asked.

One of the Arabs kicked Tom, and Yosef shuddered. He had wanted to prevent bloodshed, but now he had turned a scared and angry mob against a lone, defenseless Jew.

"The police," Yosef said. "Hand him over to the police."

Ahmed spoke into the microphone again. The robed Arabs stood down as black-clad officers rushed to the beleaguered man and dragged him away.

"Thank you," Yosef said. Together, they had averted a catastrophe.

"No," Ahmed replied. "Thank you." A sadness clouded his features. "Now I must go. I fear we shall never meet again."

The gloomy words surprised him. "What do you mean?"

But Ahmed didn't explain. "Tell Moshe Karlin to stay away from the coronation."

"What coronation?"

"The Messiah Coronation. At the Sultan's Pool. I must go. It is my fate. But Moshe is a good man; he must stay away. This will not end well."

Questions vied for attention in Yosef's mind, but he held them back. Moshe was in danger; Yosef had to warn him. "I haven't been able to reach him since yesterday. I was busy with, well, with this." He gestured at the Temple Mount around them.

Ahmed walked to the ramp at the side of the stage. "Find him," he said.

Arabs in kaffiyehs and turbans greeted him and escorted him as he walked.

Find him. Yosef felt his empty trouser pockets. His cell phone must have slipped out when the crowd had carried him overhead and shattered beneath a thousand pairs of trampling feet.

This "Messiah Coronation" did not sound like good news. In Yosef's experience, such events never were.

Ahmed and his believers grew smaller as they moved through the grounds of the Temple Mount. Somewhere beneath the lawns and pathways, the Great Temple had once stood. Yosef must have trodden on that holy site tonight, transgressing a handful of Biblical prohibitions. Now that he had averted the bombing, was he permitted to cross that hallowed ground again?

The Talmud allowed Jews to travel on the Sabbath to redeem Jewish hostages. The law also allowed them to return home, desecrating the holy day a second time. Otherwise, they might not have embarked on the sacred mission. Did the same apply to Yosef today? If Ahmed was right, another life depended on his mobility—the Prime Minister of Israel.

Yosef raced after the receding entourage. "Hold on," he cried. "Wait for me!"

CHAPTER 79

Eli descended the ramp to the Sultan's Pool that morning, a bottle of oil in his hand and a fire in his heart. *How dare Gurion!*

Eli detested false prophets. Fame motivated some, fortune others. Some were simply off their rocker. All three factors seemed to apply to Isaac Gurion. Eli Katz was the last true prophet, and Gurion would pay for his brazen lies.

A thrill of déjà vu made him shiver. This was Mount Carmel all over again. The result would probably be the same. The common folk enjoyed a good show. Rain fire and brimstone, and they'd fall to their knees. Tomorrow, they'd return to their old idolatrous ways.

That didn't absolve Eli of his task, and this time should be easier. At Mount Carmel, he had stood alone against two hundred prophets of Baal. Today, he'd face only one opponent. If only Noga could see it.

He had left her in the doctor's care after borrowing an ill-fitting set of clothes and a wad of cash and set out to meet his destiny. At a corner store on Hebron Road, he'd picked up the rectangular bottle of Yad Mordechai virgin olive oil. After confronting the false prophet, he'd anoint the true Messiah. He'd work out the details on the way.

The common folk had packed the stadium in the small

valley to capacity. They didn't seem concerned about the asteroid threat, and he understood why. Trust in the news outlets had eroded in recent years as conflicting editorials muddied the waters of truth.

Today, the People of Israel would find clarity. He felt it in his bones. Not the certainty of the Thin Voice, but a very human sensation in his gut. The Boss had a plan. Eli had learned his lessons. The world was worth saving, and the End of Death was within grasp. The Grandmaster had positioned the pieces for the final checkmate, and Eli stepped onto the board, ready to play his part. This time *would* be different. It had to be. Maybe this time, when the smoke cleared, the people would learn their lesson too.

Spectators overflowed from the seats and perched on the rocky slopes of the Hinnom Valley. Thousands of years ago, the valley had glowed red with the pyres of human sacrifice. Humanity had progressed since then, but today the valley would burn once more.

Eli halted in the main aisle between the rows of crowded seats. A black square monolith dominated the stage, rising fifty feet into the air like an alien spaceship. No sign of Gurion, or Karlin for that matter. He scanned the sea of spectators. They watched the stage and chatted among themselves.

The path ahead was clear: confront the prophet, anoint the Messiah. But where were they?

"Hey!" said a voice, and a hand waved at him a few rows back.

The man with brown curls had a rounded, pudgy face. Eli didn't know him. Was he another player in the Divine game? Eli drew near.

The man held out a fifty-shekel note. "We'll have two Maccabees," he said. "And make it snappy; the show's about to start."

"Two what?"

Did he say "Maccabees"? During the Hellenistic Era, Eli had avoided the guerrilla warriors. Look at them the wrong way and they'd accuse you of being an Antiochus sympathizer and relieve you of your head.

This pudgy man, however, seemed uninterested in ancient Jewish rebellions. He gave Eli an "are you deaf or just stupid?" look, and said, "Beers. Two of them. And a large popcorn too."

Eli glanced at the bottle of oil in his hand and understood what had happened. "I'm not selling anything." The man frowned and looked around for another vendor. "Tell me," Eli added, turning the interaction to his own benefit, "have you seen Isaac Gurion?"

"Not since we got here. Only the Prime Minister."

"Moshe Karlin?"

The question won him another "yes, stupid" look. "The one and only. He walked into the black box. Haven't seen him since. Pretty lame teaser, if you ask me." He glanced at the stage and chuckled. "Looks like his security guard didn't get the memo."

Eli turned to look at the large black structure. Sure enough, a military type in a dark suit jacket walked around the black box, testing the walls for a way in, and scratching his head.

Eli's gut writhed. The false prophet had stood him up, and a large black box had just devoured his only Messiah candidate.

Then voices murmured, and arms pointed toward the ramp. Two men entered the valley, their entourage of white kaffiyehs following at a respectful distance. One of the vanguards wore a white flowing robe; the other sported a black suit and familiar brown beard. Rabbi Yosef Lev!

Hands clapped, and people stood to get a better view of the Vice Prime Minister and his Arab companions.

"Finally," the pudgy man said. Then he swore. A woman screamed, and a dozen hands pointed at the sky.

Eli looked up. In the blue dome above burned a star, bright and large. The celestial light waxed larger every second, and a short tail stuck out behind, as though the star was heading right for them.

Not a star. An asteroid!

More voices joined the cry. Men and women launched from their seats, pushing and elbowing as they charged for the exits. Eli stepped aside and dodged the trampling herd.

He lost sight of Rabbi Yosef in the pandemonium, but as the spectators surged up the ramp and hurried out of the valley, the field cleared. Among the abandoned seats, strewn with popcorn boxes, spilled drinks, dropped shoes and scarves, three men remained at the base of the black box.

Eli joined them.

The rabbi turned at the sound of his footfalls, and his eyes widened.

"You," he said. "The biker." A short burst of joy escaped his lips. "You survived."

Eli raised the bottle of oil. "My jar of quality stuff didn't, so this will have to do."

The rabbi looked from Eli to the bottle of olive oil, and his eyes widened further.

"Are you a part of the coronation?" asked the security guard.

"I'm not with Isaac Gurion if that's what you mean, but his phony event has pushed up our schedule. We haven't been formally introduced." He put out his hand to Yosef. "Elijah of Anatot."

Rabbi Yosef released another gasp. He accepted Eli's hand, his fingers cold and thin. "I thought you'd never arrive."

"Same here."

The rabbi's lips moved as he pieced the information together. "That day at the Mount of Olives—you were there for Moshe?"

Eli gave the rabbi what he hoped looked like a wise and mysterious grin. He still was not one hundred percent sure of anything.

"I've been through a lot since then, as have we all." He looked up at the asteroid burning overhead. "And we're running out of time."

The rabbi shook his head as if waking from a trance. "This is Ahmed."

The Arab shook his hand, his expression distant, sad. "We must warn Moshe not to come here," he said. "The coronation is not what he thinks."

"Too late. He's already inside."

Ahmed turned back to the sealed black box. "Inside—but how?"

As if in answer, a panel at the front of the box fell outward like a drawbridge and slammed onto the floor of the stage with a heavy wooden *thunk*.

They stared at the black hole. Although not exactly inviting, the passageway had placed only one option on the table.

Eli had waited two thousand years for this moment, the reason for his existence. The box held the future Messiah and, probably, the last false prophet. What other surprises waited within?

The way ahead would be dangerous. His weapons included a bottle of oil and centuries of experience. But the situation was unfit for mortals.

"You three go home and take cover. I'll take this from here."

"Try to stop me," said the security agent. "The Prime Minister just disappeared on my watch."

Rabbi Yosef straightened. "Moshe might need my help. He'd do the same for me."

"No," Ahmed said. "None of you belong in there." He pulled a golden envelope from a fold of his robe. "The Shepherd invited me, not you. I have blood on my hands, but you don't. Save yourselves."

Eli sighed. "OK then." He turned toward the black doorway. "After me."

CHAPTER 80

Samira raced a wheeled trolley down the corridor of the DBS fourth-floor dormitory, peering in the doorways and distributing extra blankets. She had ten minutes to finish her rounds and take cover before the asteroid hit.

The DBS had heeded Moshe's warning and made preparations, while the rest of the country dashed for cover in panic.

A volunteer named Nir ran toward her. "There's chaos in room 439," he said, pointing down the corridor. "The monkey-men are tearing bags off the windows!"

"Here." Samira reached into her canvas shoulder bag and dumped a pack of crayons. "Let them draw on the walls. They love it!"

"Great idea!" Nir sprinted off.

"Irina's," Samira said. "Works like a charm."

Thanks to Irina's stroke of genius, a hundred prehistoric humans scrawled animals and stick-figure hunters on the dormitory walls instead of causing their usual havoc.

She hadn't seen her friend and partner since early that morning. Samira hoped she had taken cover already. They had drawn up a set of instructions for DBS Absorption Centers around the country. Now they could only wait and hope that Moshe pulled off another miracle.

Moshe had saved them from physical slavery, redeemed

them from bureaucratic limbo, and catapulted their cause to the pinnacle of power. He had also coordinated an astounding recovery from an earthquake of unprecedented devastation. If anyone could deal with a speeding asteroid, he was the man.

Out of blankets, she dumped the trolley in a corner and took the stairs to the third floor. She'd make one final round of the Call Center to check for stragglers, then crawl under the cot bed in her own room, arms over her head, and brace for impact. The asteroid would hit Jerusalem, Moshe had said, but there was no time or resources to transfer the many DBS residents to other cities.

In the Call Center, she checked the cubicles and peered through the glass window of the corner office. All clear. As she made to leave, a man blocked the doorway of the Call Center. The Arab wore white robes and a *kaffiyeh,* and for a moment fear nailed her to the spot. Had her father discovered that she was alive? Had he hunted her down to restore his tainted family honor?

She recognized the face. The man was neither her father nor a relative, but Ahmed's new friend, Dara. Now other emotions struggled in her heart.

In Ahmed, she had found a friend and true confidant. Violence had snuffed out their short first lives, and they had endured the same trauma of exploitation in their second. He had treated her with warmth and concern and given her gifts. She had imagined a future together, an escape from the terrors of her past. Together they would build a new family for their new lives. That dream had exploded into a thousand shards the moment Shmuel had identified him and pummeled him on the floor of the DBS. Her Ahmed, a murderer? That couldn't be! But Ahmed had not denied the accusation; instead, he had run away. From his crimes. From her.

She had thought of him often. Her Ahmed was no cold-blooded murderer. And yet, every day, ordinary men and women committed unimaginable violence. Who knew that better than she did? Had Ahmed fallen prey to the death machine that lurked in the shadows?

She had wondered what had become of him. Had he found a new home? Had the slave driver, Boris, and his frightening musclemen found him and hurt him? Was he dead already?

The answers had turned up on the doorstep of the DBS a few days ago. Ahmed was alive! He had new friends and a new name but had he learned nothing. She had seen through the money and the fancy new clothes and found the same death machine.

Now, Dara had turned up again, alone. She studied Dara's eyes for clues. Had the machine sucked Ahmed into the grinder again?

"Is he alive?" she said.

Ahmed's friend seemed surprised at the question. "Yeah, he's alive. Today is his coronation." He rolled his shoulders, a gesture of arrogant self-assurance, the fool. "He wanted me to give you this." Dara held out a letter.

A prickle of hurt registered inside. "Is he too important to speak to me in person?"

"Take it," Dara said. "Please. This is very important to him. If he could deliver it in person, he would have. He made me swear to hand this to you and only you."

Samira sighed. She had no time for games.

"Whatever," she said. She took the letter and shoved it into her canvas shoulder bag. "Now if you'll excuse me, I have to go."

CHAPTER 81

Alex saw his own death before his eyes. He writhed in the thug's iron embrace, kicking his legs in the air, while Boris smiled and trained the barrel of the gun at his chest. If he fired, the bullet might pass through him and hurt his henchman, and for the moment that had worked to his advantage.

The muscleman pressed his hands forward, shoving Alex's head downward and pulling his arms back. Bolts of searing pain pierced his neck and shoulders like electric shocks. He stopped struggling, and the pressure eased. Resistance was futile.

A month ago, Alex had sat in the front seat of a black Mercedes on King George Street. A motorcyclist had aimed a handgun at the windshield while a brown van had screeched to a halt in the opposite lane. In the rearview mirror, a masked thug had pulled Moshe Karlin from the backseat like a baby from a crib, then walked behind the car, holding his captive in the same immobilizing grip.

These were Mandrake's men. They would act without hesitation or mercy. He had seconds to turn the situation around.

He'd bargain with the gunman, beg him to let Irina go—Alex was the one Mandrake wanted, not her—and he'd use the diversion to surprise them. Alex opened his mouth to speak, but Boris beat him to the punch.

"I'm glad to meet you," he said. "My name is Boris." The gun relaxed in his hand, the barrel resting on his leg. "We share an employer."

Alex didn't fall for the friendly words. Boris had borrowed a page from Mandrake's playbook. Alex should expect the worst, but for now, he'd play along.

"Is this how you greet all your coworkers?"

The mustache shifted again as he smiled. "My apologies. Igor, please."

The muscleman released his grip, easing Alex to the floor, and he slid the gun from the floor.

How much had Mandrake told him? And how much of that had Boris told Irina? Had she had learned the truth? He feared that more than Boris's bullets.

His eyes flitted to Irina. She was breathing heavily, her lips pressed together, terror reflected in her eyes.

He could rush Boris. With luck, he'd overpower him before he could fire his weapon, but that hulking Igor would be close behind. Alex could handle himself in a fight, but alone and unarmed, the odds were against him. And Igor would make short work of Irina. If she was lucky.

"I've come for the girl," Boris said. "She didn't deliver the goods so she's outlived her utility. Which is where I come in. I have a little debt to settle here too. Irina and I go way back. But," he added, "not as far back as you two."

Irina's brow wrinkled as her eyes searched his. "What is he talking about?" they asked.

"Oh, yes," Boris continued, his mustache askew over his smile. "I only met Irina in her second life. But you two go back even further, don't you?"

CHAPTER 82

Moshe hovered in the dark like a hummingbird. Or an angel.

His arms were wrapping his body, and his legs had fused. An appendage pulled at his back between his shoulder blades. Did he have wings?

Was this the Spirit World that Rabbi Yosef had mentioned—the immaterial dimension between lives?

The back of his head stung. He had stumbled in the dark of the black box when something had struck him. Was this real pain or the memory of his physical body, the itch of an amputated limb?

A switch clicked, and a spotlight blinded him. Heavy footsteps approached. This was not the Spirit World; this was Gurion's web.

Moshe prepared to negotiate with his nemesis. He would offer him the world. He would beg and plead. Whatever it took, he'd get Gurion to send the civilians outside to safety.

The footsteps halted in front of him. But when Moshe hazarded a peek through his shuttered eyelids, his heart sank. His field of vision filled with a beak nose and large, sensitive eyes. This was not Isaac Gurion; this was his worst nightmare.

"Welcome back, Moshe," Mandrake intoned in his Russian accented baritone. This time, his bald abductor sported a thick handlebar mustache and a tuxedo, complete with frilly dress shirt and bowtie. The madman looked both ridiculous and terrifying. He grinned. "Did you miss me? I missed you." He stalked off into the shadows of what appeared to be a stage.

Moshe had to escape and fast. He used the respite to take in his surroundings. A white straitjacket pinned his arms to his chest. Heavy, bulky pads wrapped his legs together. The long, taut rope that suspended him from his back disappeared into the darkness above.

"Get ready for the show of a lifetime," Mandrake continued from the shadows. He chuckled. "Well, *your* lifetime."

Mandrake returned to the spotlight. A cape of black satin fell over his back, and a top hat sat at a rakish angle on his head. He adjusted the mustache beneath his nose and rapped the wooden floor twice with a silver-pommeled walking cane.

"I've waited a long time for this day. So many preparations. Things never turn out quite as one plans, do they? We'd hoped for a larger turnout, but we'll make do with this small private audience."

With a flourish of the cane, he indicated the gloom behind him. Beyond the black wooden planks of the stage, a row of three shadowy figures shifted in the darkness. Tied to their seats and gagged sat Alon, a stranger with thick hair, and… was that Rabbi Yosef? What was he doing here?

"Unfortunately," Mandrake said, "due to time constraints, we've had to trim the program down. Shall we skip to the grand finale?"

He gave the cane a sharp switch to the side, and the bottom flew off to reveal a long thin blade.

In a dark warehouse on Election Day, Mandrake had blindfolded Moshe and pretended to throw knives. This time, his tormentor would not limit his act to scare tactics.

Mandrake laughed. "Oh, Moshe. No, this isn't for you. It's for him." He pointed the blade to the left.

An upright, mirrored box sat on the stage. From large holes protruded two arms and a head with a flowing white *kaffiyeh*—the Arab boy from the billboard. Smaller holes covered the mirrors at his chest—slots for the insertion of long, thin blades. The boy stared ahead, his eyes glazed over.

"For you, Moshe," Mandrake continued, "I've prepared something special. Vitaly!" he cried. "Positions."

Footsteps thumped on the stage behind him, and wheels turned in pulleys. The rope at Moshe's back jerked upward, lifting him ten feet in the air and out of the sword's reach. His relief was short-lived.

Mandrake's bald assistant in black tied off the rope to a steel clasp on the stage floor, then pushed a large glass container the size of an elevator into view. Water sloshed in the brimming open roof as Vitaly positioned the container beneath Moshe's feet.

Oh, God, no! Moshe inhaled shallow, panicked breaths.

"Ta-dah!" Mandrake cried. He spun around, and his cape billowed behind him. "How sweet. Our two Messiahs, together for the first time. And the last."

Two messiahs? Mandrake too thought that Moshe was the Messiah, along with the poor Arab kid. But would he murder them both in front of three witnesses? With chaos and destruction about to descend on the country, he'd get away with it.

Moshe's body writhed. Soon, the entire country would burn, but his survival instinct chose "sudden pulverization later" over "slow drowning now."

"Now, for the magic," Mandrake said. "I'm old school. I don't hold with smoke and mirrors. Our audience deserves the real thing—real blood and real guts."

Moshe wriggled and strained against his bonds. His life couldn't end this way. He had to escape. Despite his efforts, he still jiggled over the watery deathtrap.

He had to create a diversion, to delay a little longer. "While there is life, there is hope," Rabbi Yosef had said. Any minute, the asteroid would hit, bringing either instant death or a lifesaving miracle.

"Aw," Mandrake said, his voice dripping with false empathy. "I know, I know. This sucks. You'll die a slow, miserable death, and I'll walk away. You think I'm a bad person, don't you? Well, step into my shoes for a moment. This isn't what I wanted. I just wanted to be loved." He leaned in and hissed. "The *goyim* made me who I am. Everywhere I went I was 'the Jew.' I mean, look at me." He tapped his beak nose. "I couldn't escape it. One look at me and they saw a cheat, a thug, a murderer. One day I stopped running. I embraced it. I became the monster. And you know what? It worked. Everybody feared 'the Jew.'"

The madman's words crowded Moshe's adrenaline-charged brain. He wasn't buying the sympathy ploy, but there was a thread of truth in the criminal overlord's story. But whereas Moshe had leveraged the same malignant projections to save lives, Mandrake used them to justify his reign of terror.

Mandrake grinned. "Thanks for listening, Moshe. I appreciate it. But now it's time to say goodbye."

He stepped up to the steel clasp on the floor and rested the sword on the rope. *No!* Moshe scrabbled for diversions to draw out the inevitable. *Think, Moshe! Keep him talking.*

"I'm not the Messiah," he said, his voice a croak in his parched throat.

Mandrake cocked his head to the side and put a finger to his lips. "Do you hear that?"

Moshe did. The distant rumble outside grew louder, the familiar patter of rotors. A helicopter circled above. Were IDF commandos about to rescue their Prime Minister? Moshe grasped at the straws of hope. *Oh, God, please!*

The chopper did not seem to bother Mandrake.

"Speak of the Devil," he said, and he chuckled. "Ladies and gentlemen, you are in luck. This is a rare honor. A rare honor, indeed!"

Moshe had that sinking feeling. Mandrake had been expecting the helicopter, just not now. The aircraft was his escape route ahead of the asteroid strike. But what was this dubious "rare honor"?

He didn't guess for long. The chopper landed on the roof of the rectangular structure with two heavy thumps. Light poured in from above as a trap door opened and closed, and shoes clanked on metal steps.

"Ladies and gentlemen," Mandrake boomed. "Prepare to meet your Maker!"

CHAPTER 83

A knocking on the cabin door disturbed the captain of the USS Ohio during the climax of his favorite movie, The Hunt for Red October. He paused the player on his iPad, pulled off his earphones, and prepared to unload his annoyance on the visitor. *What now?* The crew knew better than to disturb him on his off time. A month of latrine duty should teach the NUB a lesson.

But when he swung the steel door open, his executive officer stood in the passageway, apprehension painted over his face. His annoyance evaporated, replaced by the same nausea he had experienced only yesterday.

"Is the sea monster back?" he whispered.

"No, sir."

The captain exhaled a pent-up breath, and his nausea returned. They were on their way home and nearing for the Strait of Gibraltar. "Well, what is it?"

"Orders just came in." The XO handed him a printout of a decrypted message.

The captain read the orders, and the sinking feeling returned. After ten years in the Silent Service, he'd thought he'd seen it all, but within the space of two days, he'd been blindsided twice.

"This must be a mistake."

"I asked for confirmation, sir. Confirmation received and double-checked."

The captain swore under his breath and grabbed his captain's hat. Without a word, the officers hurried down the narrow, rounded corridor to the Command Room.

"Did you check with the other subs?"

"Yes, sir. They all received identical orders."

Dear Lord. The orders were clear and so were the ramifications. World war. Mutual assured destruction. The end of civilization.

A dozen pairs of nervous eyes greeted the officers as they burst into Command and Control and took their positions.

"Officers, open the launch tubes."

"How many, sir?"

"All of them. XO, relay the target coordinates."

"Done, sir."

The captain moved from his seat to peer over the shoulder of the launch engineer. He had launched dozens of missiles in training simulations but had never encountered coordinates like these. "What's with that extra figure, officer?"

The officer looked up. "Altitude, sir."

The captain took a few seconds to process the information. "The target is airborne?"

"Yes, sir. Well, to be more precise, in orbit."

The hotshots in the Oval Office were taking out satellites. The Trident missile had an internal guidance computer with precision correction provided by its star sighting navigation system. But hitting a satellite required accuracy beyond the missile's capabilities.

And what satellite justified that much firepower? Each missile contained twelve warheads, each with a yield of one hundred kilotons—six times more destructive force than the nuke that flattened Hiroshima. Yesterday, sea monsters; today, attacks on UFOs?

He returned to his seat. At the end of the day, he was a soldier and he'd execute his orders. He just hoped the President knew what he was doing.

"Officers," he said. "Wait for my mark. Launch commences in five minutes and counting."

CHAPTER 84

Moshe dangled over the water chamber as their visitor stepped off the metal staircase and walked to center stage. Moshe's mouth dropped open. *Prepare to meet your Maker*, Mandrake had said. In many ways, the man was just that. He was also the last person Moshe had expected to see here today.

"Hello again," the man said, in English and with his usual Texas drawl.

Moshe gawked at the silver-haired, suited juggernaut that was Reverend Henry Adams. Words eluded him. Had the reverend flown in to save him? Or had he also fallen into Mandrake's trap? The American stood beside the rabid magician, two old friends surveying their handiwork.

Adams looked over his shoulder at the three bound men. "Rabbi Yosef," he said, by way of greeting, then turned back to Moshe. "I'm sorry our arrangement has to end this way. You were doing so well. Far better than we had anticipated."

Moshe found his tongue. "Did Isaac Gurion put you up to this? Don't believe a word he says. He's a liar!"

Adams chuckled. "Oh, I know. Not a pleasant man, either. He had a way of getting ahead of himself. But this time his head got away from him." He smiled at his own joke. "He won't be bothering you again. Or anyone else. Not unless he returns from the dead as you did."

The words stunned Moshe back into silence. Gurion was dead. Adams had seen to that. But why?

"If it's any consolation, you make a much better messiah."

"But I'm not the Messiah!"

"What you are doesn't matter, only what people *think* you are."

Moshe thought he understood. "Your messiah didn't show, so you want the other messiahs dead?"

Adams sent Mandrake a bemused look. "Moshe," he said, his voice patronizing and disappointed. "We never wanted a messiah. The New Evangelical Church of America is a front, a helpful tool to part fools and their money. Our organization is larger than any one religious institution. And far, far older. Its tendrils stretch around the world, and yet each branch knows little of the others."

Adams drew near and stared up at him. "The last few centuries have been very good to us. We made tidy profits off wars and drugs. Now we've gone hi-tech. Anything can become a weapon in the right hands: airplanes, medicines, words. The most powerful by far is hope.

"Take Paradise, for example. The hope for a spiritual reward in the hereafter allows good people to endure suffering and ignore injustice in the here-and-now. And why not? This world is just a passageway. God will repay their injured souls a thousand-fold in Heaven. So, they busy themselves with their prayers and their rituals. Fixing the world isn't their job, anyway. That task belongs to the Messiah.

"And so, while believers yearn for paradise and the redeemers of tomorrow, our organization spreads its roots today."

He pointed at Moshe and snarled. "Then you came along with your resurrection. The afterlife is here. People would ask questions. 'Is this our ultimate reward?' 'Is this is the only world?' 'Should we stop praying and start paying attention?' All we needed was a messiah to come along and declare the end of history. But history must go on. Hope must go on.

Our business model depends on it. And so, the Messiahs must die."

Now Moshe did understand. "You kept the Dry Bones Society close, waiting for the Second Coming, so you could nip the Messiah in the bud. When that didn't materialize, you created your own messiah. I was a natural candidate. But when I refused to claim the title, you set up this coronation and got Gurion to lure me here."

Adams bowed his head, then circled back to Mandrake.

"It won't work," Moshe said, desperate to keep the conversation going. "I'm just one man. Others will rise up after me and complete the work I've begun."

Adams seemed amused. "Will they? Messiahs have cropped up over the ages. They all failed. Many met unpleasant deaths, and my predecessors were glad to help out with that." He winked. "But guess what happened right after the messiahs' spectacular failures. Did their believers give up or change their tactics? Oh, no. Their faith increased. They had misread the signs or miscalculated the dates. The Messiah would be back and even sooner than they thought."

The reverend—no, the Anti-Messiah—glanced at his wristwatch. "And now, history repeats itself once again. And where better than Jerusalem, the Eye of the Universe, to which all believers turn in hope. Your plan to save the planet might just work, Moshe. We appreciate your efforts on our behalf. Once the dust settles, the survivors will discover that, alas, their Messiahs have perished. The hope will go on. And we'll be there to reap the profits."

Adams turned to Mandrake. "The stage is yours." Then, to the room at large he added, "Please forgive my theatrical colleague over here, but I find that, now and then, it's best to indulge his flair for the dramatic. Enjoy the show."

Mandrake raised his sword.

"Wait!" Moshe cried.

But Mandrake didn't. He swung the blade with all his might at the rope.

CHAPTER 85

Irina stared at Alex, the gun in Boris's hand forgotten. Was it true? Had Alex known about her former life and not told her? What role had he played in that life?

"Oh, yes," Boris said. "You go way back. Isn't that so, Alex? But you didn't tell her. I understand why."

She searched Alex's eyes for the truth. His face turned pale, but he said nothing. His silence said it all. Alex was not the man she thought she knew.

Boris turned to her. "Our boss entrusted Alex with a whole new department. He placed advertisements in Lithuanian newspapers, offering secretarial work overseas for a few lucky young women. The job required no prior experience, only a photograph. The approval process was very selective. But when the lucky applicants, all pretty girls from unfortunate backgrounds, arrived in Israel, they learned that the work expected of them required neither typing nor organizational skills. Instead of the stylish business suits in the adverts, their dress code was—how shall I put it?—minimal. The office conditions were cramped, the work hours grueling. The customers many and demanding. Not the gentle sort, either. They cared little for the girls' personal safety, and they always got their money's worth."

Boris chuckled. "No, this was not their Promised Land.

But what's a poor girl to do? Their employers had taken their travel documents. They were illegal aliens employed in forbidden work in a foreign country. And they were in debt. Their handlers demanded recompense for their travel expenses. They didn't speak the language. And their shame was great. So, they shut their eyes and held their noses, resolving to endure their two years of hard labor and return home."

Irina's limbs stiffened. Often, she had fantasized about her first life. As a wealthy heiress—a modern-day princess—she flitted across the globe to exotic getaways and dodged the advances of celebrities and moguls. Then she fell into the powerful embrace of her tall husband and doted on her brood of laughing children. Had the truth been far darker?

Alex stared at the floor and swallowed hard. Had he deceived her into a hellish life of the worst human slavery? Her head shook from side to side. *No, it couldn't be.*

"One girl stood out from the others," Boris continued. "She made the most of her situation. A born organizer, she took charge of the other girls and kept them in line. She learned the language. Soon, her hard work paid off. Alex gave her more responsibility and improved conditions. A special bond formed between them, the pimp and his star performer. He fell in love. Then tragedy struck." Boris adopted a tone of fake sympathy. "His lady love used her new freedoms to escape. She alerted the authorities, and Alex's world came tumbling down. Only it didn't. Fortunately for Alex, the policeman the girl had turned to belonged to the Organization."

Tremors shuddered through Irina's body. She could guess what followed. Her former life had ended in violence, the violence that had damaged her brain and obliterated her memory. To hear Boris spell it out was almost too much for her to bear, but she needed to know, to bring closure to months of uncertainty.

Boris tutted. "Alex's boss wasn't happy. He made sure she suffered for her crimes and never escaped again. Then he let Alex clean up the mess. And what a mess it was. Alex was never the same again. But the boss had a soft spot for him."

Alex stood there, his head hung low. Irina digested the information. She had thought that once she learned the truth of her first life, the memories would come gushing back. But although the words shocked her, the tale seemed strange and foreign. That wasn't her. Those terrible things had happened to some other poor girl. For once, her amnesia was a blessing and not a debilitating curse.

The gray-haired slave driver turned to Alex. "But this fairy tale has a happy ending. Years later, Alex gets a new mission—to infiltrate the Dry Bones Society. And who does he meet right out of the gates, but his old sweetheart, back from the dead. Only, she doesn't remember him; she remembers none of it. Good old Alex thinks he's hit the jackpot. They can continue their romance where they had left off, only this time without all that unpleasant baggage. And this time, it's Alex who tries to escape."

Alex made eye contact with her. His eyes begged her to believe. He was sincere. Despite his past deeds and despite the ugly circumstances of their first meeting, he was prepared to leave it all behind. For her.

Boris sighed, his face a mask of pity. "Of course, his boss finds out, and he sends me here. But don't be sad. We're getting to that happy ending. The girl had a second chance at life, and so Alex's boss gives him a second chance, too." Boris got up, placed his gun on the kitchen table, and flopped back on the armchair. "But this time Alex has to silence the girl himself."

Every cell in Irina's body tensed. *No, he won't do it!* Alex loved her. He wouldn't kill her. But did she know him anymore? He had made her disappear before. Was he willing to die for her? She held his gaze, waiting for his signal, waiting for him to refuse.

Alex's eyes lost focus. He glanced at the gun on the table. Taking one large step forward, he picked it up and raised his arm, and the man she loved aimed a gun at her head.

CHAPTER 86

Duct tape binding him to a chair, Yosef stared at the horrific scene on the black stage above. Moshe dangled over a glass deathtrap filled with water. A magician's sawing box entombed Ahmed, who minutes ago had saved Yosef's life. This was wrong—so very wrong!—and in more ways than one.

When the Arab mob had closed in on him that morning, Yosef had accepted the inevitable conclusion. Rabbi Emden was right; Yosef was the Second Messiah.

He had resisted the idea at first. Yosef didn't want to die. And why should he? He was a simple neighborhood rabbi with a pitiful past. A recovering alcoholic didn't belong in the hallways of Knesset, never mind at the vanguard of the cosmic drama. But when hundreds of innocent lives had hung in the balance, he could not stand down.

"In a place where there are no honorable men," the Sages of the Talmud said, "be an honorable man." The police commissioner had ignored his warnings, and so Yosef had stepped up. The act might cost his life, but perhaps this was his fate. And if his destiny was to depart this world early, he'd rather perish while saving lives than cowering under his bed.

And God had blessed his path. Not only had he prevented the catastrophe, but—thanks to Ahmed of all people!—he had survived the Arab lynch mob. Then, Elijah the Prophet had sprung from the pages of the Bible. The Divine guidance he craved had arrived at last. His every cell trembled with joy. Everything would be all right. The Redemption was here!

And then everything went terribly wrong. After following Ahmed, Elijah, and Alon into the black mouth of the box-shaped structure at the Sultan's Pool, the trapdoor had snapped shut and plunged them into darkness. He heard a scuffle, felt a sharp blow to the back of his skull, and woke up bound and gagged at the foot of the black stage.

Mandrake, the crazed magician, strutted across the stage in his tuxedo. The villain had abducted Moshe on Election Day. Now he would murder Moshe before their eyes. And Yosef was helpless to stop him.

This can't be happening! Yosef belonged on that stage, not Moshe. Yosef was the Second Messiah; he must die so that the Moshe could usher in the World to Come.

Yosef struggled against his bonds to no avail. He cried out—"I'm the one you want! Take me!"—but only muffled groans reached his ears.

Just when he thought he'd reached the peak of anguish, a new character had descended the metal staircase and proved him wrong—Reverend Henry Adams!

As Yosef stared in disbelief, the reverend joined Mandrake on the stage and took charge. A sudden, desperate hope sang in Yosef's breast—Adams had swept in to rescue them from the murderous madman. Then Adams spoke, and the song fell silent.

From the start, Yosef had felt uncomfortable dealing with the clergyman. *Sitrah Achrah*, the sages of the Great Assembly had said of the resurrected Israelis—the evil Other Side. Yosef had ignored their warning and accepted hefty checks from the Evangelical Christians. But the reverend's money had helped the Society, and Yosef had made peace with the situation.

Yosef's instincts had not deceived him after all. But he had misunderstood—and far underestimated—the threat. Adams was no man of God; quite the opposite. And Yosef knew his real name.

Armilus!

Rabbi Emden had whispered the name as though the word's mere mention might attract misfortune. Yosef had not taken the myth seriously. Judaism rejected dualism. God reigned supreme. No archangel could challenge His authority.

But Adams was no demon. Who needs supernatural devils when we have human beings? This particular human being embodied all the evil and suffering in this world, and he had won.

"The stage is yours," Adams said to Mandrake. Then he turned to the captives and apologized for his colleague's theatrical flair.

Mandrake raised his sword.

Alon and Elijah shuffled and moaned on their chairs beside him. The three men—the Second Messiah, the head of Moshe's security detail, and Elijah the Prophet himself—would watch helplessly as these human monsters killed the Lord's anointed.

No, not anointed, for Elijah had missed Moshe by minutes. Yosef had spent months searching for the Messiah. All along, the Scion of David had sat right in front of his nose. He had slept in Yosef's home. They had toiled side-by-side at the Dry Bones Society, and later, mere meters had separated their ministerial offices.

Yosef should have focused his efforts on finding Elijah the Prophet, the man who had sought him out on the Mount of Olives on the second day of Moshe's new life.

Today, as with that failed first meeting, tragedy had struck at the critical moment. This time, instead of shipping Elijah off to the hospital, they would both watch, their hands tied, as murderers snuffed out all hope of redemption.

"Wait!" Moshe cried from his vulnerable perch.

But Mandrake swung the blade, severing the rope his assistant had tied to the stage floor.

Moshe's body dropped into the water and sank to the bottom. He struggled in the straitjacket, bubbles of precious air escaping his mouth. Adams and Mandrake stepped up to the glass to watch his final moments.

You can do it! Yosef willed Moshe's bonds to open, for him to slip free and rise to the surface. The escape wouldn't put him out of danger, but the reprieve would give them all another chance. *While there is life, there is hope.* Yosef had said that much to Moshe in the dark depression of his first day. Yosef had believed that then, and he clung to those words now.

CHAPTER 87

Irina stared down the barrel of the gun in Alex's hand. He wouldn't shoot her, would he? She knew him. They loved each other. He was serious about leaving his criminal past. He had pushed her to leave sooner. She should have listened to him. But now, regardless of what he wanted, did he have a choice?

She tried to divine her fate from his eyes, but she found no twinge of indecision or hesitation. He had made up his mind.

His eyes shifted sideways, a secret instruction for her to jump out of the way, then he turned the gun on the thug in the armchair.

A loud click echoed in the silence.

A smug smile spread over Boris's face. "Traitor," he jeered. "I knew it!"

Then Boris reached for his belt, and Irina knew he had another weapon.

"Run!" Alex cried. She stared at him. "Get out of here!" He lunged at Boris, slamming his fist into the seated slave driver's face and knocking the second gun out of his hand. This gun would not be empty.

With a deep roar, Igor lumbered toward the two men and pulled Alex off his boss by the shoulders.

Her first instinct had been to rush to Alex, to help him fight off the goons, but she had no delusions about her ability to tackle two hardened killers. She slipped behind the giant, rounded the kitchen wall, and ran for the front door.

As she pulled the handle toward her, an arm in a tweed coat slammed against the door, shutting the only exit. Boris snarled at her, his face uncomfortably close and murder in his eyes. Blood from his nose and upper lip had drenched his mustache, painting it red.

Irina fell backward into the entryway, then scrambled to her feet and finally, she followed Alex's advice. She ran.

Behind her, Alex gasped and grunted as he wrestled with the hulking thug. She fought back tears. No man stood a chance against that mass of muscle. A scrape of metal on the tiles told her that Boris had retrieved his gun, and his footsteps followed her.

"Go on," he said, "run." He was taunting her, taking his time. "There's nowhere to hide."

Irina wasn't sure about that. She dived into Alex's bedroom and locked the door.

She slid open the window. The cracked pavement stared back, two flights down. If it didn't kill her, the drop would break her legs, and she'd abandon Alex to fight off both henchmen alone.

No! It can't end this way! They had snuffed out her first life; she would not let that happen again. She dashed toward the closet and opened the doors. He'd discover her in a second.

A loud crash made her turn around. Boris stood in the doorway, panting. The doorframe splintered where the bolt tore through the wood. He had kicked the door in, and now he raised his arm and aimed the gun at her head.

His nose rumpling with malice, he said, "Time to die. Again."

CHAPTER 88

"Where is Prime Minister Karlin?" the President of the United States demanded.

Good question, Shmuel thought.

After setting his plan in motion, Moshe had run off to confront Isaac Gurion, while the rest of his cabinet followed the operation from the safety of the Prime Minister's Residence.

In the bunker below the Residence, Shmuel sat at the conference table of lacquered wood and put on a brave face for the camera, while world leaders stared him down from the mounted television screen.

"He had to attend to an urgent matter of life and death," he said. "He'll be back as soon as possible."

The gruff Russian President chimed in. "We're about to launch every nuclear warhead on the planet. What could be a more urgent matter of life and death?"

He had a good point. "Saving a bunch of doubting, ungrateful citizens" was not the answer they wanted to hear.

"Exactly," the American President said, agreeing for once with his Russian counterpart. "This is his show. Either he leads, or the deal is off!"

Shmuel knew what they feared. If Moshe had disappeared, who would stop the Zombie Armies? But he would not let them slip out of their commitments that easily. "Moshe's instructions are clear. He told us to continue without him, and we all know how to proceed. Remember," he added, and tried to maintain his poker face, "our Zombie Armies are already halfway to their targets."

The world leaders shifted in their seats. "Now, now," the American President said, suddenly ingratiating. "There's no need for threats. We're here to help however we can."

"Yes!" the Russian said. "Yes! And we've pulled every string to make this happen."

"You have." Shmuel exhaled a silent breath of relief. In his career as a journalist, he'd interviewed many important public figures, but he'd never had to face off the leaders of the world's superpowers together. *Moshe, where are you?*

He glanced at the countdown timer on the screen. The Time to Impact counter had dropped below five minutes.

"Professor, at your mark."

Shmuel shifted over to allow Professor Stein to face the conference camera. The bunker, added as an afterthought to the older structure of the Prime Minister's Residence, could barely contain the table, and sitting room was limited. Designed to withstand the primitive missiles of Palestinian terrorists, the bunker would not afford much protection from an asteroid strike.

The Knesset had only recently approved the construction of a new billion-shekel government compound beside the Supreme Court in Givat Ram. The command center would include a huge underground bunker to be used by the Prime Minister in times of national emergency. Little good that did them now.

And so Shmuel, Professor Stein, Sivan, Chief of Staff Eitan, and a few military technicians had squeezed into the bomb shelter along with Galit and Talya Karlin and their extended family. Avi Segal too. At the end of the world, political divisions no longer mattered.

The professor pored over the calculations on his laptop. At Moshe's request, he had devised the strategy for averting the imminent disaster, and the planet's future lay in his hands.

The professor looked up at the world leaders on the screen. "You all received my targeting instructions?"

A chorus of affirmations resounded from the leaders in the smaller squares on the screen. Each square displayed the war room of a nuclear power: The United Kingdom; France; China; India. Even Pakistan and North Korea had joined the world initiative under dire threats from their mentor superpowers.

"Good," the professor said. "Timing is critical if we're to change the asteroid's trajectory. The joint blast force might not be enough to do the job, and a mistake might shift that trajectory onto any of your home states."

There was a commotion of whispered consultations in the war rooms and expressions of surprise and dismay from the lesser leaders. Apparently, this potential side effect had not dawned on them, and the benefits of their full cooperation became crystal clear.

Professor Stein read out the list of countries and their sequence of launch times and missile locations. The checklist checked, the professor sat back in the padded-leather chair.

"Switch to orbit view," he said.

A military technician tapped at a tablet. The pictures of command centers around the world shrank to the bottom of the display. Two other feeds took their place: a live video of the speeding asteroid and a schematic of the revolving Planet Earth. A small red dot to the left indicated the approaching asteroid.

"The game is in play," the professor said. "All we can do now is wait and pray."

Shmuel glanced around for the Vice Prime Minister. They had not managed to contact Rabbi Yosef all morning. Shmuel hoped that both he and Moshe had found a safe place to weather the storm.

"God help us all," Shmuel said, and every person present answered Amen.

A cluster of small white dots rose from the schematic

Planet Earth, like shotgun pellets. Dotted lines traced their trajectories toward the larger red dot.

"China has launched," Klein said.

More white pellets left the turning planet.

"India. Pakistan." Then clusters of missiles launched from land and sea around the globe. All converged ahead of the red dot, at the point where the asteroid would pass in a few seconds.

"All armaments are in the air."

The professor gripped the armrests of his chair and sweat soaked his face. Even the slightest miscalculation would cause the warheads to miss their mark.

Shmuel glanced around the room. All eyes turned to the screen. Galit Karlin held her daughter close, her eyes watery. Avi placed a hand on her shoulder. Galit met Shmuel's eyes, and they both smiled. *He'll be fine*, their eyes said. *Moshe always is.*

CHAPTER 89

Moshe gulped air as he hit the cold water and went under. The weights on his legs dragged him down and clanked against the glass floor of the aquarium.

He struggled against the straitjacket, but it was no use. Harry Houdini might free his hands and legs and break the surface, but Moshe was no escape artist.

He needed to think outside the box. Pun intended! Gallows humor wouldn't help him now. His lungs screamed for air, but the situation was hopeless. With his legs bound to the anchor, he couldn't kick or shoulder the glass.

Precious bubbles of air fled his mouth with the effort. How had he gotten into this mess? He had only tried to make the world a better place.

A Karlin never quits.

Since he could remember, he'd struggled. Build Karlin & Son. Escape Boris's labor camp. Found the Dry Bones Society. Launch Restart.

Every now and then, he'd had an epiphany. Work fewer hours, spend more time with his loved ones. But soon enough he found another cause and off he went, trying to save the world again.

Why did he push so hard?

"Not for them," Avi had told him in a moment of anger

when Moshe had tried to stop him from marrying Galit. "You did it to prove yourself, to please those old photos on the wall."

There was truth to Avi's accusation. The tales of his forebears' former glory had lodged in his brain and driven him onward.

But he was tired of struggling. Let someone else step in and save the day. People thought he was the Messiah, but right now he needed a savior as much as anyone.

He forced his eyes open in the water. Two murky figures watched him through the glass: Mandrake, his sadistic tormentor, and Henry Adams. If that was his name. Moshe had known his debtors would come calling, but he hadn't realized that they were one and the same.

A painful ball of injustice burst in his heart. Adams, his benefactor and ally, had manipulated Moshe for his own evil ends.

His murderers would not face justice. They would fly off in a helicopter whether his plan beat the asteroid or not.

His lungs burned. Every cell of his body cried out for oxygen.

Savta Sarah was right. In the end, Death wins. No matter who you are or what you've done. Moshe had done his best. He had helped others and risen high, against the odds. His father and grandfather would be proud; he'd have to find comfort in that.

His lungs couldn't take any more. He surrendered to his breathing reflex. His final breath escaped, and chilly water rushed into his lungs.

Little Talya popped into his head. He'd never meet the young woman she'd become. He spotted Galit for the first time across the dance floor in Hangar 17 and he walked right up. "You're late," he said, the first two words he'd ever spoken to her. She hadn't batted an eyelid. "I got here as fast as I could."

These past few weeks, they'd hardly talked. He had left so much unsaid. He'd tell her… he'd say…

But his thoughts unraveled in the depths, and the world faded to black.

CHAPTER 90

The giant plucked Alex off Boris and flung him against the wall of the apartment. Alex slumped to the floor and stayed down. He waited for the thug to move closer so he could draw the final ace up his sleeve. Boris had disappeared from the couch, evening the odds but piling on the tension. The slave driver had chased Irina down the corridor, so Alex had better play that winning card soon.

The giant lumbered forward and leaned over him. Alex sprang upward and buried his fist into the thug's ample solar plexus. The larger man doubled over, expelling a breath that stank of peanuts, his eyes bulging with pain and surprise.

The blow would not have disabled Igor had Alex not slipped his fingers into a set of knuckle busters. The steel rings around his knuckles focused the impact, while the rounded grip in his palm spread the opposing force away from his own fingers.

After a lifetime at Mandrake's side, Alex had learned a thing or two.

He followed the blow with another, this time a jab to the face. The giant groaned and shifted sideways, but still didn't fall. So Alex slammed both fists onto the cowed man's spine, and he hit the tiles with a satisfying *splat*.

One down, one to go. The gray-haired bureaucrat should

make an easier opponent. Alex took one step toward the corridor when he heard a shot ring out, followed by the unmistakable *flop* of a body hitting the floor.

In the deafening silence, Alex froze.

No! Not Irina!

CHAPTER 91

Shmuel held his breath as the clusters of white dots converged on the larger red one. The live feed of the glowing asteroid went blank.

A military engineer stared at his laptop. "We've registered multiple direct hits."

The denizens of the cramped bunker glanced at each other and at the tense faces on the smaller squares on the mounted screen. The white dots had disappeared from the schematic, but the red dot remained. The missiles had found their mark, but was the full force of the planet's combined nuclear arsenals enough to divert the asteroid from its path?

Shmuel's fists whitened at the knuckles. All eyes turned to Professor Stein, who tapped at his own laptop, bobbing his head as he consulted charts and calculations.

Professor Stein looked up from his screen. "The trajectory has changed. The asteroid will miss Earth by a few miles. We did it!"

The people in the command centers jumped in the air and hugged their neighbors.

Shmuel released a pent-up breath and mopped his forehead with a handful of tissue paper. If only Moshe could have seen that! Shmuel had to let him know that the danger had passed. Citizens could leave their homes.

He reached for the desk phone and dialed Moshe's mobile number from memory. The call cut to voicemail. Was Moshe all right?

Then he glanced at the live feed and tugged Professor Stein's arm. "What is that?" He pointed at the big screen.

The bright light had faded, and the asteroid was visible again. Only now the large glowing rock had two smaller siblings, which veered away from their big brother.

Professor Stein gasped. "The blast split the asteroid into chunks." The room fell silent again, and the giddy smiles vanished. "The main bulk will miss us, but the others…" He trailed off and punched at his laptop again.

"The others?" Shmuel asked.

Professor Stein looked up from his calculations, and his face turned white. "They're heading for the Middle East. Right for us!"

CHAPTER 92

In his long life, Eli had seen empires rise and fall, cities burn and sprout from the ashes, languages transform, and accepted wisdom overturn. He'd seen kindness and joy, tragedy and suffering. He'd even experienced love. But he'd seen nothing as heartrending as what his eyes beheld now.

On the black stage, Moshe Karlin—his only messiah candidate—writhed and twisted in the watery glass chamber.

This is your fault. Eli had twiddled his thumbs at Noga's bedside. After waiting millennia for the True Messiah and receiving countless hints from the Boss, he had still not acted in time.

In his defense, this was not from lack of trying. Failing to contact the new Prime Minister, he had assisted with Noga's plan to build a grassroots awareness of the Ten Lost Tribes. The plan might have worked, had a premature apocalypse not ripped through Jerusalem. Eli's timing sucked.

But identifying the Lost Tribes was only part of his job. God sent prophets to anoint His chosen kings. Despite rushing across the city to fulfill this part of his mission, he had missed his crucial meeting by minutes.

In hindsight, he should have approached Moshe Karlin before the elections, when he was more accessible. But by then Eli had lost his way, determined to become Eli Katz, the young Internet entrepreneur, while suppressing Elijah the Prophet in the depths of his psyche. And why had he done this? To win the affections of a mortal woman.

But had there been any other way? The Elijah that Noga had met in the hospital had abandoned hope for humankind. He had despaired of redemption, inclined to let the Boss scrap humanity and start over. He had done so before.

Noga had not only messed with his mind, she had recalibrated his moral compass. The world was worth saving. But by the time he'd recovered his will to fulfill his destiny, he'd missed the boat.

It wasn't fair. It wasn't right. In the past few months, he'd discovered the secrets of the Ten Lost Tribes and the End of Death. Why would the Boss hit the reset button now? Why would He render Eli useless, his body taped to a chair of plywood and steel, while the Messiah drowned before his eyes?

Two Messiahs, as it happened. In yet another twist of cosmic irony, the details fell into place only now. Moshe, son of David Karlin, represented the tribe of Judah. The Arab kid in the magician's box stood for the Ten Tribes of Israel. Noga's research had found proof of that. But why would God kill them both?

Unless Eli had screwed up. *Was* Moshe Karlin the Messiah?

On the stage, Moshe Karlin's body twitched twice, then fell still. The show over, the magician and the suited visitor lost interest in him and moved on to their second victim.

"What's that?" said Suit, in English and with his Texas drawl. "What's he saying?"

The magician nodded to his assistant, the black-clad thug with the scar down his cheek, who walked up to the Arab boy. "It's Arabic," he said. Another Russian, by his accent.

"Kid," he said, in Hebrew. "Speak Hebrew if you have any last words." He chuckled.

Eli couldn't hear the Arab's words, but the assistant translated them into English. "He wants to ask you a question," he told the suit.

The magician and the suit exchanged glances. The magician shrugged, hefted his long thin sword, and the two men drew closer.

"He asks if you are the… Shepherd?"

The magician seemed confused, but the suit laughed and puffed out his broad chest.

"I am. Nothing like a golden ticket to make a man feel the greed." He chuckled again. "I know that you were eager to meet me, and now I've granted your wish."

The boy spoke again, longer this time.

"He says you've hurt many people, that you've turned others into killers." The henchman smiled. "He says he won't let you do that again."

The three villains had a good laugh. The boy's empty threats wouldn't save him.

Adams recovered from his fit of laughter. "You've got guts, kid. I admire that. But our time is up, and we have a flight to catch."

The magician raised his sword, positioning the sharp point at the mouth of the slat over the center of the Arab's chest. One Messiah floated, motionless, in a watery grave; the other had a sharp blade aimed at his heart. Eli couldn't bear to watch, so he closed his eyes.

On Mount Carmel, he had faced off the prophets of Baal. Despite their prayer and dance and self-flagellation, the false god had failed to answer their offering with fire. Elijah had scorned them. He dug a deep trench around his own altar and filled it with water. He turned his eyes heavenward, and the Boss answered his call. Lightning had struck his altar, igniting the wood, engulfing his sacrifice in flames, which lapped up the water too. The people had fallen to their knees and bowed. "The Lord alone is God!" they had chanted. "The Lord alone is God!"

And now, from his front row seat at the foot of the stage, Eli understood. He had a role to play. A single, final act to surpass all the miracles and wonders he had wrought over the centuries. Had the Boss led him here for this reason? Was this act the ultimate purpose of his life? He'd never know for sure. But a purpose it was, a purpose he now chose.

Elijah turned his heart heavenward. The Magic had fled, the Thin Voice fallen silent. But like Samson, defeated, blinded, and chained to the pillars of a Philistine palace, he prayed. He envisioned fire and brimstone, an explosion of heat and flame to engulf the men who sowed death and destruction. To engulf them all.

Goodbye, Noga.

His final tears streamed down his cheeks.

Please, Lord. Answer me one last time.

He found the invisible muscle at the core of his brain. *Flex! Flex! Flex!*

Nothing happened. More nothing happened. No heat, no flame. No explosion. His prayers had gone unanswered.

Eli opened his moist eyes. The three evil men, anti-Messiahs and murderers, stood over the Arab, as the magician, grinning, leaned into the hilt of the sword. The Arab boy did not cry out. Instead, he muttered a few soft words.

"What was that?" the suit said. "What did he say?"

"I don't know, sir," the henchman said. "It's Arabic. Something about *Samira.* I think that's a name."

Then, with a glint of victory in his dark eyes, the Arab smiled and balled his hand into a fist.

The world turned yellow. A fireball expanded with a whoosh, swallowing the stage, singeing Eli's eyebrows, drying his tears, and throwing him back. The chair toppled, his head hit the floor, and everything went dark.

CHAPTER 93

Irina was dead. The reality hit Alex harder than any physical blow.

In the living room of his apartment, he stood frozen to the spot beside the toppled giant. His reason to live had died with her.

You idiot! He should have taken Boris first. How had he let the thug go after her? Had he thought he'd make short work of his henchman? Now Boris had his gun. Any moment now he'd appear in the corridor to finish what he'd begun.

The ground disappeared beneath his feet, and Alex collapsed to the ground. The giant had swept his legs from under him, and his back hit the floor hard. Before he could react, the giant rolled on top of him, pinning him beneath his immense weight.

Alex swung at the bloodied face, but a large hand caught his fist and squeezed. Alex gasped as the steel grip dug into his palm. The giant grinned with pleasure, inches from his nose. Alex got in a left hook, but the giant lunged forward with both arms, pressing meaty forearms over Alex's upper arms, and the huge hands closed over his head.

The thick fingers tightened around his skull like iron clamps, the pressure increasing.

"Now this ends!" Igor roared, and his thumbs closed over

Alex's eyes, pressing them into their sockets.

Flashes of bright light exploded in Alex's head, the last sight he'd ever see. He cried out as the pressure on his cranium mounted, threatening to implode his head.

Bang!

Another shot had rung out. At once, the pressure subsided, the thumbs slipped from his eye sockets, and the bloody face dropped onto his chest. A large chunk was missing from the side of the giant's head.

Alex crawled backward from beneath the dead thug. Irina stood over him. Her arms were rigid, her face rippled with fear. A wisp of smoke rose from the barrel of the gun she held in two hands—the spare loaded Glock he had kept hidden in his cupboard.

She trained the gun on him as if considering whether to shoot him too. He'd lied to her. In a former life, he had let her die. Now that she knew the truth, the whole truth, could she forgive him? He'd turned his back on that old life, but he hadn't turned his back on her. He had risked everything to save her and start a new life together.

After three long seconds, Irina lowered the weapon. She held out her hand and helped him to his feet. Then she hugged him for all she was worth.

CHAPTER 94

Moshe retched his guts out. He knelt in a puddle of water and vomit. Shards of glass littered the floor and glinted like diamonds. Hazy light poured from the heavens like angelic rays.

The moist air smelled of roast chicken and singed hair. He had drowned in a glass elevator filled with chilly water. But now the straitjacket hung from his frame in long white scraps and only partially restrained his left arm.

He paused to fill his raw chest with air. Breathing—what a sweet, glorious sensation!

He extracted his body from the jacket, and the scraps of material that fell to the floor were stained red. *Blood?* He ran his hands over his side and back. His fingers traced a dozen shallow cuts. A small, hard object stuck to his skin. He winced as the foreign body came away in his fingers, a small silver screw. What the hell had happened?

He glanced around. A metal frame remained where the glass elevator had stood. Torn wooden boards creaked around the rough hole in the ceiling. The place looked like ground zero after a terror attack. Adams, Mandrake, and their henchman had disappeared. Moshe would not wait for them to return.

He struggled with the weights around his feet, his fingers numb and clumsy. Staggering to his feet, he took a step, and his soaked shoes kicked against chunks of blackened meat on the stage floor. Grilled chicken had rained from the sky. The paint of the stage had peeled away to reveal naked wooden panels. Smoke rose from the black patches, which grew thicker and darker toward....

Dear Lord! The magician's box had disappeared, leaving only the charred remains of the base. High above, a smoldering white bundle dangled from the lighting scaffold. The Arab boy's white kaffiyeh. Moshe felt the urge to vomit again, but he had already emptied his gut.

Oh my God. A powerful charge had detonated right where the Arab boy had sat. The explosion destroyed the glass elevator and vaporized the water, releasing Moshe from certain death.

A black top hat sat on the stage floor. Moshe leaned over and picked it up. *Ouch!* The hat singed his fingers and fell to the floor, landing right side up. Then it burst into flame.

A groan drew his attention beyond the stage. Picking up a shard of melted glass for defense, he hobbled to the edge.

Three men lay on their backs, their legs in the air, their limbs still taped to chairs. Moshe descended the stairs and got to work, slicing the bonds with the sharp glass. Alon, Rabbi Yosef, and the stranger got to their feet and rubbed their bruised arms.

"Moshe!" The rabbi wrapped him in a bear hug.

"Easy there. My back feels like a sieve."

Rabbi Yosef apologized. So did Alon.

"It's not your fault, Alon. You tried to warn me."

He gave the stranger a questioning glance. A bystander, in the wrong place at the wrong time? The man put out his hand. "Elijah," he said.

Moshe shook the hand. He'd never met an Elijah.

A loud bang overhead made them cringe. The sound came from outside, the sound-barrier crack of a hundred fighter jets.

They reached a unanimous agreement. "Let's get the hell out of here!"

They made for a bright tear in the side of the box and poured into the empty arena of the Sultan's Pool. Shielding their eyes from the searing daylight, they glanced at the skies. There was no need to point. High above them, a large fireball streaked earthward.

Oh, no! Moshe's plan had failed. The asteroid had entered the atmosphere and tore through the skies overhead, toward the rise of Mount Zion.

They ran.

CHAPTER 95

With much huffing and puffing, the tourist reached the pinnacle of the Rock of Gibraltar when he heard the boom. A thought worried him. Had his wife been right?

Too nervous to take the cable car, she had remained at the visitors' center. Her hip ruled out a hike on foot, and so she had let him "risk his neck" alone.

And risk his neck he had. The line for the cable car had been short, as had the ride, and when he'd stepped outside—oh, what a view! The Mediterranean Sea stretched out as far as the eye could see.

He'd held onto the railing, taking a moment to catch his breath, and nodded a greeting to a bushy-haired Barbary macaque that had perched on the metal fence and seemed more interested in people-watching than in the awe-inspiring vista.

The salty sea breeze filled his nostrils and refreshed his lungs. Far below, the lines of ocean swells crept over the deep blue like the slow, calming motion of distant clouds. A colorful, multi-decked cruise ship made for the Port of Gibraltar below.

Then the deep rumble had sounded, and even the monkey had jumped.

Had the cable snapped, the car's passengers plummeting

to a miserable and violent death? But the boom had come from above.

There it was! A large rounded object passed overhead, its fiery tail tracing its slow but inexorable path toward the blue horizon. The object was too large and rough for an aircraft or even a UFO. *Dear God!* That had to be the largest shooting star he'd ever seen.

Was he hallucinating? His family doctor had changed his blood pressure pills two weeks ago. No. Other visitors stood transfixed, their mouths open, their eyes and hands following the descent of the meteor. Some held phones in the air, recording the cataclysm for posterity.

Just his luck. He'd spent forty years in retail, saving up for retirement. Two months ago, he'd signed away his grocery store on the West End. The week in Gibraltar was the first trip he and his wife had embarked on, and they had planned much more: a week in the Greek isles, a weekend in Venice, and a two-week stint at a villa in Tuscany. Couldn't the end of the world wait another few months?

The flaming meteor scuttled across the heavens and disappeared into the horizon, the smoking tail still hanging in the sky. He waited for another boom. None followed. Perhaps the meteor was only passing by or had crashed in a distant land, poor buggers. By the looks of it, somewhere in the Middle East. That'll put an end to their wars—ha!

The other visitors started to talk among themselves, processing what they'd witnessed. He'd better get back to his wife. She'd regret not taking that cable car. He'd stood at the right place at the right time for the best possible view of what was surely a once-in-a-lifetime historic moment, and he had bragging rights.

As he turned to face the cable car station, however, the tone of the ambient chatter changed. Excitement had turned to concern. A young Japanese woman gasped. They were pointing again, so he turned around and made for the railing.

At the distant horizon, a white pillar rose from the sea, like a cloud. More hands pointed, this time at the waters far below. The waves retreated from the shore, sucking the cruise ship back, away from the port and out to sea. This was not a good time to be on the water.

The meteor had hit the sea. Although he was no expert in these matters, he'd seen enough Hollywood blockbusters to know what would happen next. The waters would surge back. Tidal waves. Mass hysteria.

His fellow tourists must have shared his thoughts, for they streamed toward the cable car station. He joined them. He must get off the Rock and head for high ground. As he passed the turnstile, his arms trembling and his heart rate soaring, a more practical thought crossed his mind.

He'd paid in advance for the hotel in Crete. Was it too late for a refund?

CHAPTER 96

Tom Levi couldn't believe his luck. In the holding cell at the Talpiot Police Station, he'd perched on the edge of the cot and wrung his hands. His rump hurt from the stiff, thin mattress. He'd better get used to that. According to the rough officers who had arrested him, he'd be in a cell for the rest of his life. Why had the Lord abandoned him? Then the plump woman in the blue Israeli police uniform appeared at the bars. The bunch of heavy keys jangled in her hands as she hurried to unlock the cell door.

"You're free to go," she said and bustled down the long corridor.

He followed her, joining the flow of officers and offenders. The doors of the other cells stood open, as did the gate at the end of the corridor.

"What's happening?" he asked a uniform.

"An asteroid is about to hit the city. The station isn't equipped to protect you, so you're being released."

Tom laughed out loud. God had heard his voice and seen his affliction, and now the Almighty had arranged world events to further His servant's goal.

He'd heard about the asteroid. The media had dismissed the doomsday predictions as fake news, political ploys designed to draw the public's attention away from the Prime

Minister's failings.

The midday sun smiled overhead as convicts and uniforms flooded the sidewalks of Talpiot. Tom turned his feet toward Hebron Road and the Old City. This time he wouldn't fail.

He'd been so close to his goal that morning. After infiltrating the Temple Mount maintenance team and planting his explosives, he had watched the grounds fill with Islamic usurpers. If they weren't terrorists, they were enablers who provided financial and moral support. They had no right to trample the holy grounds of the Jewish Temple; they deserved to die.

And their deaths would spark the Redemption. Vice Prime Minister Lev didn't have the guts to act, so Tom would force his hand. He had waited outside the Gate of the Tribes, remote detonator in his pocket. But just as the Temple Mount reached full capacity, the Vice Prime Minister himself had stormed the grounds.

Tom had half a mind to blow him up along with his Arab friends, but then Israeli security guards had followed Rabbi Lev inside. No Jews were to die that day; the goyim had spilled enough Jewish blood. He'd wait for the guards to leave with the misguided rabbi. Then he'd push the button.

But the first men out of the gate were Arabs. They fled to the alleys of the Arab Quarter. His quarry was escaping! He reached into his pocket when hands grabbed his arms, lifted him off the ground, and dragged him onto the Temple Mount.

To insinuate himself into the maintenance team, he had pretended to be a mute, but now he cried out. The detonator slipped from his pocket onto the large stone tiles and disappeared among the rushing feet of the crowd. Rabbi Yosef Lev had botched his plans again.

As the squad car drove him to the station, the irony hit him—the Israeli security guards were Arabs too!

The Old City walls rose over Jaffa Road. The streets stood empty. The city had taken the asteroid threat to heart. With nobody to get in his way, his job would be easy. He'd locate the detonator and complete his mission. The Temple Mount would return to rubble today, empty or not, along with that hateful golden dome.

He picked up his pace, hitching up the hem of his robe and crossing the short bridge over the Hinnom Valley. Billboards announced a coronation ceremony and displayed images of Moshe Karlin and the Mahdi. What an abomination! To display the true Messiah along with that Arab imposter. With the Temple Mount razed to the ground, rebuilding the Temple would be easy. Karlin would thank Tom and reserve for him a seat of honor at the Great Feast under the Leviathan-skin canopy.

A deafening boom overhead drew his eye beyond the billboard. The sun burned in the sky. The glowing orb seemed smaller than usual and had grown a short tail. Before his eyes, the orb waxed larger. That wasn't the sun.

Tom raced up Mount Zion. He sprinted through Zion Gate, bounded along the silent cobbled alleys of the Old City, and zeroed in on the Temple Mount.

His sandals slid over the rounded stones as he took a corner and spilled into the courtyards before the Gate of the Tribes. He searched the smooth stone tiles for the detonator.

There it is! He launched toward the small gray rectangle when a shadow passed over the courtyard and blotted out the sun. A fierce hot wind knocked him off his feet and hurled him back.

His body slammed against the far wall of the courtyard and slipped to the ground. Chips of rock and dirt pelted him like rain. Clouds of dust billowed, then dispersed. A slow groan came from his throat as he exhaled. His shoulder and hip burned. Smoke rose from his singed robes. The Gate of the Tribes and Golden Dome were no more. In their stead, fallen stones crumbled and fires raged. The flames licked at the heavens like the pillars of an immense building, a temple not of wood and stone but of fire that had descended from on high.

With a superhuman effort, he got to his feet and hobbled

forward. A fit of ecstatic laughter overcame him, and his slight frame shuddered both with great joy and bone-grinding pain.

Then water fell from the sky, wet and hard, and doused the fires. The flash shower lasted two seconds, as though God had emptied a heavenly bucket. *Strange.* The afternoon had been cloudless. The downpour soaked his tattered robes and matted his hair—and tasted of salt! As he doubted his sanity, a high-pitched whistle sounded, the terrifying whine of a Nazi V2 bomb descending on London.

He looked up, then jumped. *Splat!* Two steps away, a large fish gawked at him through dead eyes. The stone floor tile had cracked beneath the unfortunate creature. Another whistle and another squelch. This time, a tuna. Two more whistles. Three. Dozens. Tom limped to the shadow of a stone wall as fish, sharks, and a large octopus pelted the ground.

The whistles ceased. Tom hazarded a halting stroll among the piled-up wares of the unlikely fishery. He had skipped breakfast that day and lunch. Hungry as he was, he had lost his appetite for seafood of any kind.

There it came again—another whistle, but much deeper. A shadow fell over him, so he looked up. Another object fell from the heavens, but he had trouble identifying this one. It was large. Very large. He glimpsed a long, tapered neck and long lateral fins, spread like the wings of a very large bird or a passenger jet.

His last thought before that final squelch was, "I should probably get out of the way."

CHAPTER 97

A month later, Yosef jumped out of bed early in the morning, his heart racing. Today was the day.

He freshened up and hurried to the Yael Street synagogue for morning prayers. The air was redolent of palm branches and citrus fruit—the scent of the Succoth festival and new beginnings—and the leafy canopies of Sukkah booths peeked over the walls on Shimshon Street.

Returning home, he opened his bedroom cupboard to dress a second time. His wedding suit hung on the rack, immaculate within its nylon cover, dry-cleaned and tailored to his current dimensions.

Yosef had imagined that the Messiah's arrival would be sudden and unexpected, a bugle call to arms from out of the blue. But, as always, reality had surprised. As Vice Prime Minister, he had played a key role in the meticulous planning of the ceremony, along with the Prime Minister and Elijah the Prophet. But knowing every step of the way ahead today did not diminish the immense joy that filled his heart to bursting.

Dressed in his designated suit and new black fedora, he stepped into the living room and gasped.

"What?" Rocheleh asked. She ran a self-conscious hand through her flowing jet-black locks. For the historic event—one might say the *final* event of history—she had splurged on a new wig.

"You're beautiful," he said.

She blushed. Truth be told, he almost hadn't recognized her, but he kept that confession to himself; he wasn't married yesterday.

Beside her, their four boys stood at attention in identical suits and smiled from ear to ear.

"*Aba*!" Ari and Simcha cried as one. "We got you!"

They held out their new trading cards, and Yosef examined them. *Well, what do you know?* The laminated cards displayed Yosef's own visage, with a healthy dose of Photoshop.

"You've got me indeed." Yosef had his very own rabbi card. The world was ending for sure. "Shall we go?"

Outside, Baruch held the door of the limo open, and they piled into the ample back seats. The car pulled off.

"Cyndi?" Baruch asked, his eyes smiling in the rearview mirror.

"As always."

The driver pressed a button and, on the limo's speakers, Cyndi Lauper sang "True Colors."

The streets of Baka had emptied for the public holiday, the shutters of stores drawn, tables and chairs stacked behind the darkened windows of coffee shops. Even Hebron Road was desolate of traffic, like a Sabbath day in the middle of the week, and a fitting start to the Day of Complete Sabbath. The Messianic Age.

Most citizens and a swath of foreign dignitaries had already claimed their seats at the ceremony. The rest of the world would watch via live video feeds.

He who prepares on the Sabbath eve will eat on the Sabbath, the Sages said. The preparations lay in the past now. Some had been thousands of years in the making. Now humanity could sit back and enjoy the show. He only hoped that for once in the history of humankind, things would go according to plan.

There had been some thorny theological issues to iron out as well. Yosef had consulted with ancient texts and commentaries. Occasionally, he had conferred with the resurrected authors of those texts and commentaries. They had reached two conclusions.

The first insight had come from an unlikely source—the *Sitrah Achrah*. The evil Other Side. The Anti-Messiah. Armilus. Henry Adams had identified the hidden message of the Resurrection. The message reinforced everything Yosef had learned about life, the universe, and everything, and became the cornerstone of their official view of the Redemption.

Human beings only find true expression as unified wholes—thus the need to reunite bodies and souls. But physical reality has its limits. As such, the world and humanity are imperfect, incomplete. This was by design. God entrusts humans with the task of completing the world and perfecting themselves, and in doing so, they become partners in Creation.

Secondly, Maimonides was right—the Messianic Era did not break a single Law of Nature. The time for magical thinking had passed. Instead, the epoch relied on miracles of science.

The Aging Vaccination, created by Dr. Yariv Stern of the Shaare Zedek Medical Center, was a prime example. People who opted for the treatment—developed in collaboration with a Mr. Eli Katz—would, quite literally, live forever. As Isaiah had foretold, "He will swallow Death forever." The only side effect to be noted over the next few years would be a phobia for extreme sports and motorized vehicles.

The walls of the Old City towered on the horizon as the limo crossed the Hinnom Valley and joined the line of diplomatic limousines and SUVs that wrapped around Mount Zion. Traffic police manned the sidewalks and kept the approach roads to the Mount of Olives Cemetery open to VIP traffic only.

Security agents in dark suits and glasses waited for Yosef, his wife, and children outside the limo and ushered them toward the large platform at the top of the cemetery.

For the Messianic Era Induction Ceremony, the State of Israel had constructed the platform, complete with podium and microphones, beneath a protective canopy of—what else?—a Sukkah booth. But this was no ordinary booth. The sides were lined with the hide of a very large aquatic creature, previously thought extinct and roused recently from the watery depths by the same solar flare that had triggered the Resurrection and dislodged Planet Killer Seven from the Asteroid Belt. The sea monster had landed with deathly force in the Old City after the asteroid had vaporized the Mediterranean Sea. Yosef had arranged to rename the creature Leviathanosaurus.

As they climbed the path to the platform, the foothills of the Old City sprawled before them.

"Wow," the boys said as one.

Long lines of seats ran between the rows of gravestones, and the hills beyond bristled with spectators as far as the eye could see.

The murmur of the waiting masses was the susurrus of a surging ocean, excitement in their whispers and tears of joy in their laughter. This time the Messiah would not disappoint.

But who was the Messiah—or Messiahs? Yosef had discussed the matter at length with Moshe and Elijah. Surprisingly, Elijah had no idea. The prophet had lost the frequency of Divine revelation along with his miraculous powers. And although Moshe's achievements seemed to qualify him for the role, he had balked at making messianic claims of any sort. In Yosef's mind, paradoxically, Moshe's refusal to reach for that crown proved that he *was* indeed the Messiah!

After days of doubt, a solution presented itself. Their approach was simple—even trite—but seemed to be the one least likely to cause mass hysteria and pandemonium. The concept explained Elijah's failing powers too. Yosef had even found a supporting source among the ancient texts. *Yes.* The more he thought about it, the more he liked the idea. The answer had been there all along. But only after millennia of failed messiahs was the world ready to hear it.

Was their answer *the* answer—*the* solution? Who knew? Yosef craved certainty, but in the end, he'd found none. He'd learn to live without. Tom Levi had been certain of his apocalyptic plans. Perhaps a little self-doubt was a good thing after all.

The security guards deposited his family among the front rows at the foot of the platform and continued with Yosef onto the stage.

In the distance, the Old City gleamed, unrecognizable. In one fiery instant, the asteroid had vaporized the sacred grounds of the Temple Mount, obliterating the mosques, the domes, and the Western Wall, and uprooting centuries of buried history and smoldering conflict.

The flat slab of bedrock that remained solved two contentious issues. With no vestige of the hallowed Temple Mount, technically there was no way to build a third Temple. And with no Temple, the topic of sacrifices became moot. Sorry.

The clean, open space stretched from the former Western Wall Plaza to the outer edge of the Temple Mount, with no indication of where synagogue ended and mosque began. Thanks to Noga Shemer's findings regarding the Ten Lost Tribes, there was no need.

Instead, the State had earmarked the grounds for a new non-denominational structure, a memorial to centuries of bloodshed. The display would include a huge holographic model of the Jewish Temple. A Temple of Fire, indeed!

On the platform, Yosef took his seat beside the young dashing man in the black leather jacket. Yosef had suggested a more "appropriate" choice of clothing—a flowing robe, perhaps, and a pointy hat, but the prophet would have none of it. "I'm not a wizard," he had said. "Or a Greek." He didn't seem to like the ancient Greeks much.

Yosef nodded a greeting.

Elijah folded his arms. "He's late."

Yosef gazed at the endless crowds, at the hats and kaffiyehs, the skullcaps and the healthy bare heads of hair. From the first rows of seats, Rabbi Emden tipped his hat at him. Beside him sat all seven sages of the Great Council. Tears seeped unbidden into Yosef's eyes.

"Better late than never," he said. "Better late than never."

CHAPTER 98

That morning, Moshe Karlin made a detour on his way to the Mount of Olives. He had an important errand to run. The Prime Minister's cavalcade stopped outside a dusty store on the seedier side of Pierre Koenig Street in Talpiot. His mission was close to impossible. Luckily for him, he'd brought along a secret weapon.

A bell chimed as he pushed the glass door open and they walked inside. Knickknacks crowded the shelves and floor: embroidered chairs with carved armrests of polished oak, a selection of wall clocks, and, beneath the glass countertop, an array of wedding bands and diamond-encrusted rings.

The old man behind the counter looked up from his coffee and newspaper, as he had the first time Moshe had entered the pawn shop. But today a glint of suspicion sparkled in the vulture eyes beneath the wisp of cotton candy hair, and his shoulders tensed.

Moshe placed his hands on the counter. "I've come to reclaim my watch."

If the old vulture had recognized his Prime Minister, he made no sign of it. "It's not for sale." The declaration was an opening bargaining position if ever Moshe had heard one.

Moshe didn't argue. He didn't have to.

Moshe's secret weapon let out a derisive harrumph. "You

should be ashamed of yourself, young man," Savta Sarah said. By the looks of him, the storekeeper had not been addressed as a "young man" in over seventy years. "Moshe's grandfather bought that watch and passed it on to Moshe's father after him. It is a family heirloom of great *sentimental* value." Her implication: sentimental but not monetary value.

The vulture behind the counter licked his lips. Finally, he had met a worthy opponent, and he savored the challenge. He slid Moshe's old watch from beneath the glass display. He caressed the leather strap and pointed to the brand name that glittered in gold leaf.

"This, madam, I'll have you know, is a Rolex Bubbleback, 1948 Limited Edition. Few have survived to this day and none are in such pristine condition. This collector's timepiece is worth at least eighty thousand shekels."

Moshe had asked for half that amount when he'd pawned the watch to buy his freedom from Boris. In his desperation, he had settled for ten thousand.

"*Eighty thousand shekels*?" Savta Sarah gasped. "I could buy this entire store for eighty thousand shekels, including its owner."

Moshe stifled a chuckle, stepped back, and enjoyed the show. The old man gave Savta a run for her money, but even he was no match for that indomitable force of nature. In the end, Moshe had to cut the negotiation short and handed over twenty thousand shekels in crisp two-hundred-shekel notes. The wily pawnbroker had made a tidy profit. Moshe didn't mind. There was no need to create rumors that the Prime Minister was stingy. Besides, he felt sorry for him. While haggling, the old vulture had pulled out most of his remaining hair, and alarming blue veins had bulged on his forehead.

Moshe removed his golden Omega, the gift from Isaac Gurion during the honeymoon days of Moshe's early foray into politics, and he strapped on his grandfather's Rolex. The watch was heavier, the strap a little tighter, but it felt right. The timepiece was the last purchase his grandfather had made before the war had taken everything. He had sworn never to sell the watch. It was a reminder of the life he had wanted to regain. "A Karlin never quits," his father had always said. It was the motto that had kept Moshe going in his darkest hours.

Secret Service agents held the door as Moshe and Savta climbed back inside the ministerial SUV.

"Twenty thousand shekels," she said, shaking her head. "I could have got him down further if you'd let me."

"That's all right, Savta. You did very well. And we can't spend the whole day bargaining. We have another important appointment today, remember?"

CHAPTER 99

A cool morning breeze greeted Moshe at the top of the Mount of Olives when he stepped out of the SUV.

This was where it had all begun. Six months ago, he'd woken up in the ancient cemetery, naked and alone. He had lost everything. The muezzin call to prayers on the loudspeaker had sent a thrill of fear through his mind. This morning, he had arrived in a cavalcade, wearing his finest suit. The voices on the loudspeaker spoke in Hebrew, Arabic, and English, and they called every man, woman, and child to join their gathering.

Secret Service agents lined the path to the raised platform which faced the Old City below.

Galit waited on the curb, her hands clasped, looking as radiant as that first moment he had glimpsed her. She kissed Savta Sarah on the cheek, then turned to her husband.

"You're late," she said, a playful smile curling her lips.

"I got here as fast as I could."

"Daddy!"

Talya jumped up and down and hugged his waist. Moshe picked her up and mussed her thicket of dark curls.

The first two weeks after the asteroid strike had kept them both very busy. He had a country to patch up, foreign relations to mend, and international relief efforts to coordinate.

The fact that they had survived the impact at all had required some explaining, and Professor Stein was happy to oblige. As it happened, PK-7 was not an asteroid but a comet, a ball of rock *and ice*, and so the nukes had not only bumped the threat off course but broken it apart. Comets hang out in the Asteroid Belt too. Who knew?

The larger of the comet's two remaining chunks had landed in the Mediterranean Sea, which had softened the blow but still sent tsunamis racing toward every shore.

Galit had faced her own tsunami challenge—getting her parents to move out of the Prime Minister's Residence—and Moshe had not envied her. With hard work and a lot of collaboration, they completed both missions successfully.

Then Moshe did something unexpected—he took off an entire week. Instead of flying to exotic islands or hiking up north, Moshe, Galit, and Talya stayed home. No phones or emails, no Internet, only quality time together. They slept in, ate ice cream, watched movies, and played board games. Most of all, they had talked. The results were spectacular.

At the Mount of Olives Cemetery, Galit linked her arm in his, and they walked along the line of security agents.

"Ready to conquer the world?" she said.

"I'm not sure 'conquer' is the right word."

"You did save us all."

"Well," he said, noncommittally. "That still sounds a little grandiose. I suppose we did avert a global extinction event. And achieve worldwide nuclear disarmament. Within twenty-four hours and by means of a few conference calls. We can be proud of that."

"Not 'we,'" Galit corrected him. "*You.* You did all that."

As much as the idea tickled Moshe's ego, he couldn't abide the lie. "If there's one thing I've learned," he said, "it's that no one man can fix a country, never mind the world. I had a lot of help. And I'll need more yet."

Galit, Talya, and Savta made for their seats in the front row, and Moshe continued onward.

Rubi, the owlish Government Secretary, waited for him at

the ramp of the raised platform.

"Is everything in order, Rubi?" Moshe had finally yielded to his eager helper's requests, entrusting him with the logistics of the day's event.

"Yes, sir! Thank you for the honor, Mr. Prime Minister!"

"No, Rubi. Thank *you.* You've done an excellent job. And I'm sure I'll have many more projects for you in future."

Rubi swallowed hard. "Thank you, sir. I'll convey your message to the team."

Careful what you wish for, Moshe thought. He patted the man on the shoulder and continued on his way.

As he climbed the ramp to the raised platform, Jerusalem opened up like a flower in bloom. Sections of the ancient Old City walls peeled back like petals, and in the open heart of what was once the golden dome and Temple Mount, the tiny figures of innumerable people stood in white, black, and the full spectrum of colors. The hills flowed with humanity as far as the eye could see, right up to the rows of seated dignitaries among the tombstones.

At Moshe's entrance, hands clapped and voices cheered, the sound of rolling waves rushing to greet the seashore.

Two figures sat at the table of honor beside the podium, Rabbi Yosef and Elijah.

"Thank you for your patience."

"After two thousand years," Elijah said, "what's a few more minutes?"

Moshe smiled.

If anyone had asked Moshe to picture Elijah the Prophet, he would have gone for flowing robes and white beards, not jet-black hair and leather jackets. Reality never ceased to amaze.

"Is she here?" Moshe asked.

Eli smiled, touched that Moshe had remembered. "Front row," he said. He pointed to a girl with long dark hair. Noga, Eli's injured girlfriend and the discoverer of the Ten Lost Tribes, waved up at them. She and Dr. Stern sat among the dignitaries and world leaders who had turned out for the occasion.

Noga had figured out the hardest part of the Messianic equation—how to resolve the Israeli-Palestinian conflict—and for that, he was eternally grateful. If not for that, and the biker's earlier unfortunate attempt to meet Moshe and Rabbi Yosef at this very spot, Moshe might have doubted Elijah's credentials.

Moshe nodded at Irina and Alex in the second row. The day of the asteroid strike—or Day One, as people were calling it—the Russian couple had faced off another branch of Adams's criminal organization. During the confrontation, Boris and King Kong had met their end.

Moshe nodded at the new Police Commissioner in the second row. Alex's testimony had put the former Commissioner, Golan, behind bars for his collaboration with organized crime. Rooting out the Organization's tendrils would take time, but the process had begun, and Interpol would do the heavy lifting.

With the rustle of fluttering wings, a black crow alighted on the table before Elijah, cawed once, and flew off.

"What was that about?"

"An old friend," Elijah said. "He said it's time we got started."

"Right." Moshe approached the podium, cleared his throat, and the cheers rose again across the Holy City. His face appeared on projector screens along the hillsides to give even the most distant spectators a good view of the ceremony. *What to say?*

Moshe, Rabbi Yosef, and Elijah had met several times to discuss the way forward. Three things became clear. A new era had begun. They had saved the planet from extinction, brought peace to their corner of the Middle East, crippled a global consortium for organized crime, and defeated death. Secondly, they needed to mark this fact to give the people closure and guidance. Thirdly, none of the three men had a clue what they were doing.

So they'd worked with what they had.

Moshe waited for the hubbub of the murmuring crowd to settle. He had written up his thoughts earlier but decided against cue cards. From here on he'd improvise.

"My friends and fellow citizens," he said into the microphone. His amplified voice bounced off the Jerusalem hills under the warm sun of a clear autumn day. "For millennia, we have waited for the End Times. We have hoped for the end to our suffering and striving, for a brighter future of truth, peace, and justice. Some have taken advantage of that hope, cynically manipulating our beliefs to further their own greedy agendas. Today, the wait ends."

Cheers and wolf whistles rose from the masses of rapt humanity.

Moshe raised his hand for silence. "Today we mark the end of history." The ominous ring of those words ushered in total silence. "Not because time is ending. On the contrary, life is starting anew. For those who choose it, eternal life. But the story that began with two kids in God's garden has concluded, the script in which we hang our hopes and dreams on Divine intervention. *His* story has ended. *Our* story has begun."

The breeze ruffled Moshe's hair and whistled in the branches of the olive trees.

"Some have claimed that I am the Messiah." Another roar from the crowds on the hills. Moshe waited for silence. "Many have pressured me to reach for that crown myself. But I must disappoint you. No one human being can fix society. No individual can beat crime, end suffering, or fight injustice."

He drew two deep breaths and used the dramatic pause to recall the exact wording he had drafted with Rabbi Yosef and Elijah.

"I am not your Messiah. God alone is our Redeemer, and He created us all in His image. Our job is to learn from His example and to complete the process that He started. In short, to fix the world together."

Hands clapped, and the hills echoed with applause. A

chant carried on myriad voices. "Fix the World! Fix the World!"

The chant had a certain appeal. It sure beat "Undead Stay Dead!" or "Break the Dry Bones!"

Moshe smiled as the voices rose and fell. After a full three minutes, the chant subsided.

"Before we conclude the proceedings, please join me in remembering those who are no longer with us."

Moshe spoke of friends and family who had passed away during those tumultuous few months, and those who had not yet returned from death.

Moshe found Samira in the second row, and their eyes met. She smiled as tears traced shimmering trails down her face. They were both thinking of one lost friend in particular—Ahmed.

While she waited for the asteroid strike, cowering beneath her bed at the Dry Bones Society, Samira had read Ahmed's letter. He wrote of his love for her and his decision to heed her advice and not repeat the mistakes of his first life. The Messiah Coronation would bring him face-to-face with the Shepherd, he was sure of it. He promised to confront the Shepherd and end his rule of terror. Samira had not known what he had meant, but the truth soon came to light.

Forensics experts at the Sultan's Pool confirmed that Ahmed had saved Moshe's life. He had detonated a suicide vest beneath his robes, incinerating Adams, Mandrake, and their henchman. His act of self-emollition had decapitated the Hydra of organized crime, freed Moshe from his watery grave, and spared the lives of the three men the criminals had bound and gagged below the stage.

More than that, his brave words of reconciliation at the Temple Mount had set the table on which Moshe had served the tidings of the Ten Lost Tribes and helped a suffering population digest that vital dish.

Could noble actions erase a suicide bomber's past? Did saving one group of innocent lives make up for the snuffing out of another? Shmuel would say no. Moshe for one hoped, wherever the universe had blown Ahmed's soul, that this time he would find peace.

"We will remember their sacrifices forever," Moshe concluded.

He stepped back as Elijah and Rabbi Yosef took the podium. The rabbi held the long, twisted shofar—a hollowed-out deer horn—while Elijah applied his lips to the pointy end and puffed out his cheeks. The blast came deep and smooth. The single note was long and sad but determined, and as the sound waves echoed off hills and fields and homes, Moshe thought he heard the eternal city answer with hope.

Then Elijah raised a large rectangular bottle of virgin olive oil and pumped the lever of the spray nozzle. Clouds of oil wafted downwind, anointing every man, woman, and child with tiny drops of the sacred liquid. Moshe had thought this unnecessary, but Elijah was a stickler for protocol. "If they're all messiahs," Elijah had contended, "I must anoint them all." Moshe had relented. The prophet's Divine intuition and miraculous powers had disappeared for good, and Rabbi Yosef had chalked that up to this new era of human intervention. Moshe didn't have the heart to deny the prophet his anointing role too.

The proceedings concluded with the singing of the Israeli anthem, *Hatikva*. The Hope.

Od lo avda tikvatenu / Our hope is not yet lost
Hatikva bat shnot alpayim / The hope of two thousand years
Lihyot am chofshi be'artzenu / To be a free nation in our land.

The ceremony complete, Moshe led the way down the ramp, rejoined Galit and Talya, and walked the path back to the street.

"Masterful speech!" the American President said. "Well done, sir!"

"Agreed!" chimed in the Russian President. "You brought tears to my eyes."

The two world leaders had jetted in for the ceremony and become great pals. Their camaraderie had made the nuclear non-proliferation agreements easier to sign. It also helped that neither side had any nuclear arsenal to speak of. Both presidents had afforded the Israeli Prime Minister every form of aid over the past month in the relief efforts across the Mediterranean. In return, Moshe never mentioned the zombie armies.

"Have you seen our proposal? For the IGO…"

"Oh, right!" Moshe has seen the email, but not read the details. "I'll have a look as soon as possible." He hurried along the path, leaving them in his wake.

"The IGO?" Galit asked.

"International Governmental Organization. Apparently, they want me to head a unified world government."

"Wow!"

"I know. Talk about conquering the world."

"Are you going to accept?"

"I don't know. I stand by what I said—one small country is more than enough."

She chuckled, and he sensed that she wasn't disappointed. He'd spent enough time away from home and swimming against the stream. From here on, Moshe's new motto would be "delegate everything."

"Irina!" Moshe hugged his friend and her boyfriend.

She held up her hand, and a diamond twinkled on her finger. Make that fiancé. She deserved a happy ending.

Moshe teared up. "Congratulations, Irina! I mean Valentina." He kept forgetting to use her real name.

"That's OK," she said. "I'm sticking with Irina. A fresh start."

Moshe understood. "I hope you'll invite us to the wedding."

"Of course! Rabbi Yosef, perhaps you can officiate?"

The rabbi gaped for a moment. *Oops.* She had unintentionally put the rabbi in a spot. Irina wasn't Jewish. Could he marry her to Alex?

"Um," Rabbi Yosef said. "I'll look into it."

Irina jumped for joy.

Moshe thumped the rabbi on the shoulder and moved on.

He'd leave the conundrums of Jewish Law to him. That was why God had created rabbis.

A few steps down the line, a Secret Service agent held back an older Arab man.

"Hold on a moment."

"Mr. Prime Minister!" the man pleaded, then, spotting Rabbi Yosef, "Mr. Vice Prime Minister!"

"It's OK," Moshe told Alon, and he let the man draw closer.

"My son," he said, in shaky Hebrew. "You knew my son?" In his hand, he held a crumpled poster of an Arab kid wearing a black bandana and a suicide vest.

"Ahmed?"

"Yes!" He pointed to the picture. "Ahmed. My son. I am Yousef."

Yousef. Why did that sound familiar?

Moshe turned to Rabbi Yosef, whose eyes widened, and Moshe remembered what the rabbi had explained. Tradition had talked of two Messiahs. Rabbi Emden had thought that Rabbi Yosef was the doomed Messiah of Yosef, the leader of the Ten Tribes.

A shudder tingled down Moshe's spine. In Arabic, *Yosef* became *Yousef.*

"Your son saved our lives," Moshe said.

"Yes! My son." Then tears came, and the man hugged his Prime Minister and wept on his shoulder for the son he had lost. By the shaking of the man's body, it seemed he had lost his son a long time ago.

Moshe whispered to Alon to follow up with the man and see what assistance he needed. Then he moved on. He shook hands with well-wishers.

With each step, he thought of the thousands of men and women who had come before him. Through untold hardships and hopelessness, they had longed for this day, for the end of the seemingly endless road of history. Each step he took, he took for them.

At the end of the path waited a bearded man in a shiny

dark suit and top hat. He stuck out his chest, and the tails of his coat brushed the pebbly floor of the car park.

Moshe knew the man, but only in black and white, not in the full color of real life.

"Grandfather?"

The man blinked and smiled. "I thought that might be you," said the grandfather Moshe had never met. He had a thick Eastern European accent. "How many Moshe Karlins can there be?"

"Galit, this is my grandfather, Moshe Karlin!"

Moshe Karlin Senior doffed his hat and bowed. "At your service, Mrs. Prime Minister." He bent over and peered at little Talya. "And who might you be, young lady?"

Talya hid behind Moshe's leg. "Say hello to your great-grandfather, Talya."

This was too much to take in at once. "Please," Moshe said, "join us."

His grandfather obliged, and they tumbled into the back of the SUV.

"I'm proud of you, Moshe," said his grandfather. "Very proud."

"It's all thanks to you. Look." Moshe removed the Rolex from his wrist and held it out for display. "This was your watch. My father drummed that lesson in deep. 'A Karlin never quits.'"

His grandfather seemed confused. "What is this 'Karlin never quits'?"

Had his memory faded, even in the afterlife? "Your saying. The family motto. This is the watch you handed down to your son, David Karlin—my father. The last thing you bought before you lost the business in the war. And the house."

His grandfather swatted the words away with his hand. "That trinket? I won that cheap imitation shooting tins at a town fair."

"But," Moshe continued, "you refused to sell the watch. It was a reminder of the life you wanted to regain. 'A Karlin never quits,' you always said. That motto kept you going through your darkest hours."

Moshe Karlin Senior shook his head with irritation. "I didn't lose the business—my nephew, your father's cousin, took it over. Your father and his pipe dreams! He never had the head for business, always wanting to break out on his own, always arguing. He caused so much trouble that I disinherited him. The rest of the family wanted nothing to do with him either."

Moshe stared at the Rolex, the watch he'd redeemed for twenty thousand shekels. He turned to Galit, and she shrugged.

"But it's a good story," his grandfather said, jovial again.

"It is, isn't it?"

"*A Karlin never quits.* Ha! I like it. And it got you this far, didn't it?"

Moshe stared out the window as the world moved by. A better world. A world he had helped create. Did it matter that his father had been blessed with an active imagination? The lessons within his tales had stood the test of time.

He strapped the Rolex back onto his wrist. "Yes," he said. "I suppose it did."

CHAPTER 100

The attendant at the Academon Bookstore on the Mount Scopus campus of the Hebrew University of Jerusalem thought she had seen it all. Until, that is, the man with the broad gray beard and flat cap stepped up to the counter.

A bit old to be a student, isn't he? The man waited while she reviewed his list of supplies.

And what a list that was! The textbooks included first-year tomes on a wide variety of subjects ranging from astrophysics and advanced mathematics to anatomy and computer theory to anthropology and sociology. He seemed to have copied the book list for the entire Faculty of Science.

"Sir," she said, "are you sure you need all these?"

The man peered over at the list, then nodded.

"What program are you registered for?"

"I'm on the PhD track."

"For which field?"

"All of them."

"All of them?"

He nodded again, profusely, and flashed her the grin of a kid in a candy store with Mommy's credit card.

Whatever. It's his money. She made a tour of the store, sliding hardbacks from the shelves and checking off items from the list. After ten minutes, four stacks of textbooks rose from the counter and reached her nose.

She scanned each volume and rang up the total. Could he afford these on a pensioner's budget?

"How do you want to pay?"

He handed her another piece of paper. The letter, signed by the president of the university, indicated that the bearer, Rabbi Moses Ben Maimon, had been awarded a full scholarship for his studies and that she should charge his expenses to the Dry Bones Society Scholarship Program.

She checked the man's identity card, then processed the payment.

"Would you like these delivered?"

"Yes, please." He jotted down a Jerusalem address on a note, then selected three tomes with unabashed relish, looking at the crisp new books as though he intended to gobble them for lunch. He placed the books under his arm, thanked her, and turned to leave.

"Sir," she said. "If you don't mind me asking. A single PhD takes eight years on average. How are you going to finish them all?"

Maimonides smiled that boyish smile again, and he rubbed his shoulder as though massaging a vaccination wound. "I have a lot of free time, my daughter," he said. "All the time in the world."

BONUS CHAPTER

A Love and Beyond

Best Book Award 2016 Gold Medal Winner
(American Book Fest, Religious Fiction)

CHAPTER 1

On Tuesday, Dave Schwarz hit thirty and his best friend narrowly escaped a violent death.

The two events were probably unrelated, but both jolted Dave the way a sudden air pocket reminds nervous passengers that they're soaring above the clouds in a pressurized metal tube.

Realization number one: Welcome to the Middle East. Strangely, Dave never thought of his new home as the Middle East. Brutal attacks like the heavy blow to the back of the head that had nearly claimed his friend should not have surprised him.

Realization number two: I'm thirty years old and still single. In short, my life is over.

Dave shook the morbid thought from his head. This was no time for navel gazing. He perched on the edge of a bed in room 419C of the Shaare Zedek Medical Center. A plastic curtain divided the room into quarters and reeked of disinfectant and tragedy. Drops of indolent Jerusalem rain slid down the dark windowpane.

Ben's bulky form lay in the hospital bed, his eyes closed, a white bandage over his otherwise bald head, like an injured rugby fullback; the mind of an academic in the body of an East End bouncer.

According to the ward nurse, the ICU doctors had transferred Ben early Wednesday morning. He was in no mortal danger, but had his mind survived the trauma?

Dave cleared his throat. He whispered Ben's name for the tenth time in two minutes. Behind the curtain, a ventilator wheezed. A telephone rang down the hall and the nurse with the squeaky shoe continued her rounds.

Dave reached into the plastic bag from Steimatzky and placed a book on the nightstand. The Jewish War by Josephus. He had purchased the Penguin paperback at the hospital gift store on the ground floor. Ben's existing copy, a hefty side-by-side English translation of the original Greek, was thick with dog ears and split at the seams.

A bouquet of gerberas sat on the windowsill. Ben's wife had sent the flowers but it wasn't her flowing cursive that graced the message inside the card. The uneven block letters looked to Dave like a cryptic text copied by a blind scribe.

Yvette had called Dave at work half an hour ago. Would he stop by, make sure Ben was in one piece?

Dave plucked a yellow flower from the bouquet and dismembered it slowly.

If Dave lay in hospital, who would send him flowers? If he died, what would his lonely life have achieved?

"Looks bad. Doesn't it?" said Ben, his eyes still shut.

Dave almost swallowed his tongue. "No, not at all." He tossed the naked flower stem into the waste bin to join its petals. "I was thinking about myself."

"Oh," Ben said, as though that explained everything.

How long had Ben been conscious?

Dave searched the poky room for a cheerful thought.

"No shortage of Jewish doctors here." His laugh was lame even to his own ears.

"Muhammad," Ben said.

The hairs on the back of Dave's neck stiffened. He had heard anecdotes of near-death experiences but he had not expected the bright light at the end of the tunnel to be the founder of Islam.

"What?"

Ben worked his mouth, as if chewing gum. Dave scanned the headboard for an emergency button.

"Doctor Muhammad. Nice guy."

Dave exhaled, his worldview intact.

He scratched his head. Ben usually drove the conversation. A laconic Ben concerned Dave.

"I met a girl," Dave said in desperation and waited for the bomb to detonate. Ben devoured tidbits of Dave's bachelor misadventures with the voracity typical of safely married men.

The patient in the sick bed merely grunted.

Had Ben recognized Dave at all?

Dave bit his lip and drew his last card.

"You made the Jerusalem Post," he said.

Ben opened his eyes. "What did they say?"

Dave retrieved the folded printout from his shoulder bag.

"'Break-in at the City of David,'" Dave read aloud. "'An apparent break-in at the City of David Institute Tuesday night caused minor structural damage. All artifacts are accounted for, according to Dr. Erez Lazarus, curator of the museum in East Jerusalem. An employee who was present at the time sustained mild injuries. The police have opened an investigation and at this point suspect local vandals.'"

"Mild injuries," Ben mumbled and shook his head.

In a sequence of fluid movements, he sat up, propped his back against the wall with a pillow, and snatched the article from Dave's hands.

Not for the first time, Dave felt the sting of his so-called friend's so-called sense of humor.

"How long have you known I was here?"

Ben didn't look up from the article.

"And what were you doing at work so late?"

"Preparing an itinerary. Yvette's away so I wasn't rushing home. I heard a commotion outside and went to investigate. Next thing I know, I'm lying here with the mother of all hangovers. They didn't even mention my name, the bastards. Erez probably saw to that."

Dave had met Erez, Ben's boss, a number of times at the

City of David Institute, or the COD, as Erez referred to the popular tourist attraction. Erez was not known for his tact.

"You should carry a gun," Dave said, feeling suddenly vengeful.

"A gun?" Ben said, outraged. "I'm an archaeologist, Dave. Not a hit man."

Dave pictured Ben behind a heavy-duty revolver. The image made a certain amount of visual sense. His shaved head and beefy, don't-mess-with-me build called to mind the thugs of a Guy Ritchie film, rather than the rabbi's son enamored with academic nuance and scientific enquiry.

"Indiana Jones had a gun." A shameless smirk twisted Dave's lips as he said it.

"Indiana Jones." Ben lowered the printout and rolled his eyes. "God, I'm tired of that name. 'Found the Ark of the Covenant yet? Been to the Temple of Doom?' For Heaven's sake. Indiana Jones is a fictional character. Archaeology, on the other hand, is a very real, painstaking process of scientific research. Hypothesis. Excavation. Analysis. Well-founded conclusions. No stunt men. No special effects. We fight our battles in academic journals, not dark alleys… Ouch!"

Ben's hand shot to the back of his head and Dave felt a small stab of remorse. He also felt relief. This was the Ben he knew and… well, the Ben he knew.

Not that Dave was a man of adventure either. He failed to comprehend why some people tied ropes to their legs and dove off bridges, or out of perfectly good airplanes. Dave was a confirmed serotonin junkie. Any day of the year, he chose a good book, a hot cupper, and air-conditioning over jeopardy to life and limb. But the opportunity to ruffle his friend's feathers had been too good to pass up.

"What ever happened to the Ark, anyway?"

Ben raised a sarcastic eyebrow, then relented.

"Not a trace in the archaeological record. The Talmud mentions two theories. Rabbi Eliezer said the Babylonians carried it off after they destroyed the first Temple in 586 BC. Rabbi Shimon Bar Yochai claimed King Josiah hid the Ark in tunnels beneath the Temple Mount shortly before. In either event," Ben added meaningfully, "there's no mention of lost Egyptian cities or Nazi plots."

"Beneath the Temple Mount? Can't you just dig there and find out?"

"Not since Moshe Dayan gave the keys of the Temple Mount to the Waqf as a gesture of good will. Now they renovate with abandon and all we can do is sift national treasures, or fragments thereof, out of their rubble. But don't get me started on that."

Dave didn't. Instead, he asked, "When does Yvette get back from Madrid?"

"Paris," Ben said. "She'll be back tonight."

Ben's wife was, quite literally, a supermodel. She spent her days flitting between the catwalks of the world's fashion centers.

"Oh, good," Dave replied, a study of casual innocence. "So you'll both be home for Shabbat."

This was Ben's cue to invite Dave over for a Sabbath meal. Of the many banes of bachelorhood, the weekly scrabble for meal invitations pressed Dave the most. Few things were as miserable as a festive Shabbat dinner-for-one at home.

Ben didn't take the hint.

"All right," he said, "let's have it."

"Have what?"

"The girl you met."

Dave was no longer desperate enough to bare his dating soul. "Just some girl I met on Shabbat after shul."

The synagogue buffet after Saturday morning prayers was the closest Dave would get to a singles bar. The slender waterfall blond had stood beside a foldout table of herring and Jerusalem kugel—pizza slices of caramelized pasta—on plastic plates. Her free-flowing hair meant she was unmarried. The ringless fingers ruled out an engagement. But was she available?

Dave had meandered closer, a plastic shot glass of Black

Label in hand. He intercepted snatches of her conversation with a girlfriend. American accent. West Coast.

"And?" Ben said. "Tell me you made a move."

"Well…"

He had drained his glass. He placed her in his sights. The world focused around him. The moment swelled with destiny. It was now or never.

"Not as such," Dave admitted. "She's American, anyway. And probably too young."

Ben covered his face in his hands. "Dave, Dave, Dave."

"But I might know someone who knows her," Dave continued.

"Dave, oh, Dave."

"Stop it, Ben. I don't want to be the scary older guy who can't take a hint."

Ben removed his hands from his face and glared at Dave, the large, repulsive cockroach. "Why do you keep doing that?"

"Don't tell me I'm picky."

"You are picky but that's beside the point. Imagine you're a good-looking, single girl. Would you be interested in a *nebekh* who doesn't have the guts to ask you out in person?"

Dave had no sisters. He had attended Hasmonean Boys. His insights into the psyche of the fairer sex derived from acquaintances at the Hampstead Garden Suburb Hebrew Congregation, Bnei Akiva summer camps, and more blind dates than he cared to remember. Hollywood filled in the blanks. But Dave could see where this was going and he would not go down quietly.

"They want to get married, don't they?"

"True," Ben conceded. "Marriage. Kids. The whole package. But what else do they want?"

Dave shrugged. "Security?"

"Fireworks, Dave. Romance. A man to sweep them off their feet. They want to fall in love but not with Mr. Nobody. They want the leader of the pack. Mr. Numero Uno. Mr. Top Dog."

"Mr. Top Dog? You hit your head harder than I thought. What ever happened to 'just be yourself'?"

"Be yourself. But differently. You can't sit on the sidelines. You've got to put yourself out there."

"I am out there," Dave said, louder than he had intended. The plastic curtain rippled behind him and the ventilator quickened its pace.

Why do people always blame the victim? Dave looked at his watch. "Which reminds me. I've got Rabbi Levi tonight."

"Excellent," said Ben. "Here's your chance. One telephone number. That's all I ask."

"You're not dying, Ben. You don't get a last wish."

"Don't you dare leave that shul without one new telephone number."

"What if I don't fancy anyone?"

"Who cares? Think of it as practice. A game. I wish you'd just read the damned book."

Dave felt his shoulders tense. The Pickup Artist's Bible was the only paperback in Ben's library with more mileage than Josephus. In a moment of despair, Dave had agreed to read it. He had stopped on page two of the introduction.

"Ben. I'm not prowling bars for a one-night stand. I'm looking for a wife, for Heaven's sake. My soul mate. The woman who will share my life and sit at my Shabbos table."

"It's just a foot in the door," said Ben. "And girls are girls. Give her a reason to get to know you."

Dave drew a long, frustrated breath. Why did he confide in Ben in matters of the heart? Dave looked at the bouquet of flowers and remembered.

"Hypothetically speaking," he said, "if I get the number, I don't have to call it, right?"

"That's the spirit." Ben smiled, no doubt anticipating future field reports of humiliation.

Humiliation: the constant in Dave's life. How had it happened? All his childhood friends were married plus two or three kids. Somewhere along the tracks of life, Dave had derailed.

"Ben, is something wrong with me?"

Ben looked him squarely in the eyes. "You left a civilized Western country to live in the Middle East. You tell me."

~

Dave's Ford hatchback gunned down Herzog Boulevard. The light drizzle had faded into the night. In the opposite lane, a steady stream of cars flowed toward Teddy Kollek Stadium. Black and yellow scarves trailed from the windows and horns honked the Morse code of football heathens.

The football gene had skipped over Dave and he hid this aberration like a sixth finger. Only Ben shared the condition; a fact that had solidified their early friendship.

Ben would be back on his feet before long but the break-in cast an ominous shadow. Dave had visited Ben's office at the COD countless times and, over the years, he had explored every stone ruin, stairway, and tunnel. The archaeological site with its signposts and safety banisters had been, in Dave's mind, a beacon of normalcy in the sea of short fuses and itchy trigger fingers that was East Jerusalem.

Why would anyone break into the City of David? Dave could not recall any displays of gold or silver. The center's main attractions included the geological chasm known as Warren's Shaft, King Hezekiah's water tunnel, and a rooftop observatory. Although perfect for tour groups and dating activities, the COD offered little of interest to criminal elements.

Dave pressed his foot to the brake when traffic slowed at the intersection of Gaza Street and Ben Zvi.

Vandalism, the papers had written. But bodily assault was not typical of vandalism, however mean-spirited. Had Ben surprised them? Had they panicked? Botched robberies often turned violent.

Dave veered right at the light. Tchernichovsky climbed and meandered into the heart of Katamon.

Palmach. Fighter Pilots. Nili. The Jewish Brigade. Conquerors of Katamon. The street names echoed the struggles of a People returning to its Promised Land. Over the years, the four-story apartment blocks in chunky, white Jerusalem stone—a mix of Jewish slums and Christian-Arab mansions—had accumulated a patina of carbon pollution and a tenancy of students and yuppies, completing the transformation into a hive of Jewish singles.

"One phone number," Dave said, aloud.

The mantra made his task no less daunting. Dave was fairly sure that weekly Torah lectures with separate seating did not feature prominently in the Pickup Artist's Bible.

He made a left onto Emek Refaim with its trendy restaurants and boutique stores and then turned right onto Derekh Harakevet, a forgotten back road beside the grassy tracks of a defunct railway. He eased the Ford Focus into the unpaved parking lot outside his apartment building.

Dave's flat on the first floor comprised a small, square living room, tiny kitchenette, bathroom, and single bedroom.

He threw his shoulder bag onto the foldout couch that had come with the rental along with the ancient fridge, stove, and closet and went straight for the shower, maneuvering past the miniature TV, its low stand, and the rickety coffee table he'd purchased on Janglo, an email list for Jerusalem Anglos. He'd invest in real furniture after he married.

Freshly shaved, he chose an ironed shirt out of the closet when the house phone rang.

"David, darling!" The breathless voice oozed enthusiasm like crude oil. "It's your mother."

Dave cringed. His mother, the only person on the planet who called him David, packed her words with subliminal messages. The current subtext read: the prodigal son hasn't bothered to call his poor mother since the last Ice Age.

Dave lodged the portable receiver between ear and shoulder and buttoned his shirt.

"I know who you are, Mother."

"How *are* you?"

"Good. How are you?"

Dave's mental countdown started. His mother took an average of ten seconds to start poking around his love life.

The toaster oven pinged. Dave had five minutes to gobble his vegetable pâté if he was to get to Rabbi Levi's on time.

"Going out tonight?" Dave's mother asked.

Nine seconds.

"Yes," Dave said, injecting the monosyllable with enough venom to collapse a charging rhinoceros.

"A young lady?"

"No. Just a *shiur*."

"Aw, David. When are you going to get married?"

"I'll be sure to notify the media when I do."

"I don't understand why you have to be so picky."

Subtext: crowds of irresistible, eligible girls surround Dave and vie for his attention.

"This isn't a pair of socks, Mum. It's marriage. 'Til death do us part. You want me to be happy, don't you?"

"Happy?" His mother tittered. Subtext: what a quaint idea. "I didn't say happy, David, darling. I said *married*."

"Mother," Dave interrupted. Cracks appeared along the dam walls of his patience. "I really have to run."

"Your father wants to speak to you."

A short commotion on the other end produced a familiar gruff voice.

"Hello, boy. Everything all right?"

"All good. You?"

"Fine. Fine. Need anything?"

"Nope. All under control."

A muffled conversation. "Your mother says you should try to settle down soon."

"Will do."

The telephone changed hands again.

"David," his mom said, "what ever happened to that lovely girl from London you dated years ago? What was her name?"

Blood fled Dave's cheeks. Once, he had made the mistake of sharing his dating life with his mother. That's how certain he had been. He would not repeat the mistake. He could only hope and pray his mother would not remember her name. Dave himself tried never to think of it, never mind utter it out loud.

"Have to go, Mum. Sorry."

"You should take this seriously, David. You're not getting any younger."

"I'm hanging up now."

Dave replaced the receiver in the charger pad.

Little wonder he was still single, given the marital model of his parents. How had his parents ever gotten together? How had they endured thirty-five years?

The phone rang again. Deep inside Dave's brain stem, something snapped.

"What now?"

"That's a strange way to answer the phone," said a much younger female voice.

Dave slumped on the couch. "Sorry, Nat. I thought you were my mother."

"Ouch," said Nat, who had met Dave's mother. Dave had known Nat since Hasmonean Primary and she was his last remaining single friend from London.

"I'll keep it short, then," she said. "I'm hosting Friday night and you're invited."

"Great," Dave said. "Thanks."

One meal down; one to go.

"Wait a minute. Is it going to be one of those Katamon meals?"

"Well, we do live in Katamon."

"You know what I mean."

Dave heard Nat inhale. She knew exactly what he meant. Friday night was the time for family, Shabbos songs, and insights into the weekly Bible reading. It did not involve ten random singles drooling at each other and peacocking over infantile conversation.

"You know I only keep the most mature and intellectual of company. They can't help it if they're single. What do you have against single people anyway?"

"Nothing," Dave said: the single person.

"It's a small meal. Promise. One flatmate. Two select friends."

Dave hesitated. Two days before Friday night, alternatives to a miserable candlelit dinner for one were fading fast. And Nat knew her way around a kitchen.

"What can I bring to the meal?"

No stranger to bachelor culinary ineptitude, Natalie suggested he buy two large *challah* loaves.

"Oh, and we're meeting at Ohel Nechama."

Dave opened his mouth to protest. Ohel Nechama, also known as The Meat Market, topped Dave's synagogue avoidance list but he struggled to phrase his disapproval without sounding petty.

"Coming to Rav Levi's tonight?" Nat asked.

"Yes. Why?"

"No reason."

ABOUT THE AUTHOR

DAN SOFER writes tales of romantic misadventure and magical realism, many of which take place in Jerusalem. His multi-layered stories mix emotion and action, humor and pathos, myth and legend—entertainment for the heart and soul. Dan lives in Israel with his family.

Visit **dansofer.com/list-dbs3** for free bonus material and updates on new releases.

Lightning Source UK Ltd.
Milton Keynes UK
UKHW01f0641100718
325485UK00002B/540/P